About the Author

Raised an Air Force brat, **Elle James** got her work ethic from her dad, creativity from mum and inspiration from her sister. As a member of the reserves, she's travelled, managed a career, and raised three children. She and her husband even raised ostriches and emus. Ask her what it's like to go toe-to-toe with a 350-pound bird! Former manager of computer programmers, Elle is happy to write full time in NW Arkansas.

Joss Wood's passion for putting black letters on a white screen is only matched by her love of books and travelling and her hatred of making school lunches and ironing. Fuelled by coffee and craziness, Joss is a hands-on mum and, after a career in local economic development and business lobbying, she now writes full time. Surrounded by family, friends and books she lives in Kwa-Zulu Natal, South Africa with her husband and two children.

Annie West has devoted her life to an intensive study of charismatic heroes who cause the best kind of trouble in the lives of their heroines. As a sideline, she researches locations for romance, from vibrant cities to desert encampments and fairytale castles. Annie lives in eastern Australia with her hero husband, between sandy beaches and gorgeous wine country. She finds writing the perfect excuse to postpone housework. To contact her or join her newsletter, visit www.annie-west.com

Hot Heroes

Hot Heroes: Protection Detail

ELLE JAMES

JOSS WOOD

ANNIE WEST

MILLS & BOON

First Published in Great Britain 2020
By Mills & Boon, an imprint of HarperCollins*Publishers*
1 London Bridge Street, London, SE1 9GF

HOT HEROES: PROTECTION DETAIL © 2020 Harlequin Books S.A.

Hot Target © 2017 Mary Jernigan
Flirting with the Forbidden © 2014 Joss Wood
Defying her Desert Duty © 2012 Annie West

ISBN: 978-0-263-28141-5

MIX
Paper from
responsible sources
FSC® C007454

FSC
www.fsc.org

HOT TARGET

ELLE JAMES

This book is dedicated to my mother and father who taught me that the sky was the limit, and all I needed was to apply the hard work to reach for my dreams. I love you both to the moon and back.

Chapter One

Max "Caveman" Decker clung to the shadows of the mud-and-brick structures, the first SEAL into enemy territory. Reaching a forward position giving him sufficient range of fire, he dropped to one knee, scanned the street and buildings ahead through his night-vision goggles, searching for the telltale green heat signatures of warm enemy bodies. When he didn't detect any, he said softly into his mic, "Ready."

"Going in," Whiskey said. Armed with their M4A1 carbine rifles with the Special Forces Modification kit, he and Tank eased around the corner of a building in a small village in the troubled Helmand Province of Afghanistan.

Army Intelligence operatives had indicated the Pakistan-based Haqqani followers had set up a remote base of operations in the village located in the rugged hills north of Kandahar.

Caveman's job was to provide cover to his team-

mates as they moved ahead of him. Then they would cover for him until he reached a relatively secure location, thus leapfrogging through the village to their target, the biggest building at the center, where intel reported the Haqqani rebels had set up shop.

Caveman hunkered low, scanning the path ahead and the rooftops of the buildings for gun-toting enemy combatants. So far, so good. Through his night-vision goggles, he tracked the progress of the seven members of his squad working their way slowly toward the target.

An eighth green blip appeared ahead of his team and his arm swung wide.

"We've got incoming!" Caveman aimed his weapon at the eighth green heat signature and pulled the trigger. It was too late. A bright flash blinded him through the goggles, followed by the ear-rupturing concussion of a grenade. He jerked his goggles up over his helmet, cursing. When he blinked his eyes to regain his night vision, he stared at the scene in front of him.

All seven members of his squad lay on the ground, some moving, others not.

No! His job was to provide cover. They couldn't be dead. They had to be alive. He leaped to his feet.

Then, as if someone opened the door to a hive of bees, enemy combatants swarmed from around the corners into the street, carrying AK-47s.

With the majority of his squad down, maybe dead, maybe alive, Caveman didn't have any other choice.

He set his weapon on automatic, pulled his 9-millimeter pistol from the holster on his hip and stepped out of the cover of the building.

"What the hell are you doing?" Whiskey had shouted.

"Showing no mercy," he shouted through gritted teeth. He charged forward like John Wayne on the warpath, shooting from both hips, taking out one enemy rebel after the other.

Something hit him square in his armor-plated chest, knocking him backward a step. It hurt like hell and made his breath lodge in his lungs, but it didn't stop him. He forged his way toward the enemy, firing until he ran out of ammo. Dropping to the ground, he slammed magazines into the rifle and the pistol and rolled to a prone position, aimed and fired, taking down as many of the enemy as he could. He'd be damned if even one of them survived.

When there were only two combatants left in the street, Caveman lurched to his feet and went after them. He wouldn't rest until the last one died.

He hadn't slowed as he rounded the corner. A bullet had hit him in the leg. Caveman grunted. He would have gone down, but the adrenaline in his veins surged, pushing him to his destination. He aimed his pistol at the shooter who'd plugged his leg and caught him between the eyes. Another bogey shot at him from above.

Caveman dove to the ground and rolled behind a stack of crates. Pain stabbed him in the shoulder and the leg, and warm wetness dripped down both. He leaned around the crates, pulled his night-vision goggles in place, located the shooter on the rooftop and took him out.

With the streets clear, he had a straight path to the original target. Holstering his handgun, he pulled a grenade out of his vest, pushed to his feet and staggered a few steps, pain slicing through him. He could barely feel his leg and really didn't give a damn.

Two steps, three... One after the other took him to the biggest structure in the neighborhood. As he rounded the corner, one of the two guards protecting the doorway fired at him.

The man's bullet hit the stucco beside him.

Caveman jerked back behind the corner, stuck his M4A1 around the corner and fired off a burst. Then he leaped out, threw himself to the ground, rolled and came up firing. Within moments, the two guards were dead.

The door was locked or barred from the inside. Pulling the pin on the grenade, Caveman dropped it in front of the barrier and then stepped back around the corner, covering his ears.

The blast shook the building and spewed dust and

wooden splinters. Back at the front entrance, Caveman kicked the door the rest of the way in and entered the building.

Going from room to room, he fired his weapon, taking out every male occupant in his path. When he reached the last door, he kicked it open and stood back.

The expected gunfire riddled the wall opposite the door.

After the gunfire ceased, Caveman spun around and opened fire on the occupants of the room until no one stood or attempted escape.

His task complete, he radioed the platoon leader. "Eight down. Come get us." Only after each one of his enemies was dead did he allow himself to crumple to the ground. As if every bone in his body suddenly melted into goo, Caveman had no way left to hold himself up. Still armed with his M4A1, he sat in the big room and stared down at his leg. Blood flowed far too quickly. In the back of his mind, he knew he had to do something or he'd pass out and die. But every movement now took a monumental amount of effort, and gray fog gathered at the edges of his vision. He couldn't pass out now, his buddies needed him. They could be dead or dying. No matter how hard he tried, he couldn't straighten, couldn't rise to his feet. The abyss claimed him, dragging him to the depths of despair.

"CAVEMAN," A VOICE SAID.

He dragged himself back from the edge of a very dark, extremely deep pool that was his past—a different time…a terrible place. He shook his head to clear the memories and glanced across the room at his new boss for the duration of this temporary assignment. "I'm sorry, sir. You were saying?"

The leader of Homeland Security's Special Task Force Safe Haven, Kevin Garner, narrowed his eyes. "How long did you say it's been since you were cleared for duty?"

"Two weeks," Caveman responded.

Kevin's frown deepened. "And when was the last time you met with a shrink?"

"All through the twelve weeks of physical therapy. She cleared me two weeks ago." His jaw tightened. "I'm fully capable of performing whatever assignment is given to me as a Delta Force soldier. I don't know why I've been assigned to this backcountry boondoggle."

Kevin's shrewd gaze studied Caveman so hard he could have been staring at him under a microscope. "Any TBI with your injury?"

"I was shot in the leg, not the head. No traumatic brain injury." Anger spiked with the need to get outside and breathe fresh air. Not that the air in the loft over the Blue Moose Tavern in Grizzly Pass, Wyoming, was stale. It was just that whenever Caveman was inside for extended periods, he got really twitchy. Claustrophobia, the therapist had called it. Probably brought on by PTSD.

A bunch of hooey, if you asked Caveman. Something the therapist could use against him to delay his return to the front. And by God, he'd get back to the front soon, if he had to stow away on a C-130 bound for Afghanistan. The enemy had to pay for the deaths of his friends; the members of his squad deserved retribution. Only one other man had survived, Whiskey, and he'd lost an eye in the firefight.

The slapping sound of a file folder hitting a tabletop made Caveman jump.

"That's your assignment," Kevin said. "RJ Khalig, pipeline inspector. He's had a few threats lately. I want you to touch bases with him and provide protection until we can figure out who's threatening him."

Caveman glared at the file. "I'm no bodyguard. I shoot people for a living."

"You know the stakes from our meeting a couple days ago in this same room, and you've seen what some of the people in this area are capable of. As I said then, we think terrorist cells are stirring up already volatile locals. Since we found evidence that someone is supplying semiautomatic weapons to what we suspect is a local group called Free America, we're afraid more violence is imminent."

"Just because you found some empty crates in

that old mine doesn't mean whoever got the weapons plans to use them to start a war," Caveman argued.

"No, but we're concerned they might target individuals who could potentially stand in the way of their movements."

"Why not let local law enforcement handle it?" Caveman leaned forward, reluctant to open the file and commit to the assignment. He didn't want to be in Wyoming. "If this group picks off individuals, would that not be local jurisdiction?"

Kevin nodded. "As long as they aren't connected with terrorists. However, the activity on social media indicates something bigger is being planned and will take place soon."

"How soon?"

Kevin shook his head. "We don't know."

"Sounds pretty vague to me." Caveman stood and stretched.

"I set up this task force to stop a terrible thing from happening. If I had all of the answers, likely I wouldn't need you, Ghost, Hawkeye or T-Rex. I'm determined to stop something bad from happening, before it gets too big and a lot more lives are lost."

"I don't know if you have the right guy for this job. I'm no investigator, nor am I a bodyguard."

"I understand your concern, but we need trained combatants, familiar with tactics and subversive operations. As you've seen for yourself and know from experience, it's pretty rough country out here and the people can be stubborn and willing to take the law into their own hands. I'm afraid what happened at the mine two days ago could happen again."

Caveman snorted. "That was a bunch of disgruntled ranchers, mad about the confiscation of their herd."

"Agreed," Kevin said. "Granted, the Vanders family took it too far by kidnapping a busload of kids. But they knew about the weapons stored in that mine."

"Are any of them talking?"

"Not yet. We're waiting for one of them to throw the rest under the bus."

"You might be waiting a long time." Caveman crossed his arms over his chest. "People out here tend to be very stubborn."

"You're from this area," Kevin said. "You should know."

"I'm from a little farther north, in the Crazy Mountains of Montana. But we're all a tough bunch of cowboys who don't like it when the government interferes with our lives."

"Hold on to that stubbornness. You might need it around here. For today, you'll be an investigator and bodyguard. Mr. Khalig needs your help. He has an important job, inspecting the oil and gas pipelines running through this state. Contact his boss for his location, find him and get the skinny on what's going on. You might have to run him down in the backwoods."

Until he was cleared to return to his unit, Caveman would do the best he could for his temporary boss and the pipeline inspector. What choice did he have? As much as he hated to admit it, they needed help out in the hills and mountains of Wyoming. The three days he'd been there had proven that.

Caveman had met with Kevin's four-man special operations team members. One Navy SEAL, one Delta Force soldier, an Army ranger and a highly skilled Marine. Ghost, one of the Delta Force men, had been assigned to protect a woman who had been surfing the web for terrorist activity. Her daughter had been one of the children who had been kidnapped on the bus.

Caveman, Kevin and the other three members of the task force had mobilized to save the children and the three adults on board the bus. The bus driver didn't make it, but the children and the two women survived.

Kevin stood and held out his hand. "Thanks for helping out. We have such limited resources in this neck of the woods, and I feel there's a lot more to what's going on here than meets the eyes."

"I'll do what I can." Caveman shook Kevin's hand and left the loft, descending the stairs to the street below. When he'd entered the upstairs apartment, the sky had been clear and blue. In the twenty minutes he'd been inside, clouds had gathered. The superstitious would call it an omen, a sign or a portent of things to come. Caveman called them rain clouds. If he was going to get out to where Khalig was, he'd have to get moving.

GRACE SAUNDERS PULLED her horse to a halt and dismounted near the top of a ridge overlooking the mountain meadow where Molly's wolf pack had been spotted most recently. Based on the droppings she'd seen along the trail and the leftover bones of an elk carcass, they were still active in the area.

She tied her horse to a nearby tree and stretched her back and legs. Having been on horseback since early that morning, she was ready for a break. Moving to the highest point, she stared out at the brilliant view of the Wyoming Beartooth Mountain Range, with the snowcapped peaks and the tall lodgepole pines. The sky above had been blue when she'd started her trek that morning. Clouds had built to the west, a harbinger of rain to come soon. She'd have to head down soon or risk a cold drenching.

From where she stood, Grace could see clear across the small valley to the hilltop on the other side. She frowned, squinted her eyes and focused on something that didn't belong.

A four-wheeler stood at the top of the hill, halfway tucked into the shade of a lodgepole pine tree. She wondered what someone else was doing out in the woods. Most people stuck to the roads in and out of the national forest.

It wasn't unusual for the more adventurous souls to ride the trails surrounding Yellowstone National Park, since ATVs in the park itself were prohibited. Scanning the hilltop for the person belonging to the four-wheeler, Grace had to search hard. For a moment she worried the rider might be hurt. Then she spotted him, lying on his belly on the ground.

Grace's heartbeats ratcheted up several notches. The guy appeared to have a rifle of some sort with a scope. Since it was summer, the man with the gun had no reason to be aiming a rifle. It wasn't hunting season.

Grace followed the direction the barrel of the weapon was pointed, to the far side of the valley. She couldn't see any elk, white-tailed deer or moose. Was he aiming for wolves? Grace raised her binoculars to her eyes and looked closer.

A movement caught her attention. She almost missed it. But then she focused on the spot where she'd seen the movement and gasped.

A man squatted near the ground with a device in his hand. He stared at the device as he slowly stood.

Grace shifted the lenses of her binoculars to the man on the ridge. He tensed, his eye lining up with the scope. Surely he wasn't aiming at the man on the ground.

Her pulse hammering, Grace lowered her binoculars and shouted to the man below. "Get down!"

At the same time as she shouted, the sound of rifle fire reached her.

The man on the floor of the valley jerked, pressed a hand to his chest and looked down at blood spreading across his shirt. He dropped to his knees and then fell forward.

Grace pressed a hand to her chest, her heart hammering against her ribs. What had just happened? In her heart she knew. She'd just witnessed a murder. Raising her binoculars to the man on the hilltop, she stared at him, trying to get a good look at him so that she could pick him out in a lineup of criminals.

He had brown hair. And that was all she could get before she noticed the gun he'd used to kill the man on the valley floor was pointing in her direction, and he was aiming at her.

Instinctively, Grace dropped to the ground and rolled to the side. Dust kicked up at the point she'd been standing a moment before. The rifle's report sounded half a second later.

Grace rolled again until she was below the top of the ridge. Afraid to stand and risk being shot, she crawled on all fours down to where she'd left her horse tied to a tree.

Hot Target

An engine revved on the other side of the ridge, the sound echoing off the rocky bluffs.

Her pulse slamming through her body, Grace staggered to her feet, her knees shaking. She ran toward the horse. The animal backed away, sensing her distress, pulling the knot tighter on the tree branch.

Her hands trembling, Grace struggled to untie the knot.

Tears stung her eyes. She wanted to go back to the man on the ground and see if he was still alive, but the shooter would take her out before she could get there. Her best bet was to get back down the mountain and notify the sheriff. If she rode hard, she could be down in thirty minutes.

Finally jerking the reins free of the branch, Grace swung up onto the horse.

The gelding leaped forward as soon as her butt hit the saddle, galloping down the trail they'd climbed moments before.

Grace slowed as she approached a point at which the trail narrowed and dropped off on one side. With the gelding straining at the bit to speed up, Grace held him in check as they eased down the trail. She glanced back at the ridge where she'd been. A four-wheeler stood on top, the rider holding a rifle to his shoulder.

Something hit the bluff beside her. Dust and rocks splintered off, blinding her briefly. Throwing caution to the wind, she gave the horse his head and held on, praying they didn't fall off the side of the trail. She didn't have a choice. If she didn't get around the corner soon, she'd be shot.

Her gelding pushed forward, more sure of his footing than Grace. She ducked low in the saddle and held on, praying they made it soon. The bluff jutted out of the hillside and would provide sufficient cover for a few minutes. Long enough for her to make it to the trees. The shooter could still catch up, but the trail twisting through the thick trunks of the evergreens would give her more cover and concealment than being in the open. If she made it down to the paved road, she could wave someone down.

Riding like her hair was on fire, Grace erupted from the trees at the base of the mountain trail. A truck with a trailer on the back was parked on the dirt road. She slowed to read the sign on the door, indicating Rocky Mountain Pipeline Inc. No sooner had she stopped than a shot rang out, plinking into the side of the truck.

Grace leaned low over her horse and yelled, "Go, go, go!" The horse took off across a field, galloping hard.

Then, as if he tripped, he stumbled and pitched forward.

Grace sailed through the air, every move appearing in slow motion. She made a complete somersault before she landed on her feet. Momentum carried her forward and she landed hard on her belly in the tall grass, her forehead bumping the ground hard. For a moment, she couldn't breathe and her vision blurred. She knew she couldn't stay there. The guy on the four-wheeler would catch up to her and finish the job.

An engine roared somewhere nearby.

Grace low-crawled through the grass, blinking hard to clear the darkness slowing her down. When she could go no farther, she collapsed in the grass, no longer able to fight against the fog closing in around her. She closed her eyes.

It wouldn't take the gunman long to find her and end it.

Then she felt a hand on her shoulder and heard a man calling to her as if from the far end of a long tunnel.

"Hey, are you all right?" a deep, resonant voice called out.

Grace gave the last bit of her strength to pushing herself over onto her back. She made it halfway and groaned.

The hand on her shoulder eased her the rest of the way, until she lay facing her attacker. "Are you going to kill me?"

"What?" he said. "Why would I want to kill you?"

"You killed the man in the valley. And you tried to kill me," she said, her voice fading into a whisper.

"I'm not here to kill anyone."

"If you do. Just make it quick." She tried to blink her eyes open, but they wouldn't move. "Just shoot me. But don't hurt my horse." And she passed out.

Chapter Two

Caveman shook his head as he stared down at the strange woman. "Shoot you? I don't even know you," he muttered. He glanced around, searching for others in the area. She had to have a reason to think he was there to kill her.

He ran his gaze over her body, searching for wounds. Other than the bump on her forehead, she appeared to be okay, despite being tossed by her horse.

The animal had recovered his footing and taken off toward the highway.

Caveman would have the sheriff come out and retrieve the horse. For now, the woman needed to be taken to the hospital. He ran back to his truck for his cell phone, knowing the chances it would work out there were slim to none. But he had to try. He checked. No service.

How the heck was he supposed to call for an airlift? Then he remembered where he was. The foothills of the Beartooth Mountains. He didn't have the radio communications he was used to, or the helicopter support to bring injured teammates out of a bad situation.

With no other choice, he threw open the truck's rear door, returned to the woman, scooped her up in his arms and carried her to his truck. Carefully laying her on the backseat, he buckled a seat belt around her hips and stared down at her. Just to make certain she was still alive, he checked for a pulse.

Still beating. *Good.*

She had straight, sandy-blond hair, clear, makeup-free skin and appeared to be somewhere between twenty-five and thirty years old. The spill she'd taken from her horse could have caused a head, neck or back injury. If they weren't in the mountains, where bears, wolves and other animals could find her, he would have left her lying still until a medic could bring a backboard, to avoid further injury. But out in the open, with wolves and grizzlies a real threat, Caveman couldn't leave the woman.

He shut the door and climbed into the driver's seat. The man he was supposed to meet out there would have to wait. This woman needed immediate medical attention.

As soon as he got closer to the little town of Grizzly Pass, he checked his phone for service. He had enough to get a call through to Kevin Garner. "Caveman here. I have an injured woman in the backseat of my truck. I'm taking her to the local clinic. You'll have to send someone else out to meet with Mr. Khalig. I don't know when I'll get back out there."

"Who've you got?" Kevin asked.

"I don't know. She was thrown from the horse she was riding. She hasn't been conscious long enough to tell me her life history, much less her name."

"Grace," a gravelly voice said from the backseat.

Caveman glanced over his shoulder.

"My name's Grace Saunders." The woman he'd settled on the backseat pushed to a sitting position and pressed a hand to the back of her head. "Who are you? Where am I?"

"I take it she's awake?" Kevin said into Caveman's ear.

"Roger." He shot a glance at the rearview mirror, into the soft gray eyes of the woman he'd rescued. "Gotta go, Kevin. Will update you as soon as I know anything."

"I'll see if I can find someone I can send out to check on Mr. Khalig," Kevin said.

His gaze moving from the road ahead to the reflection of the woman behind him, Caveman focused on Kevin's words. "I found a truck and trailer where his office staff said it would be, but the man himself wasn't anywhere nearby."

"I suspect that truck and trailer either belong to

the dead man or the man who was doing the shooting," the woman in the backseat said.

"Dead man?" Caveman removed his foot from the accelerator. "What dead man? What shooting?"

"I'll tell you when we get to town. Right now my head hurts." She touched the lump on her forehead and winced. "Where are we going?"

He didn't demand to know what she was talking about, knowing the woman needed medical attention after her fall. "To the clinic in Grizzly Pass." He'd get the full story once she had been checked out.

"I don't need to go to the clinic." She leaned over the back of the seat and touched his shoulder. "Take me to the sheriff's office."

Caveman frowned. "Lady, you need to see a doctor. You were out cold."

"My name is Grace, and I know what I need. And that's to see the sheriff. *Now.*"

He glanced at her face in the mirror. "Okay, but if you pass out, I'm taking you to the clinic. No argument."

"Deal." She nodded toward the road ahead. "You'd better slow down or you'll miss the turn."

Caveman slammed on his brakes in time to pull into the parking lot.

Grace braced her hands on the backs of the seats and swayed with the vehicle as it made the sharp turn. "I was okay, until you nearly gave me whiplash." She didn't wait for him to come to a complete stop before she pushed open her door and dropped down from the truck, crumpling to the ground.

Out of the truck and around the front, Caveman bent to help, sliding his hands beneath her thighs. "We're going to the clinic."

She pushed him away. "I don't need to be carried. I can stand on my own."

"As you have so clearly demonstrated." He drew in a breath and let it out slowly. "Fine. At least let me help you stand upright." He slipped an arm around her waist and lifted her to her feet.

When she was standing on her own, she nodded. "I've got it now."

"Uh-huh. Prove it." He let go of her for a brief moment.

Grace swayed and would have fallen if he'd let her. But he didn't. Instead he wrapped his arm around her waist again and led her into the sheriff's office.

With his help, she made it inside to the front desk.

The deputy on the other side glanced up with a slight frown, his gaze on Caveman. "May I help you?" His frown deepened as he looked toward the woman leaning on Caveman. "Grace?" He popped up from his desk. "Are you all right?"

"I'm fine, Johnny. Is Sheriff Scott in? I need to talk to him ASAP."

"Yeah. I'll get him." He glanced from her to Caveman and back. "As long as you're okay."

Anger simmered beneath the surface. Caveman glanced at the man's name tag. "Deputy Pierce, just get the damn sheriff. I'm not going to hurt her. If I was, I would have left her lying where her horse threw her."

The deputy's lips twitched. "Going." He spun on his heels and hurried through a door and down a hallway. A moment later, he returned with an older man, dressed in a similar tan shirt and brown slacks. "Grace, Johnny said you were thrown by your horse." He held out his hand. "Shouldn't you be at the clinic?"

Grace took the proffered hand and shook her head. "I don't need to see a doctor. I need you and your men to follow me back out to the trail I was on. Now."

"Why? What's wrong?" Sheriff Scott squeezed her hand between both of his. "The wolves in trouble?"

"It's not the wolves I'm worried about right now." She drew in a deep breath. "There was a man. Actually there were two men." She stiffened in the curve of Caveman's arm. "Hell, Sheriff, I witnessed a murder." She let her hand drop to her side as she sagged against Caveman. "I saw it all happen…and I was too far away…to do anything to stop it." She sniffed.

"You have to get out there. Just in case he isn't dead. It'll get dark soon. The wolves will find him."

"Is that why you were riding your horse like you were?" Caveman asked.

She nodded. "That, and someone was shooting at me. That's why Bear threw me." Her head came up and she stared at the sheriff. "I need to find Bear. He's running around out there, probably scared out of his mind."

Sheriff Scott touched her arm. "I'll send someone out to look for him and bring him back to your place." He glanced at Caveman. "And you are?"

"Max Decker. But my friends call me Caveman."

The sheriff's eyes narrowed. "And what do you have to do with all of this?"

Grace leaned back and stared up at the man she'd been leaning on. "Yeah, why were you out in the middle of nowhere?"

"I was sent to check on a Mr. Khalig, a pipeline inspector for Rocky Mountain Pipeline Inc. I was told he'd been receiving threats."

"RJ Khalig?" the sheriff asked.

Caveman nodded. "That's the one."

"He's been a regular at the Blue Moose Tavern since he arrived in town a couple weeks ago. He's staying at Mama Jo's Bed-and-Breakfast," Sheriff Scott added.

Grace shook her head. "I'll bet he's the man I saw

get shot. He appeared to be checking some device in a valley when the shooter took him down."

"What exactly did you see?" Sheriff Scott asked.

"Yeah," Caveman said. "I'd like to know, as well."

GRACE'S INSIDES CLENCHED and her pulse sped up. "I was searching for one of the wolves we'd collared last spring. His transponder still works, but hasn't moved in the past two days. Either he's lost his collar, or he's dead. I needed to know." Grace took a breath and let it out, the horror of the scene she'd witnessed threatening to overwhelm her.

"I was coming up to the top of a hill, hoping to see the wolf pack in the valley below, so I tied my horse to a tree short of the crown of the ridge. When I climbed to the crest, I saw a vehicle on a hilltop on the other side of the valley. It was an all-terrain vehicle, a four-wheeler. I thought maybe the rider had fallen off or was hurt, so I looked for him and spotted him in the shade of a tree, lying in the prone position on the ground, and he was aiming a rifle at something in the valley." She twisted her fingers. "My first thought was of the wolves. But when I glanced down into the valley, the wolf pack wasn't there. A man was squatting near the ground, looking at a handheld device.

"When I realized what was about to happen, I yelled. But not soon enough. The shooter fired his shot at the same time. The man in the valley didn't have a chance." She met the sheriff's gaze. "I couldn't even go check on him because the shooter must have heard my shout. The next thing I knew, he was aiming his rifle at me." She shivered. "I got on my horse and raced to the bottom of the mountain."

"And he followed?"

She nodded. "He shot at me a couple of times. I thought I might have outrun him, but he caught up about the time I reached the truck and trailer Mr. Decker mentioned. He shot at me, hit the truck, my horse threw me and I woke up in the backseat of Mr. Decker's truck." She inhaled deeply and let it all out. "We have to go back to that valley. If there's even a chance Mr. Khalig is alive, he won't be by morning."

"I'll take my men and check it out."

Grace touched his arm. "I'm going with you. It'll take less time for you to find him if I show you the exact location."

"You need to see a doctor," the sheriff said. "As you said, I don't have time to wait for that." He glanced at Caveman. "Do you want me to have one of my deputies take you to the clinic?"

Grace's lips firmed into a straight line. "I'm not going to a clinic. I'm going back to check on that man. I won't rest until I know what happened to him. If you won't take me, I'll get on my own four-wheeler and go up there. You're going to need all-terrain vehicles, anyway. Your truck won't make it up those trails."

The sheriff nodded toward his deputy. "Load up the trailer with the two four-wheelers. We're going into the mountains." He faced Grace. "And we're taking her with us."

"I'll meet you out at Khalig's truck in fifteen minutes. It'll take me that long to get to my place, grab my four-wheeler and get back to the location." She faced Caveman. "Do you mind dropping me off at my house? It's at the end of Main Street."

"I'm going with you," Caveman said.

"You're under no obligation to," she pointed out.

"No, but when you find an unconscious woman in the wilderness, you tend to invest in her well-being." His eyes narrowed. He could be as stubborn as she was. "I'm going."

"Do you have a four-wheeler?"

"No, but I know someone who probably does." Given the mission of Task Force Safe Haven, Kevin Garner had to have the equipment he needed to navigate the rocky hills and trails. If not horses, he had to have four-wheelers.

"I'm not waiting for you," Grace warned.

"You're not leaving without me," he countered.

"Is that a command?" She raised her brows. "I'll have you know, I'll do whatever the hell I please."

Caveman sighed. "It's a suggestion. Face it, if your shooter is still out there, you'll need protection."

"The sheriff and deputy will provide any protection I might need."

"They will be busy processing a crime scene."

"Then, I can take care of myself," Grace said. "I've been going out in these mountains alone for nearly a decade. I don't need a man to follow me, or protect me."

The sheriff laid a hand on her arm. "Grace, he's right. We'll be busy processing a crime scene. Once you get us there, we won't have time to keep an eye on you."

"I can keep an eye on myself," she said. "I'm the one person most interested in my own well-being."

Caveman pressed a finger to her lips. "You're an independent woman. I get that. But before now, you probably have never had someone shooting at you. I have." He took her hand. "Even in the worst battlefield scenarios, I rely on my battle buddies to have my back. Let me get your back."

For a moment, she stared at his hand holding hers. Then she glanced up into his gaze. "Fine. But if you can't keep up, I'll leave you behind."

He nodded. "Deal."

SHE GAVE THE truck and trailer's location to the sheriff and the deputy. Because she didn't want to slow them down from getting out to the site, she was forced to accept a ride from the man who'd picked her up off the ground and carried her around like she was little more than a child.

A shiver slipped through her at the thought of Caveman touching her body in places that hadn't been touched by a man in too long. And he'd found her unconscious. Had she been in the city, anything could have happened to her. In the mountains, with a shooter after her, she hated to think what would have happened had Caveman not come along when he had.

If the killer hadn't finished her off, the wolves, a bear, a mountain lion could have done it for him. Much as she hated to admit it, she was glad the stranger had come along and tucked her into the backseat of his truck.

"We'll meet you in fifteen minutes," Grace said to the sheriff.

He tipped his cowboy hat. "Roger." Then he was all business back on the telephone before Grace made it to the door.

Once outside, Grace strode toward Caveman's truck, now fully in control of the muscles in her legs. She didn't need to lean on anyone. Nor did she need help getting up into the truck.

Caveman beat her to the truck and opened the passenger door.

She frowned at the gesture, seeing it as a challenge to her ability to take care of herself.

"Just so you don't think I'm being chauvinistic, I always open doors for women. My mother drilled that into my head at a very young age. It's a hard habit to break, and I have no intention of doing that now. It's just being polite."

Grace slid into the seat and gave a low-key grunt. "You don't have to make a big deal out of it," she said through clenched teeth.

Caveman rounded the front of the truck, his broad shoulders and trim waist evidence of a man who took pride in fitness. She'd bet there wasn't an ounce of fat on his body, yet he didn't strut to show off his physique. The man had purpose in his stride, and it wasn't the purpose of looking good, though he'd accomplished that in spades. And he was polite, which made Grace feel churlish and unappreciative of all he'd done for her.

When he slid into the driver's seat beside her, she stared straight ahead, her lips twisting into a wry smile. "Thank you for helping me when I was unconscious. And thank you for giving me a ride to my house." She glanced across at him. "And thank you for opening my door for me. It's nice to know chivalry isn't dead."

His lips twitched. "You're welcome." Twisting

the key in the ignition, he shot a glance toward her. "Where to?"

She gave him the directions to her little cottage sitting on an acre of land on the edge of town. She hoped Bear had found his way home after his earlier scare. The town of Grizzly Pass was situated in a valley between hills that led up into the mountains. Grace had ridden out that morning from the little barn behind her house.

As she neared the white clapboard cottage with the wide front porch and antique blue shutters, she leaned forward, trying to see around the house to the barn. Was that a tail swishing near the back gate?

Caveman pulled into the driveway.

Before he could shift into Park, she was out of the truck and hurrying around to the back of the house.

Her protector switched off the engine and hurried after her. "Hey, wait up," he called out.

Grace ignored him, bent and slipped through the fence rails and ran toward the back gate next to the barn, her heart soaring.

Bear stood at the gate, tossing his head and dancing back on his hooves.

She opened the gate and held it wide.

Bear slipped through and turned to nuzzle her hand.

Grace reached into her jeans pocket and pulled out the piece of carrot she'd planned on giving Bear as a treat at the end of the day. She held it out in the palm of her hand.

Bear's big, velvety lips took the carrot and he crunched it between his teeth, nodding his head in approval.

Wrapping her arms around his neck, Grace hugged the horse, relieved he wasn't hurt by the bullet or by wandering around the countryside and crossing highways. "Hey, big boy. Glad you made it home without me." She held on to his bridle and leaned her forehead against his. "I bet you're hungry and thirsty."

Bear tossed his head and whinnied.

With a laugh, Grace straightened and walked toward the barn. Bear followed.

Inside, she opened the stall door. Bear trotted in.

She removed Bear's bridle and was surprised to find Caveman beside her loosening the leather strap holding the girth around the horse's middle. "I can take care of that," she assured him.

"I know my way around horses," he said, and pulled the saddle from Bear's back. "Tack room?"

"At the back of the barn. I can handle the rest. I just want to get him situated before we leave."

"No problem." He took the saddle and carried it to the tack room. Caveman reappeared outside the stall. "I'll be right back."

"I'm leaving as soon as I'm done here."

"Understood." He took off at a jog out of the barn.

With her self-appointed protector gone, Grace suddenly had a feeling of being exposed. Shrugging off the insecurity, she went to work, giving the horse food and water, and then closed the stall.

From another stall, she rolled her four-wheeler out into the open. She hadn't ridden it in a month and the last time she had, it had been slow to start. She'd had to charge the battery and probably needed to buy a new one, but she didn't have time now. She'd promised to meet the sheriff in fifteen minutes. Already five had passed.

The next five minutes, she did everything she knew to start the vehicle and it refused.

Just when she was about to give up and call the sheriff, a small engine's roar sounded outside the barn.

She walked out and shook her head.

Caveman sat on a newer-model ATV. "Ready?"

"Where did you get that?"

"My boss dropped it off." He checked the instruments, revved the throttle and looked up. "I thought you'd be gone by now."

"I can't get mine to start, and we're supposed to be there in five minutes."

"Let me take a look." He killed the engine and entered the barn.

Okay, so she wasn't that knowledgeable about mechanics. She knew Wally, who had a small-engine repair shop in his barn. He fixed anything she had issues with. That didn't mean she couldn't take care of herself.

"Your battery is dead." Caveman glanced around. "You got another handy?"

She shook her head. "No. Fresh out."

"Got a helmet?"

She nodded. "Yeah, but I won't need it if I can't get my ATV started."

He spun and headed for the barn door. "You can ride on the back of mine," he called out over his shoulder.

Grace's heart fluttered at the thought riding behind Caveman, holding him around the waist to keep from falling off. "No, thanks. Those trails are dangerous." She suspected the danger was more in how her pulse quickened around the man than the possibility of plunging over the edge of a drop-off.

"I grew up riding horses and four-wheelers on rugged mountain trails. I won't let you fall off a cliff." He held up a hand. "Promise."

She frowned. But she knew she only had a few minutes to get to the meeting location and relented, sighing. "Okay. I guess I'll put my life in your hands." She followed him out of the barn and closed the door behind her. "Although I don't know why I should trust you. I don't even know you."

Chapter Three

Caveman settled on the seat of the ATV and tipped his head toward the rear. "Hop on."

Grace fitted her helmet on her head and buckled the strap beneath her chin. "Wouldn't it make more sense for me to drive, since I know the way?"

"Actually, it does." He grinned, scooted to the back of the seat and glanced toward her, raising his brows in challenge.

Still, Grace hesitated for a moment, gnawing on her bottom lip.

God, when she did that, Caveman's groin clenched and he fought the urge to kiss that worried lip and suck it into his mouth. The woman probably had no clue how crazy she could make a man. And he was no exception.

Finally, she slid onto the seat in front of Caveman. "Hold on." She thumbed the throttle and the four-wheeler leaped forward.

Caveman wrapped his arms around her waist and pressed his chest to her back. Oh, yeah, this was much better than driving.

Grace aimed for the back gate to the pasture, blew through and followed a dirt road up into the hills, zigzagging through fields and gullies until she crossed a highway and ended up on the road leading to Khalig's truck and trailer. Another truck and trailer stood beside the original, this one marked with the county sheriff logo. Sheriff Scott and Deputy Pierce were mounted on four-wheelers.

Grace nodded as she passed them, leading the way up the side of a mountain, the trail narrowing significantly. There was no way a full-size truck or even an SUV could navigate the trajectories. Barely wide enough for the four-wheeler, the path clung to the side of a bluff. The downhill side was so steep it might as well be considered a drop-off. Anyone who fell over the edge wouldn't stop until they hit the bottom a hundred or more feet below.

Now not so sure he'd chosen the right position, Caveman wished he had control of steering the ATV. He tightened his arms around Grace's slim waist, wondering if she had the strength to keep them both on the vehicle if they hit a really big bump.

Caveman vowed to be the driver on the way back down the mountain. In the meantime, he concentrated on leaning into the curves and staying on the ATV.

As they neared the top of a steep hill, Grace slowed and rolled to a stop. "This is where I tied off my horse."

The sheriff and deputy pulled up beside them. Everyone dismounted.

Fighting the urge to drop to a prone position on the ground and kiss the earth, Caveman stood and pretended the ride up the treacherous trail hadn't been a big deal at all. "You rode your horse down that trail?"

She nodded. "Normally, I take it slowly. But I had a gunman taking shots at me. I let Bear have his head. I have to admit, I wanted to close my eyes several times on the way down."

The sheriff nodded toward the ridgeline. "Was that your vantage point?"

She nodded, but didn't move toward the top. "The shooter was on the ridge to the north."

Sheriff Scott and the deputy drew their weapons and climbed. As they neared the top, they dropped to their bellies and low-crawled the rest of the way. The sheriff lifted binoculars to his eyes.

Caveman stayed with Grace in case the shooter was watching for her.

A couple minutes later, Sheriff Scott waved. "All

clear. Grace, I need you to show me what you were talking about."

Grace frowned, scrambled up to the top and squatted beside the sheriff.

Caveman followed, his gaze taking in the valley below and the ridge to the north. Nothing moved and nothing stood out as not belonging.

Grace pointed to the opposite hilltop. "The shooter was over there." Then she glanced down at the valley, her frown deepening. "The man he shot was in the valley just to the right of that pine."

The sheriff raised his binoculars to his eyes again. "He's not there."

"What?" She held out her hand. "Let me see."

Sheriff Scott handed her the binoculars. Grace adjusted them and stared down at the valley below. "I don't understand. He was in that valley. Hell, his truck and trailer are still parked back at the road. Where could he have gone?" She handed the binoculars back to the sheriff. "Do you think he was only wounded and crawled beneath a bush or something?" She was on her feet and headed back to the ATV. "We need to get down there. If that man is still alive, he could be in a bad way."

The sheriff hurried to catch up to her. "Grace, I want you to stay up here with Mr. Decker."

She'd reached the ATV and had thrown her leg over the seat before she turned to stare at the sheriff. "Are you kidding? I left him once, when I could have saved him."

The sheriff shook his head. "You don't know that. You could have ended up a second victim, and nobody would have known where to find either one of you." He touched her arm. "You did the right thing by coming straight to my office."

When the lawman turned away, Grace captured his hand. "Sheriff, I need to know. I feel like I could have done something to stop that man from shooting the other guy. I know it's irrational, but somehow I feel responsible."

The way she stared at the sheriff with her soft gray eyes made Caveman want the sheriff to let her accompany him to the valley floor.

"You promise to stay back enough not to disturb what could potentially be a crime scene?" Sheriff Scott asked.

She held up her hand like she was swearing in front of a judge. "I promise."

The sheriff shot a glance at Caveman. "Mr. Decker, will you keep an eye on her to make sure she's safe?"

"I will," Caveman said. He wanted to know what was in that valley as well, but if it meant leaving Grace alone on the ridge, he would have stayed with her.

"Fine. Come along, but stay back." Sheriff Scott and the deputy climbed onto their four-wheelers and eased their way down a narrow path to the valley floor.

Caveman let Grace drive again, knowing she was better protected with his body wrapped around her than if she'd ridden on the back.

At the bottom of the hill, Grace parked the four-wheeler twenty yards from the pine tree she'd indicated. "We'll see a lot more on foot than on an ATV."

"True." Caveman studied the surrounding area, careful to stay out of the way of the sheriff and his deputy.

"Grace," the sheriff called out.

She and Caveman hurried over to where the sheriff squatted on his haunches, staring at the dirt. He pointed. "Is this the spot where he fell?"

Grace glanced around at the nearby tree and nodded. "I think so."

The sheriff's lips pressed together and he pointed at the ground. "This looks like dried blood."

Caveman stared at the dark blotches, his belly tightening. He'd seen similar dark stains in the dust of an Afghanistan village where his brothers in arms had bled out.

"Got tire tracks here." Deputy Pierce stared at the ground a few yards away.

The sheriff straightened and walked slowly toward the deputy. "And there's a trail of blood leading toward the tracks."

Caveman circled wide, studying the ground until he saw what he thought he might find. "More tracks over here." The tracks led toward a hill. Without waiting for permission, Caveman climbed the hill, parallel to the tracks. As the ground grew rockier, the tracks became harder to follow. At that point, Caveman looked for disturbed pebbles, scraped rocks and anything that would indicate a heavy four-wheeler had passed that direction.

At the top of the hill, the slope leveled off briefly and then fell in a sheer two-hundred-foot drop-off to a boulder-strewn creek bed below. Caveman's stomach tightened as he spotted what appeared to be the wreckage of an ATV. "I found the ATV." He squinted. What was that next to the big boulder shaped like an anvil? He leaned over the edge a little farther and noticed what appeared to be a shoe... attached to a foot. "I'm sorry to say, but I think I found Mr. Khalig."

Grace scrambled to the top of the hill and nearly pitched over the edge.

Caveman shot out his hand, stopping her short of following the pipeline inspector to a horrible death. "Oh, dear Lord."

Wrapping his arm around her shoulders, Caveman pulled her against him.

She burrowed her face into his chest. "I should have stayed."

"You couldn't," Caveman said. "You would have been shot."

"I could have circled back," she said, her voice quivering.

"On that trail?" Caveman shook his head. "No way. You did the right thing."

Sheriff Scott appeared beside Caveman. "Mr. Decker's right. You wouldn't be alive if you'd stopped to help a man who could have been dead before he went over the edge."

Grace lifted her head and stared at the sheriff through watery eyes. "What do you mean?"

"We noticed footprints and drag marks in the dirt back there," Deputy Pierce said.

The sheriff nodded. "I suspect the killer came back, dragged the body onto the ATV and rode it up to the hill. Then he pushed it over the edge with Mr. Khalig still on it." He glanced over at the deputy. "We'll get the state rescue team in to recover the body. The coroner will conduct an autopsy. He'll know whether the bullet killed him or the fall."

"Is there anything we can do to help?" Grace asked.

Sheriff Scott nodded. "I'd like you to come in and sign a statement detailing what you saw and at what time."

"Anything you need. I'll be there." Grace shivered. "I wish I'd seen the killer's face."

"I do, too." The sheriff stared down at the creek bed. "Murder cases are seldom solved so easily." He glanced across at Grace. "You might want to watch your back. If he thinks you could pick him out in a lineup, he might come after you."

Grace shivered again. "We live in a small town." Her gaze captured the sheriff's. "There's a good chance I might know him."

"If the law isn't knocking on his door within twenty-four hours," Caveman said, "he might figure out that you didn't see enough of him to turn him in."

"In which case, he'd be smart to keep a low profile and leave you alone," the sheriff added.

"Or not." Grace sighed. "I can't stay holed up in my house. I have work to do. I still haven't found my wolf."

"It might not be safe for you to be roaming the woods right now," the sheriff said. "By yourself, you present an easy target with no witnesses."

Grace's shoulders squared. "I won't let fear run my life. I ran today, and Mr. Khalig is dead because I did."

Caveman shook his head. "No, Mr. Khalig is dead because someone shot him. Not because you didn't stop that someone from shooting him. You are not responsible for that man's death. You didn't pull the trigger." The words were an echo from his psychologist's arsenal of phrases she'd used to help

him through survivor's guilt. Using them now with
Grace helped him see the truth of them.

He hadn't detonated the bomb that had killed
his teammates, nor had he pulled the trigger on the
AK-47s that had taken out more of his battle buddies.
He couldn't have done anything differently other
than die in his teammates' place by being the forward element at that exact moment. He couldn't have
known. It didn't make it easier. Only time would help
him accept the truth.

"THERE IS SOMETHING you could do for me," the sheriff said.

Grace perked up. "Anything." After all that had
happened, she refused to be a victim. She wanted
to help.

"Go back down, get in my service vehicle and let
dispatch know to call in the mountain rescue crew.
Johnny and I will stay and make sure the wolves
don't clean up before they get here."

"Will do," Grace said. "Do you need me to come
back?"

"No. We can handle it from here. You should head
home. And please consider lying low for a while
until we're sure the killer isn't still gunning for you."

"Okay," Grace said. Though she had work to do,
she now knew she wasn't keen on being the target of
a gunman. She'd give it at least a day for the man to

realize she hadn't seen him and couldn't identify his face. "You'll let me know what they find out about the man down there?"

"You bet," Sherriff Scott said. "Thank you, Grace, for letting us know as soon as possible."

But not soon enough to help Mr. Khalig. She turned and started back down the hill. Her feet slipped in the gravel and she would have fallen, but Caveman was right beside her and helped her get steady on her feet. He hooked her elbow and assisted her the rest of the way down the steep incline.

At the bottom, he turned her to face him. "Are you okay?"

She nodded. "I'm fine, just a little shaken. It's not every day I witness a murder."

His lips twisted. "How many murders have you witnessed?"

"Counting today?" She snorted. "One." With a nod toward the ATV, she said, "You can drive. I'm not sure I can hold it steady." She held up a hand, demonstrating how much it trembled.

"Thanks. I would rather navigate the downhill trail. Coming up was bad enough." He climbed onto the ATV and scooted forward, allowing room for her to mount behind him.

At this point, Grace didn't care that he was a stranger. The man had found her unconscious, sought help for her and then gone with her to show the sheriff where a murder had taken place. If he'd been the shooter, he'd have killed her by now and avoided the sheriff altogether.

She slipped onto the seat and held on to the metal rack bolted to the back of the machine, thinking it would be enough to keep her seated.

"You need to hold on around my waist," Caveman advised. "It's a lot different being on the back than holding on to the handlebars."

"I'll be okay," she assured him.

Caveman shrugged, started the engine and eased his thumb onto the throttle.

The ATV leapt forward, nearly leaving Grace behind.

She swallowed a yelp, wrapped her arms around his waist and didn't argue anymore as they traversed the downhill trail to the bottom.

When she'd been the target of the shooter, she hadn't had time to worry about falling off her surefooted horse. Now that she wasn't in control of the ATV and was completely reliant on Caveman, she felt every bump and worried the next would be the one that would throw her over the edge. She tightened her hold around his middle, slightly reassured by the solid muscles beneath his shirt.

For a moment, she closed her eyes and inhaled the scent of pure male—a mix of aftershave and raw, outdoor sensuality. It calmed her.

Although she'd always valued her independence, she could appreciate having someone to lean on in this new and dangerous world she lived in. Before, she'd only had to worry about bears and wolves killing her. Now she had to worry about a man diabolical enough to hunt another man down like an animal.

By the time they finally reached the bottom and made their way back to the parked trucks, Grace's body had adjusted to Caveman's movements, making them seem like one person—riding the trails, absorbing every bump and leaning into every turn.

When the vehicles came into view, she pulled herself back to the task at hand.

Caveman stopped next to the sheriff's truck and switched off the ATV's engine.

Grace climbed off the back, the cool mountain air hitting her front where the heat generated by Caveman still clung to her. Shaking off the feeling of loss, she opened the passenger door of the sheriff's vehicle, slid onto the front seat, grabbed the radio mic and pressed the button. "Hello."

"This is dispatch, who am I talking to?"

"Grace Saunders. Sheriff Scott wanted me to relay a request for a mountain rescue team to be deployed to his location as soon as possible."

"Could you provide a little detail to pass on to the team?" the dispatcher asked.

Grace inhaled and let out a long slow breath before responding. "There's a man at the bottom of a deep drop-off."

"Is he unconscious?"

The hollow feeling in her chest intensified. "We believe he's dead. He's not moving and he could be the victim of a gunshot wound."

"Got it. I'll relay the GPS coordinate and have the team sent out as soon as they can mobilize."

"Thank you." Grace hung the mic on the radio and climbed out of the sheriff's SUV.

"Now what?" Caveman asked. He'd dismounted from the four-wheeler and stepped up beside the sheriff's vehicle while she'd been talking on the radio.

She shrugged. "If you could take me back to my place, I have work to do."

Caveman frowned. "When we get there, will you let me take you to the clinic to see a doctor?"

"I don't need one." Her head hurt and she was a little nauseated, but she wouldn't admit it to him. "I'd rather stay home."

"I'll make a deal with you. I'll take you home if you promise to let me take you from there to see a doctor."

She sighed. "You're not going to let it go, are you?"

He crossed his arms over his chest and shook his head. "Nope."

"And if I don't agree, either I walk home—which

I don't mind, but I'm not in the mood—or I wait until the sheriff is done retrieving Mr. Khalig's body."

His lips twitched. "That about sums it up. See a doctor, walk home alone or wait for a very long time." He raised his hands, palms up. "It's a no-brainer to me."

Her eyes narrowed. "I'll walk." She brushed past him and lengthened her stride, knowing she was too emotionally exhausted to make the long trek all the way back to her house, but too stubborn to let Caveman win the argument.

The ATV roared to life behind her and the crunch of gravel heralded its approach.

"You might also consider that by walking home, you put yourself up as an easy target for a man who has proven he can take a man down from a significant distance. Are you willing to be his next target?"

His words socked her in the gut. She stopped in her tracks and her lips pressed together in a hard line.

Damn. The man had a good point. "Fine." She spun and slipped her leg over the back of the four-wheeler. "You can take me to my house. From there, I'll take myself to the clinic."

Caveman shook his head, refusing to engage the engine and send the ATV toward Grace's house. "That's not the deal. I take you home. Then I will take you to the clinic. When the doctor clears you to drive, you can take yourself anywhere you want to go."

"Okay. We'll do it your way." She wrapped her arms loosely around his waist, unwilling to be caught up in the pheromones the man put off. "Can we go, already?"

"Now we can go." He goosed the throttle. The ATV jumped, nearly unseating Grace.

She tightened her hold around Caveman's waist and pressed her body against his as they bumped along the dirt road with more potholes than she remembered on the way out. Perhaps because she noticed them more this time because she wasn't the one in control of the steering. Either way, she held on, her thighs tightly clamped around his hips and the seat.

By the time they arrived at her cottage, she could barely breathe—the fact having nothing to do with the actual ride so much as it did with the feel of the man's body pressed against hers. She was almost disappointed when he brought the vehicle to a standstill next to her gate.

Grace climbed off and opened the gate. The distance between them helped her to get her head on straight and for her pulse to slow down to normal.

He followed her to her house. "We'll take my truck. Grab your purse and whatever else you'll need."

When she opened her mouth to protest, he held up his hand.

"You promised." He frowned and crossed his arms over his chest again. "Where I come from, a promise is sacred."

Her brows met in the middle. "Where *do* you come from?"

His frown disappeared and he grinned. "Montana."

Caveman started toward the house, Grace fell in step beside him. "Is that where you were before you arrived in Grizzly Pass?"

His grin slipped. "No."

She shot a glance his direction. A shadow had descended on his face and he appeared to be ten years older.

"Where *did* you come from?"

He stared out at the mountains. "Bethesda, Maryland."

There was so much she didn't know about this man. "That's a long way from Montana."

"Yes, it is." He stopped short of her porch. "I'll be in my truck when you're ready." Before she could say more, he turned and strode toward the corner of her house.

For a moment, Grace allowed herself the pleasure of watching the way his butt twitched in his blue jeans. The man was pure male and so ruggedly handsome he took her breath away. What was he doing hanging around her? Since she was being forced to ride with him to the clinic, she'd drill him with questions until she was satisfied with the answers. For starters, why did he call himself Caveman? And what was the importance of Bethesda, Maryland, that had made him go from being relaxed and helpful to stiff and unapproachable?

Caveman disappeared around the corner.

Grace faced her house, fished her key from her pocket and climbed the stairs. She opened the screen door and held out the key, ready to fit it into the lock when she noticed something hanging on the handle. It rocked back and forth and then fell at her feet.

She jumped back, emitting a short, sharp scream, her heart thundering against her ribs. With her hand pressed to her chest, she squatted and stared at the item, a lead weight settling in the pit of her belly as she recognized the circular band with the rectangular plastic box affixed to it.

It was the radio collar for the wolf she'd been looking for earlier that day, and it was covered in blood.

Chapter Four

Caveman had been about to climb into his truck when he heard Grace's scream. All thoughts of Bethesda, physical therapy and war wounds disappeared in a split second. He pulled his pistol from beneath the seat and raced back around the house to find Grace sitting on the porch, her back leaning against the screen door, her hand pressed to her chest.

"What's wrong?" His heart thundered against his ribs and his breathing was erratic as he stared around the back porch, searching for the threat.

"This." She pointed toward something on the porch in front of her. It appeared to be some kind of collar. Her gaze rose to his, her eyes wide, filling with tears. "This is the collar for the wolf I was looking for when I ran across the murder scene."

"What the hell's it doing here?"

"It was hanging on the handle of the door. Someone put it there."

"Do you have any coworkers who would have brought it to you?" Caveman reached out a hand to her.

She laid her slim fingers into his palm and allowed him to pull her to her feet and into his arms. "It has blood on it and it's been cut."

"Why would someone put it on your doorknob?" he asked.

She drew in a deep breath and let it out. "I was out in the mountains where I was because I was following the signal for this collar. It had stopped moving as of two days ago. The only other people aware of the wolf's movement, or lack thereof, were my coworkers on the Wolf Project out of Yellowstone National Park. This collar belonged to Loki, a black male wolf out of Molly's pack. I rescued him as a cub when his mother had been killed by a local rancher." Her jaw tightened, she drew herself up and gave him a level stare through moist eyes. "We suspected he was dead, but had hoped of natural causes. That someone brought me the collar without a note of why it was covered in blood leaves me to think all kinds of bad things."

"You think the shooter who killed Khalig might have killed the wolf?"

"If he didn't kill the wolf, I think he wants me to believe he did."

"And he left the collar as a warning or a trophy?"

Grace stared down at the offensive object and nodded. "What else am I supposed to think? Unless someone else owns up to leaving the collar on my back porch doorknob, I can only imagine why it was left." She bent, reaching for the collar.

Caveman grabbed her arm to keep her from retrieving it. "Leave it there for the sheriff. They might be able to pull fingerprints from the plastic box."

Grace straightened. "Why do people have to be so destructive and heartless with nature?"

"I don't know, but let's get you inside, just in case the shooter is lurking nearby."

Grace shot a glance over her shoulder. "Do you think he might be out there watching?" A shiver shook her body.

"He could be." Caveman held out his hand. "Let me have your key."

She pointed at the porch near the collar. "I dropped it."

Caveman retrieved it from the porch and straightened. "Let's go through the front door." Slipping his arm around her, he shielded her body with his as much as possible as he led her around the house to the front door. There he opened the screen door. Before he fit the key into the lock, he tried the knob. It was locked. He fit the key in the knob, twisted and pushed the door open. "Let me go first."

She nodded and allowed him to enter first, following right behind him.

Closing the door behind her, he stared down into her eyes. "I want to check the house. Stay here."

Again, she nodded.

Caveman moved from room to room, holding his 9-millimeter pistol in front of him, checking around the corners of each wall before moving into a room. When he reached the back door, he checked the handle. The door was locked. As far as he could tell, the house hadn't been entered. "All clear," he called out.

"The sheriff will be busy up in the hills until they retrieve the body," Grace said, walking into the kitchen, her arms wrapped around her body. "I don't like the idea of leaving the collar on the porch."

"Do you have a paper bag we can use and maybe some rubber gloves?"

"I do." She hurried into a pantry off the kitchen and emerged with a box of rubber gloves and what appeared to be a paper lunch bag. Setting the box of gloves on the counter, she pulled on a pair. "These won't fit your big hands. I'll take care of the collar."

He opened the back door and looked before stepping over the collar and standing on the porch. He used his body as a shield to protect Grace in case the shooter had her in his sights. Given the killer had good aim with a rifle and scope, he could be hiding in the nearby woods, his sights trained on her back door.

Grace scooped up the collar by the nylon band and dropped it into the paper bag, touching as little as possible.

Once she had the collar in the bag, she nodded. "I'll grab my purse. We can drop this off at the sheriff's office."

"On the way to the clinic," Caveman added.

Her lush lips pulled into a twisted frown. "On the way to the clinic." The frown turned up on the corners. "You are a stubborn man, aren't you?"

He grinned and followed her back into the house, locking the door behind him. "I prefer to call it being persistent."

She walked back through the house. "If you give me just a minute, I'd like to wash my hands and face."

"Take your time. I'll wait by the front door."

Grace turned down the hallway and ducked into the bathroom, closing the door behind her.

Caveman waited in the front entrance, staring at the pictures hanging on the walls. Many were of wolves. Some were of people. One had a group of men and women standing in front of a cabin, all grinning, wearing outdoor clothing. Another photo was of Grace, maybe a few years younger, with a man. They were kissing with the sun setting over snowcapped peaks in the background. She looked young, happy and in love.

Something tugged at Caveman's chest. He'd assumed Grace was single.

The door opened to the bathroom and Grace appeared, her face freshly scrubbed, still makeup-free. She'd brushed her hair and left it falling around her shoulders the way it was in the picture.

"You have some interesting pictures on your wall." Caveman nodded toward the wolves.

She nodded. "I'm living my dream job as a biologist working on the Wolf Project, among others. The pictures are of some of the wolves I've been tracking for the past five years."

Caveman pointed toward the group picture.

Grace smiled. "Those are the crew of biologists working in Yellowstone National Park. We keep in touch by phone, internet and through in-person meetings once a month."

"Do you live alone?" Caveman asked, his gaze on the picture of her kissing the man. "Should I be concerned about a jealous husband walking through the door at any moment?"

The smile left Grace's eyes. "Yes, I live alone. No, you don't have to worry." She grabbed a brown leather purse from a hallway table and opened the front door. "I'm ready."

"I take it I hit a sore spot," he said, passing her to exit the house first.

"I'm not married, anymore."

But she was once. Caveman vowed not to pry. Apparently, she wasn't over her ex-husband. Not if she still had his picture hanging in her front entrance.

Grace paused to lock the front door and then turned to follow him toward the truck. "For the record, I'm a widow. My husband died in a parasailing accident six years ago."

GRACE CLIMBED INTO the passenger seat of Caveman's truck. "You really don't have to take me to the clinic. I've been getting around fine for the past couple of hours without blacking out. I could drive myself there, for that matter."

"Humor me. I feel—"

"Responsible," she finished for him. "Well, you're not. You've done more than you had to. You could have dropped me off at the sheriff's office earlier today and been done with me."

"That's not the kind of guy I am."

She tilted her head and stared across the console at him. "No, I got that impression." She settled back in her seat, closed her eyes and let him take control, something she wasn't quite used to. "Well, thank you for coming to my rescue. If you hadn't been there…" She shivered. What would have happened? Would the shooter have caught up to her and finished her off like he'd done Mr. Khalig?

A hand touched hers.

She opened her eyes, her gaze going to where his hand held hers and warmth spread from that point throughout her body. She hadn't had that kind of reaction to a man's touch since Jack had died, and she wasn't sure she wanted it.

"I'm glad I was there." Caveman squeezed her fingers gently, briefly and let go. "I'm sorry about your husband."

"Yeah. Me, too. We were supposed to be doing this together." She shrugged and let go of the breath she hadn't known she was holding the whole time Caveman's hand had been on hers. "But that was six years ago. Life goes on. Turn left at the next street. The clinic is three blocks on the right."

They arrived in front of the Grizzly Pass Clinic a few minutes before it was due to close. "I doubt they can get me in."

"If they can't, where's the nearest emergency room?" Caveman shifted into Park and stepped down from the truck. Rounding the front of the vehicle, he arrived in time to help her down.

"The nearest would be in Bozeman, an hour and a half away."

"Guess we better get inside quickly." He cupped her elbow and guided her through the door.

Fortunately, the doctor had enough time left to check her over while her self-appointed bodyguard waited in the lobby.

"You appear to be all right. If you get any dizzy spells or feel nauseated, you might want to call the EMTs and have them transport you to the nearest hospital for further evaluation. But so far, I don't see anything that makes me too concerned." He offered her a prescription for painkillers, which she refused. "Then take some over-the-counter pain relievers if you get a headache."

She smiled. "Thank you for seeing me on such short notice."

"I'm glad I was here for you." He walked her to the door. "Have you considered wearing a helmet when you go horseback riding?"

"I have considered it. And I might resort to it, if I continue to fall off my horse." She might also consider a bulletproof vest and making the helmet a bulletproof one if she continued to be the target of a sniper. She didn't say it out loud, nor had she told the doctor why she'd fallen off her horse. The medical professional had been ready to go home before she'd shown up and he wasn't the one being shot at.

When she stepped out of the examination room into the lobby, she found Caveman laughing at something the cute receptionist had said. The smile on his face transformed him from the serious, rugged cowboy to someone more lighthearted and approachable. The sparkle in his eyes made him even more handsome than before.

A territorial feeling washed over Grace. Suddenly she had a better understanding of the urge the alpha wolf had to guard his mate and keep her to himself. Not that Caveman was Grace's mate. Hell, they'd just met!

But that didn't stop her fingers from curling into her palms or her gut from clenching when the receptionist smiled up at the man.

"Are you ready to take me home?" Grace asked, her voice a little sharper than usual.

Caveman straightened and turned his smile toward her, brightening the entire room with its full force. Then it faded and his brows pulled together. "What did the doctor say?"

"I'm fine. Can we go now?" She started for the door, ready to leave the office and the cute, young receptionist as soon as possible.

Grace was outside on the sidewalk by the time Caveman caught up with her and gripped her arm. "Slow down. It might not be safe for you to be out in the open. Care to elaborate on the doctor's prognosis?"

"He said I'm fine and can carry on, business as usual." She shook off his hand.

"No concussion?"

"No concussion. Which means you can drop me off at my house, and your responsibility toward me is complete."

He nodded and opened the truck door for her. "If you don't mind, I'd like to stop by my boss's office for a few minutes. I need to brief him on what happened. He might want to hear what you have to say."

"Now that we're not being shot at, and I'm not dying of a concussion, maybe you can answer a few questions for me."

"Shoot." He winced. "Sorry. I didn't mean the pun."

She inhaled and thought of all the questions she had for this man. "Okay. Who's your boss?"

"The US Army, but I'm on temporary loan to a special task force with the Department of Homeland Security. I'm reporting to a man named Kevin Garner."

"I've seen Kevin around. I didn't know he was heading a special task force."

"It's new. I'm new. I got in a couple days ago, and I'm still trying to figure out what it is I'm supposed to be doing."

"Army?" That would explain the short hair, the military bearing and the scars. "For how long?"

"Eleven years."

"Deployed?"

He nodded, his gaze on the road ahead. "What is this? An interrogation?"

"I've been all over the mountains with you and I don't know who you are."

"I told you, I'm Max Decker, but my friends call me—"

"Caveman." She crossed her arms over her chest. "Why?"

"Why what?"

"Why do they call you Caveman?"

"I don't know. I guess because I look like a caveman? I got tagged with it in Delta Force training, and it's stuck ever since."

"Army Delta Force?" She looked at him anew. "Isn't that like the elite of the elite?"

He shrugged. "I like to think of it as highly skilled. I'm not an elitist."

"And you're assigned to the Department of Homeland Security?" She shook her head. "Who'd you make mad?"

His fingers tightened on the steering wheel until his knuckles turned white. "I'd like to know that myself."

"Wait." Her eyes narrowed. "You said you came from Bethesda. Isn't that where Walter Reed Army Hospital is located?"

A muscle ticked in his jaw. "Yeah. I was injured

in battle. I just completed physical therapy and was waiting for orders to return to my unit."

"And you got pulled to help out here." It was a statement, not a question. "Any you carried me to your truck." She raked his body with her gaze. "I don't see you limping or anything."

"I told you. I finished my physical therapy. I've been working out since. I'm back to normal. Well, almost."

"What did you injure?"

He dropped his left hand to his thigh. "My leg."

"Gunshot?"

"Yeah."

"I'm sorry." She dragged her gaze away from him. "I didn't mean to get too personal."

"It's okay. When you're in the hospital, everyone gets pretty damned personal. I'm used to it by now."

"It had to be hard."

"What?"

"The hospital."

His replaced his hand on the steering wheel, as he pulled into the parking lot of the Blue Moose Tavern. "At least I made it to the hospital," he muttered.

Grace heard his words but didn't dig deeper to learn their meaning. She could guess. He'd made it to the hospital. Apparently, some of his teammates hadn't.

Sometimes recovering from an injury was easier

than recovering from a loss. She knew. Having lost her husband in a parasailing accident, she understood what it felt like to lose someone you loved.

From what she knew about the Delta Force soldiers, they were a tightly knit organization. A brotherhood. Those guys fought for their country and for each other.

Grace realized she and Caveman had more in common than she'd originally thought.

Chapter Five

Caveman got out of the truck in front of the Blue Moose Tavern, his thoughts on the men who'd lost their lives in that last battle. For a moment, he forgot where he was. He looked up at the sign on the front of the tavern and shook his head.

Like Grace had said, life moves on. He couldn't live in the past. Squaring his shoulders, he focused on the present and the woman who'd witnessed a murder. Kevin would want to hear what she had to say. Since the man who'd been shot was most likely RJ Khalig, it had to have something to do with the threats the man had reported, the reason Garner had sent Caveman out to find the pipeline inspector.

A pang of guilt tugged at his insides. If he hadn't delayed his departure, arguing over his assigned duties, would he have found Khalig before the sniper?

He shook his head. When he'd arrived at the base

of the trail, he wouldn't have been able to find the man without GPS tracking and an all-terrain vehicle. *No.* He couldn't have gotten to Khalig before the shooter.

Grace was out of the truck before Caveman could reach her door. She sniffed the air. "I didn't realize how hungry I was until now."

Caveman inhaled the scent of grilled hamburgers and his mouth watered. "Let's make it quick with Garner. If you're like me, you haven't eaten since breakfast this morning."

"And that was a granola bar." She glanced toward the tavern door. "They make good burgers here."

"Then we'll eat as soon as we're done upstairs." Caveman waved a hand toward the outside staircase leading up to the apartment above the tavern.

Grace rested her hand on the railing and climbed to the top.

Caveman followed closely, once again shielding Grace's body from a sniper's sights.

Before they reached the top landing, the door swung open. Kevin Garner greeted them. "Caveman, I'm glad you stopped by." He stepped back, allowing them to enter the upstairs apartment. Once they were inside, he closed the door, turned to Grace and held out his hand. "I've seen you in passing, but let me introduce myself. Kevin Garner, Department of Homeland Security."

"Grace Saunders. I'm a biologist assigned to the Wolf Project, working remotely with the National Park Service out of Yellowstone."

"Interesting work." Garner shook her hand. "I'm glad you stopped by. I wanted to hear what happened today. The last thing I knew, you were recovering from being thrown by your horse, and Caveman needed a four-wheeler to go back into the mountains. Care to fill me in on what's happened since you got up this morning?"

Grace spent the next five minutes detailing what she'd seen on that ridge in the mountains and what had followed, taking him all the way to her back porch and the present she'd received.

She held out the paper bag with the dog collar inside. "Can I assume you have some of the same capabilities or access to the same support facilities as the sheriff's office?"

Garner took the bag, opened it and stared inside, his brows furrowing. "What do you have here?"

"The collar for number 755. Loki, the wolf I was tracking when I went up in the mountains this morning."

"I don't understand." His glance shot from Grace to Caveman and back to Grace. "Where's the wolf?"

Her lips firmed into a tight line. "Most likely dead. But I haven't seen the body to confirm." Grace nodded toward the bag. "That was left on my back porch as a gift."

"We suspect that whoever killed Khalig might have killed the wolf and decided to leave this on Grace's back porch," Caveman said.

Kevin's brows twisted. "Why?"

His jaw tightening, Caveman glanced toward Grace. "Possibly as a warning to keep her mouth shut about the murder she witnessed."

Kevin stared at the collar. "Or he might be a sadistic bastard, trying to scare her. Otherwise, why would he kill the wolf?"

"Target practice?" Grace suggested, her face pale, her jaw tight.

"Could he be one of the local ranchers who has lost livestock because of the reintroduction of wolves to the Yellowstone ecosystem?" Garner asked.

Grace nodded. "He could be."

"Or he could be a game hunter wanting a trophy for his collection," Caveman said. "Why else would he remove the collar?"

Grace frowned. "You think he killed the wolf before he took out Mr. Khalig?"

Caveman caught Grace's gaze and held it. "You said, yourself, the collar had been stalled in the same location for two days. He had to have killed the wolf two days ago."

"And he retraced his steps to where he'd killed

him just to retrieve the collar?" Grace shook her head. "Doesn't make sense. I saw him kill Mr. Khalig. You'd think he'd get the hell off the mountain and come up with an alibi for where he was when I witnessed the murder."

"Unless he's cocky and wants to play games with you," Caveman said.

Grace shivered and wrapped her arms around her middle. "That's a lot of assumption."

"Still, if this guy thinks he can get away with the murder, and he's flaunting that fact by gifting you with this collar, you need to be careful," Garner said. "If he thinks you can identify him, he might take it a step further."

Grace turned and paced away from Garner and Caveman. Then she spun and marched back. "I don't have time to play games with a killer. I have work to do."

Caveman closed the distance between them and gripped her arms. "And who will do that work if you're dead?"

She stared up at him, her gray eyes widening. "You really think he'll come after me?"

"He already has once, right after the murder. If he left that collar, that makes two times."

"Three's a charm," Grace muttered, raising her hands to rest on Caveman's chest. Instead of pushing him away, she curled her fingers into his shirt. "What am I supposed to do?"

Garner tapped an ink pen on a tabletop where he had a map of the area spread out. "Khalig had received threats. I hadn't been able to pinpoint from whom. I have to assume whoever was threatening him had to have a gripe with the pipeline industry."

"What kind of threats?" Caveman asked.

"Someone painted 'Go Home' on his company truck's windshield two days ago. Yesterday, he had all four tires slashed. I tried to talk him out of going out into the field until we got to the bottom of it, but he insisted he had work to do."

Caveman raised his brows and stared down at the woman in his arms. "Sound familiar?"

"Okay." Grace rolled her eyes. "I get the point." She stepped back, out of Caveman's grip. "I don't know anything about the pipeline. Except that it goes through this area. Supposedly it's buried deep and not in an active volcanic location."

"There's been quite a bit of controversy about the pipelines and whether or not we should even have them. Activists love a cause," Garner said. "With oil prices going down, a lot of pipeline employees are out of work. That makes for some unhappy people who depended on the pipeline companies for their jobs. Then there are the ranchers who are angry at the pipeline companies having free access to cross their lands."

"And there are the ranchers who are mad at the government interfering with grazing rights on government property," Caveman added. "Like Old Man Vanders, whose herd was confiscated because he refused to pay the required fees for grazing on federally owned land."

Garner nodded. "That's what stirred up a lot of folks around here. There's a local group calling itself Free America. We found empty crates in the Lucky Lou Mine with indication they'd once been full of AR-15 rifles. We think the Free America folks have them and might be preparing to stage an attack on a government facility." Garner raised a hand. "I know. It's a lot to take in. Thus the need for me to borrow some of the best from the military."

Grace shook her head. "I had no idea things were getting so bad around here." She snorted. "With all that, don't forget the ranchers angry with the government for reintroducing wolves to the area. I know I get a lot of nastiness from cattlemen when they find one of their prize heifers downed by a wolf pack."

Caveman crossed his arms over his chest. "Since Khalig is a pipeline inspector, is it safe to assume the shooter targeted him because of something to do with the pipeline?"

"That would be my bet. But that doesn't negate the

possibility that Khalig might have stumbled across something secret the Free America militia were plotting."

"He was checking some kind of instrument," Grace reiterated. "From what I could tell, he didn't appear to be afraid or nervous about anything. He straightened, still glancing down at his equipment, when the shooter took him down."

"For whatever reason he was murdered," Garner said, "we don't want anything to happen to you, just because you witnessed it."

Grace stiffened. "Don't worry about me. I can take care of myself."

"Do you own a gun?" Kevin asked.

Her chin tilted upward. "I do. A .40-caliber pistol."

"Do you know how to use it?" Caveman asked.

Her gaze shifted to the wall behind him. "Enough to protect myself."

"Are you sure about that?"

"I know how to load it, to turn off the safety and point it at the target."

"When was the last time you fired the weapon?" Caveman asked.

Her cheeks reddened. "Last year I took it to the range and familiarized with it."

Caveman's eyes widened. "A year?" He drew in a deep breath and let it out slowly. "Lady, you're no expert."

Her lips firmed and she pushed back her shoulders. "I didn't say I was. I said I knew how to use my gun."

"It's not enough," Garner said.

Grace turned her frown toward the DHS man. "What do you mean?"

Garner's gaze connected with Caveman's.

Caveman's gut tightened. He knew where Garner was going with what he'd just stated, and he knew he was getting the task.

"You need protection," Garner turned toward Grace.

She flung her hands in the air. "Why won't anyone believe me when I say I don't need someone following me around?" Those same hands fisted and planted on her hips. "I can take care of myself. I don't need some stranger intruding in my life."

"I wasn't going to suggest a stranger," Kevin said.

"Well, the sheriff's department has their hands full policing this area and finding a murderer," Grace shook her head. "I wouldn't ask them to babysit me, when I have my own gun."

"You need someone to watch your back." Garner held up a hand to stop Grace's next flow of words. "I wasn't going to suggest a stranger." He shifted his glance toward Caveman.

His lips twitching on the corners, Caveman couldn't help the grin pulling at his mouth when he stared at the horrified expression on Grace's face. Suddenly, being in Wyoming on temporary duty didn't seem so bad. Not if he could get under the skin of a beautiful biologist. As long as when it was all said and done, he could return to his unit and the career he'd committed his life to.

"YOU WANT *HIM* to follow me around?" Grace waved her hand toward Caveman. "He doesn't even want to be in Wyoming." She narrowed her eyes as she glared at Garner. "And you said you wouldn't suggest a stranger. I didn't know this man until sometime around noon today when I found myself loaded in the backseat of his truck like a kidnap victim." She shook her head. "No offense, but no thanks."

Garner's brows dipped. "Am I missing something? I thought you two were getting along fine."

Oh, they had gotten along fine, but she couldn't ignore the sensual pull the man had on her. "You are missing something," Grace said. "You're missing the point. I don't need a babysitter. I'm a grown woman, perfectly capable of taking care of myself." Perhaps the more she reiterated the argument, the more she would begin to believe it. Today had shaken her more than she cared to admit.

"Agreed," Garner said. "In most cases. But based on the evidence you've presented, you have a sniper after you. Who better than another sniper to protect you? Caveman is one of the most highly trained soldiers you'll ever have the privilege to meet. He understands how a sniper works, having been one himself."

Grace glanced at Caveman. Was it true? Was he a sniper as well as a trained Delta Force soldier?

He nodded without responding in words.

Her belly tightening, Grace continued to stare at this man who was basically a war hero stuck in Grizzly Pass, Wyoming.

"He's the most qualified person around to make sure you're not the next victim," the Homeland Security man said.

"But I—" Grace started.

"Let me finish." Garner laced his fingers together. "I'll speak with the sheriff's department and ask them if they have someone who could provide twenty-four/ seven protection for you."

Grace shook her head. "They don't have the manpower."

"Then I'll query the state police," Garner countered.

"They're stretched thin." Grace wasn't helping herself by shooting down every contingency plan Garner had.

"Look, Grace." Garner lifted her hand. "Let Caveman protect you until I can come up with an alternative." He squeezed her hand. "What's it going to hurt? So you have to put him up for a few nights. You have enough room in your house."

Caveman chuckled. "I promise to clean up after myself. And I can cook—if you like steaks on the grill or carryout."

She chewed on her bottom lip, worry chiseling away at her resistance. "You really think I'm at risk?"

Garner held up the paper bag and nodded. "Yes."

"And you can't always be looking over your shoulder," Caveman added. "I respect your independence, but even the most independent of us need help sometimes. I'll do my best not to disturb your work and stay out of your way as much as I can. The fact is, a killer has taken one life and he's left his calling card on your door. If I was you, I'd want a second pair of eyes watching out for me."

"What do you say?" Garner pressed.

Grace's lips twisted and her eyes narrowed as she stared at Caveman. She didn't want to be around him that much. He stirred up physical responses she hadn't felt since her husband died. It confused her and made her feel off balance. But they were right. She couldn't keep looking over her shoulder. She needed help. "I still want to get out and check on the other wolves."

"We'll talk about it," Caveman said.

"We'll do it," she insisted. "And I won't be confined to my house."

"We'll talk about going out in the woods. And I promise not to confine you to your house." He waved his hand out to the side. "We're having dinner at the tavern today. See? I can be flexible."

Another moment passed and Grace finally conceded. "Okay, but only for the short term. I'm used to living by myself. Having another person in my house will only irritate me."

"Fair enough." Garner grinned. "I'll see what I can do to resolve the situation so that you don't need to have a bodyguard."

"Thank you." Grace's stomach rumbled loudly, her cheeks heated and she gave a weak smile. "As for eating, *clearly* you know that I'm ready."

Again, Caveman chuckled. "Let's feed the beast. We can talk about where to go from here, over a greasy burger and fries."

Her belly growled again at the mention of food. "Now you're talking."

Garner walked them to the door and held it open. "Be careful and stick close to Caveman. He'll protect you."

"What about the collar?" Grace asked.

"I'll get it to the state crime lab. If they can lift prints, they'll be able to run them through the nationwide AFIS database to see if they have a match. I'll let you know as soon as I hear anything."

"Thanks, Kevin." Grace held out her hand.

He took it, his lips lifting on one corner. "You're welcome. I'm glad you'll be with Caveman."

Caveman was first out the door of the upstairs loft apartment, his gaze scanning the area, searching for anything, or anyone, out of the ordinary or carrying a rifle with a scope. Apparently satisfied the coast was clear, he held out his hand to Grace. "Stay behind me."

"Why behind you?" she asked.

"The best probability of getting a good shot comes from the west." He pointed toward the building on the south. "The buildings provide cover from the north to the south. And I'm your shield from the west. The staircase blocks the shooter's ability to get off a clear shot."

His explanation made sense. "But I don't want you to be a shield. That means if the killer takes a shot, he'll hit you first."

"That's the idea. If that happens, duck as soon as you hear the shot fired. If I'm hit and go down, he'll continue to fire rounds until he gets you."

"Seriously. You can't be that dense." She touched his shoulder, a blast of electricity shooting through her fingers, up her arms and into her chest. "I don't want you to take a bullet for me."

"Most likely the shooter won't be aiming for me. If I'm in the way, he'll wait for me to move out of the way so that he can get to you."

"That makes me feel *so* much better," she said, her voice strained. "We don't know that he'll come gunning for me, anyway."

"No, we don't. But are you willing to take the risk?"

Grace sighed. "No." What use was it to argue? The longer they were out in the open, the longer Caveman was exposed to Grace's shooter. "Hurry up then, before I pass out from hunger."

A chuckle drifted up to her. "Bossy much?"

"I get cranky when my blood sugar drops."

"I'll try to remember that and bring along snacks to keep that from happening." Caveman paused at the bottom of the stairs, hooked her arm with one of his hands and slipped the other around her shoulders.

Her pulse rocketed and she frowned up at him. "Is that necessary?"

"Absolutely. My arm around you makes it hard for anyone to distinguish one body from the other. Especially at a distance." His lips quirked on the edges. "I'll consider your reaction more of the low blood sugar crankiness."

Again, shut up by a valid argument, Grace suffered in silence. Although suffer was a harsh word when in fact she was far from suffering, unless she considered unfulfilled lust as something to struggle with.

Caveman opened the door to the tavern and waved her inside.

"Grace, it's been a while since you were in." A young woman with bright blond hair and blue eyes greeted them. "Would you like a table or to sit at the bar?"

"Hi, Melissa. We'd like a table," Grace responded.

"Hold on, just a minute. Let me see if there's one available." She disappeared into the crowded room.

"Is it always this busy?" Caveman stared around the room, his brows rising.

"As one of two restaurants in town, yes. The other one doesn't serve alcohol."

"I understand." He glanced around the room. "Do you know most of the people here?"

"Most," she said. "Not all. It's a small town, but we have people drift in who work on the pipeline or cowboys who come in town looking for work."

Caveman nodded. "It was like that in Montana, where I'm from. Everyone knew everyone else."

Melissa appeared in front of them. "I have a seat ready, if you'll follow me. Is this a date?" she asked, her gaze shooting to Grace.

"No," Grace replied quickly. She wasn't interested in Caveman as anything other than a bodyguard to keep her safe until they caught the killer.

"Oh? Business?" She turned her smile on Caveman.

"You could say that," Grace said.

"Yes, strictly business," Caveman agreed.

"That's nice." Melissa's eyelids dropped low. "In town for long?"

"I don't know," Caveman said.

Grace wasn't sure she liked the smile Melissa gave to Caveman, or that she was openly flirting with him when Grace was on the other side of the man. She wanted to call the girl out on her rude behavior, but was afraid she'd look like a jealous shrew. So she kept her mouth shut and seethed inwardly.

Not that she cared. Caveman could date any woman he wanted. Grace had no hold on him and would never have one. She'd sworn off men years ago, afraid to date one or form a bond. The men she'd been attracted to in the past had all died of one cause or another. The common denominator was their relationship with her.

Though she was a biologist and didn't believe in ghosts or fairy tales, she couldn't refute the evidence. Men who professed an affection for her died. What did that say about her? That she was a jinx.

The first had been her high school sweetheart, Billy Mays, who'd died in a head-on collision with a drunk man. The second had been when her husband, Jack, who'd died in a freak parasailing accident on their honeymoon in the US Virgin Islands. The third had been Patrick Jones, a man she'd only dated a few times. He'd died when he'd fallen off the big combine he'd been driving, and had been chopped into a hundred pieces before anyone could stop the combine.

Since then, she'd steered clear of relationships, hoping to spare any more deaths in the male population of Grizzly Pass, Wyoming. Which meant staying away from any entanglements with Caveman, the handsome Delta Force soldier who was only there on a temporary duty assignment. When he'd completed his assignment, he'd head back to his unit. Wherever that was. Even if she wasn't cursed, a connection with Caveman wasn't possible.

This meant she had no right to be jealous of Melissa's flirting with Caveman. The waitress was welcome to him.

Yeah, maybe not. The woman could have the decency to wait until Grace wasn't around.

In the meantime, Grace would have his full attention. She might as well find out more about the man, to better understand the person who would be providing her personal protection until a murderer was caught and incarcerated.

She hoped that was sooner rather than later. It was hard to take a seat across the table from the soldier who made her pulse thunder. It reminded her of everything she'd been missing since she'd given up on men.

Chapter Six

Caveman leaned across the table and captured Grace's hand in his. He'd been watching her glancing right and left as if searching for an escape route from the booth. "Hey. I really don't bite."

She gave him a poor attempt at a smile. "Sorry. I guess I've been alone so much lately that being in a crowded room makes me antsy."

"Concentrate on the menu." He picked up one and opened it. "What are you going to have?"

"A bacon cheeseburger," she said without even looking. "They make the best."

"Sounds good." He closed the menu without having looked. "I'll have the same."

A harried waitress arrived and plunked two cups of ice water on the table. "What can I get you to drink?"

"A draft beer for me."

"Me, too," Grace said. "And we're ready to order."

The waitress took their order and left, returning a few minutes later with two mugs filled with beer.

Caveman lifted his. "To finding a killer."

"Hear, hear." Grace touched her mug to his and drank a long swallow.

"I don't know too many women who like beer," Caveman said.

"And you say you're from Montana?" Grace snorted. "Lots of women drink beer around here."

He nodded. "It has been a while since I've been back in this area of the country. Hell, the world."

Grace set her mug on the table, leaned back and stared around the tavern. "Is it hard coming back?"

He nodded. "I feel like I have so much more to accomplish before I retire from the military."

"More battles to be fought and won?" Grace asked.

"Something like that." More like retribution for his brothers who'd lost their lives. He wanted to take out the enemy who'd lured them into an ambush and then slaughtered his teammates. Caveman shook his head and focused on Grace. "What about you? Are you from this area?"

She nodded. "Born and raised."

"Why don't you go live with your folks while the police search for the murderer?"

She laughed. "My work is here. My parents left Wyoming behind when my father retired from ranching. They live in a retirement community in Florida. They're even taking lessons on golfing."

"Are you an only child?"

A shadow crossed her face. "I am now."

"Sorry. I didn't mean to bring up bad memories."

"That's okay. It's been a long time. My little brother died of cancer when he was three. Leukemia."

"I'm so sorry."

"We all were. William was a ray of sunshine up to the very end. I believe he was stronger than all of us."

The waitress reappeared carrying two heaping plates. She set them on the table in front of them, along with a caddy of condiments. "If you need a refill, just wave me down. Enjoy."

She was off again, leaving Caveman and Grace to their meals.

Caveman gave himself over to the enjoyment of the best burger he'd ever tasted. "You weren't kidding," he said as he polished off the last bite. "I've never had a burger taste that good. What's their secret?"

"They grill them out back on a real charcoal grill. Even in the dead of winter, they have the grill going." Grace finished her burger and wiped the mustard off her fingers.

Caveman waved for the waitress and ordered two more draft beers and sat back to digest. "Do you mind my asking what happened to your husband?"

A shadow crossed her face and she pushed her fries around on her plate. "I told you, he died in a parasailing accident."

"You couldn't have been barely out of college six years ago."

"That's where we met. We were both studying biology. He went to work with Game and Fish, I landed a job with Yellowstone National Park. A match made in heaven," she whispered, her gaze going to the far corner of the room.

"That must have been hard. Was it on a lake around here?"

Her lips stretched in a sad kind of smile. "No, it was on our honeymoon in the Virgin Islands," she said, her voice matter-of-fact and emotionless.

Her words hit him square in the gut. "Wow. What a horrible ending to a new beginning." He covered her hand with his. "I'm sorry for your loss."

She stared at the top of his hand. "Like I said. It was a long time ago."

"You never remarried?"

She shook her head. "No."

"Didn't you say life goes on?"

"Yes, but that doesn't mean I had to go out and find another man to share my life. I'm content being alone."

Caveman wasn't dense. He could hear the finality of her statement. She wasn't looking for love from him or any other man. Which was a shame. She was beautiful in a natural, girl-next-door way. Not only was she pretty, she was intelligent and passionate about her work. A woman who was passionate about what she did had to be passionate in bed. At least that was Caveman's theory.

He found himself wondering just how passionate she could be beneath the sheets. His groin tightened and his pulse leaped at the thought. "You sound pretty adamant about staying alone. Don't you want to fall in love again?"

"No." She said that one word with emphasis. "Could we talk about something else?"

"Sure." He lifted his mug. "How about a toast to the next few days of togetherness."

"Okay. Let me." She raised her mug and tapped it against his, her gaze meeting his in an intense stare. "To keeping our relationship professional."

Caveman frowned. He didn't share her toast and didn't drink after she'd said the words. Though he knew he'd only be there until he got orders to return to his unit, he didn't discount the possibility of getting to know Grace better. And the more he was with her, the more he focused on the lushness of her lips and the gentle swell of her hips. This was a woman he could see himself in bed with, bringing out the same intensity of passion she displayed for her wolves.

Hell, he could see her as a challenge, one he'd

meet head-on. Maybe she only *thought* she liked being alone. After a week with him, she might change her mind.

The thought of staying with her for the night evoked a myriad of images, none of which were professional or platonic. He had to remind himself that he was there to work, not to get too close to the woman he was tasked with protecting. She obviously had loved her husband. Six years after the man's death, she had yet to get over him.

He could swear he'd felt something when he touched her. An electric surge charging his blood, sending it pulsing through his body on a path south to pool low in his belly. Riding behind her on the ATV, his arms wrapped around her slim waist, he'd leaned in to sniff the fresh scent of her hair, the mountain-clean aroma reminding him of his home in Montana.

He'd take her to her house, make sure she got inside all right and then he'd sleep on the porch or on the couch. The woman was hands-off. He didn't need the complication a woman could become. Especially one with sandy-blond hair and eyes the gray of a stormy Montana sky.

They didn't talk much through the remainder of their dinner. Before long, they were on their way to her house, silence stretching between them. The thought of being with this desirable woman had Caveman tied in knots.

His fingers wrapped tightly around the steering wheel all the way to her house. When he pulled up in her drive, he wondered if he should just drop her off and leave. She had temptation written all over her, and he was a man who'd gone a long time without a woman. Grace was not the woman with whom to break that dry spell.

Chapter Seven

Caveman pulled up the driveway in front of Grace's house, shoved the gear into Park and climbed down from the truck.

Grace pushed her door open and was halfway out when he made it around the front of the truck to help her down. With his hand on her arm, he eased her to the ground. "How are you feeling?"

The color was high in her cheeks, but she answered, "Fine. Really. No dizziness or nausea. I don't see any reason for you to stay the night here. I'll lock the doors and sleep with my gun under my pillow."

He shook his head, the decision already made. "No use shooting your ear off. I'm staying."

She frowned, pulled the keys from her pocket and opened the door. "I can take—"

"I know. I know. You can take care of yourself." Hell, she'd given him the out he needed. Why was he arguing?

She unlocked the door and entered.

Caveman stopped her before she got too far ahead of him. "Do you mind if I have a look around before you get comfortable?" he asked.

"Are you going to do this every time we enter my house?" she asked.

He nodded. "Until the killer is caught."

"Be my guest." She stepped into the hallway and made room for him to pass.

He slipped by, pulled his gun from beneath his jacket and made a sweep of the house, checking all the rooms. By the time he'd returned from the back bedrooms, Grace had left the front hallway.

He followed sounds of cabinet doors opening and closing in the kitchen where he found Grace, nuking a couple of mugs in the microwave.

"I hope you like instant coffee or hot tea."

"Coffee. Instant is fine."

The microwave beeped and she pulled the mugs out, set them on the counter and plunked a tea bag in one of them. "I'd drink coffee, but I don't want to be up all night. How do you do it?"

"Do what?"

"Sleep after drinking coffee?" she asked.

"You learn to sleep through almost anything when you're tired enough. Including a shot of caffeine."

She scooped a couple of spoonfuls of instant coffee into the hot water, dropped the spoon into the mug and set it on the kitchen table. Then she fished in the cupboard pulling out a bag of store-bought cookies. Carrying the cookies and her tea, she took the seat across from Caveman.

"So what's your story?" Grace dropped a teabag into her mug of hot water and dipped it several times.

The aroma of coffee and Earl Grey tea filled Caveman's nostrils and it calmed him without him actually having taken a sip. He inhaled deeply, took that sip and thought about her question.

Sitting in the comfort of her kitchen, the warm glow of the overhead light made the setting intimate somehow. Her gray-eyed gaze was soft and inviting, making him want to tell her everything there was to know about Max Decker. But he wouldn't be around long enough to make it worth the effort. She was part of the job. He was going back to his unit soon. No use wasting time getting to know each other. "I don't have a story."

"We've already established that you're from Montana." She raised her tea to her lips and blew a stream of air at the liquid's surface.

The motion drew his attention to the sexiest part of her face—her lips. Or was it her eyes?

"It's not a secret." He lifted his mug and sipped on the scalding hot coffee, more for something to do. He really hadn't wanted the drink.

She tipped her head to the side. "What did you do before the military?"

Grace wasn't going to let him get away with short answers. He might as well get the interview over with. "Worked odd jobs after high school. But I left for the military as soon as I graduated college."

Her gaze dropped to the tea in her cup. "Married?"

Cavemen felt his lips tug upward at the corners. "No."

"Ever?" Grace met his gaze.

"Never."

"Never have?" Her eyes narrowed. "Or never will?"

"Both."

Grace lifted her mug to her lips and took a tentative sip of the piping hot liquid and winced. "How long have you been away from your unit?" she continued with the inquisition.

Caveman sighed. "Fourteen weeks, five days and thirteen hours."

"But who's counting?" Grace smiled, the gesture lighting her eyes and her face.

Wow. He hadn't realized just how pretty she was until that moment. Her understated beauty was that of an outdoorsy woman with confidence and intelligence.

"Some say you either love the military or hate it? Which side of the fence are you on?" she asked.

His chest swelled. "Yeah, there have been some really bad times, but being a part of the military has been like being a part of a really big family. It's a part of me."

"I'll take that as a 'Love it.'"

Turnabout was fair play. She didn't have the corner on the questions market. Caveman told himself, he wanted to learn more about her because the information might help him keep her safe. But that wouldn't be totally true. He really was interested in her answers. He leaned back in his seat. "What about you?"

GRACE STIFFENED. "Nope. This interrogation is all about you. If I'm to trust you, I need to know more about you."

Caveman's lips quirked upward on the corners. "That's an unfair advantage."

"I never said I was fair. I am, however, nosy." She grinned and eased her mug onto the table to let the tea cool a little before she attempted another sip. "How are you with horses?"

He frowned. "Why?"

She pushed to her feet. "I need to feed and water my gelding. He's probably a little skittish after being shot at today." Grace started for the back door.

Caveman reached it before her. "You know, you

put yourself in danger every time you step out into the open."

"I know, but I put my livestock in danger by not feeding or watering them. I'm going out to take care of my horse. You can come or finish your coffee. Your choice."

"Coming." He opened the door and stepped out on the porch. After a cursory glance in both directions, he waved her out onto the porch and slipped his arm around her. "Just stay close to me. Don't give a shooter an easy target."

As much as she hated to admit it, she liked the feel of Caveman's arm around her. Though she knew a shooter could kill them both, if he really wanted to, she felt safer with the man's body next to hers.

Inside the barn, Bear whinnied and pawed the stall door.

"I'm coming," Grace said. She scooped a bucket of grain from the feed bin, opened the stall door and stepped inside.

Caveman grabbed a brush and entered with her.

Bear's nostrils flared. He pawed the ground and tossed his head, as if telling Grace he wasn't pleased with the other human entering his domain.

"Bear doesn't like strangers."

Caveman didn't get the hint. Instead he stood in the stall with the brush in his hand, not moving or getting any closer to the horse.

Grace opened her mouth to ask Caveman to leave, but he started speaking soft, nonsensical words in a deep, calming tone.

Bear tossed his head several times, not easily won over, but he didn't paw the ground or snort his dissent. Soon the animal lowered his head and let Caveman reach out to scratch behind his ears.

"I'll be damned," Grace whispered.

Caveman covered Bear's ears. "Shh. Don't let that foulmouthed biologist scare you," he whispered.

The horse nuzzled the man's chest and leaned into the hand scratching his ear.

"So, not only are you a Delta Force soldier, you're a horse whisperer?" Grace snorted.

"I told you. I'm from Montana."

"And one of those odd jobs just happened to be on a ranch?"

He grinned. "Yes and no. I grew up on a ranch. I worked there during the summers for spending money."

"A cowboy. My mother warned me about getting involved with a cowboy."

"From what you said, your father was one."

"Exactly why she warned me." Though her mother was still crazy in love with her father, even after over thirty years of marriage.

"Why cowboys?" Caveman asked.

She met his gaze head-on. "They tend to like their horses better than their wives."

"Horses don't talk back as much, or make you fold laundry."

Grace chuckled. "I've had my share of sassy horses."

"Okay, so they don't make you clean the house."

"And I've cleaned my share of stalls." She crossed her arms over her chest and raised her eyebrows. "Care to try again?"

"I can sell a horse that's giving me a hard time, thus getting money for my trouble. Getting rid of a woman costs a heck of a lot more than ditching a horse."

"Okay, you got me on that one," Grace said. "But a horse won't be warming your bed and giving you children."

"Most of my married friends don't have sex more now that they're married. In fact, the kids suck the life out of their wives' sex drive."

"But your buddies have someone to come home to. People who care about them."

"Sometimes. Then there are the Dear John letters they get when in a hellhole fighting the enemy with their hands tied behind their backs by politicians. Meanwhile the wife back home has been having an affair with the banker next door."

Grace's brows rose. "Cynical much?"

Caveman shrugged. "I've seen some of the toughest soldiers commit suicide because they can't go home to salvage the relationship."

Caveman had worked himself up a rung on Grace's perception ladder with his horse trick. But she wasn't ready to fall for the big guy, yet. And despite her mother's warning not to fall for a cowboy, she had a soft spot in her heart for them, since her father had been one.

Hell, a man who had a way with animals, who'd been raised a cowboy, was a war hero and looked as good as Caveman could easily find his way beneath her defenses. If she wasn't careful, he might be the next victim of her curse.

Grace held out her hand. "I can take care of Bear."

He handed her the brush. "I'll haul the water."

"Not necessary. As soon as he's done eating, I'll let him out in the pasture. There's a trough in the paddock." She rounded the horse to the other side and went to work brushing his coat.

Caveman's presence raised the temperature of every blood cell in Grace's body. Fully aware of his every move, she knew when he left the stall. She let out a sigh and relaxed a little as she worked her way toward the horse's hindquarters.

The stall door squealed softly, announcing Caveman's return. He'd retrieved a currycomb and went to work on Bear's tangled mane and tail. Soon the horse was fully groomed, full of grain and ready to be turned loose in the pasture.

Yeah, the soldier had gone up another rung. Not every man would take the time to groom a horse. Not every man knew how to do it right.

She'd have to talk to Caveman's boss and ask him to send someone else. How would she approach the request? *Please send someone who isn't quite as drool-worthy. Maybe someone who is happily married, has a beer belly, belches in public and is not at all interesting.*

Grace hooked Bear's halter and led him through the barn and out to the gate.

Caveman moved ahead of her and had the gate open before she got there.

She let go of Bear's halter and the horse ran into the pasture, straight for the water trough.

Grace backed up, trying to get out of the way of the gate. Her foot caught on the uneven ground and she tipped backward.

Caveman caught her in his arms and hauled her up against his chest. "Are you all right?"

No, she wasn't. Cinched tightly to the man's chest, she could barely breathe, much less think. She tried to tell herself that the malfunctioning of her involuntary reflexes had nothing to do with how close Caveman was to her. Neither were his arms, which were hooked beneath her breasts, causing all kinds of problems with her pulse and blood pressure. "I'm fine. Seriously, you can let go of me."

For a long moment, he stared down at her, his arms unmoving. "Anyone ever tell you that your eyes sparkle in the moonlight?"

And there went any measure of resistance. "No." Whether her one-word answer was in response to his question or in response to her rising desire, she refused to pick it apart.

"They do," he said. "And your lips clearly were made to be kissed."

Her heart hammering against her ribs, Grace watched as Caveman lowered his head, his mouth coming so close to hers she could feel the warmth of his breath on her skin. She tipped her head upward, her eyelids, sweeping low, her pulse racing. Dear Lord, he was going to kiss her. And she was going to let him!

A BREATH AWAY from touching his mouth to hers, Caveman came to his senses. What was he thinking? This woman had nearly died that day. He was responsible for her safety, not for making a pass at her. As much as he wanted to kiss her, he shouldn't. It would compromise his ability to remain objective. Then why had he mentioned how her eyes sparkled and how her lips were meant to be kissed?

Because, man! He wanted to kiss her. With a deep sigh, he untangled his arms from around her.

Grace opened her eyes and blinked. Even in the moonlight, Caveman could see the color rise in her cheeks. She stepped out of his reach, careful not to trip again, straightened her blouse and nodded. "Thanks for catching me. In the future, I'll do my best not to fall."

As she headed back to the house, he followed closely behind her, using his body as a shield. Should the shooter decide to follow her to her home, he wouldn't have a clear target. He'd have to go through Caveman first.

Once inside the house, Grace gathered a blanket and pillow, handed them to him and pointed to the couch. "You can stay on the couch."

The couch beat his truck and the front porch, but it might still be too close.

Grace disappeared into the only bathroom in the house.

Caveman could hear the sound of the shower and his imagination went wild, picturing the beautiful biologist stripping out of her clothes, stepping into the shower and water running in rivulets down her naked body.

He left the blanket on the couch and slipped out onto the front porch. Yeah, sleeping on the hard, wood planks with a solid wood door locked between them would be the right thing to do. Knowing she'd be in the bed down the hall made his groin tight and guaranteed he wouldn't sleep any better than the night before when he'd caught a few hours cramped in the front seat of his truck.

Tomorrow, he'd speak with Kevin about assigning another one of the team members to watch over Grace. Apparently, he'd been too long without a woman. What else would make him so attracted to Grace when he'd only known her a few hours?

The door behind him opened and Grace stuck her head through the screen door. "The shower's all yours."

She wore a baggy T-shirt that hung halfway down her thighs. If she had on shorts, the shirt covered them. And when she turned to the side, her shirt stretched over her chest.

Caveman sucked in a breath and his jeans got even tighter.

She wasn't wearing a bra beneath the shirt. The beaded tips of her nipples made tiny tents against the fabric.

What had she said? Oh, yes. The shower was all his. He really should have told her he didn't need one and that he would sleep outside. But no, that might require more explanation than he was prepared to give. And it might scare her to think the man who was supposed to protect her wanted to jump her bones. "I'll be there in a minute."

"Okay." She started to turn, paused and then faced him. "Thank you for rescuing me today."

"You're welcome." *Now, go straight to your bedroom and lock your door.* Caveman clenched his fists to keep from reaching out and dragging her into his arms. "Have a good night," he said, his voice huskier than usual.

Again, she started to turn, changed her mind and stepped through the door, closed the distance between them. When she stood in front of him, she raised up on her toes and brushed her lips across his cheek. Before Caveman could react, Grace turned and ran back into the house.

He groaned and adjusted the tightness of his jeans. Yeah, he wouldn't get much sleep. When he could move comfortably again, he walked out to his truck, grabbed his duffel bag from the backseat and returned to the house, locking the front door behind him. He made another pass through the house, checking all of the doors and windows with the exception of Grace's bedroom.

When he was certain the house was locked down, he entered the bathroom, shucked his clothes and turned on the cold water. After several minutes beneath the icy spray, he was back in control, his head on straight and his resolve strengthened.

Grace Saunders was off-limits. Period. End of subject.

He lay on the couch, his gun close by, and stared at the ceiling for the next few hours. Finally, in the wee hours of the morning he fell asleep and dreamed of making love to a beautiful, sandy-blond-haired biologist who loved wolves. Even in his dream, he knew he was treading the fine line of professionalism, but he couldn't resist. The crow of a rooster jolted him away as the gray light of predawn edged through the window.

He had breakfast on the table by the time Grace emerged from her bedroom.

"You're kind of handy to have around." She yawned and stretched. "Not only do you rescue damsels in distress, you can scramble eggs? You'll make someone a great wife."

"Don't get used to it. I cooked out of self-defense." He handed her one of the two places of fluffy yellow eggs. "I was starving."

She smiled and padded barefoot to the table. "What's the plan for today?"

"I thought we'd stop by the tavern and see if Kevin and his computer guy have come up with any potential murder suspects."

"You think they might have more than the sheriff and his deputies have come up with?"

"Hack, Kevin's computer guy, is a pretty talented techie. He's been following up on the Vanders family and their connections in the community. He might have found someone who was as trigger-happy as the Vanders."

Grace chewed on a bite of toast and swallowed. "What's wrong with people? In the past, all we had to complain about was the weather and taxes. Now people are shooting at each other. Last night all I could think about was Mr. Khalig's family. Did he leave a wife and children behind? People who loved him and looked forward to his return?"

Her face was sad, making Caveman want to wrap his arms around her and make everything okay. But he couldn't. No amount of hugging would bring back a dead man. Hugging was a bad idea, anyway. He'd promised himself that he'd steer clear of temptation.

Caveman looked down to keep from staring at Grace's sad eyes. He poked his fork at his eggs. "Not everyone is bad or crazy."

"You're right." She chuckled. "I was lucky enough one of the good guys was there when I needed someone." She ate the rest of her eggs and toast with a gusto most women didn't demonstrate.

Caveman finished his breakfast, as well. When he reached for her plate, she held up her hand. "I'll take care of the dishes since you cooked." She took his plate to the sink, and filled it with water and soapsuds.

Having grown up on a ranch where his mother worked outside as much as his father did, Caveman couldn't stand by and not help. He grabbed a dry dish towel and stepped up beside Grace. "You wash, I'll dry. We'll get it done in no time."

She smiled, and it seemed like the sun chose that moment to shine through the window.

Caveman forced himself to focus on the dish in his hand, not the sun in Grace's hair.

When they were done, and the dishes were stacked neatly in the cabinet, Grace disappeared into her bedroom and came out wearing boots and a jacket, her hair brushed neatly and pulled back into a ponytail.

Caveman liked her hair hanging down around her shoulders, the long straight strands like silver-gold silk swaying back and forth with each step. Lord help him, he was waxing poetic in his head. His buddies back in his unit would have a field day if they knew. "Come on. We need to stop by the sheriff's office and give him your official statement and see what else they can tell us about the shootings."

"I hope they were able to retrieve Mr. Khalig's body."

Caveman stepped out on the porch and searched the tree line and shadows for movement before he allowed Grace out of the house. "I spoke briefly with Kevin on the phone. They did. He's with the coroner in Jackson. They'll provide a report as soon as they can."

Grace locked the front door and followed Caveman to the truck.

Within ten minutes, they were inside the sheriff's office.

Grace gave her statement. The sheriff recorded the session and made notes. When she was done, he stared across the table at her. "I'd like to think you'll be okay. Since you didn't see who it was, you can't identify the shooter. For your sake, I hope he lays low and leaves you alone."

"I wish I *had* seen him. I'd rather know and be hunted than not know. As it is, it could have been anyone." She pushed to her feet.

The sheriff did too and held out his hand.

She ignored the hand and hugged the older man. "Thank you, for all you do. Give your wife my love."

Caveman felt a stab of envy for the hug the sheriff was getting from the pretty biologist.

Sheriff Scott hugged her back and patted her back. "You be careful out there. Can't have our favorite wolf lady getting hurt."

Caveman gave his brief statement of how he'd found Grace and thanked the sheriff.

"Where to?"

"Operations Center," Caveman said, a little more brusquely than he intended. That jolt of envy for a friendly hug Grace had given the sheriff had set Caveman off balance. He barely knew Grace. Perhaps the hit he'd taken to his leg and all the morphine he'd had during the operation and recovery had scrambled his wits. He needed to get his head on straight. Soon. He wasn't going to be around long enough to get to know the woman, nor was he in the market for a long-term relationship. He had a unit to get back to.

But the sway of Grace's hips, and the way she smiled with her lips and her eyes, seemed to replay in his head like a movie track stuck in replay mode.

By the time they had debriefed Kevin and Hack, the computer guru, they'd missed lunch and the evening crowd had begun to gather at the tavern below.

"Want to grab something to eat before we head back to my house?" Grace's lips twisted into a wry grin. "I don't cook often, and I'm certain it was a fluke you actually found something in the refrigerator for breakfast."

"Sure," Caveman said. "Then we can stop at the store for some groceries, if it's still open when we're done."

"I'm game."

For the second time in the past two days, Caveman and Grace entered the tavern and asked for a seat in the dining area.

"If you ever want to find out what's going on, you need to people-watch in the tavern or go to the grocery store. Mrs. Penders knows all of the gossip."

"Then we're definitely going to the store next."

"Hi, Grace, good to see you again. Who's this?"

Grace smiled at a pretty, young waitress with bleach-blond hair. "Lisa Lambert, this is Max Decker. You can call him Caveman. He's a...friend of mine."

Lisa grinned. "Caveman? Is that a statement on how you are with the ladies?" She winked. "Nice to meet you." She held out a hand.

Caveman shook it, and gave Lisa a smile. "Nice to meet you, Lisa."

"You know, if it's all the same to you," Grace said. "I'd like to get the food to go and eat it at home."

"We can do that," Lisa said. She took their order and hurried to the back. She returned a few minutes later with two glasses of water and a smile. "The cook said it will take him ten minutes."

"Great." After Lisa left, Caveman leaned toward Grace. "See anyone here that might be your killer?"

She glanced around the room. "I see a bunch of people I've known all my life. I find it hard to believe any of them could be a killer. I grew up with some of them, went to church on Sunday with others and say hello to others at community functions."

"Anyone who might have a beef with the pipeline inspector?"

Grace studied the people. "Some of the men worked on the pipeline. Maybe the ones who were laid off are angry because Mr. Khalig still had his job? I don't know. I work with wolves, not pipeline workers."

"What about the property owners the pipelines cross?" Caveman asked.

"Maybe. I'm not sure who they are, though. The pipelines cross the entire state. Mr. Khalig was on federal land when he was shot."

A few minutes later, Lisa returned with a bag filled with two covered plates.

Handing her several bills, Caveman told her to keep the tip. He had turned to leave when he heard a commotion behind him.

"I don't care what you say!" a slurred male voice yelled over the sound of other patrons talking.

Caveman spun toward the bar to see a man leaning with his back to the bar. "The BLM isn't a law unto themselves. You have no right to confiscate a man's herd or have him arrested for trespassing on the land his cattle have grazed on since his great-great-grandfather settled this area."

"If the man doesn't pay the grazing fees for his animals, and he doesn't remove them from federal property, he forfeits them to the government," another man said, his voice lower. "It's in the contract he signed."

A pause in general conversation allowed Caveman to hear the man's quiet response. "Who are the two arguing?"

"The man at the bar is Ernie Martin," Grace said. "He poured all his money into raising Angora goats, counting on the subsidies the government gave ranchers for raising them. The subsidies were cut from the federal budget, and now he's facing bankruptcy."

"And the other guy?" Caveman prompted.

"Daryl Bradley. He's a local Bureau of Land Management representative. They sent him in to feed information to the agency on how it's going out here. They had a man who wouldn't pay his grazing fees try to shoot the sheriff. It's been pretty volatile out here. *You* should know. I heard you had a hand in rescuing the school bus full of kids just the other day."

He nodded. "Vanders was the man who tried to shoot the sheriff. And it was his sons who kidnapped the kids. That could have turned out a whole lot worse than it did."

Grace nodded. "It was bad enough old Mr. Green died. He was a good man."

Caveman nodded. "Thankfully, all of the kids survived."

Grace shook her head. "I never would have thought members of our little community could be that desperate they could kill a kind old man and kidnap a bunch of innocent kids."

"It ain't right," Ernie shouted. "How's a man supposed to make a living when the government is out to squeeze every ounce of blood from his livelihood? The land doesn't cost the government anything to maintain. *We* fix the fences. *We* provide the water and feed for the cattle. And the BLM collects the money. For what? To fund some pork belly program nobody wants or needs."

"The BLM hasn't raised the fees in years," Daryl said. "We haven't even kept up with inflation. It was time."

"That's taxation without representation. Our forefathers dumped tea in a harbor to protest the government raising taxes without them having a say in it." Ernie slammed his mug on the bar, sloshing beer over the top. "It's time we take back our country, the land our grandfathers fought to protect, and boot the likes of you out."

Daryl stood, pushing back his chair so hard it tipped over and crashed to the floor. "Is that a threat?"

"Call it whatever you want," Ernie shouted. "It's time we took matters into our own hands and set things straight in the US."

A tall, slender man rose from his chair and ambled over to the fray. "Oh, pipe down, Ernie. You're just mad because they cut the government subsidies for Angora goats."

Grace leaned close to Caveman. "That's Ryan Parker. Owns the Circle C Ranch."

"Yeah, you're right, I'm mad." Ernie poked a finger toward Ryan. "I sold my cattle to invest in those damned goats. It's like they timed it perfectly to close me down. I've already had to sell half of my land. It won't be long before I sell the other half, just to pay my mortgage and taxes." He puffed out his chest. "The government has to understand the decisions they make affect real people."

"That's why we go to the voting booths and elect the representatives who will take our message to Washington." Ryan waved toward the door. "Go home, Ernie."

"And what good will voting do?" Ernie shouted. "You're not in much better shape. What has our government done for you? You had to sell most of your breeding stock to make ends meet. How are you going to recover from that? Not only that, you didn't have a choice on that pipeline cutting through your property. What if it breaks? What if it leaks?

Your remaining livestock could be poisoned, the land ruined for grazing."

"Or we could all die in the next volcanic eruption. We can't predict the future." Ryan crossed his arms over his chest. "No one made you sell all of your livestock to invest the money in goats. Any ranch owner worth his salt knows not to put all his eggs in one basket."

"So now you're saying I'm not worth my salt?" Ernie marched across the floor and stood toe-to-toe with Ryan.

Caveman tensed and extended a hand to Grace. "Might be getting bad in here. Are you ready to go?"

Her gaze was riveted on the two men shouting at each other. "Think we should do anything to stop them?"

"My job is to protect *you*, not break up a barroom fight."

"I didn't go to war to fight for your right to collect subsidies from our government." Ryan glared down at Ernie. "You made a bad financial decision. Live with it."

"Why, you—" Ernie swung his fist.

Ryan Parker caught it in his palm and shoved it back at him. "Don't ever take a swing at me again. I won't let it go next time."

Ernie spat on Ryan's cowboy boots. "You're one of them."

"And if you mean I'm a patriot who loves my country and fought to keep it free for dumbasses like you, then yes. I'm one of them. What have you done for your country lately, Ernie?"

Ernie rubbed his fist. If his glare was a knife it would have skewered Ryan through the heart. "I might not have joined the military, but I'm willing to fight for my rights."

"And what rights are those? The right to raise goats at the taxpayer's expense?" Ryan shook his head. "Get a real life, Ernie. One that you've earned, not one that you've gambled on and lost."

Ernie's face turned a mottled shade of red. He reached into his pocket, his eyes narrowing into slits.

Grace started toward the man before Caveman realized what she was doing.

He leaped forward and grabbed her arm, pulling her back behind him.

"But Ernie's going to do something stupid," Grace said. "Ryan's one of the good guys."

"I'll handle it," Caveman said between clenched teeth. "Stay out of it," he ordered and strode toward the angry man.

"You'll see." Ernie eased his hand out of his pocket, something metal and shiny cupped in his palm. Based on the size and shape, it had to be a knife. "You and every other governmental tyrant will see. Just you wait, Parker." Ernie's brows drew together and he took a step toward Ryan. "You'll see. We'll have a free America again. And it won't be because you went to fight in a foreign country. We'll bring the fight back home where it belongs."

"What do you mean?" Ryan stood his ground.

Caveman also wanted to know what the belligerent Ernie meant by bringing the fight home, but he wasn't willing to wait for the angry drunk to explain.

Ernie started forward, cocked his arm, preparing to thrust his hand at Ryan.

Caveman popped Ernie's wrist with his fist in a short, fast impact that caused the man to drop the knife. "Sorry. Didn't mean to bump into you," he said and kicked the knife beneath a table, out of Ernie's reach.

Clenching his empty hand into a fist, Ernie glared at Caveman and then turned his attention back to Ryan. "It won't be long. And you'll see."

Two other men stepped between Ernie and Ryan. "You've said enough," one of the men muttered.

"That's fine." Ernie snorted. "I'm done here." He turned toward the door and pushed his way through the crowd that had gathered around him and Ryan. "Move. Get out of my way."

As the tavern returned to its normal dull roar of voices, Caveman made his way back to where he'd left Grace. "What was Ernie talking about, *bringing the fight back home*?"

Grace's brow formed a V over her nose. "I'm not sure. We've heard rumblings about a militia group forming in the area. But that's the first I've heard anyone actually talk about bringing the fight here." She glanced around as if looking at the crowd with fresh eyes.

"Who were the guys who stopped Ernie?" Caveman looked for the men, but didn't see them. They'd disappeared into the crowd and Ryan had stepped up to the bar to pay his bill.

"That was Quincy Kemp and Wayne Batson. Quincy was the one who spoke to Ernie. He's not the nicest or most reputable individual in Grizzly Pass. But he does make good sausage. All of the hunters go to him to have their antlers mounted and the meat turned into steaks, sausage or jerky."

"He's a butcher *and* a taxidermist?" Caveman asked.

"Yes. He has a shop in town, but he lives off the grid. His home is up in the hills. He uses wind and solar power and hunts for his food."

"Pretty good shot?"

"I'd say he'd have to be to feed himself and his family." Her lips pulled up on the corner. "As for Wayne Batson, he nearly went bankrupt when ranching got too expensive. He sank a lot of money into making his place a sportsman's paradise, building high fences around his ten-thousand-acre ranch and stocking it with exotic deer, elk, wolves and wild-cats. He also has one of the most sophisticated out-door rifle ranges in the state. Men come to train on his range and hunt on his land."

"Maybe we should ask the sheriff to check their alibis."

"Wayne and Quincy are highly skilled hunters." Grace smiled. "But, if we were looking for the best hunters in the area as our potential shooter, you'd have to question half the people in this county alone. You know how it is. Most men in these parts grew up with a guns in their hands. They're all avid hunters and are good with a rifle and scope. We even have a man from here who became the state champion rifle marksman."

"You're right. It was the same in Montana. I guess I've been in other parts of this country too long, where most people wouldn't know how to load a gun, much less shoot one."

"Most of them don't need one to survive." She gathered her purse. "We should go. I need to log my notes into the project database and notify my boss of the loss of Loki."

Normally, Caveman would have held the door for Grace, but he wanted to go out first and scan the parking lot for danger before he allowed her to leave the relative security of the tavern.

He stopped in the doorway and looked around.

Three men stood near a truck talking in hushed voices, their faces intense. One of them was Ernie Martin. The other men had their backs to Caveman, but based on the one's greasy brown hair and slouchy blue jeans, he appeared to be Quincy Kemp, the local meat processor and taxidermist. The other had the swaggering stance of the man Grace had called Wayne Batson.

"What's going on," Grace asked, her breath warming Caveman's shoulder, sending a thrill of awareness through him.

"Ernie, Wayne and Quincy are having a conversation."

"I'm not afraid of them," she said.

He looked around for any other threats. The sun had set and the gray of dusk provided enough light to make their way to their truck, but not enough to see into the shadows. "Stay close to me. When we get to the truck, get in and stay down. Don't provide any kind of silhouette."

"I'm still not quite convinced the shooter is actually after me anymore. He has to know by now that I couldn't identify him. Otherwise someone would have been knocking at his door."

"That doesn't mean he won't take pleasure in keeping you guessing. A man who'd hang a dead wolf's collar on your door might go to the trouble of continuing to scare you." Caveman handed her up into the passenger seat. "Even if you're not scared of him, I might be. For you, of course." He winked, his hand on the door. "Again, stay down until we're back at your house."

She rolled her eyes, but complied, doubling over in her seat, bringing her head below the dash, out of sight of any passerby, or shooter aiming at the truck.

Caveman climbed into the truck, started the engine and pulled out of the Blue Moose parking lot onto the road headed toward Grace's house.

Chapter Eight

"I feel silly bending over this long." Grace lay over, her face near the sack of food, the smells making her mouth water. "Are we there yet? My stomach is rumbling."

"Rather silly than sorry," he said.

"Easy for you to say. You're not the one scrunched over your seat." She straightened for a moment and worked the kink out of her neck. "Seriously, this is nuts. I went all day without anyone making a move. Nobody is going to shoot at me at night."

A sharp tink sounded and a hole appeared in the passenger seat window a few inches away from Grace's head. "What the hell?" She reached out her hand to touch the round hole. Splinters of glass flaked off at her touch.

"Get down!" Caveman yelled and swerved into the middle of the road.

Someone was shooting at them! Caveman jerked,

his hand, twisting the steering wheel to the right. He cursed and held on, straightening the truck before he plowed into a ditch and flipped the vehicle.

Caveman steadied the vehicle, slammed his foot on the accelerator and sped forward. When he glanced at the matching holes in the window, his heart stopped for a second. Those were bullet holes. Had Grace been leaning a few inches forward in her seat, those bullets would have hit her in the head.

His gut clenched.

Grace lay doubled over, her head between her knees to keep from being seen by the enemy. "Should we go straight to the sheriff's office?" she asked from her bent position.

"Probably, but I'm not sure what that will accomplish since the sheriff will have gone home by now," Caveman said.

"Should we go to my house? We could call the sheriff from there." The shooter already knew where she lived and had been there the day before.

"Is there anywhere else we could go?" Caveman asked.

Grace shook her head. "We could drive up to the park at Yellowstone and see if they can fit us into one of the cabins."

"And if they can't?" Caveman glanced across the console at her.

"We could drive on into Jackson Hole. There's bound to be a hotel there."

"That's a lot of driving late at night."

"Then we go to my place," she decided. "I don't like leaving my horse for too long, anyway. If this guy shoots wolves, he doesn't have a sense of compassion in dealing with animals. He could decide to hurt my horse."

"Almost there," Caveman pulled into her driveway and shone the headlights at her small cottage. Nothing seemed amiss. Then he drove around the side of the house and shone the headlights at the small barn. The lights reflected off the horse's eyes, but everything appeared normal.

He parked at the rear of the house.

"I know," Grace said. "I'm to stay put while you check it out." She sighed. "I'm sorry about your window."

"Don't worry about it. I'm glad you weren't hit." He pushed open the door to his truck. The overhead light illuminated Grace's pale face and worried eyes.

He reached over and touched a hand to her cheek, wanting to take her into his arms, as if by doing so he could protect her from whoever was shooting at her. "If you had any doubts the shooter is after you, I hope you're convinced now."

"I am," she said, quietly. "Completely." She covered his hand with hers and leaned into his palm.

"But why? I still don't have a clue who it is. It's not like I'm a threat to him."

"Doesn't matter at this point. What does matter is that we get you inside that house safely before the gunman has the chance to get here from his previous location."

"Caveman?"

"Yeah."

"Thanks for being here for me."

Caveman pressed his lips together. "Don't thank me until the gunman is caught." She was still in danger and he could be the best bodyguard around, but a skilled sniper could take someone out from up to four hundred yards away.

He wasn't sure what they'd do next. He didn't see any other option but to stay inside the house, avoid all the windows and pray whoever was shooting wouldn't get lucky and hit Grace. Though he'd only known her a very short time, he wouldn't want anything to happen to the dedicated biologist.

Chapter Nine

Grace felt strange running for the door of her house. This was Grizzly Pass, Wyoming, not some village in a war-torn nation. People didn't shoot at you for no reason.

Unless you witnessed a murder, and the killer was crazier than a rabid skunk, and fired on you when you were driving home from town.

Ducking low, Grace ran up the porch steps.

Caveman was right behind her, using his body as a shield to protect hers, again. Was he insane?

When her hand shook too much to insert the key in the lock, Caveman took the key from her and opened the door. With his palm on the small of her back, he hurried her through and closed the door behind them.

She rounded on him, realizing too late that she hadn't given him much room to get in the door and close it. She stood toe-to-toe with the man, feeling the heat radiating off his body. "Why do you keep doing that?"

He raised his hands to cup her elbows. "Doing what?"

"Using your body to shield mine? You don't have to take a bullet for me." She touched his arm. "You hardly know me."

He gave her a half smile. "Let's just say, what I know, I like and admire." His lips twitched and his eyes twinkled. "You're the first woman I've met who likes beer. What's not to love about you?"

Her heart warmed at his playful words. If she wasn't such a deadly jinx, she'd be tempted to flirt with the man. "Well, don't do it, again. I don't think I could live with myself if something happened to you because of me." She set her purse on the hall table and would have walked away, but Caveman took her hand and laced his fingers with hers.

"Sweetheart, I'm here to protect you. I'm not going to leave you exposed to a sniper's sights."

"I'm not your sweetheart, and you should wear a bulletproof vest if you're going to be around me." She stared up into his eyes, her own stinging. Her chest ached with an overwhelming fear for his life. "I don't want to be the cause of another death."

"You have to stop beating yourself up." He raised her hand to his lips, pressed a kiss to her knuckles and sent sparks shooting through her veins. "Khalig didn't die because of you."

"I know." She stared at where his lips had been. She wished he would claim her mouth instead of wasting kisses on her fingers. But, no, that wouldn't work. Grace shook her head. "I can't do this to you."

"Do what?"

"Nothing." She pulled her hand free and turned away.

Caveman caught her arm and pulled her around to face him. "Do what to me?" He cupped her cheek in his palm. "Drive me crazy? Too late. For some reason, I'm insanely attracted to you. But every time I think I'm about to kiss you, you pull away, or my head gets screwed on straight. Well, I'm tired of doing the right thing. I swear your eyes are saying yes, but the next thing I know, you're running. Is it something I said? Is it my cologne? I'll change it."

Grace rested her hand on his chest as tears welled in her eyes. "Don't say nice things. Don't try to kiss me."

"Why not?" He brushed his thumb across her lips. "You're beautiful. And I might be reading too much into your body language, but I think you want to kiss me, too."

Yes, she did. But now, she couldn't. "I can't do this to you."

He stepped closer, bringing his body nearer to

hers, the warmth crushing her ability to resist. "Can't do what to me? Talk to me, Grace. You're not making sense."

"I can't curse you."

He leaned his head back, his brows forming a V in the center of his forehead. "Curse me? I don't understand."

"I'm cursed. If you kiss me, I'll jinx you. I don't want something terrible to happen to you." She curled her fingers into his shirt, knowing she should push him away, but she couldn't. Now that they were so close, her brain stopped thinking and her body took over. She wanted, more than anything, for him to kiss her.

"Let me get this straight. You think that by kissing me, you'll jinx me?" He stared down at her for a long moment. Finally, he said, "What in the Sam-dog-hell are you talking about?"

Her brows lifted and her lips twitched. "Sam-dog-hell?" She gave a shaky laugh.

"Don't change the subject." He brushed his thumb across her lips again, his glance shifting to his thumb's path. "I was just about to kiss you."

"I didn't change the subject. And you can't kiss me." She was saying one thing while she allowed him to tip her chin up, her lips coming to within a breath of his. "Kissing me is a really bad idea," she whispered.

"Damn it, Grace, if kissing you is a bad idea, then color me bad. I have to do it." He bent to claim her lips. "Curses be damned," he muttered into her mouth, sliding his tongue between her teeth, claiming her tongue with a warm, wet caress that curled Grace's toes.

She pressed her body against his, longing to be closer, their clothes just one more barrier to overcome so that she could be skin-to-skin with this big soldier who'd take a bullet for a relative stranger. What had she done to deserve him?

Nothing. So how could she stand there kissing him, knowing it would put him in mortal danger? Grace pushed against his chest, though the effort was only halfhearted and less than convincing.

His arms tightened and then loosened. "If you really want me to let go, just say the word." He stared down into her eyes. "Otherwise, I'm going to continue kissing you."

She fell into his gaze, her heart hammering against her ribs. Slowly, her hands slid up his chest to lock behind his head, pulling him down for that promised kiss. "If you die, I'll never forgive myself."

He chuckled. "I'll take my chances." Then he kissed her until her insides tingled and she forgot the need to breathe. When he raised his head, she lowered her hands to the buttons on his shirt, working them loose as fast as her fingers could push them

through the holes. Her goal was to get to the skin beneath, before her brain kicked in and reminded her
why she shouldn't be kissing him and whatever else
might come next.

As she reached for the rivet on his blue jeans, he
captured her hands in his. "Are you sure about this?
You know I want it, but I don't want you to do something you'll regret later."

She caught her lower lip between her teeth and
stared down at the button on his jeans, wishing he
hadn't stopped her, praying her brain wouldn't kick
in. "You're a soldier, right?" she said.

"Yes. So?"

"You've lived through some pretty serious battles, I assume?"

"Again, yes."

"You can take care of yourself, right?"

"I can."

"Then kiss me and tell me you'll be all right."

"Grace, no one is guaranteed to live to old age."
He threaded his hands through her hair. "We have
to live every day like it could be our last."

"Yeah, but I don't want your life to be cut short
because of me."

"Let *me* make that choice. The only decision you
need to make is whether you want to make love here,
against the wall or take it to the bedroom?"

Her pulse raced, and her breathing grew ragged.

"Here. Now." She ripped open the button on his jeans and dragged the zipper down.

Caveman grabbed the hem of her shirt, pulled it up over her head and dropped it on the hall table. Then he bent to kiss her neck, just below her ear. He nibbled at her earlobe and trailed his lips down the length of her neck. Continuing lower, he tongued the swell of her right breast, while pushing the strap over her shoulder and down her arm.

Past anything resembling patience, Grace reached behind her and unclipped her bra. Her breasts freed, she shrugged out of the garment and it fell to the floor.

Caveman cupped both orbs in his hands and plumped them, thumbing the nipples until they hardened into tight little beads. He bent to take one into his mouth, sucking it deep, then flicking it with the tip of tongue.

Grace moaned and arched her back, wanting so much more. They still had too many clothes on. She shoved her hands into the back of his jeans, cupped his bottom and pulled him close. His shaft sprang free of his open fly and pushed into her belly.

"I want to feel your skin against mine," he said, his words warm on her wet breast.

"What's holding you back?" she managed to get out between ragged gasps.

"These." He flipped the button of her jeans through

the hole and dragged the denim down her legs. Dropping to his haunches, he pulled off her cowboy boots and helped her step free. As he rose, he skimmed his knuckles along her inner thigh, all the way up to the triangle of silk covering her sex.

His gaze met hers as he hooked the elastic waistband of her panties and he dragged them over her hips and down her thighs.

Her body on fire, Grace couldn't take it anymore. She pushed his jeans down his legs and waited for him to toe off his boots, kicking them to the side. He shucked his pants, pulling his wallet from the back pocket before he slung them against the wall. Then they were both naked in the hallway of her home.

A cool waft of air almost brought her back to her senses.

Before it could, Caveman retrieved a condom from his wallet, tossed the wallet on the hallway table and handed her the packet. "We might need that."

"I'm glad *someone* is thinking," she said. She sure wasn't. Grace tore open the foil, rolled the condom over his engorged shaft all the way to the base. Sweet heaven, he was hard, long and so big, her breath caught and held.

Caveman tipped her chin and brushed a light kiss over her lips, then scooped her up by the backs of her thighs and wrapped her legs around his waist. Pinning her wrists to the wall above her head, he pressed his shaft to her damp entrance. "Slow and easy, or hard and fast?"

Her eyes widened. No man had ever asked her how she liked it. Not even her husband. She assumed it was up to the guy to establish the pace.

She only took a moment to decide. With her body on fire, her channel slick and ready, there was only one choice. "Hard and fast."

He eased into her, let her adjust to his thickness and then pulled out. Dropping his grip on her wrists, Caveman held her hips, his fingers digging into the flesh. Soon, he was pumping in and out of her, moving faster and faster, their movements making thumping sounds against the wall.

Grace held on to his shoulders, her head tipped back, her breath lodged in her chest as wave after wave of sensations ebbed through her, consuming her in a massive firestorm of desire. When she thought it couldn't get any better, he hit the sweet spot and sent her catapulting over the edge. She held on, riding him to the end.

One last thrust and he drove deep inside, pressing her firmly against the wall, his staff throbbing inside her. He leaned his forehead against hers, his breaths short and fast, like a marathon runner's.

A minute passed, and then two.

Grace didn't care, she teetered on the brink of a

euphoric high. He could do it all again, and she'd be perfectly happy.

Caveman tightened his hold around her and carried her into the master bedroom, where he laid her on the bed. In the process, he lost their connection.

Grace ached inside, the emptiness leaving her cold. But not for long.

He slipped onto the mattress behind her and pulled her back to his front. His still-hard shaft nudged her between her legs and pressed against her entrance, sliding easily inside. Slipping his arms around her, he held her close, driving the chill from the air and her body.

She could be content to lie with him forever. After making love against the wall and being completely pleased, she could imagine how much more satisfying making love in the comfort of a bed might be.

If he stayed with her through the night, she vowed to find out before morning.

Pushing all the niggling thoughts of her curse to the back of her mind, she snuggled closer, giving him time to recuperate before she tested his ability to perform more than once in a night.

A CURSE. CAVEMAN had wanted to laugh off Grace's mention of it, but she'd been very adamant to the point she'd held him at arm's length. Until she couldn't fight the attraction another minute. He felt a twinge of guilt for teasing her into abandoning her cause and making love to him.

"So why is it you think I will be cursed?" he said, nuzzling the back of her ear.

She stiffened in his arms.

Caveman could have kicked himself for bringing it up after the most amazing sex he'd had in a very long time. "Never mind. I'm not very superstitious, anyway."

For a long time, she lay silent in his arms.

He began to think she'd gone to sleep.

"My high school sweetheart died in a head-on collision the night after I lost my virginity to him," she said. "He was eighteen."

Caveman kissed the curve of her shoulder. "Could have happened to anyone."

"That's what I thought." She inhaled deeply and let it out. "My husband died on our honeymoon. The day after we got there. We went parasailing. The cable holding his chute to the boat broke. He had no way to control the parachute. It slammed him into a cliff and he crashed to the rocks below. He was only twenty-four."

"Just because two of the guys you cared about died doesn't mean you are cursed."

She snorted softly. "A couple years ago, I decided to get back into the dating scene. I met a nice man. We dated three times. After our third date, I didn't hear from him for a few days. I called his cell phone number. A woman answered. I asked where he was. She broke down and cried, saying he'd died in a farming accident."

"Grace, you can't blame yourself for their deaths. Sometimes your number is just up. Those cases were all unrelated and coincidental."

"No, they were related. I cared about all three of them. The common denominator was me." She eased away from him, turned and faced him, her head lying on the pillow, her hand falling to his chest. "I haven't had a date since. I keep on friendly but distant terms with the men in my life." Her gaze shifted from his eyes to where her hand lay on his chest. "Until you." She looked up again. "Now...dear Lord, I've cursed you."

He kissed her forehead and pulled her into his arms. "You aren't cursed and nothing's going to happen to me just because we made love tonight."

Grace rested her cheek against his chest, her head moving back and forth. "I shouldn't have risked it. You've been good to me, rescuing me when I was thrown from my horse. This is no way to repay you."

"I didn't ask for payment. I made love to you because I find you intelligent, sexy and brave."

"Not brave," she said, burying her face against his chest. "I ran when Mr. Khalig was killed."

"You had no choice."

"I did. I chose to run."

"You chose to live." He pressed a kiss to her forehead. "Sleep. Tomorrow is another day."

"Tomorrow's another day," she echoed. Her hand slid down his chest to touch him there. "But there's still tonight."

And just like that, he was ready. He jumped out of the bed, ran to where he'd left his wallet in the hallway and returned with protection for round two.

Later, while Grace slept, he slipped from the bed and used the phone in the hallway to call Kevin before midnight. He filled him in on the bullets fired at Grace in his truck. "We will make a full report to the sheriff in the morning. Did the coroner get a positive ID on the body?"

"Yes. It was RJ Khalig."

Caveman's chest tightened. "I should have gotten there sooner."

"How could you have?" Kevin asked. "You didn't know where 'there' was."

His head told him the same, but the man was his assignment and he'd let him down. "Anything on his cause of death?"

"He definitely had a gunshot wound to the chest. The coroner is still trying to determine whether or not it was enough to kill him, and whether he was alive or dead when he fell over the cliff."

Caveman walked into Grace's living room and

nudged the curtain aside to look out at the street in front of her house. "My bet is that he was dead. Whoever shot him went back to finish the job." Moonlight shone down on the grass, the driveway and the street. Nothing moved. No vehicles passed.

"We'll know when the coroner's report is complete. In the meantime, how's Ms. Saunders?"

His pulse leaped and his groin tightened. Ms. Saunders was amazing. "Holding her own, but scared."

"She has every right to be." Kevin said something, but the sound was muffled. "I need to go. My wife is getting jealous of my job."

"Sorry to call so late."

"Don't be. I'm here for you. It's like I told you in the beginning, there's a lot more going on than meets the eye. I have a feeling this area is a powder keg waiting for someone to light the fuse."

As much as he would like to disagree with his new boss, he couldn't. In his gut, he knew the man was right.

"Stop by the loft in the morning," Kevin said. "Maybe Hack will have something on the men who were arguing in the tavern earlier."

"Will do." Caveman ended the call.

A sound drew his attention from the scene through the front window to the woman standing in the doorway to the living room. She stood in the meager light from the moon edging its way around the curtains. Her sandy-blond hair tumbled around her shoulders, her lips were swollen from his kisses and she'd loosely wrapped the sheet from the bed around her naked body.

"For someone who wasn't sure she wanted to make love, you're sending all the wrong signals." He chuckled and stalked toward her, his eyes narrowing as he got closer.

"I woke up, and you were gone."

"Not far. I couldn't leave, knowing there was a beautiful woman keeping the sheets warm."

"The sheets are cold." She lifted her arms to wrap around his neck. As she did, the sheet drifted down past her hips and floated to pool at her ankles.

"Mmm. Perhaps I need to warm them again." He bent, scooped her up into his arms and carried her back to the bedroom. "I'm out of condoms," he said, as he laid her out on the bed and climbed in beside her.

"We'll make do." She touched his cheek. "I just hope that since you're not going to be around for longer than this assignment lasts, you will be immune to the curse."

He turned his face into her hand and kissed her palm. "You're not cursed. And what if I stick around longer?" Now that he was in Wyoming, and the trouble Kevin had mentioned was turning out to be very real and imminent, he didn't see a pressing need for him to return to his unit, just to be sidelined until his leg was 100 percent and he could pass a fitness test. He could stay in Grizzly Pass and get to know Grace a little better, make love to her again...and again.

"Seriously." She brushed her lips across his. "Promise me that you won't fall in love with me. Not that you are or anything. But just to be safe, please...promise me."

His heart twisted. Promise not to love her? Hell, he'd only just met her. How could he fall in love with her so quickly? He kissed her palm again. "Don't you think it's a little early to think about love?" He pressed his lips to the tip of her nose. "Lust, I can understand—"

She touched a finger to his lips. "Please. Just promise."

Caveman opened his mouth to comply, but the words lodged in his throat. "I—" The words she wanted to hear refused to leave his lips. He couldn't even think them. Not love Grace? His twisting heart seemed to open into a gaping void at the thought of leaving Grizzly Pass and never talking to her again. He looked around the room, searching for the right words, knowing there weren't any. His gaze paused at the window. Light shone around the edges of the curtain, a bright white light getting lighter by the moment. He shot a glance at the clock on the night-stand. Was it already morning?

The green numbers on the digital clock read 12:36.

His pulse leaped, he grabbed Grace and rolled to the far side of the bed and off, taking her with him. Just as they landed hard on the floor, a loud crashing sound filled the air, the bed slid toward them, and the mattress upended and slammed them against the wall. Drywall crumbled, sending the ceiling and loose insulation cascading down around them, filling the air with dust so thick Caveman wouldn't have been able to see his hand in front of his face. If he could get his hand free to raise to his face. He and Grace were trapped between the mattress and the wall, unable to move.

Chapter Ten

Grace struggled to turn her head to the side, pulled her face out of a pillow and gasped for air. Something heavy lay on top of her and the mattress held her tightly against the wall. "Caveman?"

He coughed, making his body wiggle against hers, explaining the weight lying across her. "Grace? Are you all right?"

"I think so," she said. "But it's hard to breathe."

An engine sounded really close and the smell of exhaust warred with the dust filling her lungs. "What happened?" she whispered, barely able to draw in enough air to activate her vocal cords.

"I think someone crashed into your house."

"Dear God. How?" She tried to draw in a deep breath, but with everything smashing her to the floor and wall, she couldn't. The darkness surrounding her was nothing compared to the dizzying fog of losing consciousness. If they didn't get out of there soon, she'd suffocate.

"I...can't...get up." Caveman twisted his shoulders, his hands pressing down on her, searching for something else to brace against and finding nothing.

"Just push against me," she said.

"I'm sorry." He braced a hand on her chest and shoved himself backward, sliding down her body, inch by inch. As he moved past her chest, she was able to get a little more air to her lungs. She dragged it in, uncaring that it was filled with dust. The oxygen cleared her brain.

"I'm out," Caveman said.

She heard the sound of boards being kicked to the side. Then she heard the engine revving and the metal clank of gears shifting; the pressure eased off the mattress and her.

She lay for a moment, letting air fill her lungs. Then she struggled to push the heavy mattress off her.

Suddenly the bed shifted and fell away from her.

Caveman leaned down, extending a hand.

Grace took it and let him draw her to her feet and into his arms.

He held her for a long time, smoothing his hand over her hair. Finally, he pushed her to arm's length and swept his gaze over the length of her. "Are you all right? No broken bones, concussion, abrasions?"

She shook her head and stared around at the disaster that was her bedroom. "Maybe a bruised tailbone, but nothing compared to what it could have been if you hadn't thought so quickly." The front wall was caved in, the ceiling joists lay on the floor, electrical wires sparked dangerously close.

"Where's your breaker box?" Caveman asked.

"In the kitchen."

He scooped her up into his arms and waded through the splintered two-by-fours and broken sheets of drywall until he reached the intact hallway. There, he set her on her feet, grabbed her hand and led the way to the kitchen.

Grace took him to the breaker box in the pantry.

He flipped the master switch, shutting off all electricity to the house. "Gas?"

"Propane tank out back."

Caveman hurried to the front hallway and returned a minute later wearing his jeans. He handed her the clothes she'd shed earlier, her boots and her purse. "Put these on and stand out on the porch while I shut off the gas to the house."

Grace dressed on the back porch, shivering in the cold.

Caveman returned and put his arm around her.

"What happened?" she asked, trembling uncontrollably.

"Someone drove my truck into the house."

"Oh, no. Did it ruin your truck?"

Caveman chuckled. "You were almost killed and you're worried about my truck? Sweetheart, you have to get your priorities straight."

"You were in the same place I was. Which means you were almost killed, as well." She leaned into him, slipping her arm around his waist. "If you hadn't noticed the lights headed our way…"

"Sorry about the rough landing, but at least we're alive."

"The driver?" she asked.

"Took off. I'm sure he's long gone by now." With his arm still around her, he led her down the back porch stairs and away from the damaged house. "We can't stay here tonight."

"We could go to my folks' place. I have a key." Grace laughed, the sound more like a sob. "If you want to dig it out. It's somewhere in my jewelry box on my dresser…"

"Beneath all the rubble." Caveman shook his head. "Hopefully Kevin can help us out."

"I can't believe someone drove your truck into my house." She turned back. "I can't leave it like this. What if it rains?"

Caveman stared up at the clear night sky. "It's not supposed to rain for a couple days. We can come back in the morning and see what we can salvage." He steered her toward the front of the house where his truck stood, the front end smashed in, one of the tires flat. "We'll have to take your vehicle, unless you want to wait while I attempt to change that flat."

"We'll take my SUV." Grace fished in her purse, pulling out her keys. She handed them to Caveman. "I'd drive, but I'm not feeling very steady right now."

"Don't worry. I'll get us there."

Sitting in the passenger seat of her SUV didn't make her feel any better. Nothing about what had happened in the last thirty-six hours felt right.

Except making love to Caveman. And he wasn't much more than a stranger. A stranger who'd saved her life three times now. That had to make up for the fact that they'd known each other such a short amount of time.

"I think it's time to wake the sheriff." Caveman turned the key in the ignition.

It clicked once, but the engine didn't turn over.

Caveman's hand froze on the key, his brows descending. "Grace, get out."

"But we can't take your truck. It's damaged."

"Just get out. Now!" He reached across the seat, pulled the handle on her door and shoved her through. "Run!"

The pure desperation in his tone shook Grace out of the stunned state she'd been in since her world had come crashing down around her. Her feet grew wings and she ran faster than she had since the high school track team. She didn't know where she was going, as long as it was away from the vehicle.

Twenty feet from her old but trusted SUV, the world exploded around her for the second time that night. She flew forward, landing hard on the ground, the air forced from her lungs, her ears ringing.

She lay for a moment, trying to remember how to breathe.

"Caveman," she said and pushed up to her knees. "Caveman!" she shouted, but couldn't hear an answering response due to the loud ringing in her ears. She ran back to the burning hulk that had been her SUV. He'd been so adamant about getting her out of the vehicle he hadn't had time to get himself out.

Grace reached for the door handle of the burning vehicle. She couldn't leave him in there, she had to get him out. The heat made her skin hurt. Right before her hand touched the metal handle, a voice shouted.

"Grace!"

The sound came to her through her throbbing ears and over the roar of the fire. She turned toward it.

Caveman rounded the edge of the blaze and ran toward her. He pulled her away from the flames and held her close.

Several minutes passed, neither one of them in a hurry to move away.

A siren sounded in the distance and then another. Soon the yard was filled with emergency vehicles.

The sheriff's deputy was first on the scene, followed by all of the vehicles belonging to the Grizzly Pass Volunteer Fire Department.

The Emergency Medical Technicians checked Grace and Caveman. Other than a few scrapes and bruises they'd live to see another day.

Soon the blaze was out.

Grace checked on her horse in the pasture on the other side of the barn. The fire had been in the front yard. The barn had sustained no damage, but her horse galloped around the paddock, frightened by the sirens and the smoke.

Caveman helped her catch the horse and soothe him. When she finally released him, he ran to the farthest point away from the smoke.

Grace made certain he had sufficient water before she returned to the front of the house. She and Caveman gave a detailed description of the bullets fired on their way home, and what had happened to her house and finally her vehicle. Caveman borrowed a cell phone from the deputy and placed a call to Kevin. The DHS agent offered to let them sleep in the loft above the tavern until they could come up with another arrangement.

The sheriff appeared shortly after they'd finished their account. He wore jeans and a denim jacket and looked like he'd just gotten out of bed.

Grace and Caveman recounted their story again for the sheriff's benefit.

"Grace, the man who killed Mr. Khalig is definitely after you. Do you know where you're going from here?"

"The Blue Moose Tavern."

The sheriff frowned. "They're closed."

"We'll be staying in the apartment above the tavern tonight," Caveman said.

"Come. You can ride with me," the sheriff said.

"Please." Grace didn't care who she rode with as long as there was a shower and a clean bed wherever they landed. Grace climbed into the back of the sheriff's vehicle. Caveman slid in next to her and pulled her into the crook of his arm. He was covered in dust and soot, but she didn't care. She was equally dirty, but alive. She nestled against him, but when she closed her eyes, images of the fire burned through her eyelids. Her pulse quickened and her heart thudded against her ribs.

"It's okay. We're going to be okay," Caveman said in that same tone he'd used on her horse. It worked on humans just as well.

Grace felt the tension ease. "I thought you were still in my SUV."

"I got out right after you." He smoothed his hand over her hair. "What's important is that we're both okay."

"I have my men watching the roads leading into and out of town," the sheriff said. "If someone is still out and about, they'll bring him in for questioning."

"Whoever did this will be long gone, if he's smart," Caveman said.

The sheriff glanced at them in his rearview mirror. "Whoever it was is getting more serious about these attacks."

"The question is why?" Grace said. "I couldn't see him from the distance when he killed Mr. Khalig. He should know by now."

"No search warrants have been issued," the sheriff said. "I haven't called anyone in for questioning. He's in the clear. As far as we know, it could have been anyone."

"What good does it do to kill me?" Grace shivered. "I'm nobody. Just a biologist."

Caveman tightened his arm around her. "Who happened to be in the wrong place at the wrong time and witnessed a murder."

"And escaped before the shooter could kill you, too." Sheriff Scott glanced back at her in the rearview mirror. "You're the one who got away."

Another tremor shook Grace's body. "I can't keep running."

"You can't get out in the open and give him something to shoot at." Caveman held her close. "I won't let you."

"I won't stand by and let him get away with destroying my home, my car and my life."

Caveman frowned. "What do you propose to do?"

She shook her head. "I don't know, but I'll think of something." Snuggling closer, she laid her cheek on his chest. "After a shower and some sleep."

THE LOFT ABOVE the Blue Moose Tavern was a fully furnished apartment with a single bedroom, bathroom and a living room with a foldout couch. The living area had been transformed into an operations center with a bay of computers and a large folding table covered with contour maps.

Kevin and Hack, his computer guru, waited in front of the tavern when the sheriff dropped off Caveman and Grace. The two DHS employees led the tired pair up the stairs. After a quick debriefing, Kevin offered Grace clothes his wife had sent and sweats and a T-shirt for Caveman. "We'll help you sift through the debris at your house tomorrow. For tonight, we hope this will do." Kevin's wife had also sent along a toiletries kit with a tube of toothpaste, shampoo, soap and toothbrushes still in their packages.

Grace gathered the kit, the clothes and a fresh towel. "This is one of those times when I'll gladly claim the 'ladies first' clause." She disappeared into the bathroom leaving the men to discuss the events of the day.

"I don't like it," Caveman said as soon as Grace was out of earshot.

"I don't blame you," Kevin agreed.

"There have been too many near misses today and we have yet to identify who's doing it."

"Do you think maybe there's more than one person involved?" Kevin asked.

"I don't know. But what I do know is that whoever it is knows something about weapons and explosives. He wired Grace's ignition with a damn detonator." Anger bubbled up inside him, spilling over. Caveman stalked away from Hack and Kevin, his fists clenched. He needed to fight back, but he didn't have a clue who he was fighting against. He spun and strode back to where Kevin stood. "If I hadn't gone with my gut when the vehicle didn't start, Grace wouldn't be in this apartment now. If I hadn't been there when she came barreling out of the mountains and was thrown by her horse, she'd be dead."

Kevin nodded. "We're still trying to trace the crates we found in the abandoned mine. Someone did a good job transporting them so that no one could identify their origin. We did a count, though, and based on the empty boxes, there were one hundred AR-15s in those crates. You don't hide one hundred AR-15s just anywhere. Someone has an armory around here and they're stockpiling weapons and ammunition."

"And the infrared satellite images we had from a week ago indicated fifteen individuals who helped unload those weapons. The Vanders family would account for at least four of those heat signatures, which leaves eleven."

"Hell, that's half the people in this county," Caveman said.

"I know this town is small, but there are a lot of outlying homes and ranches comprising the entire community of Grizzly Pass." Kevin scrubbed his hand down his face. The shadows under his eyes made him appear much older. "People are preparing for something. It's our jobs to stop them before they hurt others."

Caveman paced the room again, thinking. "This Free America group. Who are the members?"

"We don't know for certain," Hack said. "LeRoy Vanders and his sons admit to being members. They're talking about who else."

"What about the loudmouth last night in the tavern? Ernie Martin," Caveman shot out.

Kevin nodded. "He's one we're watching."

"I've tapped into his home internet account and his cell phone." Hack pulled out his chair and sat at the bank of computers, bringing up a screen. "His computer is clean, and I'm not finding any significant connections on the cell numbers he calls. If he's communicating with the group, he's doing it in person or on a burner phone I can't trace." He tapped several keys, booting the computer to life.

"You don't have to stay and work through the night," Caveman said. "I'm with Grace. All I want right now is a shower and some sleep."

"Do you want one of us to stand guard while you get some rest?" Kevin asked.

"No." Caveman wanted to be alone. With Grace. "The sheriff will have a deputy swing by every half hour until daylight. We should be all right."

Kevin straightened. "Then we'll leave you to get some rest. The sofa folds out into a queen-size bed. You can find sheets and blankets in the chest at the end of the bed. Help yourselves to anything in the refrigerator. I had it stocked with drinks and snacks."

"Thanks." Caveman could hear the shower going in the other room.

Hack powered the computer off and followed Kevin to the door.

"If you need me, give me a call. I can be here in five minutes." Kevin held out his hand. "Bet you weren't counting on so much activity in Wyoming. Were you?"

Caveman shook the man's hand. "No, I thought this would be a mini vacation and I'd be on my way back to my unit."

"And now?"

"I'm beginning to understand your concerns." And he couldn't leave, knowing Grace was in trouble.

"So you'll stay a little longer?"

"As long as you need me and my unit doesn't."

Kevin nodded. "Glad to hear it. We need good soldiers like you."

"I'll do what I can."

"I'm only five minutes away, as well," Hack said. He held up his cell phone. "Call, if you need me."

"Roger." Caveman closed the door behind the two men and twisted the dead bolt lock. Not that a dead bolt would have stopped a truck from crashing through Grace's bedroom wall. He hurried to the back of the apartment, stripping off his dirty clothes and kicking off his boots. The shower was still going when he stepped through the bathroom door.

He pushed the curtain aside and slipped into the tub.

"I wondered how long it would take you to get rid of those two." Grace turned around, her body clean and glistening beneath the spray. "I was beginning to prune." She slid a handful of suds over his chest, making mud out of the dirt, soot and dust.

Caveman didn't care. She could smear mud all over his body if she wanted as long as her hands were doing the smearing. She poured shampoo into her palm and lathered his hair.

With his hands free to explore, he lathered up and smoothed his fingers over her shoulders and down to her breasts, where he tweaked the nipples into tight buds. Moving lower, he cupped her sex and parted her folds, strumming the nubbin of flesh between.

She moaned and widened her stance. "No protection," she said, her voice catching in her throat as he flicked her there again.

"This isn't about me."

Grace moaned again, her hand sliding over his shoulders, washing away all of the grime, dirty bubbles carrying it down the drain. "Not all about me." She wrapped her hands around his shaft and stroked the length of him.

It was his turn to groan.

Touching and testing the sweet spots, they felt their way to an orgasm that left Caveman satisfied and frustrated at the same time. First thing in the morning, he'd hit the local drug store for reinforcements. This woman's appetite rivaled his own, and he didn't want to be caught unprepared.

By the time they'd explored every inch of each other's body, the water had cooled to the point of discomfort.

Caveman turned off the shower, grabbed a towel

and gently dried Grace. She returned the favor and sighed, her face sad.

"Why so sad?" he asked. "Didn't you like that?"

"Too much." She took his hand and led him to the bed. "I'm going to miss it when you're gone."

"Who said I'm going anywhere?"

"You know what I mean." She lay down on the bed and scooted over, making room for him. "You said it yourself. You're only going to be here for a short time."

"What if I decide to stay?" He might not have a job to go back to in the army. If the Medical Review Board didn't clear him, he'd be discharged, or given a desk job. He'd rather move back to Montana or Wyoming than take a desk job.

Grace's brows descended. "You can't stay. Look what nearly happened tonight. You were almost killed."

"But I wasn't. And neither were you."

She snuggled closer, her eyes drooping. "I'm too tired to argue about it. Just keep your promise, and don't do something stupid like fall in love with me." Her voice trailed off and her breathing grew steadier.

Caveman brushed a strand of hair away from her cheek and bent to kiss her. "I never made that promise. And it might be too late." Never in a million years, would Max "Caveman" Decker have guessed he would fall in love with a woman after knowing her for less than a week. But the thought of leaving and going back to his unit didn't hold the same appeal. In fact, even the mention of leaving made him feel like someone had a hand on his heart, squeezing the life out of him.

Maybe it was too soon for love, but only time would tell. Caveman wasn't so sure he'd have the time to find out, if Khalig's killer had his way with Grace. Tonight would have been the end of her had Caveman left when he'd originally wanted. Now, he couldn't leave. Not as long as Grace was in danger.

Chapter Eleven

Grace slept until after ten the following morning.
When she woke, she stretched her arm across the
bed, expecting to feel a naked body next to hers.
When she didn't, she opened her eyes.

Caveman was gone.

For a moment, panic ripped through her. After all
that had happened, she'd begun to rely on him to rescue her. Then she reminded herself he wouldn't have
left without saying goodbye. Not after last night.

They'd shared more than a near-death experience,
they'd connected on a level even more intimate.

Male voices sounded through the paneling of the
bedroom door.

Grace bolted to a sitting position, dragging the
sheet up over her bare breasts. She'd forgotten that
the living area was being used as the command center for the DHS representatives. They'd probably
been there for at least an hour, while she'd slept in.

Her cheeks heated. She wondered if Caveman had risen before they arrived to spare her the embarrassment of the team finding them in bed together.

She rose, grabbed the clothes Kevin's wife had provided and slipped into the bathroom. Five minutes later, she was dressed, had her hair pulled back into a neat ponytail and had brushed her teeth. She was ready to face the world. Or at least Kevin's team. She opened the door to the bedroom and stepped out.

The group of men standing around the array of computer monitors turned as one.

Heat rose into Grace's cheeks. Did they know she and Caveman had slept naked in the next room? Did she care? She squared her shoulders and forced a smile to her face.

In addition to Kevin, Caveman and Hack, three more men were in attendance. All there to witness Grace emerging from the back bedroom. Yeah, not what a woman wanted that early in the morning. "Good morning."

"Grace." Kevin stepped forward. "I trust you slept well?"

She nodded, her gaze going to the three men she didn't recognize.

Kevin turned to them. "Grace, have you met the other members of my task force?"

"No, I have not."

He turned to a big man with red hair and blue

eyes. "This is Jon Caspar, US Navy SEAL. They call him Ghost."

Ghost shook her hand. "I've seen you around. Nice to meet you."

Kevin moved to the next man, who was not quite as tall as Ghost, but had black hair and ice-blue eyes. "Trace Walsh, aka Hawkeye, is an Army Ranger."

Grace shook hands with Hawkeye. "Pleasure to meet you."

He grinned. "The pleasure's all mine."

Caveman grunted behind her. If she wasn't mistaken, it was a grunt of anger, maybe jealousy? Her heart swelled.

The last man Kevin introduced had really short auburn hair and hazel eyes. Almost as tall as Ghost, he looked like he could chew nails and spit them out. "This is Rex Trainor."

"My friends call me T-Rex." The man stuck out a hand. "I'm with the US Marine Corps."

When T-Rex shook her hand, he nearly crushed the bones.

Introductions complete, Grace glanced at the computer monitors. "Am I missing something?"

Kevin shook his head. "Not at all. We were just going through some of the most likely suspects who live in the area."

"Like?" She stepped up beside Caveman and looked over Hack's shoulder at pictures of people on the different monitors. Some of them were mug shots, others were driver's license pictures or photos from yearbooks. She recognized most of them, having lived in the area for the majority of her life. Small-town life was like that.

"Quincy Kemp and Ernie Martin," Caveman said.

"Mathis Herrington, Wayne Batson," Kevin added.

"And, of course, Tim Cramer and the Vanders family, who have already been detained." Hack tapped the keys on the computer keyboard. "We've been trying to find the connection between all of them."

Grace yawned and stretched, her muscles sore from everything that had happened over the past couple of days. "Has anyone thought to ask Mrs. Penders at the grocery store?"

Four of the five men frowned.

Ghost grinned. "That's where my girl, Charlie McClain, goes when she wants to know what's going on. Mrs. Penders seems to have her finger on the pulse of everything going on in town."

"I'll go question her." Caveman turned toward the door. "Mrs. Penders is her name?"

Grace held up her hand. "You can't just barge in and interrogate the woman. She likes to gossip, not answer a barrage of very pointed questions. Since my house was destroyed last night, she'll be eager to hear all of the details straight from the horse's mouth. Give a little, get a lot." She glanced down at the clothes Kevin's wife had loaned her. "Kevin, tell your wife thank you for the loaner. I'll get them back as soon as I dig my wardrobe out from under the rubble."

"She said to keep them as long as you need them," Kevin said. "And we plan to help with the cleanup."

"Thanks, but I'd rather you found the killer." She drew in a deep breath and let it out. "I don't know how much longer I can play this game with him, before he scores." *With my death.* "Now, if you will excuse me, I'm going across the street to talk to Mrs. Penders and buy a few supplies I might need in the cleanup process."

"I'm going with you," Caveman said.

Grace shook her head. "You can't. Mrs. Penders will be more likely to talk if I'm alone."

"You can't waltz around town like anyone else." Caveman gripped her arms. "You have a killer after you. One who is a crack shot with a rifle and scope."

Placing a hand on his chest, Grace smiled up at him. "Then I'll zigzag, or whatever it is you trained combatants do to run through enemy territory."

The other men chuckled. Not Caveman.

His face hardened. "It's not a joke."

Her smile fading, Grace nodded. "I know. It's not every day you have someone drive a truck into your bedroom, or have someone shooting at you. I'll be careful and look for trouble before I cross the street."

"I'm walking you across the street."

Her first instinct was to argue, but one glance at Caveman's face and she knew she would lose that argument. And frankly, she liked having him around. "Okay." She walked to the door and followed Caveman down the steps to the street.

He looped his arm around her shoulders, pulling her close to his body. They probably appeared to be lovers who couldn't get enough of each other. After last night, the look fit Grace. She wondered if Caveman felt the same, or if he truly only thought of her as a temporary distraction until he returned to his unit.

At the corner of the grocery store, Grace stopped and placed a hand on Caveman's chest. "This is where I get off. I'll see you as soon as I get all of the information I can out of Mrs. Penders."

"I'll be right here. All you have to do is yell if you need me."

"Thank you." Then, before she could talk herself out of it, she leaned up on her toes and pressed her lips to his. It was meant to be a quick show of appreciation. However, she was more than gratified when Caveman took the kiss to the next level.

He cinched his arm around her waist, crushing her to his body, his lips claiming hers in a kiss that stole her breath away and made her knees turn to gelatin. Had Caveman not been holding her, she would have melted to the ground. When he set her away from him, she swayed.

She raised a hand to her lips. "Wow."

He chuckled, the warm, deep resonance of the sound heating her from the inside out. "I don't like you standing out in the open for long." He turned her toward the grocery store entrance, gave her bottom a pat and sent her on her way. "Hurry back. I have more where that came from."

She ran her tongue across her bottom lip, tasting him.

"On second thought, forget going inside. We can drive out to the local lake and make out in the backseat of my pickup."

She laughed. "You're not making this easy."

He held up his hands. "What am I supposed to make easy?"

"Letting go of you when you leave Grizzly Pass."

"Maybe that's my plan."

Her smile faded. "You have to, eventually."

"Let's not talk about that now. In fact, take your time inside. Don't come out until you see me walk by the windows. I want to look around town."

She snorted. "That won't take long."

"Exactly. So take all the time you need. Just don't come outside until I'm here to protect you."

She nodded. Grace wanted to run for the door, zip in, suck information out of Mrs. Pender's brain in record time and return for another of those soul-defining kisses.

She'd warned him not to fall in love with her, but maybe she'd been warning the wrong person. Grace needed to take her own advice. Perhaps the curse was on anyone *she* fell in love with, not who fell in love with her.

With no time to contemplate her thoughts, she stepped into the store and greeted the female store owner with a smile. "Good morning, Mrs. Penders."

"Grace, honey, I was shocked to hear someone bulldozed your house last night. What can I do to help?"

OUTSIDE, LEANING ON a light post, Caveman studied the people who entered and exited the small store. The only one of its kind in town, it had the corner on the market. If people wanted more than what the Penderses offered, they had to drive thirty minutes to an hour to the nearest big town. Too far for a loaf of bread or a gallon of milk.

After a few minutes, he pushed away from the light post and walked to the end of the block—still within a reasonable distance to listen for a scream or see someone entering the store who might appear to be there for nefarious reasons rather than to buy a can of soup or a loaf of bread.

From his vantage point at the street corner, he could see to the end of Main Street. A storefront on the opposite side had a stuffed bear outside on the sidewalk. Not the teddy bear of the fake fur, cotton-filled variety. No, this was an eleven-foot tall grizzly, professionally mounted by a skillful taxidermist. He stood on his hind legs, his front legs outstretched, the wicked claws appearing to be ready to swipe at pass-ersby. And the mouth was open, every razor-sharp tooth on display. Yes, Quincy Kemp was very good at making the carcasses appear alive.

With a quick glance toward the grocery store to make certain Grace hadn't ended her information-gathering mission early, he turned toward the meat processing and taxidermist shop.

The door stood open; the scents of cedar, pepper and the musk of animal hides filled his senses, bringing back memories of a similar place in Caveman's hometown. In states where hunting was the major pastime of residents and tourists, every town seemed to have one of these kinds of stores.

A man emerged from a back room, wiping his hands on a towel. "What can I do for you?"

Caveman recognized him as Quincy Kemp. "I heard you made jerky."

"You heard right," Quincy said with one of the best poker faces Caveman had encountered.

"Do you happen to have buffalo or venison jerky?"

The man nodded and pulled a plastic butter tub from beneath the counter, opened it and selected a strip of jerky. "Try before you buy. I don't do refunds. This is buffalo."

Caveman popped the piece of jerky in his mouth and then chewed and chewed. The explosion of flavors made his mouth water.

Quincy crossed his arms over his chest, lifted his chin and looked down his nose at Caveman. "Well?"

"Good. I'd like to purchase a pound of the buffalo jerky."

While Quincy weighed several strips of the flavored, dried meat, Caveman wandered around the store. Besides a glass case of jerky and a refrigerated case of raw meat labeled Beef, Venison, Buffalo, Elk and Red Deer, there were numerous animals mounted on the wall.

"Did you do all of these?" Caveman waved at the lifelike animals staring down at him from shelves and nooks along the wall.

Quincy slipped the strips of jerky into a plastic bag and sealed it before answering. "Yeah. That'll be fifteen bucks."

Caveman fished his wallet out of his pocket, which reminded him he needed to hit the store for a refill of condoms. He placed a twenty on the counter. "What kinds of animals have you done?"

"What you see."

Caveman had noticed the bear, bobcat, rattle snake, elk, moose and coyote. "What about mountain lion?"

"I've done a couple."

"Bobcat?"

He shrugged. "Four."

"Is there an open season on bobcat and mountain lion?"

The man's eyes narrowed. "Do you have a point?"

"Just wondering. I might like to buy a hunting license while I'm here."

Quincy slapped the change on the counter and pushed the plastic bag of jerky toward Caveman. "Hunting season isn't open until the fall. If that's all you want, I don't have time to talk. I have work to do."

Caveman lifted the bag of jerky and grinned. "Thanks."

Quincy didn't wait for Caveman to leave the store before he returned to the back room.

Caveman would like to have followed the man to the back to see what job he was all fired up about. The man looked like someone who could chew nails. Not that he scared Caveman, but he wouldn't take kindly to being followed.

But then, Caveman could claim he wanted to see Quincy's work in case he wanted the man to stuff his next trophy kill. Not that Caveman ever killed just for the trophy. He hunted back in Montana, but always ate what he bagged.

Easing behind the counter, Caveman worked his way to the door leading to the back of the building. Quincy had left it open, presumably to hear for customers entering the shop.

Through the door was a workroom filled with hides and tools of the taxidermist trade. A short corridor led to a workshop in the back. The meat packaging plant was probably at the end of the hallway.

Quincy was nowhere to be seen.

Caveman studied the hides, curious about what the taxidermist did.

"Hey!" Quincy emerged from a door in the back. "What are you doing back here?"

Startled by the man's abrupt appearance, Caveman snapped around, his legs bent in a ready stance, his fists clenched in a defensive reflex. "I had a question for you."

"Well, take it out to the front. Nobody comes back here, but me."

"Sorry." Caveman held up his hands in surrender. "I didn't touch anything."

"Doesn't matter. You don't belong back here." Quincy marched toward him.

Caveman backed through the door, pretending to be afraid, but ready to take on the man if he pushed him too far. "I wanted to know if you could stuff a wolf I hit on my way into town. I threw him in the back of my truck, hating to waste a good-looking hide. I think he'd look really great in my man cave back home in North Carolina."

"Man, you need to get rid of the carcass. It's illegal to keep a wolf, dead or alive, in the state of Wyoming."

"So you wouldn't stuff him? What if I sneak him in here at night? Could you?"

"Hell, no. I don't plan on spending the next five years in jail. Been there, done that. I'm never going back. I'd die before I let them take me back."

"Okay. I totally understand. No worries. I'll find someone else to do it."

"You won't."

"Won't what?"

"Find another taxidermist. No one will touch a wolf, unless the government commissions it."

"Well, there goes my idea for a centerpiece in my living room." Caveman raised a hand in a half wave. "I guess that's all I needed to know. I must say, I'm disappointed."

Quincy's mouth formed into a tightly pressed line and his eyes narrowed.

Caveman waved the bag of jerky again. "Thanks

again for the jerky and all the information on taxidermist rules in Wyoming." He left the shop and strolled down the street toward the tavern, his gaze on the grocery store where he'd left Grace.

When he was far enough away from Quincy's shop, Caveman crossed the street and waited outside the grocery store, chewing on the buffalo jerky he'd purchased from Quincy, wondering what the man might be hiding in the back of his building. Perhaps he'd bring it up to Kevin and let the boss decide who he could send in to check. At this point, from what Caveman could tell of his role with Task Force Safe Haven, his primary purpose was to protect Grace from a killer. Kevin and the others could do the sleuthing to find out if what was happening in Grizzly Pass was a terrorist plot to take over the government.

"MARK RUTHERFORD SHOULD be available to help you fix the damage to your house. He's a good handyman and carpenter. And Lord knows he could use the work," Mrs. Penders said. "What with his daddy having to pay the additional grazing fees when he just forked out a wad of cash to install a new pump in his well. I'm sure Mark would appreciate the extra income."

"I'll check with him as soon as I assess the damage. I just can't understand why someone would deliberately crash into my house."

"Are you sure it wasn't an accident?"

"No, it was deliberate. He broke into the truck and drove it into my bedroom wall as if he knew I was in bed." Grace glanced around the store. "I'll need some trash bags and cleaning supplies."

"Sweetie, let me help you."

"Oh, I can't take you away from the register."

"There's no one in the store right now. I want to help." Mrs. Penders locked the register and led the way down the aisle of cleaning supplies, plucking off a couple bottles of disinfectant spray and cleaner. "I don't know what's going on in town, what with the Vanderses going crazy and kidnapping a busload of little ones. And now someone's murdered Mr. Khalig. He came into the store the other day for a bag of butterscotch candies." She smiled sadly. "Such a nice man. I imagine his wife will be devastated."

"Who would want to kill Mr. Khalig?"

Mrs. Penders rounded the end of the cleaning supplies aisle and started up the one with paper products and boxes of trash bags. She grabbed one of the boxes, read the front and put it back, selecting one with a larger number of bags. "Mr. Khalig worked as an inspector for the pipeline. If he doesn't approve what's going on, the pipeline shuts down. He could have reported some safety issues. Some people think he's the reason they got laid off."

"Did he ever say anything about any safety issues?" Grace asked, taking some of the cleaning supplies from Mrs. Penders. They walked back to front of the store and set the items on the counter.

"I could use some paper plates and disposable cutlery. I have a feeling my electricity will be off and on as they work on my house."

Mrs. Penders turned and led the way to the plastic forks and spoons. "Mr. Khalig wasn't allowed to discuss his work on account of confidentiality. But I could tell he wasn't happy with what he was finding. He started out warm and friendly. The longer he was here, the quieter and more secretive he became. And he kept looking over his shoulder, like someone was watching him." Mrs. Penders sighed. "And somebody had to have been, in order to shoot him from a distance. Poor, poor man. How awful."

"How do you know all of this?"

Mrs. Penders carried the boxes of spoons and forks to the counter and gave Grace a smile. "I just do. As for who, there are quite a few people I can think of. All of them worked for the pipeline and lost their jobs. The sheriff should start there. I mean look at what happened with Tim Cramer. He lost his job with the pipeline, his wife filed for divorce and now he's in jail. He was so desperate he helped with that kidnapping."

"He couldn't have been the one to kill Mr. Khalig. He was in jail when it happened."

"True. But there are others on the verge of bankruptcy, losing their homes and destroying their families." Mrs. Penders clucked her tongue. "Such a shame. I wish that pipeline had never crossed this state."

"Most of those who worked for the pipeline would have moved out of state to find jobs by now."

"Yes, but they wouldn't be as desperate." Mrs. Penders unlocked the register. "It's as if someone is sabotaging this area and the people in it."

"Who would do that, and why?" As Mrs. Penders rang up Grace's purchases, Grace put them into a bag. "We don't have anything here anyone would want."

"Maybe they want the pipeline to fail, but then maybe not, if they shot the inspector who could have shut down the whole thing." Mrs. Penders took Grace's money and handed her the change. "Then there are the folks who are tired of everything to do with the government. They would prefer to have the entire state of Wyoming secede from the United States. Bunch of crazies, if you ask me. Even scarier, they're a bunch of armed nut jobs."

"Do you know any of them?"

"Nobody comes out and says they're part of the group Free America. But I have my suspicions."

"Who?"

The older woman glanced around to make sure no one else was in the store. "I think Ernie Martin, Quincy Kemp, Don Sweeney and Mathis Herrington belong to that group. I'm sure there are a lot more who aren't as vocal. Some not from this county, but a county over."

"If they aren't telling you, how do you know?"

The older woman lifted her chin. "I have ears. Sometimes they run into each other in the store while I'm stocking shelves. I can hear them talking. In fact, I'm pretty sure they're having some meeting tomorrow night."

Butterflies erupted in Grace's belly. "Where?"

Mrs. Penders shrugged. "I don't know. Ernie and Quincy were in here buying lighter fluid and briquettes earlier today for a barbeque. They said something about getting together at the range."

"Range?" Grace's mind exploded with possibilities. "As in front range? Good Lord, that could be almost anywhere." Or maybe… "Or do they mean like a gun range?"

A mother carrying a baby in a car seat walked into the store.

The store owner smiled at the woman. "Good morning, Bayleigh, how's Lucas?"

The young mother smiled. "He's finally sleeping through the night."

"That's wonderful. Are you here for that formula you ordered?"

"I am," Bayleigh answered.

Mrs. Penders raised her finger. "One minute. I'll get it from the back."

"Please, take your time," Bayleigh said. "I have other shopping to do."

Grace gathered her bags. She couldn't take up any more of Mrs. Penders's time. "Thank you for everything, Mrs. P."

"Let me know if you need anything. Remember to check with Mark Rutherford. He's got time on his hands and probably can start right away on the repairs."

"I'll do that." Grace paused at the entrance, a frown pulling at her brows. A meeting at the range. When she spotted Caveman waiting outside, she pushed through the door and hurried toward the man who made her heart beat faster. "We need to talk to the team."

Chapter Twelve

Caveman paced the length of the operations center.

"How do you propose we get an invite to that meeting tomorrow evening?" Kevin asked. "We're not even sure what Mrs. Penders meant by 'the range.'"

"I'd bet my last dollar it's Wayne Batson's gun range," Ghost said.

Hack nodded. "He has the fences and security system in place to hold off an initial attack. And his computer system has a helluva firewall. I've yet to hack into it."

"Sounds like someone with something to hide," Caveman said.

"Why don't we just walk in?" Grace asked.

All five men turned toward her.

"Walk in?" Kevin asked. "What do you mean?"

"By now, everyone in town will know I've been the target of a shooter and someone who likes crashing trucks into my house. What if I ask Wayne to give me some time on his range, maybe even shooting lessons?"

"No way," Caveman said. "Putting you on a rifle range with a bunch of loaded weapons is a recipe for getting shot. What if the shooter is Wayne or one of his buddies?"

"So, I take my bodyguard and announce it to the world I'm going to the range. The sheriff knows, everyone in town knows. If someone shoots me at the range, they'll have to shoot Caveman, too. They might get away with an accident killing one person, but they won't get away with killing two."

Anger tinged with a healthy dose of fear bubbled up inside Caveman. "So who shall we offer up as the one?" He shook his head. "It's too dangerous."

Grace turned toward Kevin. "At the very least, we go in, find the weaknesses of Batson's security system, leave and come back at night when we can slip in under the cover of darkness."

Caveman couldn't believe what she was saying. If one of Batson's friends was the shooter, he'd have no trouble lining up his sights and taking her down. "There is no 'we' in slipping back into Batson's property." He poked a finger at her. "*You're* not going anywhere."

"But I'm the one with the big target on my back."

Crossing his arms over his chest, he refused to back down. "Exactly. Now you're beginning to understand."

Her frown deepened and her cheeks reddened. "Don't patronize me, Max Decker. I'm the one who has to keep looking over her shoulder. I'm the one whose house is now a wreck. I have the biggest stake in finding the killer. I deserve to go."

"But you don't deserve to die." His face firmed and his eyes narrowed. "You're not going."

Her chin lifted. "Then I'll go without you. I need practice with my .40-caliber pistol, and I don't need your permission." She started for the door. "Gentlemen, I have a house to sift through and arrangements to make to get me onto Batson's rifle range." She sailed past Caveman and almost made it to the door when he grabbed her arm and yanked her back.

"We need to talk," he said. He couldn't let her walk out the door unprotected and waltz into the enemy's camp. If Batson was truly the enemy. "Let's at least talk this through before we go off half-cocked."

"I'm done talking." She glared at the hand on her arm. "Let go of me."

"Grace." Kevin stepped over to where they stood by the door. "We need to make a plan. We also need to understand who we're dealing with. What motivation does Wayne Batson have to host a Free America meeting on his range?"

"Maybe he's training recruits for the takeover of the government," Ghost offered. "The message Charlie picked up off that social media site was clear. They're planning a takeover of something."

"Why would Batson lead the charge?" Kevin asked. "He has to have a reason."

Grace pressed her fingers to the bridge of her nose. "I don't know. Wayne Batson seems to be the only person in the county who has pulled himself up out of hard times. When he was faced with bankruptcy, he found investors and turned his ranch into a sportsman's paradise. Why destroy a good thing by plotting against the government?"

"Having been in a bad situation, maybe he harbors animosity toward the government for some reason," Hawkeye said. "You never know what will push a man over the edge and make him think he has to take control of the world."

"Are you saying we might be barking up the wrong tree?" Grace asked. "That Batson might not be our guy? His ranch with the rifle range might not be the meeting place?"

Kevin shook his head. "No. I think you're on to something."

"Then what's your plan?" She planted her fists on her hips. "If I take Caveman with me to practice my shooting skills, we can at least get inside and look around."

Caveman turned toward Kevin. "What do you have in the way of communications equipment? We had the radio headsets we used when we stormed the Lucky Lou Mine in the rescue attempt to save the kidnapped kids. Could we have something like that? And do you have any kind of webcam we can hide in a pen?"

Kevin grinned. "You must have me mistaken with the CIA."

Hack spun in his chair and opened his mouth to say something.

Before he could, Kevin held up his hand. "As a matter of fact, I invested some of the project funding in just what you're talking about. We have a webcam button we can attach to your shirt. Hack will get you two wired up."

Grace smiled. "Thank you."

Caveman wasn't happy about the situation, but he could either shut up and go, or send someone else with Grace. The woman was going whether or not he wanted her to. And because he found himself just a little bit protective of her, he didn't trust anyone else to take care of her as well as he would. Not that the others weren't fully capable. They just didn't have the connection he had with her.

Hack went to a footlocker in the corner, unlocked the combination lock and pulled out radio headsets and a small case with a little white button. "Doesn't look like much, but it sends a pretty clear picture to our computer." He handed it to Grace. "The idea is to replace a button on a shirt, so it will take a little bit of sewing skills." He handed her a small sewing kit like the ones found in hotel rooms.

"I can handle that." She glanced at Caveman. "Since your shirt has the buttons and you'll know better what to look for, you should have the camera on you. I can sew this onto your shirt."

"I'm pretty handy with a needle and thread, if you'd rather I did it," he offered.

"No use taking off your shirt. Let me call Batson and see if we can even get onto the range this afternoon."

Hack looked up the Lonesome Pine Ranch and passed her the contact number.

Grace pulled her cell phone from her purse, entered the number and waited.

Part of Caveman wished no one would answer or, if they did, they wouldn't allow her to book time on the gun range.

"This is Grace Saunders. I've had some troubles lately with someone following me."

Caveman snorted softly. Grace had conveniently left off the fact that someone was not only following her, but trying to kill her.

"Thank you. Yes, I'm okay," Grace said. "The sheriff suggested I call and see if I could get some time on the range to practice with my pistol. The sooner the better. I was hoping to get out there this afternoon. It will be two of us. Me and my…boy-friend." She paused, nodding at whatever the person on the other end of the call was telling her. "That would be great. Four o'clock works perfectly. Yes, we'll bring our own guns. I'll see you at four. Thank you." She clicked the end call button and looked across at Caveman. "We're on for four o'clock. I might have to dig my pistol out from under the rub-ble of my bedroom."

"I have one you could use," Kevin offered.

"If I can't find mine, I'll take you up on the offer," Grace said. "In the meantime, I'd like to get some-thing going on the cleanup effort at my house. I don't want to wait until it rains and ruins even more of my belongings."

For the next few hours, Grace was on the phone with an insurance adjuster and a handyman.

Caveman took her out to her house to meet with the adjuster. Once the man left with a page full of notes, Caveman started sorting through broken boards and crumbled drywall to get to Grace's night-stand where she kept her pistol. He helped her locate the boxes of bullets she'd need at the range.

They cleared enough debris to allow her to get into her drawers and closets to pack several suitcases.

Without a way to lock her home, she couldn't stay in the house until the wall was back up.

Grace called Mark Rutherford, the handyman Mrs. Penders had recommended. He showed up, surveyed the damage and gave her an estimate on how much it would cost to fix it. He'd only take a week to clear the debris and rebuild the wall. He'd need the better part of the next week to do the finishing work on the inside and outside.

Throughout the day, he watched Grace handle the disaster of her house with calm and patience, talking to the handyman and the adjuster with a smile and a handshake. The sheriff came out to survey the damage in the daylight and take pictures of the house and the truck. When she told him she'd be going out to Wayne Batson's range for target practice, he nodded.

"It's a good idea to be proficient and have confidence in the handling of your own weapon."

She didn't tell him why she'd chosen Batson's range or that there might be a meeting of the Free America group there the next night.

Caveman was tempted, but he figured she didn't want the sheriff to try to talk her out of it.

His gut clenched all day. He was torn between calling the whole thing off and going through with the plan. If they could get in and out without being shot and killed, they could bring back enough information for the task force team to enter the secure ranch compound. The team could find out what the rebel group was planning and maybe determine who might have killed Mr. Khalig.

After the sheriff left, Caveman brought a mug of hot cocoa out to the porch for Grace and insisted she sit for a few minutes. She chose the porch swing and sat far enough over for Caveman to join her. "How did you make hot cocoa?"

Caveman grinned. "I found a camp stove in a closet."

For a few minutes, they shared the silence, sipping cocoa and staring at the caved-in portion of her home.

"Why would a rebel group like Free America want to kill a pipeline inspector? They don't work for the government. They contract out to the big oil companies." Grace sighed. "I hope we're not wasting our time going out to the Lonesome Pine Ranch, chasing a wild goose."

"If you're concerned, why don't you stay in town and let me go alone? The activities of the Free America group are a concern of Task Force Safe Haven. Kevin's responsibility as an agent with the Department of Homeland Security is to keep our homeland safe. If this group is planning to take a government facility that would be considered an act of terror. We have to investigate. This is the first real information we've received on when and where they will meet. We have to check it out. But you don't."

"If they have anything to do with Mr. Khalig's death and the subsequent threats to my life, I sure as hell have to go. I refuse to continue playing the victim. It's time I fought back."

Caveman took her empty cup and set it on the end table beside the swing and put his next to it. Then he took Grace's hands in his. "I want you to promise you won't do anything that will make Batson or his employees think we're spying on him. If he is part of this rebel group, he might want to keep it under wraps. In which case, he might go to all lengths to keep that secret."

"I promise I will do my best not to draw unnecessary attention. We'll get in there, and get out with the data your team needs to do what they have to do to protect our nation."

"Then we'd better get going. Your appointment is for four o'clock." He stood, pulled her to her feet and into his arms.

She rested her hands on his chest. "Are you going to kiss me?"

He chuckled. "I'm thinking about it."

Her hands slipped up around his neck. "Stop thinking, and start kissing."

"Do you still think your curse will be the death of me?"

"Not if we don't fall in love."

If her curse was real, he was doomed. In the short amount of time he'd been with Grace, she'd found her way into his mind, body and soul. He knew there would be no going back. Convincing her that she wouldn't kill him with a crazy curse would be the first challenge. Figuring out where they'd go from Grizzly Pass would be the second.

She laced her fingers at the back of his head and pulled his head down to hers. "Now, are you going to kiss me?"

"Damn right, I am." His lips crashed down on hers, his tongue pushing past her teeth to caress hers. This was what he'd wanted all day.

Grace didn't hold back. Her tongue twisted and thrust, her body pressing tightly to his.

When he had to breathe again, Caveman rested his cheek against her temple. "I worry about you," he whispered.

"You don't have to. I can make my own decisions and live with the consequences of my actions."

His chest tightened as if someone was squeezing him really hard. "If you're fortunate enough to live."

GRACE CLENCHED HER hands in her lap, as she stared at the road ahead, with every intention of staying alive. As far as she was concerned, she was going to get in some target practice with her handgun. Then she'd leave. If they just happened to find out more about a certain antigovernment organization, so be it. She'd keep those little gems of information to herself until she was off the Lonesome Pine Ranch and back where it was safe.

She had no problem letting the trained soldiers handle the major spying mission, although she would love to be a fly on the wall and listen in on the Free America meeting. After all, it was her country, too. She didn't appreciate terrorists trying to take over the land of the free and the home of the brave.

But she wasn't trained in combat tactics and would slow them down. She'd help them more by gathering information that would help them infiltrate after dark.

She'd sewn the webcam button onto Caveman's shirt and watched as he tucked the radio communication device in his ear. She put one in hers as well, but she wasn't as confident using it. She turned her head away from Caveman. "Can you hear me?"

"Loud and clear," he said.

"We can hear you, too," Hack said from his desk in the operations center.

Grace grinned. "I feel like I fell into a spy movie."

"Yeah, well, this isn't make-believe. Stick to the script and keep a low profile."

"Got it." Grace's heartbeat sped as Caveman

pulled up to the gate of the Lonesome Pine Ranch and punched the button on the control panel.

"Grace Saunders and Max Decker here for range practice," he said into the speaker.

"Welcome. Please drive through." The giant wrought-iron gate swung open.

Caveman pulled through the gate.

Grace glanced over her shoulder as the big gate closed. Her breath caught in her throat. For a moment, she felt like an animal caught in a trap. Forcing a calm she didn't feel, she smiled over at Caveman. "Ready for some target practice?"

"You bet." He laid his hand over the console.

Grace placed hers in his for a brief squeeze before he returned his grip to the steering wheel.

Signs for the gun range directed them to turn before they reached the big house perched on top of a hill. The road ended in a small parking area. Wayne Batson waited for them, a holster buckled around his hips. In his cowboy boots, jeans and leather vest, he looked like a man straight out of the Old West.

A shiver rippled across Grace's skin. What if this man was the one who'd been shooting at her? Would he take the opportunity now to kill her? Maybe she'd been a little too naive to think a killer wouldn't shoot her in broad daylight even when the sheriff knew where she was going.

Instead of an old-fashioned revolver in the holster, Wayne had a sleek, dark-gray pistol, probably a 9-millimeter by the size and shape.

Grace pasted a smile on her face and climbed out of the truck. "Good afternoon, Mr. Batson. Thank you for letting me come out for some target practice on such short notice."

"My pleasure," he said. "I hear you're having a little trouble and want to make sure you can defend yourself."

She nodded. "I've had this gun since I graduated from college, but I don't get nearly enough practice with it."

"No use having one if you don't know how to use it properly," Batson said.

"I told her the same." Caveman stepped up to Batson and held out his hand. "Max Decker. You must be Wayne Batson, the owner of Lonesome Pine Ranch?"

Batson nodded and shook his hand. "It's been in the family for over a century. I hope to keep it in the family for another century." He glanced from Caveman to Grace. "Show me what you have in the way of firepower."

Grace pulled out the case with her .40-caliber H&K pistol. It was small, light and fit her hand perfectly.

Caveman brought out a 9-millimeter Glock.

Batson assigned them lanes on the range and

handed them paper targets. Once the targets were stapled in place, they stood back at the firing position.

Batson joined Grace in her lane. "How often do you fire this weapon?"

"At least once a year."

"That's not nearly enough to feel comfortable holding and aiming." He demonstrated the proper technique for holding a pistol and then had her show him the same.

"How's it been here at the Lonesome Pine since you turned it into a big game hunting ranch?" Grace asked.

"Business is good," he answered, his tone clipped.

Grace lined up her sites with the target. "Lot of people from out of state?" She squeezed the trigger, remembering not to anticipate the sound and slight movement of the gun. The pungent scent of gunpowder reminded her of her father and the first time he'd taken her out to shoot. As his only daughter, he wanted her to be safe and know how to defend herself should she have to. Her heart squeezed hard in her chest. Her father would be horrified to know she'd been the target of a killer. He'd be on the first plane back to Wyoming from their retirement home in Florida.

Grace refused to call them and tell them she was in trouble. They'd fly back in an instant and place themselves in the line of fire. She'd be damned if she let some low-life killer touch her family. Now if only she could stay alive so they didn't come back to a funeral.

She studied Wayne Batson out of the corner of her eye.

He was tall, muscular and lean. The man would have been incredibly handsome, but for the slight sneer on his lip that pushed him past handsome to annoyingly arrogant.

She fired several rounds, adjusting her aim, working for a tighter grouping.

Batson holstered his gun and turned toward Caveman. "Do you have any questions?"

Caveman gave him a friendly smile. "I have one. Do you have many locals come out to fire on your range, or is it mainly the out-of-towners?"

Grace ejected her magazine and made slow work of loading bullets, wanting to hear every word of the conversation between Batson and Caveman.

"I get locals who need a place to practice with real targets at specific distances. They come to improve their skills for hunting season, just like my out-of-towners. The only difference is that the locals can come more often."

"How do you keep the game contained inside the perimeter?" Caveman asked, while reloading his magazine.

"You might have noticed on your drive in, we

have high fences surrounding all ten thousand acres. It's one of the largest fully contained game ranches in the state. We offer guided hunts of all kinds."

"A client could select the preferred prey?"

Batson nodded. "My clients can be very specific."

"You've stocked the ranch with animals, and they can choose what they want to hunt?" Caveman asked.

"Yes."

Caveman smacked the magazine into the grip of his pistol and stared across at Batson. "The fences keep all of them in?"

"Only the best materials were used," Batson said. "We have high-tech monitoring to detect breeches so that we can get to the exact location and fix them quickly."

"That had to cost," Grace said.

"My clients pay."

"Then why bother with a range like this if your big game hunts are paying the bills?"

"I've learned diversification is important. When all we had were cattle and horses, we had some hard times. I almost lost the ranch to the government for back taxes. I promised myself I'd never get in that situation again. I will not let the government take my family home, like they're trying to take the Vanderses'."

"You sound pretty adamant," Grace said.

Batson's jaw tightened. "I am."

Grace fit her magazine in the grip of her handgun and slammed it home. She stared down the barrel at the target and squeezed the trigger. Five rounds fired made five little holes on the silhouette target where the heart would be on a man. All her father's lessons came back with a little practice.

"Nice," Caveman commented. He brought his weapon up, aiming it downrange. "One other question for you, Mr. Batson."

"Shoot."

Caveman fired five rounds, hitting the silhouette target in the head, the holes the bullets made in such a tight grouping they appeared to be one big hole. He turned toward Batson with a friendly smile. "What do you prefer, handgun or rifle?"

Grace had been ejecting her magazine from her pistol. When she heard Caveman's unexpected question, she fumbled the magazine and it fell to the dirt.

Batson's eyes narrowed. For a moment, Grace didn't think the game ranch owner would answer the question.

"It depends on several things—how close I plan to get to the target, how accurate I want to be and how intelligent my quarry is." He touched a hand to his ear where he had a very small Bluetooth earpiece. "What is it, Laura?" He listened for a moment and then spoke. "Fine, let them in." His gaze returned to Grace. "Pardon me. It seems the sheriff wants to see me."

"The timing couldn't be better," Caveman said. "It's starting to get dark and we need to head back to town."

"Good." Batson nodded. "I don't usually leave guests on the range without supervision."

"Then we'll head out." Grace left the magazine out of her pistol, pulled back the bolt and inspected the chamber to make sure it was empty. Then she laid the weapon in its case. "Thank you for allowing us to come out on such short notice."

They shook hands with Batson and stowed the gun cases in the backseat of Caveman's truck.

The sheriff's vehicle was pulling up as they drove away. Grace slowed and started to lower her window.

"Just wave and keep driving," Caveman advised.

"Won't the sheriff think that strange?"

"I'm not concerned about what the sheriff thinks." Caveman waved her forward. "I want to use the time he keeps Batson occupied to leave slowly and capture as much information as I can about the security system used around the perimeter."

Grace slowed, nodded and pulled past the sheriff as she headed down the road toward the gate.

Caveman studied the fences and the gate, making comments aloud about the cameras located at the top of the gate pillar, aimed at the road.

Once they were through the gate, Grace crept along the highway, moving slowly enough Caveman could study the fencing. "I didn't notice it before, but stop for a minute."

Grace glanced in the rearview mirror. Nobody was behind her so she pulled to the side of the road and stopped. "Why are we stopping?"

"I want to test a theory." He opened his door, reached toward the ground and came up with a rock the size of a golf ball. Then he tossed it toward the fence wire. When the rock hit the fence, a shower of sparks shot out.

Grace gasped. "It's electric."

"Pretty expensive fencing for a game ranch."

"That'll keep the game in," Grace said.

Caveman's eyes narrowed to slits. "And uninvited guests out."

Wayne Batson had more than a game ranch on his huge spread: he had a locked-down compound capable of keeping out nosy people. As Grace drove back to town, a chill spread over her body. Her friendly community of Grizzly Pass had a darker side she never knew existed.

Chapter Thirteen

It was late by the time Caveman finished debriefing the team. He learned Kevin had sent the sheriff out to the Lonesome Pine Ranch to run interference for them so that they could leave unimpeded.

"While you two were on the inside, we had a drone flying over," Kevin said. "Between the information you two collected and the footage from the drone, we'll have our hands full tonight, determining the best way we can get in before the meeting tomorrow."

"Could we grab a bite to eat before we start?" Caveman asked.

"We can do better than that," Kevin said. He held out a key. "I got you two a suite at Mama Jo's Bed-and-Breakfast a couple blocks away. You can eat, catch some sleep and come back in the morning to see what we found."

"You don't need us?" Grace asked.

"With four of us looking at the monitors, it will be crowded enough. And you two have already done enough. Get some food and rest. Tomorrow will be another day. We'll brief you on the plan then."

Hack chuckled. "We hope to *have* one by then. I anticipate pulling an all-nighter."

Caveman would have liked to have stayed and looked over the drone images, but he was hungry, and he bet Grace was, too.

They called down to the tavern and ordered carryout. A few minutes later they left the team, collected their food and drove to the quaint Victorian house just off Main Street. They had all of the second floor, which consisted of two bedrooms, a shared bathroom and a sitting room, complete with a television and a small dining table.

"I'm going to hit the shower before I eat," Grace said. "I feel dusty from being out on the range this afternoon."

"Want company?" Caveman asked.

"What do you think?" She smiled, dragged her shirt up over her head and dropped it on the floor. Turning, she walked into the bathroom, half closed the door and then dangled her bra through the opening.

Caveman was already halfway out of his clothes, tripping over his boots as he kicked them off.

The next minute, he was in the shower with Grace,

lathering her body, rinsing, kissing and repeating the process until they had the bathroom steaming. They made love under the warm spray and stayed until the water chilled. By the time they'd dried, the night had settled in on Grizzly Pass. Traffic slowed on Main Street and folks went home to their families.

Caveman and Grace ate their dinner and then moved to the king-size bed where they made love again. Nearing midnight, they lay in each other's arms, sated, but not sleepy.

"We should go back to the operations center and see if they've discovered anything new," Grace said.

Caveman sighed and brushed his lips across hers. "I know you're right. But I can't help it. I don't want our time together to end."

"Me, either." She sighed, too, and kissed him hard.

He would have stayed right where he was, with Grace's warm body pressed against his, but they weren't done for the night. Caveman rolled out of the bed and extended his hand. "Ready?"

She shook her head, laid her hand in his and let him pull her to her feet. "I'll only be a minute." Grace grabbed her clothes and hurried into the bathroom.

"I'll call and let Kevin know we're coming," Caveman said. He made the call to learn Kevin, Hack, Ghost, T-Rex and Hawkeye were still up and poring over the videos. They'd noted a few items of interest they wanted to show Caveman. "Good," he said. "We'll be there soon."

He dressed quickly, pulled on his boots and waited by the window. From their room, he had a good view of Main Street and the front of Quincy Kemp's meat packing shop. It was dark, like most of the businesses in town at that hour. He wondered what was in the back of Quincy's shop that the man hadn't wanted Caveman to see. Could he have the wolf carcass, preparing it to be stuffed? And, if he did, he would know who killed it. Or was he hiding the AR-15s in one of his freezers behind big slabs of meat?

Dressed in a black turtleneck shirt and black jeans, Grace stepped up beside him and looked through the window. "What are you looking at?"

"Quincy's place. I went there while you were with Mrs. Penders. He didn't want me in the back of his building. He was pretty adamant about it. Which makes me think he has something to hide."

"What are you thinking?" She pulled on her boots and straightened. "Want to go there first?"

"I can send another member of the team to investigate."

"Why? They have enough on their plates. Obviously, Kemp isn't in his shop now. Not with all of the lights out, and no one moving around. We could get in, do a little spying and leave with no one the wiser."

His lips quirked on the corners. "You realize you're talking about breaking and entering."

"We're not stealing anything," Grace argued.

"It's still illegal."

"You're right." She chewed on her bottom lip. "You can't afford to be caught. It might get you in trouble with the military."

He didn't like the calculating look in her eyes. "What are you thinking?"

"That I'm brilliant, and you don't have to commit a crime. You could keep watch outside while I go in and poke around. That way you aren't in on the crime. If I'm caught, I'll be the only one charged."

"Have you heard of aiding and abetting?" Caveman countered.

She shrugged. "You just have to deny everything. I'll tell them I snuck off, leaving you wondering where I'd gone. It will all be on me."

"I'm surprised you would even consider it." He reached for her hand. "I took you for a by-the-books kind of woman."

Her lips thinned into a tight line. "I was, until someone started shooting at me. Desperate times call for...you know."

"Desperate measures." Caveman didn't like Grace's plan at all, but his gut told him Quincy was hiding something in the back of his shop. "Look, you're not going anywhere without me."

She smiled up at him, her brows rising in challenge. "Then I guess you'll be breaking the law with me, because I'm going into Quincy's place to see what he was hiding from you."

He slipped his arm around her waist and kissed her. "You're a stubborn woman, Grace Saunders."

"I have to be in my line of business."

"I'll bet you do." He kissed her again and then turned to scan what he could see of the street and buildings around Quincy's shop. Other than the tavern, the town of Grizzly Pass had more or less rolled up its sidewalks.

Grace headed for the door. "If we're going to do this, we should get moving."

Caveman shrugged into his jacket and followed. "Stay close."

"I told you, I don't like you playing the role of my bullet shield." She pulled on a dark coat and swept her hair up into a ponytail.

"Humor me, will you?" He grabbed her hand and led her out of the bed-and-breakfast, hugging the shadows of the building to the corner where it connected to Main Street. The road was clear of people and vehicles as far as Caveman could tell, but he didn't know who might be watching from any of the buildings.

"Come on." He looped his arm over her shoulder

and pulled her close. "We're just lovers on a late-night stroll."

"I like the sound of that," Grace whispered. "It would be even better if we weren't on someone's hot target list."

They crossed the street and walked past Quincy's place, turned down the next street and slipped into the back alley behind the meat packaging store.

Fortunately, the light over the back entrance was burned out, leaving the area completely in shadows.

Caveman slipped a knife from his pocket and pushed the blade in between the door and the jamb. With a few jiggles, he disengaged the lock, opened the door and hurried both of them inside.

Grace lifted her cell phone and shone the built-in flashlight around the room. The very back of the building was the meat packaging area with stainless-steel tables, sinks and refrigerators. The scents of blood, raw meat and disinfectants warred with each other.

Caveman checked the big walk-in freezers first. Finding nothing inside other than slabs of meat and big carcasses, he closed the doors. A quick survey of the rest of the room revealed nothing unusual or suspicious.

Quickly moving on, he led the way to a long corridor with a door on either side. This area separated the meat processing operations from the taxidermy workroom. He tried the handles. One was locked, the other wasn't. He pushed it open, only to find a variety of cleaning supplies: mops, aprons, bottles of disinfectant and various packaging supplies. The room was nothing more than a closet with shelves. Caveman checked the walls and floors for hidden doors.

"Anything?" Grace asked from the hall.

"Nothing." He left the supplies closet, locking it behind him.

Moving to the door across the way, Caveman used his knife to disengage the lock. Inside, he found an office with a desk, file cabinet and shelves. This room wasn't much bigger than the janitor's closet. Neither room was as wide as the shop front or the meat processing rear.

Caveman exited the office for a moment and walked into the taxidermy work area. It was as wide as the meat processing area, but square.

Grace gasped.

"What's wrong?"

She pointed to the hide of what appeared to be a black wolf. Tears welled in her eyes. "Loki." She shook her head, her fists bunching. "The bastard killed Loki."

Caveman pulled her against him and held her for a brief moment. "I'm sorry. But we have to keep moving."

"I know." She wiped a tear from her cheek and

pushed away, turning her back to the wolf she'd raised from a pup.

Caveman's heart pinched at her sadness, but they had bigger, more immediate problems. "The office and supply room aren't as deep as the two work rooms. Where's the rest of the space?"

He hurried back into the office and checked the walls. In the back corner, on the far side of a large filing cabinet, was a wall with a pegboard attached. On the board, different tools hung neatly. Everywhere else in the office boxes were stacked on the floor, blocking access to the walls, except in front of the pegboard lined with tools.

Caveman pushed the pegboard and the entire wall moved just a little. He tapped on the wall, creating a hollow sound. Running his fingers along the outer edge of the pegboard he traced one end and then the other. Halfway down the right side, his finger encountered a hidden latch. He released it and the pegboard and wall swung toward him.

"I'll be damned," Grace muttered behind him.

He glanced back at the woman standing in the doorway of the office. "Could you keep an eye on the hallway while I go in to check it out?"

Grace nodded. "Okay, but don't be too long." She shot a nervous glance over her shoulder. "I have a bad feeling about this."

"I'll hurry." He ducked into the room, shining his cell phone flashlight at the far walls, looking for windows to the outside. When he didn't locate any, he flipped the light switch on the wall and studied the contents of the room, his stomach clenching into a vicious knot.

Racks filled with guns stood in short, neat rows. Shelves lined the walls loaded with boxes of ammunition.

"I think I found at least half of the AR-15s here in this room."

"Uh, Max…" Grace's voice sounded strained behind him, closer than if she'd been in the hallway. "We have a problem."

Caveman turned to face her.

She stood with her head tilted backward, a darkly clothed arm wrapped around her neck, her eyes wide and frightened.

In the split second it took Caveman to realize what had happened, he was already too late.

Two probes hit him in the chest and a charge of electricity ripped through his body. He clenched his teeth to keep from crying out. Then he fell, his muscles refusing to hold up his frame.

"Caveman!" Grace screamed.

Unable to control his fall, he hit his head against

the corner of a low cabinet and blackness engulfed him in a shroud of darkness and pain.

GRACE FOUGHT AGAINST the hands holding her, desperate to get to Caveman.

The man with the Taser moved forward, his head and face concealed in a ski mask, his hands in leather gloves. He yanked Caveman's wrists together behind his back and slipped a zip tie around them, cinching it tightly. Then he rolled Caveman onto his side, pulled the probes out of his chest and nodded. "He's down."

A jagged cut on Caveman's temple oozed blood onto the floor.

Grace wanted to go to him, but the man holding her was so much stronger than she was, and his arm around her throat squeezed just hard enough to limit her air intake. Gray fog crept in on the corners of her vision. *No.* She couldn't pass out. She had to find a way to extricate herself and Caveman from this dangerous situation.

"What do we do with them?" one of the men asked.

"Boss wants them." Even with the mask, the man was easy to recognize just by his low, gravelly voice.

"Quincy," Grace said. "Don't do this. You won't get away with it."

"Shut up." Quincy backhanded her, his knuckles slamming into her cheekbone.

Grace's head whipped back with the blow and pain knifed through her. She fought the dizzying spinning in her head that threatened to take her down. "What are you going to do with us?"

"That's not for me to decide," he said.

"So you do the dirty work of capturing us, committing a crime to do it, and your boss sits back and lets you take the rap?"

He backhanded her again, this time hitting her in the mouth, splitting her lip. "You should have stayed out of this. Now, you'll pay the price for meddling."

Her jaw ached and the coppery taste of blood invaded her mouth. Anger roiled inside, pushing aside the wobbly feeling of an oncoming faint.

Caveman lay on the floor, his body still, and Grace could do nothing. The man holding her was a lot bigger and stronger. And there were two of them to one of her. Outnumbered and overpowered, she didn't have a choice. But she had to do something.

"You know you won't get away with this. There's probably a sheriff's deputy driving by as we speak."

Quincy's lip curled back in a snarl. "No one knows you're back here, and no one can see inside this part of the building. Even if the police came in, I'd be legally in the right. You two trespassed on private property. Last I checked, breaking and entering was illegal. I could shoot you and claim self-defense. Now, enough talk." He shoved a rag in her mouth, then threw a pillowcase over her head and down her arms. "Take her out to the van."

The big man holding her scooped her off her feet, slung her over his shoulder where she landed hard on her belly, the breath knocked out of her lungs. She couldn't see anything through the fabric of the pillowcase, but she could tell the man was carrying her back the way they'd entered the shop. When they stepped out of the building, cool night air wrapped around her legs. The sound of a metal door sliding sideways gave her renewed determination to break free. She kicked and struggled, bucking in the man's grip.

Finally, she was flung away from him, landing on what she was sure was the floorboard of a commercial van. She hit the surface hard, her head bouncing off the metal.

Then something was stuck up against her arm and a jolt of electricity sliced through her. Her body went limp and her struggles ceased. But she could still tell a little of what was going on. Someone tied her wrists behind her back with a zip tie. Another body was dumped onto the floor beside her.

It had to be Caveman.

With her wrists bound and a pillowcase wrapped loosely around her head, her body in a catatonic state, she could do little to free herself or her head so that she could see. She vowed that as soon as she regained control of her muscles, she'd work her way out of the case and zip tie.

Meanwhile, she was conscious. She listened, trying to gauge which direction they were headed and how far they were going. She could tell when they left the back alley and emerged on paved highway. She guessed they were headed south on Main Street. If only she could get up, throw open the door and scream. Alas, she could barely wiggle her toes by the time she was certain they'd driven out of the little town.

Would they take them out to a remote location, shoot them and leave their bodies to rot?

Grace's chest tightened. She couldn't let that happen. All of this was her fault. If she hadn't witnessed the killer shooting at Mr. Khalig, none of this would be happening to her and Caveman.

Caveman.

He was the innocent bystander in all of this. And because she'd allowed him to get past the walls she'd erected around her heart, he would die.

She squeezed her fist, anger fueling her. When her toes tingled, she wiggled them. Slowly, the feeling came back to her legs and arms. She was able to roll onto her side, but she couldn't lift her arms to pull off the pillowcase. Instead, she scooted along the floor, trying to maneuver her way out of the fabric covering her head.

They had been traveling ten minutes when she finally made it out of the pillowcase.

Lifting her head, she looked around the interior of an empty utility van with metal sides and floors. The two men who'd captured them sat in the front seat, staring out the window as they slowed for a stop.

Grace tried to see what they were seeing. It appeared to be a gate of some sort.

The van lurched forward and the tires crunched on what sounded like gravel.

With little light to see by, Grace searched the interior of the van for something sharp to break the zip tie holding her wrists tightly together behind her. No sharp edges stuck out, no tools lay on the metal floor.

And Caveman lay as still as death.

She inched her way over to him and laid her face close to his. For a long moment she held her breath, praying he was still alive. Then she felt the warmth of his breath against her cheek. Her heart swelled with joy. He was still alive.

Somehow, she had to get them both out of the van and away from their captors.

The gravel road ended, but the van continued to move forward on a much bumpier, hard-packed road.

Several times, Grace tried to sit up, only to be flung across the van floor. She was better off lying on her side, praying they'd stop before she was bounced to death.

Caveman groaned softly and his legs moved. "Grace?" he whispered.

"I'm here," she replied softly, so as not to draw attention from the men in the front seats.

"Where are we?"

"We're in the back of a van and have been on the road for over twenty minutes as far as I can guess. Other than that, I'm not sure where we are. Based on the road conditions, I'd bet we're way out in the boondocks."

"Have they said what they're going to do with us?"

"No." She glanced at the back of the driver's head. "Quincy said something about it wasn't up to them. The boss would decide."

"So he's not in charge."

The van came to a jerky stop.

Grace waited for them to start up again, but they didn't. The engine switched off and the two men climbed out. A moment later, the side door slid open and moonlight shone into the interior.

Grace blinked up at the men.

Quincy had taken off his ski mask, but the other man hadn't. They grabbed Grace by her upper arms and dragged her out of the van and onto her feet.

"Hurt her, and I'll kill you," Caveman said, his voice little more than a feral growl.

Quincy snorted. "That would be really hard to do when you're all tied up, now wouldn't it?"

They grabbed Caveman by the arms and slid him out of the van, dumping him on the ground at their feet.

He rolled to his side, bunched his legs and pushed to his feet. "What now?"

"Now, the fun begins," another voice said from behind Quincy and his accomplice. A big man wearing a combat helmet, camouflage clothing and carrying a military-grade rifle stepped between their two captors. His face was blackened with paint and he sported a pair of what appeared to be night-vision goggles pushed up onto his helmet.

"What do you mean, 'now the fun begins'?"

"I told you. I provide all kinds of prey for my clients—elk, lion, moose, bear and…human."

Grace gasped, a heavy, sick feeling filling her belly. "You can't be serious."

"Oh, I'm serious, all right."

Grace squinted, trying to see past the paint. "Wayne?"

The man sneered. "Surprised?"

"Actually, I am." She shook her head. "Why would you risk losing everything you have by killing people? You won't get away with it for long?"

"I've been getting away with it for the past five

years. I'll continue to get away with it as long as no one finds the bodies. *Your* bodies."

"You're insane."

"No, I'm tired of the government stealing what's mine. I'm tired of working my butt off for the pittance you make off cattle, only for the government to steal every cent I make by charging an insane amount of taxes."

"You've been selling human hunts for the past five years?" Grace shook her head. "How did no one know this?"

"The people who work for me know not to say anything. And the people we hunt don't live long enough to tell."

"Was Mr. Khalig one of your *hunts*?" Grace's stomach churned so hard she fought to keep from losing her dinner.

Wayne snorted. "Hell no. He was a paid gig. And an easy target."

"Paid gig?" What was wrong with the man? He acted like killing a man was no worse than being paid to perform on stage.

"*Highly* paid gig." Wayne shifted his rifle to his other hand. "But that's not why we're here tonight."

"Why are we here?" Caveman asked, his gaze direct, the shadows cast by the bright moon making him appear dangerous.

"You two are going to be a little training opportunity for my men. A little night ops search-and-destroy. You get a chance to run. They get to practice and test their night hunting skills with live animals."

"That's like shooting lions in a zoo. Where's the sport in that?"

"Oh, there will be sport. We're going to let you loose, give you a little bit of a head start, and then we're coming after you."

"Unarmed?" Caveman goaded. "How is that a training exercise?"

"I can't turn over a loaded weapon to a trained soldier. How would we explain so many people with gunshot wounds?" Wayne nodded to Quincy. "Release them."

Quincy frowned. "Now?"

"Now." Wayne fixed his stare on Caveman. "If you make a move toward me or my men, I'll put a bullet in Ms. Saunders." He nodded. "Take her and leave. You'll only have five minutes to get as far as you can, before we come after you." He glanced down at his watch.

"Three minutes on foot won't get us far," Caveman pointed out.

"You're lucky I'm giving you that." He looked again at his watch. "Four minutes thirty-five seconds."

"Aren't you going to cut the zip ties?" Grace's

pulse hammered so loudly in her ears she could barely hear herself think.

"Not my problem." Wayne Batson raised his brows. "Four minutes fifteen seconds."

"Grace, come on." Caveman pushed her with his elbow and herded her away from Batson.

She hurried with Caveman toward the tree line. Her last glimpse of the three hunters was the image of Quincy and the other man dressed in the combat helmet, multi-pocketed vests and camouflage clothing. They were in the process of loading ammunition magazines into their vests.

And she thought getting away from the men would be hard enough. *Staying* away from Wayne Batson and his thugs, while their hands were tied behind their backs, would be a lot more of a challenge than she could imagine.

Chapter Fourteen

They jogged into the tree line. Caveman's leg hurt like hell, but he refused to slow them down. "We have to get as far away from them as possible and find a rock hill or cliff to put between us and them. Are you able to run for long?"

"I can hold my own," Grace said. "I'm used to hiking in the hills. When I'm not working, I train to run half marathons."

Caveman snorted. "I'll have a hard time keeping up with you. Why don't you lead the way?"

"Do you think we're on Batson's ranch?" she asked, jogging alongside Caveman while they were on a fairly wide path between trees.

"That's my bet. Not only do those fences keep people out, they keep his pets in."

"Any chance we can get out of these zip ties?" she asked.

"As soon as we reach that outcropping of rocks.

We have to put something solid and impenetrable between us and them for cover as well as concealment against their night-vision goggles." He glanced across at her face in the moonlight. "Can you run faster?"

"I'm game," she said, though her breathing had become more labored.

Caveman increased his speed, glancing back often enough to make certain Grace kept up. He was aiming for the base of the mountain he'd glimpsed through gaps in the trees. It appeared to be right in front of them, but looks could be deceiving, especially at night.

The full moon helped them find their way, but it also made it all too easy for Batson and his gang to see them. The sooner they made it into the hills, the better.

He figured the five-minute head start had long since expired and still they hadn't reached the relative safety of the mountain.

A crash behind him brought Caveman to a halt.

Grace lay on the ground, struggling to get to her feet. "Don't wait on me. I'll catch up," she insisted.

"Like hell you will." He squatted next to her. "Grab a sturdy tree branch or a jagged rock."

She did, rolled over to hand it to him and then worked herself to a sitting position. "What are you going to do with it?"

"I'm going to try and use it as a saw." He nodded. "But we have to keep moving. Lean on me to get up."

She leaned her shoulder against him and pushed herself to stand.

"Ready?" he said.

"Go." Grace followed him, keeping closer this time.

While he ran, Caveman rubbed the small tree branch against the plastic of the zip tie. It wasn't much, but he hoped with enough friction, it would eventually cut through.

They emerged in a small opening in the forest, finding themselves at the base of a bluff.

Caveman glanced each direction, then turned north toward a large outcropping of boulders. If they could get behind them, they could stop long enough to break the zip ties. But they couldn't stay long. They had to go deep into the mountains and stay alive long enough for Kevin and the team to figure out they were in trouble.

A sinking feeling settled low in his belly. Though he'd given Kevin a heads-up that they'd be over to review drone footage, he hadn't given him a definitive time. All they could hope for was that Kevin would get worried when they didn't show up within thirty minutes of the call. Still, the team wouldn't know where they'd gone, or where to start looking.

Their best bet was to avoid the hunters long enough

to make it back to one of the perimeter fences. Then they'd have to figure out how to get through it and fast enough they could make it to a road and catch a ride to town. Timing would be crucial since Batson had the fence wired to tell him exactly where the breech occurred.

Caveman kept his thoughts to himself. Grace had enough to worry about just staying a step ahead of Batson and his gang.

In order for them to reach the giant boulders for cover, they would have to cross a wide-open expanse, flooded by bright moonlight.

"I don't know how close they are. When we start out across the open area, run as fast as you can and zigzag to make it harder for someone to sight in on you." He gripped Grace's arms. "Are you okay?"

She nodded, breathing hard. "I'll be fine. Let's go." With a deep breath, she took off running across the rocky terrain, dodging back and forth, leaping over brush and smaller boulders.

Caveman was right behind her, hoping the hunters hadn't yet caught up to them.

A shot rang out, kicking up the dirt near Caveman's feet. He ran faster, changing directions erratically, hoping the gunmen couldn't get a bead on him and take him out.

Grace had just made it to the boulder when another shot rang out. She stumbled and fell against the huge rock, righted herself and slipped out of sight.

Caveman dodged once more to the right, then sprinted the remaining ten steps and dove behind the boulder.

Grace was on her knees, breathing hard, but rubbing the zip tie against a jagged stone jutting out of the hillside.

"We don't have time to break these. We have to keep moving," Caveman warned.

The zip tie snapped. "I'm ready." She grabbed a sharp rock and pointed to a flat one. "Put your hands here." She quickly positioned him, then put all of her weight behind the sharp rock and cut through his zip tie.

Caveman took her hand and ran for a ravine thirty feet from where they were standing. Together, they climbed the side of the hill, working their way over the rocks upward to a ridge. If they could drop over the other side, they'd have a chance of staying out of range of the rifles. He wasn't sure how much longer Grace would last. His sore leg ached and he worried it slowed him down too much. They didn't have weapons and they couldn't fight back. He had to keep them moving.

Grace slipped beside him and slid several feet down the hillside and stopped abruptly when her foot hit a tree root. "Damn." She doubled over, clutching at her leg. She pushed to her feet, but fell back as soon as she put weight on her foot.

Caveman slid down next to her, his gaze scanning the bottom of the ravine. "What's wrong?"

"I think I've sprained my ankle." She looked up at him. "Don't stop. You have to keep going. Get help."

He pressed his lips together. "Grace, I'm not leaving without you." He bent, draped her arm over his shoulder and lifted her. "Come on. We're not stopping here."

Together, they limped up the side of the steep hill, slipping and sliding on the loose gravel. When they reached the top of the ridge, Caveman studied the other side. There was a steep drop-off close to where they stood and a trail leading down the other side. If they were careful, they might make it down to the bottom before the others caught up to them. From there, he could see the fence in the distance. And, if he wasn't mistaken, the cutaway between a stand of trees had to be the highway. "See that?"

"The fence," Grace said through gritted teeth. "Think we can make it?"

"I don't think it, I know it." With his arm around her waist, he hurried down the trail toward the bottom of the hill, knowing this trail was the path of least resistance and it would make it far too easy for the hunters to spot them from a distance and catch up to them all too quickly. They only had to get close enough to sight in on them.

A good sniper would be able to pick them off at two-hundred meters. A great sniper would be able to take them out at four-hundred. If they could get down to the trees before the hunters topped the ridge, they might have a little more of a chance to make it to the fence. At that point, they'd have to figure out how to keep from getting electrocuted.

HOPPING ON ONE foot all the way down the side of a hill wasn't getting them where they needed to be fast enough. And every time she bumped her right foot, pain shot through her, bringing her close to tears. She refused to cry. Not when they needed every bit of their wits about them to escape the insanity that was Wayne Batson. "Leave me," she begged. "I don't want you to die because of me."

"Not up for discussion," he said, grunting as he took the brunt of her weight and hurried her along. "Save your breath and mine."

She knew any further argument would be ignored and took his advice to save him further aggravation. They rounded several hip-high boulders as they neared the bottom of the hill. A shot rang out and pinged off one of the boulders.

A sharp stinging sensation bit Grace's shoulder. "Ow!"

"Get down!" Caveman pulled her down behind the boulder. He looked ahead to the next big rock. "Can you crawl to the next one?"

"Probably faster than I could walk it by myself."

"Then go, while I distract them."

"What do you mean 'distract them'?" she asked, hesitant to leave him, even for a moment.

He shed his jacket and hung it on a stick. "Ready? Go!" He ran the stick up over the top of the rock.

Grace crawled as fast as she could over rocks, gravel and brush, bruising her knees, but not caring. When she made it to the next rock, she rolled behind it and called out, "Made it!" She sneaked a peek around the edge in time to see Caveman make his dash to join her.

He hunkered low and ran, diving behind the rock as two more shots echoed off the canyon walls. "Are you all right?" he asked, his attention on the hill above them.

"A little worse for the wear, but alive." She pressed a hand to the stinging spot on her shoulder and winced. When she brought her hand back in front of her, she grimaced. It was covered in dark warm liquid she suspected was her blood. She hid her hand from Caveman. If she was badly wounded, she wouldn't have been able to move her arm. Now wasn't the time to faint at the sight of blood.

"Right now, they have the advantage with their

night-vision goggles. They can see us, but we can't see them."

She snorted. "They have all the advantages. They have the guns. We're unarmed."

He glanced behind them. "We could try for the tree line, but it's a long way."

"And I move too slowly." She shook her head. "Leave me here. Go for help. It's the only way."

"I'm not leaving you."

"Then what do you suggest?"

He glanced around the moonlit area. "The fence is two football fields away. Even if we could make it there, we don't have a way to cut through."

"Then that's out," she said.

"We've run out of places to hide. This is the last large boulder between us and them."

"True."

"We only have one choice." He drew in a deep breath and let it out. "We wait until they come to us."

Grace nodded, knowing the odds were stacked against them, but unwilling to admit defeat. She wouldn't go down without a helluva fight. "Then we have to be prepared."

"You're willing to stick it out?"

She chuckled. Her ankle hurt like hell, she was bleeding and she didn't know if she'd live to see another sunrise. "Seems like our only recourse. So,

Army Special Forces dude, what can we do to get ready to rumble?"

"Stay here."

She laughed out loud. "Like I could get up and dance a jig?"

"You know what I mean. Don't poke your head out. Stay behind the rock so that I don't have to worry about what's happening while I'm not here."

She frowned. "Not here? Where are you going?" Grace reached out and touched his arm. "You can't leave the safety of the boulder. They'll shoot you."

He took her hand in his and looked down into her eyes. "I'm not dying today. I'm going to debunk your curse."

"Sweetheart, I hope and pray you do." She wrapped her other arm around his neck and pulled him close. "I'd really like to spend a little more time with you. Two days is not nearly enough."

"I'm thinking a life time won't be enough." He kissed her hard, his tongue sweeping across hers. Then he pulled away. "Now, I have to see what I can come up with. I'll be back."

"I'm counting on it," Grace whispered.

The night stood still. Not even the crickets or coyotes sang in the dark.

Caveman got up on his haunches, breathed in and out, then dove toward a stand of trees nearby.

The crack of gunfire rang out.

Grace flinched and strained her eyes, searching for movement in the shadows. She could hear the crunch of leaves and the snapping of sticks. Caveman was moving.

Another shot pierced the silence. This one seemed closer, though it was hard to tell when the sound bounced off the hillsides.

With her breath lodged in her throat, Grace waited for Caveman's return. She gathered stones, rocks and anything she could use as a weapon, no matter how puny they seemed compared to a high-powered rifle. She even scraped up a pile of sand next to her.

Then Caveman came running toward her. Just as he was about to make it behind the boulder, gunfire sounded so close, Grace yelped.

Caveman fell behind the boulder, his arms loaded with sticks and what looked like half a tree. He lay still for a moment, his breathing ragged.

"Are you okay?" Grace crawled toward him, pushing aside the sticks and brush.

"I'm fine, just winded." He drew himself up to a sitting position. "They're getting closer." He handed her several long sticks. "They aren't much, but you can use them like spears. The hunters have to come around the boulder to get to us. That's when we surprise them with these."

"What if they swing wide?"

"Hey, I'm trying to be positive. Help me out."

He kissed her cheek. "Seriously, we could do with the power of positive thinking. It's just about all we have left."

"Okay, I'm positive they can swing wide and stay out of spear range, but I'm willing to try anything. I'm not ready to leave this world."

"Good, because we're going to play dead," Caveman said.

"What?"

"You heard me. We're going to play dead. It's risky, but we don't have any other way to lure them in." He grabbed some of the bigger rocks and stones, placing them in circle around them where the boulder would not provide protection. "We'll lie as flat as we can against the ground, thus we won't present much of a target. They will have to come closer to finish us off. That's when we hit them. Got it?"

"Got it."

"Now, before they get any closer, we need to assume the dead cockroach position with our spears at our side." He waited while she lay on her back, her hand on her the spear.

Grace's pulse thumped hard in her veins, her breath came in shaky gasps. In her mind, she told herself she was not ready to die. She wanted to live. To kiss Caveman and make love to him again in the comfort of a bed.

"Shh." Caveman pressed a finger to his lips and laid down beside her. "They're coming."

Grace lay as still as death, her breath caught in her throat, trying not to make even the sound of her breathing.

As she remained there counting what could possibly be the last beats of her heart, she heard another sound. A *thump, thump, thumping* sound that started out soft, but grew louder with each passing minute.

"What the hell?" Caveman started to sit up. The crack of a gunshot sounded so close, it could have been right beside them.

Caveman dropped back down on his back and groaned loudly.

"Are you okay?" Grace whispered.

"I'm fine. That was for effect."

The thumping grew louder. "What's that sound?"

"I hope it's what I think it is."

"What?"

"The cavalry arriving to save the day."

Another shot rang out, and another, each getting closer. One kicked up rocks near Grace's hand. Another pinged against the boulder, ricocheted off the surface and hit the ground so near to her head she swore she could feel the whoosh of air.

Grace finally recognized the thumping sound as that of helicopter rotors churning the air. A bright light pierced the night, shining down to the ground.

"Stay down," Caveman said. "That light will make their night-vision goggles useless. I'm going after them."

"But you're unarmed," she cried out. She rolled onto her stomach and watched as Caveman disappeared into the darkness surround the ray of light.

A burst of gunfire ripped through the air, followed by an answering burst from the helicopter above.

Grace rose to her knees, her heart in her throat. Where was Caveman?

Chapter Fifteen

The helicopter was taking on fire. Caveman didn't want to get in the way as they fired back. He watched as the beam of light played over the ground.

There. One of the men stood near a tree, aiming his weapon toward the chopper.

Caveman was torn between going after him and staying close to Grace. If he let the man shoot at the helicopter, he could kill the men inside and possibly bring the helicopter down. A burst of semiautomatic gunfire erupted from the aircraft. The man caught in the beam of light dropped to the ground and lay still.

More shots rang out.

Caveman wanted to go after the hunters, but the light from the helicopter was blinding him, as well. Then a shot hit the bulb on the light and it blinked out. The chopper swung around and lowered to the ground.

Giving his eyes a few moments to adjust to the

moonlight, Caveman hunkered low to the ground near a tree a couple yards from where Grace lay. A movement alerted him to someone moving nearby. He recognized the man as Quincy Kemp.

When the meat packer walked within three feet of Caveman's position, he raised his rifle, aiming at Grace.

Caveman swung the limb he'd been holding as hard as he could. The limb caught the man's arm, tipping the rifle upward as it went off.

Caveman struck again, catching Quincy in the chin, knocking him backward so forcefully he fell, hitting his head against a rock. The man didn't move.

Grabbing the rifle from the ground, Caveman searched the darkness for the last man standing. His gut told him it was Wayne Batson.

Shouts sounded off in the field near the helicopter. The silhouettes of men disengaged from that of the aircraft, all running toward Caveman's position. Still, he couldn't see Wayne. Where had he gone? Had he run as soon as the helicopter showed up?

Then a movement near the giant boulder caught his attention. Wayne Batson stepped out of the shadows and pointed his rifle at Grace where she lay on the ground. "Come any closer and I kill the girl!"

Caveman froze, his heart slammed to a stop. *No. Not Grace!* He wanted to shout. But he was afraid any movement would push Batson over the edge and he'd pull the trigger. The man was crazy. You couldn't reason with crazy.

Batson reached down, bending over Grace's inert form. Then the ground beneath him erupted.

Grace jerked the spear she'd been holding up into the man's belly. She rolled to the side at the same time, sweeping her good leg out to catch Batson's.

Batson pitched forward, falling onto the makeshift spear. He screamed out loud, and pulled the trigger on his rifle. The shots hit the dirt. He toppled to the ground beside Grace, losing his hold on the weapon. Grace tried to get away, but the man grabbed a handful of her hair.

Caveman lunged forward, kicked the rifle out of Batson's reach and slammed his foot into the man's face.

Batson flew backward, letting go of Grace's hair, and lay motionless.

Caveman scooped Grace up off the ground and held her in his arms, crushing her against him. "Sweet Jesus, woman. I thought I'd lost you!"

She wrapped her arms around his neck and pulled him close for a kiss. "I wasn't going anywhere without you. I told myself, I had to get out of this so that I could kiss you."

"Please. Kiss me all you want, because that's what I want, too."

"Caveman? Grace?" Kevin Garner's voice called out. "Are you two okay?"

Caveman broke off the kiss long enough to say, "We're alive." And he went back to kissing her.

"Are there anymore bogies? We counted three."

Grace broke their kiss this time. "Three were all there was. By the way. Thanks. Your timing was impeccable." She grinned at Kevin as the DHS man stepped out of the tree line and approached them.

"The sheriff's on his way," Hack said, emerging from the tree line, dressed in a bulletproof vest and helmet. He was carrying a satellite phone and an AR-15. "Thank goodness we decided to run the drone tonight, or we might not have found you."

Grace laughed. "Thank God for drones and Hack." She turned to Caveman. "As much as I love when you hold me close, you can set me on my own feet. Or foot."

Caveman shook his head. "If it's all the same to you, I'd rather get you back to town and have a doctor look at your ankle and that shoulder. You're bleeding all over me."

"Take the chopper," Kevin said. "We'll stay here and wait for the sheriff."

Caveman glanced across at Kevin. "Thanks."

Kevin smiled. "If you still want to go back to your unit at the end of the week, I'll make it happen."

Grace shot a look up at him.

Caveman shook his head. "If it's all the same to you, I'd like to stay and see this operation through to the end." His gaze dropped to Grace. "I'm just getting to know the locals. I'd like to get to know them a little better. Maybe something will come of it."

Kevin clapped a hand on his shoulder. "Yeah. They have a way of growing on you. As you can see, we can use all the help we can get."

"Count me in," he said. "In the meantime, I'll see that Miss Saunders gets to a doctor."

"You do that. When you're both rested up, stop by the loft for a debriefing."

"You got it." Caveman carried Grace to the helicopter.

"Isn't your leg bothering you?" Grace asked.

"What leg? I don't feel a thing except the beat of my heart."

She snorted. "The Delta Force soldier is a closet poet?"

"Hey, don't knock it." He set her in the seat and buckled the seat belt around her, his fingers grazing her breasts. Then he handed her a headset, helping her to fit them over her ears.

He climbed in next to her, buckled his belt and positioned a headset over his ears.

"Where did Kevin get a helicopter?" Grace asked into her mic.

"I think it's the one they used in the hostage rescue." He leaned over the back of the seat toward the pilot. "How did you get here so quickly?"

"I was still in town, waiting for some replacement parts I got in today," the pilot said into the headset. "I was due to fly out tomorrow, but I think I'll be delayed yet again."

As the chopper rose from the ground, the gray light of predawn crept up to the edge of the peaks.

Caveman stared down at the men on the ground, standing guard over the hunters who'd gambled their lives on an evil sport and lost.

"Think they'll live to testify?" Grace asked, her voice crackling over the radio headset.

"I hope so. I'd like to know who paid Batson to shoot Khalig."

"Me, too."

"Somehow, I don't think we'll get that answer from Batson."

"No, he wasn't looking so good," Grace said, her face pale, her brow furrowed. "If he dies, that will be the first man I've ever killed."

"And hopefully the last."

Her lips firmed. "I refuse to feel bad about it. The man was pure evil."

"Agreed." He squeezed her hand. "In the meantime, I have more work to do. We still don't know why Mr. Khalig had been killed and who had paid Wayne Batson to do the job."

Grace nodded. "True."

Caveman tipped her chin up and stared down into her eyes. "Do you still believe you're cursed?"

Grace shrugged. "I have to admit, you dodged death enough in the past couple of hours it makes me think you're the only man who could possibly break the curse."

"You're not cursed."

"Okay. Maybe I'm not." She laid her hand in his, silence stretching between them. "Caveman?"

"Yes, sweetheart?" Despite talking into a radio, he'd never felt closer to her.

"Do you believe in love at first sight?" she asked.

"I didn't." He squeezed her hand and raised it to his lips. "Not until I met you."

"Excuse me," another voice sounded in Caveman's ear.

He shot a glance toward the pilot and grimaced.

"I hate to break up your little lovefest, Caveman, but we're about to land. I suggest you save the rest of it until you get her alone."

"Thanks, I will."

The chopper landed, Caveman climbed out and lifted Grace out, but refused to set her on her feet until they were clear of the rotors.

Grace insisted they watch until the helicopter lifted off. Then she turned to Caveman. "Let's get to the doctor and back to the room. I think there's a shower calling my name."

"I hear my name in there, too."

"Darn right, you do."

He lifted her into his arms and kissed her, glad he'd been stuck with this strange assignment out in the wilds of Wyoming. This woman seemed to be his perfect match with the potential to be the love of his life. He planned on exploring that theory. One kiss at a time.

* * * * *

FLIRTING WITH THE FORBIDDEN

JOSS WOOD

Vaughan and I have been married for twenty years this year and he's my biggest fan, my best friend and my favourite travelling companion. He's also pretty hot... This book is dedicated to him to say thanks for making me coffee every morning, for being a brilliant dad, for loving me so much and for the fun that is our life.

PROLOGUE

Eight years earlier...

NOAH FRASER LOOKED at the crown moulded ceilings above his head and tried not to think about the action in his pants—hmmm, at least he wasn't wearing a kilt. Truthfully, he could understand what was happening in his pants far more easily than he understood the mess in his head. Lust was easy, and there was a straightforward and time-honoured process for getting shot of it. But since the obvious was out of the question—it required a great deal more privacy than he currently had—he knew he had to distract himself.

He'd spent a lot of the past five years feeling horny—thanks to several tours of duty in dusty countries with little to no female interaction—and he'd learned a couple of techniques to relieve the frustration. Running through the process of dismantling his favourite weapon, the MP5 submachine gun, in the field usually did the trick.

Safety check. Check.

Noah banged his head back against the arm of the couch and cursed softly. What he really wanted was to get naked with that annoyingly sexy bundle of energy beyond the bedroom door. He was head-over-heels in *lust* with her...and a whole bunch of *like*. He could handle the lust...sorta, kinda... but the like had him tied up in knots.

It was a time of firsts for both of them. He was her first

bodyguard and hers was the first body—and what a body it was too!—he'd guarded. His mission was to keep her safe, and apparently hers was to crack the inscrutable façade he'd been told to present. It wasn't easy keeping his demeanour deadpan, because she was funny and smart and had a dry sense of humour that he deeply appreciated. He'd soon realised that she was winding him up by practising her flirting skills on him and it had started a battle of wills between them: she tried to get a reaction out of him and he refused to give her one. He still wasn't sure what the score was, but if they had to judge the competition by his frustration levels then she was streaks ahead.

Release bolt by vigorously slapping the cocking lever out of the indent. Check.

Okay, slight improvement…not much, but some. Noah, curled up on her too-small couch, glared at the closed door and cursed himself for being a fool…and for being unable to concentrate. Concentration, focus, control—control was his thing.

Pull out the locking pin…

His mind drifted again. She had the most amazing smile… and a 'shoot-all-the-blood-to-his-groin' body! Firm, toned, luscious, sweet…young.

Noah pulled the pillow over his head and silently screamed into the fabric. *Nineteen*, for crying out loud! He couldn't believe he was losing his mind over a teenager. He was a flippin' moron. Morgan Moreau was too young and she was his principal. His principal! Six months out of the unit, he was new to bodyguarding and the CFT Corporation, but he was pretty sure that sleeping with his principal was high up on the list of bodyguarding no-no's.

Since he had no intention of getting his ass fired over a piece of ass, no matter how sexy and tempting it was, he pulled the pillow away from his face, heaved in a deep breath and opened his eyes.

'Crap!' he yelled, scuttling up into the corner of the couch.

'Some bodyguard you are. I could've stabbed you in the heart,' Morgan drawled.

'You're naked,' Noah croaked, dimly aware that the saliva in his mouth had dried up. It had probably joined his blood as it sprinted south.

Naked, naked, naked, his body panted. *Yeah, baby!*

Noah was unable to stop his eyes from scanning her body. Perky breasts, a flat stomach, a Brazilian… Oh, he was a dead man…a Brazilian.

What was he thinking?

'You have amazing powers of observation,' Morgan said, her sexy mouth curving upwards. Her voice was perfect for the bedroom: gravelly, low, sexy.

'Why…? What…? How…?'

Morgan perched on the edge of the couch and placed her elbow on her knee, immensely at ease in her nakedness—which ratcheted up his level of panic. 'I thought you were brighter than that, Noah. I'm here, you're here—let's have some fun.'

Noah, his last two brain cells working overtime, narrowed his eyes at her. 'Subtle.'

'Straightforward,' Morgan countered. 'So, what do you say?'

They could… Who would know? They could have a couple of nights of uncomplicated sex, and when they'd hunted down the group of fanatics threatening her famous and wealthy family he'd return to the field and they could both move on with their lives. He'd move on to another job and she'd pull the same thing on another guy…

Noah frowned at the thought. While he believed in equality, the thought of Morgan getting naked with someone else left a sour taste in his mouth. It was on the tip of his tongue to warn her not to do this with anyone else, but he bit the words back.

Which was weird. He didn't like being controlled, hated people telling him what to do, so why did he want to do that to her? This was all too confusing; he'd had his fair share of sexual encounters but this was out of his ken. Way, *way* out. Outer Hebrides out.

He dropped his eyes to her chest and realised that she had the most amazing nipples—pink and succulent. All he had to do was reach for her arm and tumble her onto his lap. One little tug...

Nineteen. His job. Nineteen.

She was entrancing. Look at those eyes...the colour of bold green glass...

Nineteen. Job. Principal! He'd get his ass fired. Noah craned his neck and, yes, *her* ass was more gorgeous than he'd imagined.

Noah, as hard as stone, rolled to his feet and yanked his shirt up and over his head, thinking he'd get her to cover up, but instead he just stared at what she offered. Who would know? Truly, who would ever know?

His brain was back-pedalling, but he was facing a gorgeous naked girl who was offering herself on a plate, and the fact that he actually liked her as well was a nice bonus. When had he last genuinely *liked* a girl?

Walk away, Fraser, just walk away...

Then he remembered that he'd never had a halo that needed polishing.

Morgan felt his hand encircle her wrist, and as he launched her up into his hard body she closed her eyes in sheer, pure relief. For one moment she'd thought that this strong, quiet, sexy Scotsman was about to say no, that he was genuinely thinking about walking away. But suddenly he was hard under her hands, and his mouth on hers was an absolute revelation.

He kissed her as if he owned her, as if she was—just for this moment in time—his and only his. His mouth was hot, silky, sexy. Morgan felt his fingers digging into the skin on her hips and she wished that he would do something with them… Instead he just kissed her: long, liquid slides that tasted like heaven-coated sin.

Then Noah placed his hands under her butt and lifted her up and—oh, oh, *oh!*—onto his jeans-clad erection. The muscles in his arms bunched and she slid her hand up and down that tanned skin, briefly tracing the Celtic cross tattoo on his shoulder. Dropping her head, she kissed that smooth skin while he carried her back to her bedroom with an ease that astounded her.

A strong, sexy Scotsman… She couldn't believe that this was happening. Finally!

Noah lowered her down to the cool white sheets of her bed and loomed over her, his mouth going to her breast and pulling it into his mouth. Then he slid a hand between her legs and she arched off the bed as hot, sexual power pulsed through her. He slid a finger inside her and lifted his head to look into her face.

'So hot, so wet,' he muttered. 'You are a soldier's dream, lass.'

Morgan lifted her head and then smacked it against the bed as he built up a fire inside her that threatened to consume her.

'Can't believe I waited so long,' she growled to herself. 'Man, you're good at this.'

His finger stopped, his mouth pulled away from her breast and cool air drifted over her wet flesh. It was hot and muggy outside, but she knew that she'd crashed into an emotional iceberg.

'Sorry. I didn't mean to say that,' she muttered as he withdrew from her and rolled himself away.

'Were you hoping I wouldn't notice?'

'Kind of,' Morgan admitted.

He was trying to control himself; she could see that. He opened his mouth to say something and snapped his words back, his eyes sparking dangerously.

'So, how does this work? Did you decide that your virginity was something you no longer needed and I was handy?'

No! Yes! Kind of… How did she explain that she felt comfortable with him? Safe? From the moment she'd met him she'd known that he was authentic, solid. In her world, she didn't encounter those characteristics that often. He made her feel grounded, real…special.

And it didn't hurt that he had a hard, droolworthy body.

'I just thought…you…me…it would be fun.'

'Fun, huh?' Noah ran his hand through his hair and shook his head in disgust. 'Morgan, just what the hell do you think you're doing?'

'Why are you so angry?' Morgan demanded, pulling a sheet up and around her. Every inch of her skin was now blushing and she felt humiliated and confused. Why was this a problem? She was offering her body, not asking him to do her laundry.

'You don't just give it away—especially to someone like…' Noah trailed off. 'Damn it! Don't you have a boyfriend? Surely you've had offers? I see how those guys you hang out with look at you!'

Her blood cooled at the thought. 'None of them can keep their mouths shut and, trust me, my hooking up with someone would be huge news. And a very big feather in someone's cap.'

Since she hadn't slept with any of the society boys—sons of her mother's friends, acquaintances and connections—she knew that she was a fish to be hooked, a prize to be won. She wouldn't give any of those poncey, wishy-washy pseudo-men the satisfaction.

Noah looked ill—green—and Morgan's heart dropped like a brick. Only *she* could make a guy nauseous with an offer of sex.

'So you went trawling, huh?'

Trawling? Morgan frowned. Was he nuts? He was a far

better choice on any weekday and twice on Sundays. 'No, I— What's your problem anyway?'

'Just trying to figure out where I am in the pecking order. Above the pool boy but below the riding instructor? What comes next? Are you going to offer to pay me?'

Okay, now he was way off course. 'Stop being a jerk, Noah! Look, I like you, and I thought that you might like me...just a little. I thought that we were almost friends, and I'd rather do it with an almost-friend than someone who sees me as a prize.'

But Noah wasn't listening. He swore, his Scottish accent becoming rapidly more pronounced.. 'I knew this was a bad idea. What is *wrong* with me? I cannot believe that I let my libido override my common sense, my professionalism. Acting with integrity, my ass. She'd knock me into next year if she knew.'

Who? What on earth was he talking about?'

Noah shook his head as if to clear it and glowered at her. 'Put some clothes on. This isn't going to happen. Not now, not ever.'

Noah took one last look at her, then swore softly again as he turned and walked out of the room, slamming her bedroom door behind him.

Morgan winced and cursed the tears that stung her eyes. 'Guess that's a big old Scottish no, then.'

Curling into a ball, she lay on her bed and stared out through the open sash window. Sleep refused to come, and when she did manage to drift off she woke up to a stranger in her flat.

Noah had left and in his place was a female bodyguard— just in case, Morgan thought grimly, she was so desperate to get laid that she seduced the next male bodyguard who was assigned to her.

If losing her virginity had been the goal, then half the

population in the world could have sorted her out. But she didn't want half the population…

Stupid man; she wanted *him*.

CHAPTER ONE

NOAH FRASER DODGED past a couple kissing and ran his hand across his prickly jaw. His eyes flicked over the waiting crowds, mentally processing faces against his internal data bank, and nobody blipped on his radar until he saw a tall, thin man with his hands in the pockets of his expensive trousers.

He frowned and wondered what was so important that Chris had to meet him here.

Twenty hours ago he'd boarded a plane at the Ministro Pistarini International Airport just south of Buenos Aires, after a week spent doing a full-spectrum security analysis for a museum. He'd identified threats and risks and then provided them with solutions to plug the holes. It was a part of the business they were trying to grow and it was lucrative.

Because he was a frugal Scot, he still felt guilty that he'd upgraded his seat to business class, but he just hadn't been able to face the thought of wedging his six-foot-three frame into a minuscule economy class seat to spend thirteen hours in cramped misery. As Chris kept reminding him, business class also allowed him to review his files in privacy, to catch a couple of twenty-minute power naps, to drink good whisky. He'd worked hard for a long time, he told himself, and he—the business—could afford it.

Noah rolled his shoulders as he made his way through

Customs, looking forward to a decent shower, a beer and to sleeping for a week.

Of course sleeping for a week was a pipedream; he was working all hours of the day to build his company, and sleep was a luxury he just couldn't afford. Self-sufficiency and financial independence were a lot higher up on Noah's list of priorities than sleep.

Who knew why he was being met by Chris, his oldest friend, partner and second-in-command at Auterlochie Consulting? Something must be up. He swallowed as dread settled over him. The last time Chris had met him at the airport it had been because Kade, one of their best employees, had committed suicide. God, he didn't want to deal with something like *that* again...

'No one has died,' Chris said quickly and Noah wasn't surprised that he'd read his mind.

They'd learnt to read each other's faces—sometimes their thoughts—in dusty, unfriendly situations and it was a trait they'd never lost.

Noah did a minor eye-roll as Chris shook his hand and pulled him into that one-armed hug he did so well. Only Chris could get away with that kind of PDA; when you'd saved a guy's life you had to overlook his occasional sappiness.

Noah adjusted the rucksack on his shoulder as they made their way across the terminal. 'What's up?'

Chris jammed his hands in his pockets and gestured towards the nearest coffee shop. 'I'll explain. You look like hell.'

Noah grinned wryly. 'Nice to see you too.'

Ten minutes later Noah was slumped into a plastic seat at one of the many generic restaurants scattered throughout the hall. He sent his friend a sour look and took another sip of his strong black coffee. By his estimation he'd been awake for more than thirty hours and he was feeling punchy.

'How did the assessment go?' Chris asked.

'Brilliant. They took all my suggestions on board and paid the account via bank transfer before I left the office. The money should be through already.'

'It is. I checked. It's easy money, Noah.'

'And we can do it with our eyes closed. If we start getting a reputation for providing solid advice at a good price, I think we could double our turnover—and soon too.'

'We've already exceeded our initial projections for the business. In fact, we're doing really well.'

'We can do better. I want to build us into being the premier provider of VIP protection and risk assessment in the UK.'

'Not the world?' Chris quipped, gently mocking his ambition as he always did.

Chris was less driven than he was, and had his feet firmly placed on the ground. It wasn't a bad thing. Noah had enough ambition for both of them. They were great partners. Chris was better with people: he had an easy way about him that drew people in. Their clients and staff talked to Chris; he was their best friend, the elder brother, a mate. Chris was the touchy-feely half of their partnership.

Noah was tough, decisive and goal-orientated; the partner who kicked butt. He called it being disciplined, reasonable, responsible and dedicated in everything he did. Chris called it being a control freak perfectionist. And emotionally stunted. Yeah, yeah...

Well, that was what happened when you grew up far too fast... Noah ran a hand over his face as if to wipe away the memories of his childhood, of picking up the pieces when his mother died, the wrench of losing his brothers. He pulled in a breath and along with it control.

He *was* in control, he reminded himself. It was a long time ago that he was sixteen and had felt the earth shaking under his feet.

He saw Chris's insightful look and summoned up a smile. 'I've scheduled world domination for next year,' he quipped.

'What was the response when you told our employees that we wanted them to do a mandatory session with a psychologist every six months?'

'They grumbled, but they understood. Kade's death has rocked them all. You *do* know that we'll have to do it too.'

Noah blanched. 'Hell, no.'

'Hell, yes. Kade was our responsibility and we didn't pick up the signs. What if we're working too hard, trying to keep too many balls in the air, and we miss the signs in someone else? We have to be as mentally healthy as—*more* mentally healthy than—any of our employees, Noah. That's non-negotiable.'

Since Chris was the healthiest, most balanced person he knew, Noah didn't have to be a rocket scientist to know that Chris was talking about him. Chris thought he was too stressed—working like a demon, juggling far too many balls. He knew that Chris was worried about him burning out, but he also knew that that he was nowhere near the edge...

Working hard never killed anyone—and besides, he'd been to the edge before and he knew what it looked like. He was still miles away.

Chris slapped the folder he'd been holding onto the table and pushed it towards him. Flipping open the cover, Noah looked down into the laughing face of a green-eyed blonde. She was standing between her famous mother and father, her brother behind them. The most successful family on planet earth, he thought. Rich, successful, close. A unit.

He felt a pang of jealousy and told himself that despite the fact that he had not been part of his brothers' lives for most of their formative years he was now, and they weren't doing so badly.

Noah concentrated on the photo below him. Morgan... she'd grown up. She was wearing a tight, slinky cream dress that stopped inches below her butt and revealed her giraffe-long legs. Her blonde hair was pulled back into a smooth ponytail and her naturally made-up face was alight with joy. She looked fantastic. Happy, charismatic.

Hot.

Doing a stint as her bodyguard had nearly killed him. Apart from that one incident he'd never before or since needed the same amount of control and determination as he'd summoned the night he'd walked away from the gloriously naked Morgan Claire Morrisey Moreau.

Noah flipped through the papers in the file. 'Floor plans of the Forrester-Grantham hotel in New York. Photos of the Moreau jewellery collection... I thought the Moreaus were Amanda's clients—have always been CFT's clients?'

Amanda. Their ex-boss and his ex-lover. As petite and as dangerous as a black widow spider, she looked like every other ball-breaker businesswoman in the city.

Except that Amanda *actually* broke balls. She'd certainly tried to go for his when she'd found out that he was leaving the CFT Corporation to start a company that was in direct competition with hers.

That hadn't been a day full of fun and giggles.

'Well, as you know, James Moreau and I went to school together,' Chris said.

Noah shrugged off his tiredness to connect the dots. James Moreau: CEO of Moreau International, brother to Morgan and son to Hannah 'Queen of Diamonds' Moreau and Jedd Moreau, one of the world's best known geologists.

Moreau International owned diamond and gemstone mines, dealt in the trading of said gems—especially diamonds—and had exclusive jewellery stores in all the major cities around the world. Hannah, as the face of the company, had always been a target, and CFT routinely provided her and Jedd with additional bodyguards when they needed more protection than their long-term driver/guards. That protection was only extended to James and Morgan and other high-ranking executives within MI when MI's security division or CFT received a particular threat, or were monitoring a situation where extra protection was needed.

Eight years ago, just after he'd left the SAS, Noah had been unlucky enough to end up guarding the nineteen-year-old Morgan for a week because a well-funded but stupid militant environmental group had been protesting MI's involvement with mines in a nature reserve in Uganda. Huge threats had been issued until it had been pointed out that it was an oil company mining for natural gas and not MI looking for gems.

Morgan had never been in any real danger, but no one had been prepared to take the chance. As the rookie, he'd got the so-called 'creampuff' assignment to guard the teenager. He'd never told anyone that it had probably been one of the best weeks of his life. Sure, he'd vacillated between wanting to wring her neck and fantasising about her, which had been off-the-scale inappropriate since she'd been his principal and he'd been six years older than her—and a million years in experience. But he'd laughed—internally—been relaxed in her company and had enjoyed her scalpel-sharp mind.

Noah felt heat creep up his neck and he stared at the fingers that gripped his coffee cup. He'd lost his mind that night...well, almost. He'd nearly risked everything he had—his sole source of income at that time—to make love to her. The consequences of his actions still made his blood run cold. If CFT had found out he would have been canned and would never have been able to get another job in security again. And security was what he did—what he'd trained for—the only skill he'd had at that time.

He'd left the army, his first and only love, to find a better-paying job so that he could put his two younger brothers through college. CFT had offered him a fantastic salary which he'd nearly thrown away to sleep with Morgan Moreau.

Who'd just wanted him to break her duck!

Chris's voice pulled him back to the here and now. 'I've

been working on James to send some business our way, told him we've expanded into security analysis, and he's thrown us a bone.'

'Oh, yay,' Noah deadpanned.

'If we pull it off it gives us an in at Moreau and we want them as clients.' Chris reminded him. 'World domination, remember? Moreau's is a good place to start.'

'I know, I know... Okay, what is it?' He tapped Morgan's picture. 'Does she need a bodyguard again? Who has her family upset this time?'

'She doesn't need protection.'

'Good.' Noah lifted an eyebrow at Chris. 'What's the job?'

'Every five years the Moreaus host a grand ball for charity, and they combine the ball with an exhibition of the family collection of jewels—which is practically priceless. Some of the biggest and the best diamonds and jewels collected over generations of wealthy Moreaus,' Chris explained. 'There has been a massive increase in armed robberies at such jewellery exhibitions, and James wants a complete, intensive threat analysis. I know it's a puffball assignment, but you just need to head to New York for a meeting, have a look at their current security arrangements, check out the hotel—do what you do best. With luck we'll get the contract to oversee the security, based on your report. But for now, it's just a couple of days in New York and we have an in with Moreau.'

'When is this meeting?'

'In the morning. I have you booked on a flight leaving in an hour.'

'Why can't you go? You're James's mate, not me.' Noah groaned. 'I'm beat.'

'I've got a meeting scheduled with another client, and you are far better at security assessments than I am. You're brilliant at planning operations, getting in and out of places and situations you shouldn't be, and you can see stuff from a criminal perspective.'

'Thanks,' Noah said dryly.

Noah pushed his chair out and stretched his long legs. He linked his hands behind his head in his favourite thinking posture, his eyes on Morgan's photograph which lay between them on the grubby table. Gorgeous eyes and slanting cheekbones, and she had a wide, mobile mouth with a smile that could power the national electrical grid.

Noah licked his lips and forced his thoughts away from that dangerously sexy mouth. Slowly he raised his eyes to Chris's face. He leaned forward and rested his arms on the table. 'Why don't you just shoot me now?'

'It's an option, but then I'd be out of a partner. It's a few days, Noah, in an exciting city that you love.'

'Clothes?'

'Bag in the car. I went to your flat and picked out some threads.'

Noah swore and flipped the cover of the folder closed. 'Guess I'm going to New York.'

'Atta boy.'

Noah narrowed his eyes at his partner. 'You're a manipulative git.'

Chris just grinned.

Sapphires, rubies, pearls. Diamonds. The usual suspects. And then there were the less common gems that sparked her imagination. Alexandrite that changed from green in daylight to red under incandescent light. Maw Sit-Sit, the same green as her eyes. Almandine Garnet, purplish red and the neon blue of Paraiba tourmaline.

Having access to the gemstone vaults of Moreau International was a very big perk as a jewellery designer, and it allowed Morgan the chance to offer her very high-end clients one-of-a-kind pieces containing gemstones of exceptional quality.

Morgan looked up at Derek, their Head of Inventory, and the security guard who'd accompanied the jewels to her airy, light-filled design studio on the top floor of the

Moreau Building on Fifth Avenue from the super-secure
fourth floor that housed the jewellery vaults. Morgan knew
that there was another vault somewhere in the city, and others in other places of the world, which housed more gemstones. Her mother didn't believe in keeping all their precious
eggs in one basket.

'I'll take the Alexandrite, the tourmaline and both garnets.' Morgan scanned the cloth holding the jewels again.
'The fifteen-carat F marquise-cut yellow diamond and I'll
let you know about the emeralds. Thanks, Derek.'

Derek nodded and stepped forward to help Morgan replace the jewels in their separate bags. She signed an order
form as Derek spoke.

'I have some apparently amazing Clinohumite coming in
from a new mine in Siberia. Interested?'

Interested in the rare burnt orange gems that she could
never get enough of? *Duh.* 'Of course! I'll owe you if you
can sneak a couple of the nicer ones to me before you offer
them to Carl.'

Carl was Head Craftsman for MI's flagship jewellery
store which was on the ground floor of the building. A rival
to Tiffany and Cartier, Moreau's made up the third of the
'big three' jewellery stores in New York City. Carl had his
clients and so did Morgan, and they shared one or two others. They happily waged a silent war, competing for the best
of the Moreau gems that were on offer. And for the clients
with the deepest pockets.

'I'll offer you two per cent above whatever Carl offers for
the Clinohumites. Don't let me down, Derek, I want those
stones.' She might be a Moreau, but her business was separate to the jewellery store and the gemstones. She had to buy
her stones at the going rate and sell at a profit…and that was
the way she liked it.

'Of course. I owe you for designing Gail's engagement
ring. She still thinks I'm a god.'

Morgan laughed. 'I'm glad she loves it.'

Even though he had a hugely responsible job at Moreau's, he would never have been able to afford the usual prices Morgan commanded. Sometimes she thought that the money she charged for her designs was insane but, as her mother kept insisting, exclusivity had its price, and the Moreau price was stratospheric.

Morgan heard the door to her studio click closed behind Derek and his guard and sat down on a stool, next to her workbench. She twisted a tanzanite and diamond ring on her finger before resting her chin in the palm of her hand.

Morgan Moreau Designs. She couldn't deny that being a Moreau had opened doors that would have been a lot harder to break down if she hadn't possessed a charmed name associated with gemstones. But having a name wasn't enough; no socialite worth her salt was going to drop squillions on a piece of jewellery that wasn't out of the very top drawer. Morgan understood that they wanted statement pieces that would stand out from the exceptional, and she provided that time and time again.

It was the one thing—probably the only thing—she'd ever truly excelled at. She adored her job; it made her heart sing. So why, then, exactly, wasn't she happy? Morgan twisted her lips, thinking that she wasn't precisely unhappy either. She was just…feeling 'blah' about her life.

Which was utterly ridiculous and she wanted to slap herself at the thought. She was a Moreau—wealthy, reasonably attractive, popular. She ran her own business and had, if she said so herself, a great body which didn't need high maintenance. Okay, she was still single, and had been for a while—her soul mate was taking a long time to make an appearance—but she dated. Had the occasional very discreet affair if she thought the man nice enough and attractive enough to bother with.

She had a life that millions of girls would sell their souls for and she was feeling sorry for herself? *Yuck*.

'Earth to Morgan?'

Morgan looked up and saw her best friend standing in the doorway of her studio, her pixie face alight with laughter. Friends since they were children, they'd lived together, travelled together and now they worked together...sort of. Riley was contracted to design and maintain the window displays of the jewellery store downstairs. She was simply another member of the Moreau family.

'Hey. I'm about to have coffee—want some?'

Riley shook her head. 'No time. Your mother sent me up here to drag you out of your nest. She wants you to come down and join the charity ball planning meeting.'

'Why? She's never included me before.'

'You know that's not true. Every year she asks if you want to be involved, and every year you wrinkle your pretty nose and say no.'

'You'd think she would've got the message by now,' Morgan grumbled. Organising an event on such a scale was a mammoth undertaking and *so* not up her alley. She'd just make an idiot of herself and that wasn't an option. Ever.

She'd felt enough of an idiot far too many times before.

'Well, she said that I have to bring you down even if I have to drag you by your hair.'

'Good grief.'

Morgan stood up and stretched. She took stock of her outfit: a white T-shirt with a slate jacket, skinny stone-coloured pants tucked into black, knee-high laceup boots. It wasn't the Moreau corporate look, but she'd do.

Morgan walked towards the door and allowed it to close behind her; like all of the other rooms in the building, entrance was by finger-scan. Keys weren't needed at Moreau's.

'Did you get your dress for Merri's wedding?' Riley asked as they headed for the stairs.

'Mmm. I can't wait. We're hitching a lift with James on the company jet, by the way. He's flying out on the Thursday evening.'

'Perfect.'

And it was… Their friend Merri was getting married in her and Riley's hometown of Stellenbosch, South Africa, and Morgan couldn't wait to go home. She desperately missed her home country; she'd love to return to the vineyards and the mountains, the crisp Cape air and the friendly people. But if she wanted to cement her reputation for being one of the best jewellery designers in the world—like her grandfather before her—then she needed to be in fast-paced NYC. She needed clients with big money who weren't afraid to spend it…

And talking of exceptional, she thought as they stepped out of the lift onto the fifth floor, where Hannah and the New York-based directors of MI had their offices, she had to start work on the piece Moreau International had commissioned her to design and manufacture that would be sold as part of the silent auction at the charity ball. Maybe that was why Hannah wanted her at the meeting…

CHAPTER TWO

MORGAN WATCHED AS her glamorous, sophisticated mother stepped out of her office in a lemon suit, nude heels and with a perfectly straight platinum chin-length bob.

'I need a decision about the jewellery for the auction,' Morgan announced as Hannah approached them. 'Do you have any gemstones in stock that you want me to use? What do you want me to design? Diamonds? Emeralds? Rubies? Classic or contemporary? Is that why you want me at this meeting?'

'Hello to you too, darling,' Hannah said in her driest tone. 'How are you?'

Morgan waved an elegant hand in the air. 'Mum, we had coffee together this morning; you didn't say anything then about me having to come downstairs.'

'It's a conference room, not a torture chamber, Morgan,' Hannah replied, her tone as dry as the martinis she loved to drink. 'Nice photo of you in the *Post*, by the way.'

Since she hadn't been out recently, Morgan wasn't sure where she'd been photographed. 'Uh…where was I?'

'At the opening night of that new gallery in Soho.'

Her friend Kendall's new gallery; she'd popped in for five minutes, literally, and it couldn't go undocumented? *Sheez!* But she was, very reluctantly, a part of the NYC social scene, and because she was a Moreau whenever she made an appearance she was photographed extensively. Many of those photographs ended up in the social columns and online.

Hannah folded her arms and tapped her foot. Good grief, she recognised that look.

'Morgan, it's time we talked about you joining Moreau International in an official position.'

Morgan sighed. 'Has six months passed so quickly?'

They had an agreement: Hannah was allowed to nag her about joining the company every six months. For the last twelve years they'd had the same conversation over and over again.

'I've decided that I want you to be MI's Public Relations and Brand Director.'

Run me over with a bus, Morgan thought. PR and Brand Director? That was a new title. 'Mum, I'm happy doing what I'm doing—designing jewellery. You and James are doing a fabulous job with MI. You don't need me.'

And she was damned if she was going to take a job away from a loyal MI employee who was way more qualified for the position than she'd ever be. And—funny, this—she actually wanted to get paid for what she *did*, not who she was.

But she had to give Hannah points for being persistent. She'd been trying to get her to work for MI since she was sixteen—shortly after they'd received the happy news that Morgan was just chronically dyslexic and not selectively stupid.

It had only taken her mother and a slew of medics, educational psychologists and shrinks to work that out. Everyone had been so pleased that they'd found the root cause of her failing marks at school, her frustration and her anger.

The years of sheer hell she'd lived through between the time she'd started school and her diagnosis had been conveniently forgotten by everybody except herself.

Water under the bridge, Morgan reminded herself. And she knew her mum felt guilty for the part she'd played in the disaster that had been her education.

Morgan knew that it hadn't been easy for her either. She'd

been thrust into running MI in her mid-thirties, when her adventure-seeking husband had decided that he didn't like the corporate life and wanted to be MI's chief geologist, discovering new mines. Hannah, with her MBA in business and economics, had taken over the role of MI's CEO, juggling its huge responsibilities with two children, one of whom had made her life a great deal more difficult by her inability to meet her mother's and teachers' expectations.

How often had she heard variations on the theme of, 'She's such a bright child; if only she would try harder.'

Nobody had ever realised how hard she'd always been trying, how incredibly frustrating it had been not to meet her goals and everybody else's. Had they honestly believed that she didn't want to learn to read and write properly? That she'd enjoyed being the class freak?

Ages eight to sixteen had been a suck-fest of epic proportions. Finally being diagnosed as being chronically dyslexic had freed her, a little, from the shame and guilt she'd felt for years. She'd started to believe that her learning disabilities weren't her fault and her relationship with her family—well, mostly with her mother—had rapidly improved. Her mum was still a controlling corporate queen, and she still marched to the beat of her own drum, but they'd found a way back to each other—even if they did have to have this conversation every six months.

Morgan knew that she wasn't stupid, but she also knew that working for MI would require computers and reading and writing reports. While she *could* do all of that, she just took longer than most—okay, a lot longer—and the corporate world couldn't and wouldn't wait that long. And shouldn't…

Until she was the best person for a job, she wouldn't take it. Not to mention that her dyslexia would become an open secret; she wouldn't be able to keep it under wraps. Wouldn't that be fun? She could just see the headlines: *The ultimate dumb blonde… Gorgeous but thick… With her looks and money, who needs brains anyway?*

She'd heard them all before—even from someone she'd loved…

Morgan shuddered. *No, thank you.* Call her stubborn, call her proud, but she wasn't going to expose herself to that much ridicule again.

Besides, designing jewellery was her solace and her joy—her dream job. If only Hannah would see that and get off her back about working for MI her relationship with her mum would be pretty much perfect.

Morgan took her mum's hand and squeezed. 'I love you for the fact that you believe I should play a bigger part in MI, but I am neither qualified nor suited for the corporate world, Mum. I don't *want* to be part of that world. I'm happy being on the fringes of MI.'

'I will wear you down someday.' Hannah sighed loudly. 'On another subject, I want you to haul out your designer dresses and start creating hype around the ball at social events.'

Morgan gagged. '*Ugh*. Don't I do enough already?'

'Hardly.' Hannah sniffed. 'One function every two weeks and cutting out early isn't good enough to promote your business, and not nearly good enough to promote the ball. You need to charm more people than you're currently doing. Darling, you are a social disgrace. How many invitations did you turn down this week alone?'

Morgan shrugged. 'Ten…twelve?'

'Helen, my personal publicist, said that you were invited to at least twenty-five, maybe more. Soirées, charity dinners, afternoon teas, breakfasts…'

Morgan tipped her head and counted to ten, then thirty, before attempting to speak rationally. 'Mum, I have a business to run, designs to get out the door. I work, just like you do. Okay, I don't oversee a multinational company but I work. Hard.'

'You're a Moreau; you should be out more. Can you start going to some more formal parties? The benefits, the politi-

cal fundraisers, the balls? That is where the money is, darling—the people who can actually afford the price of the
ball tickets. We need to target the people who have the *real*
money, and they are at the more sedate functions.'

Sedate meaning deadly dull. 'Don't nag me, Mother. You
know I hate those stuffy functions where the conversation is
so…intense. The situation in Syria, the economy, the plight
of the rainforests.'

'Because, you know, those issues *aren't* important…'
Riley said, her tongue in her cheek.

Morgan glared at her. 'I feel…' She wanted to say *stupid*
but instead said, 'I feel out of place there.'

Like all the other issues related to her dyslexia, it had
taken her many years to conquer her social awkwardness and
to decode social cues. She still battled with new situations,
and she knew that many people took her occasional lapses
of concentration and her social shyness as self-absorption
and disinterest. Nothing could have been further from the
truth. She generally loved people, but she could never tell if
they loved her back.

When she added that to her 'I wonder if he sees me or
just the family money' concerns, dating was a bit of a nightmare…

And, really, she would rather have a beer in a pub in jeans
and a T-shirt than be in a ballroom in shoes that hurt her feet.

Riley smiled at her and Morgan recognised the mischie-
vous glint in her eyes.

'You poor child…being forced to dress up, drink the best
champagne in the world and eat the finest food at functions
that are by invitation only. It's almost abuse—really, it is.'

Morgan's searing look promised retribution for Riley's
teasing and her encouragement of her mother's campaign to
get her to be the reigning young socialite of New York City.

Morgan wrinkled her nose at her mother. 'You and James
just do it so much better than me. You're suave and sophisticated and far more charming than I'll ever be—with or with-

out the big D. Look, we've discussed my contribution to the ball so can I go now?' Morgan asked hopefully.

'No, I'd still like you to attend this first planning meeting with Riley, Jack—our PR director—and the new consultant James has appointed to assess security,' Hannah said as they walked down the carpeted passage to the boardroom.

On the walls either side were framed photographs of the Moreau collection of jewels.

'Why can't Moreau's own Chief of Security handle it? He always has,' Morgan said, because she felt she should show *some* interest.

'Since the last Moreau ball there have been a number of armed robberies on jewellery exhibitions.' Hannah rapped her fist against the frame that held a picture of the Moreau Diamond—a gem Morgan's three times great-grandfather Moreau had bought from a broke Russian aristocrat and which had once been owned by Elizabeth of Russia. 'Fifty-three carats, D-colour, flawless. Worth more than five million dollars. You want to risk it getting stolen?'

When she put it like that…

'Our jewellery collection is priceless, Morgan, so James has contracted Auterlochie Consulting to look at every security hole we have and to plug it. Their best operative will be in charge…'

Auterlochie…Auterlochie… Why did she know that name?

'In you go, darling, and smile!'

Hannah placed a hand on her back and she bared her teeth at her mother as she stepped into the conference centre. Her hand still on the doorknob, she looked around—and her head jerked back as dazzling blue eyes connected with hers.

Deep brown hair… Auterlochie… A deep Sean Connery voice explaining that it was a town in the Scottish Highlands, situated on a loch, and he'd once visited it with a friend. Two young boys had fished and explored the icy banks there, and he'd told her when he opened his business it would be called Auterlochie something.

It was the one of the longest sentences he'd strung together, and Morgan had been enthralled by his Scottish accent and the light of determination in those fantastic cobalt eyes... Noah Fraser.

Morgan's heart splattered as it hit the floor. *Bats on a broomstick.*

She stepped back behind the door and squeezed her eyes shut. Eight years and she still wished she could acid-wash the memory out of her brain.

'Excuse me. I really need to go to the bathroom.'

'Oh, Morgan? Right now? The meeting...'

Hannah's voice followed her down the hall.

In the upscale visitors' bathroom where she'd fled after Hannah had dropped her verbal meteor strike, Morgan sat on the lid of a toilet and stared at her hands. She knew she had to get moving, get to the meeting, or her mum would hunt her down like a rabid fox but she didn't know if she could face Noah Fraser again.

She'd rather flush herself down the toilet bowl.

'Morgs?' A fist rapped on the door. 'You in there? Your mum is *not* a happy camper.'

Morgan leaned forward and flipped the lock to open. Riley pulled the door open and frowned. She sent her a pointed look. 'Why are you hiding out in the bathroom?'

Morgan bit the inside of her cheek. 'Did you meet Noah Fraser?'

'The security guy? Yes. Very intense, very hot.'

Morgan swore and dropped her face to her hands.

'And the problem is...?'

Morgan briefly explained her history with Noah and Riley lifted her hands in confusion. 'So you made a move on the guy and he said no? It was a long time ago, Morgan.'

Morgan knew that if there was anyone who would understand what she was about to say Riley was it. They'd been friends forever and she had witnessed Morgan's constant struggles with the system. Shortly after the incident with Noah she'd moved in as Morgan's flatmate. Riley had watched her struggle through college to get her diploma in Gemology and Jewellery Design—it had taken her double the time to get as anyone else, even with a scribe—and she knew the challenges she faced on a daily basis and had supported her through the hard times.

'Okay, I need more details. So tell me about Mr Melt-My-Panties. And hurry up—your mother is going to have both our hides soon.'

'When I was nineteen the parents had some kidnapping threats made against them by some weird group and Noah was assigned as my bodyguard.'

'Uh-huh…'

'After a week of hanging with him I threw myself at him—actually, I threw my *naked* self at him.' Morgan nodded at Riley's wince. 'He kissed me, discovered I was a virgin, and then he declined the offer. I was so humiliated. I liked him—felt so at ease with him despite the fact that he hardly spoke—and his rejection felt like—'

'Like what, hon?'

'I can't explain it, and I don't know why, but his rejection made me feel swamped with shame. Every emotion I'd ever experienced with my dyslexia—the lack of self-belief, the fear of judgement—dropped on me like a ton of bricks. It was horrible. He made me feel worthless again. And now is not the time to tell me that nobody can make me *feel* worthless!'

'Okay. No lectures. Did he know that you were dyslexic?'

'No, I was very careful to keep it from him. For that summer I was Morgan without the big D. That's what made it even harder, I think… He rejected me anyway. Around him I was the most normal I had ever been and it still wasn't enough. I still can't think of that night without feeling cold and clammy.'

'Oh, honey… Well, you know you're not worthless. You've worked hard to climb out of that pit of feeling *less than* and not valued. Why are you letting those feelings, and that man, chase you into a bathroom stall? You're better than that.'

She *was*, dammit. 'I know that…' she muttered.

'Then get your butt out of there and pick up your chin. You'll be fine. Me, I'm not so sure.' Riley wiggled her butt.

Morgan lifted her hands in query. 'What's the matter with you?'

'I think my panties are starting to melt…can I hit on him?'

'Sheez, Ri!' Morgan snapped. 'No, you can't hit on him! I mean, yes, you can… *Aarrgh!*'

Riley's chuckles followed her out of the bathroom.

This time he'd sent *her* running.

Judging from her hasty retreat and her *oh, crap!* look, nobody had told her he would be at the meeting. While he hadn't expected Morgan to attend this meeting, at least he'd been prepared to run into her. And he'd had a six hour flight to practise his *oh-it's-you* face.

He understood her belting out of the room; he'd fought the same impulse himself. That and the inclination to grab her and pick up where they'd left off years ago. She'd be naked, of course…

Noah looked down at the table he was sitting at and concentrated hard. Thirty-three years old and he was grateful that his crotch was hidden from view by a sleek boardroom table.

Get a grip, Fraser. Distraction… Years ago he'd used firearm drills; now he just flipped open his iPad and checked his emails. Ten minutes later he glanced at his watch and stifled a frustrated sigh. The meeting still hadn't started.

He'd made Morgan run off screaming into the… Well, not the night, but he still couldn't blame her. It wasn't his finest memory and *he* hadn't been naked…with a Brazilian… *Do not go there, Fraser.*

He glanced over to the corner, where Hannah Moreau and her son James, who'd just entered the conference room, were standing. He'd met James once before, and despite the fact that he was one of the richest men in the world he rather liked the guy. He was smart, decisive, and didn't give off an air of being precious.

He also knew, from Chris, that he played a cracking game of touch rugby, didn't play polo, and could talk to miners and millionaires with equal ease. He couldn't help hoping that Morgan had turned out equally well.

Not that he cared—much—one way or the other.

Noah saw the conference door open and didn't realise that he'd sucked in his breath. The arty-looking redhead stepped through the door first, and exchanged a look with James that was part defiance, part attraction—something cooking there—and then Noah focused his attention on the figure in the doorway.

'Sorry I kept you waiting, everybody. Hi, James.'

James Moreau whirled around and immediately crossed the room, pulling Morgan into his embrace. Morgan's butterscotch-coloured head rested on his chest and she closed her eyes as she returned the hug. When she opened them again she looked straight at him—now utterly composed— with those clear, deep green eyes, and it was his turn to feel something akin to exposed and vulnerable…as if she'd cracked him open and his every thought, emotion, fear was there for her to read.

In another reality—the one where he wasn't losing his mind—Noah remembered his manners and forced himself to his feet, taking a moment to pull his thoughts together and to display his usual expression. He called it inscrutable; Chris called it bored indifference. He pulled in a shallow breath and made himself relax while Morgan shook hands with the others in the room. He watched her interact and knew that her smile wasn't as wide as it could be, that the muscles in her slim shoulders were taut with tension, that she was trying to delay the moment of having to acknowledge his presence.

Well, he wasn't entranced with the idea either. Entranced with *her*, yes. With the reality of being entranced by her...no.

He didn't do entranced.

'Noah,' James said, placing a hand on Morgan's stiff back and urging her towards him, 'I don't know if you remember my sister Morgan?'

Since the memory of her naked is forever printed on my retina, I should think so.

Noah's mouth twitched, and when Morgan glared at him he thought that she'd worked out what he was thinking. 'Of course. Nice to see you again, Morgan,' he said, in his smoothest, blandest voice.

Wish you were naked, by the way.

'Noah,' Morgan said. Her eyes flicked over him, narrowed, and then she gave him a 'you're a bug and I'm desperate to squash you' look.

What was her problem? He hadn't asked her to proposition him... Was she still annoyed because he'd said no? *Come on, it was eight years ago—get over it, already.*

Noah held her defiant stare. He'd perfected his own implacable, don't-mess-with-me stare in the forces, and it had had more than a couple of recruits and higher-ranking officers buckling under. When Morgan started to flush he knew had he won their silent battle of wills. This time.

'Take a seat everyone.'

Noah turned back to the table and pulled out the chair next to him for Morgan, gestured her into it. She narrowed her eyes at him, yanked it back another couple of inches in a flouncy display of defiance and dropped into it. Noah could smell her scent, something light and fresh, and felt a rush of blood heading south, making him feel almost light-headed. She still wore the same perfume and it transported him back to that night so long ago, when he'd tangled with temptation and by the skin of his teeth escaped.

'Right, the first item of business...' Hannah said, in a crisp, no-nonsense voice when they were all seated and looking at her expectantly. 'I'm handing over the responsibility of the ball to you, Morgan, and it's not under discussion. Make me proud.'

CHAPTER THREE

WHEN SHE WAS very tired, stressed or emotional Morgan saw dots in front of her eyes and the letters on a page danced and shuffled about. However, this was the first time the room had ever moved, that faces had bopped and objects jiggled.

Morgan closed her eyes and wondered if she had imagined the last thirty seconds. She'd thought she'd heard her mother say that she wanted her to take over the organising the Moreau Charity Ball—the most anticipated ball on the international social scene, held once every five years, displaying the full collection of gemstones and jewellery the Moreau family had acquired over many generations.

There were only three thousand guests attending, five hundred of whom were invited by Hannah herself from among their loyal customers, long-time business associates and preferred suppliers. For the rest, whether they were royalty or the average Joe, they had to place a bid for a double ticket and the highest bids won the highly sought after tickets.

It was outrageous how much people were prepared to pay for a double ticket. Simply inconceivable… And that was why, along with the auction, the Moreau Charity Ball raised tens of millions for the various causes they supported around the world.

But for their money their guests expected the best enter-

tainers, visually stunning dress sets, Michelin star quality
food—the whole gilt-plated bang-shoot.

It was rich, it was exclusive, it was the social highlight
of the half-decade. And if you wanted to be part of the experience then you paid, stratospherically, for the privilege
of being there.

And Hannah wanted *her* to run it? Morgan felt her throat
constrict. She lifted her left hand and didn't realise that she
was groping for Noah's hand until his strong fingers encircled her palm and squeezed.

'Breathe,' he told her, his voice authoritative even though
it was pitched at a volume only she could hear. 'Again; in
and out. There you go.'

Morgan felt the room settle as oxygen reached her brain
and lungs. When she thought she could speak she licked her
lips and considered removing her hand from Noah's strong
grasp. But since it seemed to be her only tenuous link to reality, she left it exactly where it was.

Morgan made herself look at her mother, who had the
slightest smile on her face. 'Is this a joke?'

'Not at all,' Hannah replied. 'I'd like you to plan, organise and execute the ball.'

'But—'

'Riley will help you with the creative side—help you pick
the theme, do the design. You both have an amazing streak of
creativity and I know that it will look visually spectacular.'

Morgan shook her head, wishing she could speak freely
and say exactly what was on her mind. *I don't do well with
reading reports, writing reports, analysing spreadsheets.
You know this! I've worked really hard to conquer my dyslexia, but it's still there and it becomes a lot worse when I'm
stressed. This ball will stress me out to the max! I don't want
to mess this up; it's too important for me to be in charge of.*

Hannah's eyes softened but determination radiated from
her face. 'Honey, I know that you will be fine. I know that
you also have your own commissions, your own business to

run, so the full resources that are available to me are available to you too. We'll hire you a PA for this project; she'll type your reports and be your general gopher. James will keep an eye on the finances and you'll liaise with Jack regarding the promotion and advertising of the ball. Noah will draw up plans to keep the jewels safe, and I'll be on the other end of a mobile. You just have to co-ordinate, make decisions, boss people about.'

'You're good at that,' James inserted with an easy grin.

And in a couple of sentences her mother, without announcing to the room that she had a problem reading and writing, waved away her biggest concerns.

Morgan reluctantly pulled her hand out from Noah's and flushed, because she could sense those deep blue eyes on her face. What must he think of her? she wondered. That she was a candidate for an upmarket loony bin?

'Why are you bowing out, Hannah?' Riley asked, as forthright as ever.

Hannah picked up her pen and tapped the point on the stack of papers in front of her. Morgan saw a quick, secret smile on her face and frowned. It was a good question, and one she was sure she knew the answer to… Three, two, one…

'I need a break—to step away from the business for a while.'

There it is and here we go again…Morgan thought. Now they were getting to the bottom of things. Every ten years or so her parents decided that they should try and live together again. They loved each other, but they loved each other more when they had continents between them. They refused to accept that while they adored each other they just couldn't live together. How many times had her father moved in and out of the Stellenbosch farmhouse and, later, the Englewood mansion?

Morgan sent James a quick eye-roll and he responded with a faint smile.

'Jedd and I have realised that we've been married nearly forty years and we want to spend more time with each other. He's going to try to be a little less of a mad geologist and I'm going to accompany him on his travels. So I need you, Morgan, to organise the ball for me.'

Morgan expelled her pent-up tension in a long stream of air. If this was about her parents' marriage then she gave her mum a week and she'd be on the company jet back home. Hannah couldn't go five minutes without checking her email or applying her lipstick. Her father spent weeks in jungles without making contact, sleeping in tents and hammocks and, she suspected, not washing much.

A week, maybe two, and Hannah would be back and yanking the ball's organisation into her beautifully mani-cured hands. Fine by her. She just had to ride it out.

What a morning, Morgan thought. Noah, the ball, her parents; she felt as if she was in sensory and information overload.

'Right, down to business,' Hannah said sharply.

Morgan frowned and held up her hand. 'Whoa! Hold on, there, Mum.' Morgan narrowed her eyes at her beautiful, wilful mother. If she gave her mother an inch, she'd gobble her up. 'I will sit in on this first planning meeting and then I will decide how involved I want to become—because I know that you will whirl back in here in two weeks' time and take over again.'

Blue eyes held green and Hannah's mouth eventually twitched with a smile. She nodded, looked around the table and pulled on her cloak of business. 'Okay. Now, we've wasted enough time on our family drama. Back to work, everyone.'

By the end of the two-hour meeting Morgan felt as if her head was buzzing. She desperately needed a cup of coffee and some quiet. Just some time to think, to process, to deal with the events of the morning.

She wanted to run up to her studio, lie down on her plush raspberry love seat and just breathe. But instead, because Hannah had asked her super-nicely, she was accompanying Noah to the Forrester-Grantham Hotel—the oldest, biggest and most beautiful of Manhattan's hotels. It had the only ballroom in New York City big enough to accommodate the ball's many guests, and the fact that it was lush, opulent and a six-star venue made it their instinctive hotel of choice.

Morgan had been delegated, by her mother, to introduce Noah to the hotel's Head of Security and discuss the current security arrangements for the ball.

Yippee.

Riley, the last to leave, closed the door behind her and Morgan was left alone with Noah. She watched as he unfurled his long body and headed for the refreshment table in the corner. He placed a small cup beneath the spout of the coffee machine and hit the button marked 'espresso'. He was different, Morgan thought. His body, under that nice grey suit, still seemed to be as hard as it had been eight years ago, but his hair was longer, his face thinner. Okay, he was older, but what felt so different? Maybe it was because now he radiated determination, a sense of power…leaving no one in doubt that he was a smart, ambitious man in his prime.

Noah snagged two bottles of sparkling water from the ice bucket, held them loosely in one hand as he picked up the small cup and brought it back to the table. To her surprise, he slid the cup and a bottle towards her.

'You look like you need both,' Noah said, pushing away the chair next to her with his foot and resting his bottom on the conference table so that he faced her. He picked up a bottle of water, twisted the cap off and took a long sip.

Morgan lifted the cup to her lips, swallowed and tipped her head so that it rested against the high back of the leather chair. Her mind skittered over all the questions she wanted to ask him: where did he live? He wasn't wearing a ring but was he married? Involved? Why had he said no to her all those years ago?

She opened her mouth to say…*what?*…and abruptly closed it again.

The right corner of Noah's mouth lifted and Morgan felt her irritation levels climb. 'What are you smirking at?' she demanded.

'You, of course.'

Of course.

'Well, stop it! Why?'

Noah lifted one shoulder and looked at her as he put the water bottle to his lips. Lucky water bottle… *Really, Morgan! Do try to be less pathetic, please.*

'You're sitting there thinking that politeness demands that you have to talk to me and the only thing you want to talk about is why I walked away so long ago.'

The ego of the man! The arrogant, condescending, annoying son-of-a… He was *so* right, damn him.

'I haven't thought of you once since you left,' she said, with a credible amount of ice in her voice.

'Liar,' Noah said softly, his eyes sparking with heat. 'You've *also* wondered what it would've been like…'

Also wondered? Did that mean that he had too? And why was she even having this conversation with him? In fact, why was he talking at all? The Noah she knew needed pliers and novocaine to pull words out of him.

'Well, I see that you've grown some social skills. Have you found that talking is, actually, quite helpful to get your point across?'

See—she could do sarcastic. And quite well. *Hah!*

'My partner nagged me to improve.'

His partner? Who was she? How long had they been together? Did they have children?

Noah laughed softly. 'You have the most expressive face in the world. Why don't you just ask?'

'Ask you what?' Morgan feigned supreme indifference. 'I have no idea what you mean.'

'Again...*liar*. When I say partner I mean Chris—my business partner.'

Single! Yay! Her girl-parts did a stupid happy dance and she mentally slapped them into submission because he hadn't really answered the question.

'And you?'

Morgan lifted her perfectly arched dark brown eyebrows at him. She knew that they were the perfect contrast to her blonde hair. And they made her eyes look greener than they actually were. 'That has nothing to do with you.'

Noah grinned and disturbed the million bats squatting in her stomach.

'You are such a duchess.'

Morgan bared her teeth at him. 'And don't you forget it. And, just to make it clear, I do not—*ever*!—want to discuss Cape Town.'

'It's a nice city.'

Morgan growled. 'What we *did* in Cape Town.' She pushed out the clarification between clenched teeth.

'*We* did? All *I* did was kiss you—you were the one who was naked and hoping to get lucky.'

She was going to kill him...slowly, with much pleasure.

Morgan ground her teeth together. How was this *not* discussing the issue? Did he not understand the concept of letting sleeping dogs lie? Obviously not.

Noah pushed his hair away from his face and rubbed his hand across his jaw. 'As much fun as it is, exchanging barbs with you, I do need to say something about Cape Town.'

Please don't. I've been humiliated enough.

Noah looked at her with serious eyes. 'I should've handled it—you—the situation—better, Morgan.' He held up a hand as her mouth opened and she abruptly shut it again. 'It took guts to do what you did and I was cruel. I'm sorry.'

Morgan realised that she was wearing her fish-face and snapped her teeth together. He was apologising? Seriously?

'So, that's all I have to say.'

Ah… It was more than enough and, quite frankly, she'd still prefer to pretend it had never happened. But she had to respect him for apologising, although she had played her own part in the train wreck that had been that night.

She rubbed her suddenly sweaty palms against her thighs. 'Okay, then. Wow. Um…thanks. I suppose I should apologise for hitting on you naked. I was rather…in your face.'

'A woman who looks like you should never apologise for being naked,' Noah said, humour sparking in his eyes.

It made her want to smile at him and she wasn't quite ready to do that. Nearly, but not quite yet.

'Can we…*ahem*…put it to bed?' he asked.

Morgan rolled her eyes at the very unsubtle pun.

Way past time to change the subject, Morgan thought. 'Mum said something about you being on your own? That you're not with CFT any more?'

Noah nodded. 'I have my own company doing pretty much the same thing CFT are doing. Except that we're branching out into security analysis; this is our first job for MI. I'm here to make recommendations about what systems should be put in place to secure the collection. That's the first step. Hopefully it'll lead to us installing those systems.'

'Are you good at it?'

'Very.'

'Okay, then.' Morgan twisted her ring around her finger and half shrugged. 'Today aside, I don't have much to do with the ball, but I would hate to see anything happen to the collection. It's fabulous; the gems are magnificent and the craftsmanship is superb.'

'Nothing to do with the ball? I think your mum has other ideas.' Noah finished his bottle of water, carefully replaced the cap and placed it on the table. 'If we get the job to install the systems then I will make damn sure that nothing happens to the collection. My business would be ruined if a diamond chip went missing, and that's not a risk I'm prepared to take.'

Morgan went cold at the thought of losing the collection. The value of the pieces meant nothing to her, but the fact that her family was the custodian of Elizabeth of Russia's diamond ring, a pearl won by an eighteenth-century Maharani wife, and the first diamond to come out of the first Moreau mine, meant a great deal. They were valuable, sure, but they were also historically important.

But if Noah was in charge of securing them then she knew that they would be fine. He exuded an air of capability and competence and, like all those years ago, when she'd felt secure enough to hand herself over to him, she felt confident about the collection's safety.

Noah was reliable and proficient.

Everything she wasn't—outside of her design studio. He was a living, breathing reminder of why she could never organise the ball. She would be stepping so far out of her comfort zone... A million things could go wrong and probably would and she'd be left holding the can. Nope, this was her mum's baby and would remain so.

Besides, she so didn't need the stress, the responsibility or the hassle of dealing with the sexy and not-so-silent-anymore Noah Fraser, with his sexy Scottish burr and sarcastic smile.

'Come on—time to go,' Noah said, standing up.

He watched as she uncrossed her legs and stood up. He looked her up and down and his eyes crinkled in amusement.

'Looking good, Duchess. Of course not as good as you looked back then—'

'I was nineteen,' Morgan protested, conscious that she'd picked up more than a pound since she'd been a perfect size four. 'Anyway, I'm that not much bigger.'

'You're not big at all, Duchess; you know you look great. My point was back then you were naked.' Noah placed a hand on her back and pushed her towards the door. 'Naked is always hard to beat.'

'Taxi, Miss Moreau?'

Morgan sent Noah a look in response to the doorman's question.

He shook his head slightly and jammed his hands in the pockets of his pants. 'No, thank you. It's a beautiful afternoon; we'll walk.'

'Enjoy the rest of your day, Miss Moreau. Sir…'

Noah fell into step with Morgan as she turned right and headed to the traffic lights to cross Park Avenue. It was moments like this when he was reminded just how famous the people he protected actually were. When the doormen and staff of one of the most famous hotels in the world recognised you and greeted you by name, as numerous people had Morgan inside the hotel, you had pull, clout—a presence.

Morgan, surprisingly, took it all in her stride. She'd greeted some of the staff by name, introduced herself to others. She didn't act like the snob he'd expected her to be.

'Amazing hotel. I've never been inside before,' he commented as they waited for the light to change so that they could cross the road.

A taxi driver directly in front of them leaned out of his window and gestured to the driver of a limousine to move and a transit van dodged in front of another cab, which resulted in a flurry of horns and shouted insults out of open windows.

New York traffic…crazy. And they drove on the wrong side of the road.

Morgan, adjusted the shoulder strap of her leather bag, looked back at the imposing entrance to the hotel and smiled. 'Isn't it amazing? I love it.'

'A couple of the staff nearly fell over to greet you. Must be crazy, being so well known.'

'Oh, I've been going there since I was a little girl; for tea, for dinner, for drinks—and of course we host the ball here every five years. It's a great place.'

'Great, yes. Safe? I'll be the judge of that.'

Morgan grinned. 'Oh, you and my Mum are going to get along just fine.'

It was a stunning spring afternoon for a walk back to the MI offices.

'Hey, Morgan. Over here!'

Noah turned around and a camera flash went off in his face. He cursed.

'Who's the dude, Morgan?'

A paparazzo, wearing an awful ball cap and a fifty-thousand-dollar camera, popped up. Seeing Morgan's thundercloud face, he lifted an eyebrow in her direction.

'This is why I hate going anywhere with you in New York,' Noah complained in his best petulant tone. 'Nobody ever pays any attention to *me*!'

Morgan looked startled for about two seconds before her poker face slid into place. 'Are you whining?' she demanded, not totally faking her surprise.

'I've been nominated for three BAFTAs *and* I've won a BSA but do I get the attention? No!'

Both Morgan and the pap looked puzzled. 'A BSA?' the pap asked, confused.

'British Soap Awards. And you call yourself a pap? Your UK counterparts would kick your ass!'

'Who are you again?'

It went against every cell in his body, but Noah forced himself to toss his head like a prima donna. 'Oh, that's just wonderful!' He looked at Morgan. 'I've wasted enough time—can we please go now?'

Morgan's lips twitched. 'Sure.'

Noah gripped Morgan's elbow and turned her away.

She sent him an assessing look from under her absurdly long lashes. 'Who *are* you again?'

Noah grinned. 'He's going to spend the next couple of hours combing through photos of Brit celebrities before he realises that he's been hosed.'

Morgan grinned. 'Excellent. Quick thinking, soldier. It won't stop him from printing the picture, but it did stop him from hassling me further.'

'Cretin.'

'Um…is there anyone back home that might get upset by seeing us together? If there is, you should give them a heads-up.'

Who would care if his photo appeared in a society column? It took a moment to board her train of thought. Ah…a wife, partner, girlfriend or significant other. He thought he saw curiosity in her eyes about whether he was involved with someone or not.

'I'll bear that in mind.'

Frustration flicked across her face at his reply. Yep, definitely interested—which was, in itself, interesting.

'Does that happen often? The cameras in your face?'

Morgan jabbed the 'walk' button to cross the road. 'All the time. It's deeply annoying and I wish they'd leave me alone.'

'Well, you *are* one of the world's wealthiest heiresses.'

Morgan's pulled a face as they crossed the famous street. 'Moreau International is wealthy—me, not so much. And I'm not that much of a social butterfly. Much to my mother's despair,' Morgan said quietly as she pulled oversized Audrey Hepburn sunglasses out of her black bag and slipped them on. 'Would you believe me if I told you that I'd rather pound a stake into my ear than attend a soirée or a cocktail evening?'

He wouldn't, actually. Look at her—she radiated confidence, class and poise. She was Morgan Moreau and her blood ran very blue. Unlike his, which was of the cheap Scottish whisky variety.

You're a long way from home, lad. Remember that.

'Then why do you do it?'

Morgan sent him a surprised look, opened her mouth to

reply and shut it again. She dodged around a group of teen-agers looking in a storefront window and looked resigned. 'So, what did you think of Sylvester Cadigan?' she asked a few moments later.

Change of subject, but he'd circle back round to her later. 'He seems competent. He wasn't happy that I demanded a complete and detailed dossier of the security arrangements they put in place for the last ball. He thought that I was questioning his professionalism.'

'Weren't you?' Morgan sent him a direct look with those bottle-green eyes.

'Sure I was. I don't trust anyone.' Especially when it was *his* rep on the line. 'I'll have a lot more questions for him tomorrow, after I've reviewed the dossier he's emailing me.'

'Do you need someone from Moreau to attend that meeting?' Morgan asked as they approached the gold and white façade of Moreau's Gems.

'No. We're going to investigate entrances and exits, look at the surveillance system. I think I can manage without someone holding my hand.'

'Good,' Morgan said, and gestured to the building in front of them. 'MI's flagship store, established in 1925.'

Noah looked at the façade of the jewellery store and swallowed down his impressed whistle. The very wide floor-to-ceiling window was lavishly decorated in a 1920s theme, Noah guessed. There were feather boas, deckchairs with tipped-over champagne bottles, strings of pearls hanging from or wrapped around silver ice buckets. Brooches pinned to berets left in sand, discarded chiffon dresses under a spectacular emerald and diamond necklace. Rings scattered in beach sand.

He hadn't passed the window when he'd arrived that morning, going directly to the separate doors that led up to the MI corporate offices. The window was fantastic and made him want to explore the store and see what other treasures were hidden within. And that, he supposed, was exactly the point.

'Amazing.'

'Riley's work,' Morgan replied proudly. 'She's utterly marvellous at what she does. She changes the display every month and she keeps it top secret. On the first of every month we all traipse down here, along with a horde of shoppers, to see what she's done. It's like Christmas every month.'

'She's very talented.'

'All the big stores keep trying to steal her away but she's loyal to us. Although she and James knock heads continuously. She demands carte blanche to do what she wants with the windows; James demands that she runs her designs past him first.' Morgan waved at a store employee through the glass. 'Having Riley and James in the same room is fabulous entertainment. They argue like mad. I can't wait to hear her ideas on themes for the ball.'

Oh, God, here comes the girly stuff. 'Themes? What's wrong with putting on some fancy duds and showing up?'

'*Pffft!* You sound just like my father. How would that be different from the other sixty balls happening in the city alone? We organise the *Moreau Ball,* not just *a ball.*'

Morgan turned away and headed to the MI entrance further down the street.

'How long will you be in New York for?' she asked, super-casually.

It was the first vaguely personal question she'd asked him and he wondered if he had imagined the flicker of attraction cross her face.

He was pretty sure *his* attraction had flashing neon bulbs and a loud hailer.

'If I get all the information I need I'll try and fly out tomorrow evening. I'll draw up my report, with recommendations and time-frames, then email it to you, James and your mother,' he said as they stepped up to the entrance of MI and the automatic doors swished open.

A guard gestured him to move away from Morgan; he stepped up to sign in at the security desk and to be patted down for the second time that day. Then he followed Morgan through the metal detectors and on to the bank of elevators.

'I'll arrange security clearance for you so you can swipe your way through,' Morgan said as they waited for a lift. 'Where are you staying tonight?'

The lift doors opened and they stepped inside. He could smell her scent, feel her heat, and their eyes collided in the floor-to-ceiling mirrors as he answered her question. 'In the MI company flat in the Lisbon Building, on West and Fifty-Seventh Street.'

'I know where it is. I live in the apartment above it. James, when he stays in town, is above me in the penthouse. My parents are in the family house in Englewood Cliffs.'

Noah shook his head. 'Never heard of it. Where is that?'

'Northern New Jersey, Long Island. About…hmm…ten miles from downtown Manhattan.' The tip of her pink tongue peeked out from between her luscious lips. It made him wonder what that mouth would feel like, how that tongue would taste. Still the same? Better?

'So, I'm single.'

Morgan looked confused. 'Okay. Thanks for sharing that.' 'You?'

Where was this going? 'Um…me too.'

Noah placed his shoulder against the mirror and couldn't believe what he was about to say next. His accent deepened as he spoke softly. 'Do you know something?'

'What?'

'MI have not, officially, signed any contract, so I'm technically not affiliated or contracted to MI yet. I don't think we're going to be working together, because you don't seem to have much inclination or willingness to organise this event…'

'Try *none*—and can you tell my mother that?' said Morgan, then frowned. 'And your point is…?'

'My point is that, technically, I can do this...' Noah stepped closer to her, placed his hands on her hips and dropped his head so that his mouth lined up with hers. 'I want to see if you taste the same.'

Morgan's eyes widened as her hands came up to rest on the lapels of his suit jacket. 'Uh...what are you doing?'

'Kissing you. Because we're both single, we're not linked by business, and because I want to,' Noah whispered against her lips.

They were as soft as they looked, as piquant as he remembered. They softened under his and he lifted his hand to push it under the weight of her hair, encircling her slender neck with his large, hard hand. Morgan whimpered and arched towards him, her hands snaking up his chest to link behind his neck. She stood up on her tiptoes and his tongue darted out to touch hers.

All sense of propriety and sensibility left him as he spun her around and pushed her up against the wall. His hand roamed the backs of her legs and under her butt cheeks as he lifted her hips into his erection, felt her breasts flatten against his chest. She was so hot, so feminine, and she was as into this kiss as he was.

All he could think was, where had he found the strength to walk away all those years ago? He wanted her—now—and considered pulling her to the floor...except that they were in a lift and the doors could open at any second...any freakin' second.

Noah pulled his hands off her butt and yanked his mouth off hers. He backed away—two steps, big deal—and tried to control his heaving breath. Morgan looked no better: shell shocked, kiss-bruised lips, strips of colour across her cheekbones. Anybody who saw them now would know exactly what they had been up to.

Morgan kept her eyes on his face and when the lift opened onto the executive floor, where they'd been earlier, she watched him get out. When Noah realised she wasn't following him he placed his hand on the door to keep it open and looked back at her.

'You aren't getting out here?'

'I'm going up to my studio. Top floor. Bye. And, Noah?'

'Yeah?'

'That was one helluva kiss.'

CHAPTER FOUR

MORGAN HAD DELIBERATELY not thought about his kiss all day. Well, she'd tried not to think of his kiss… Okay, truth: she hadn't thought of much besides his kiss!

To put it another way, she'd done little more than stare out of the window for the whole afternoon.

She was glad to be home, glad to be in her apartment where she could drop all manner of pretence and admit that Noah's lips on hers had rocked her to her core. She staggered over to her plump red and white striped couch, dropped her bag to the floor and sank down into its welcoming softness.

She'd kissed Noah Fraser.

Inside her body, every single cell she possessed was in revolt. A picture of the little molecules on a protest march flashed in her head…grumpy little cells each carrying placards with various sayings like: *Do Him!*, *We Want Orgasm Reform!*, or simply, *Sex! Now!*

She couldn't argue.

Her body craved Noah, and she wished she could use the excuse that she'd had none for a while…but she had, surprisingly, not so long ago. It hadn't been 'rock my world' sex, but it had been nice, pleasant, fulfilling and, best of all, very, very discreet.

With her high profile she valued discretion. She just hadn't realised that in that case *discreet* had been a synonym for married. She'd been surprised and shocked when—at the last minute, admittedly—she'd decided to attend a cocktail party she'd said she wouldn't be at. He'd been there with his very beautiful, very thin Venezuelan wife and they'd both known that her tipping a glass of red wine into his lap, accidentally on purpose, had been a poor substitute for her slapping him into next year.

Morgan placed her thumb on one eye and her index finger on the other and pushed.

She had kissed Noah Fraser. Again.

Actually, kissed was totally the wrong word… She'd inhaled him, Frenched him…devoured him. She could still feel his long fingers searing through her pants, the rasp of his two-day beard, the silkiness of his hair as she pulled it through her fingers.

He kissed liked a dream, like a man should kiss: with authority, skill, strength and tenderness. If he made love like he kissed… Morgan whimpered as she felt the pool of heat and lust drop to her womb. She was minutes off an orgasm and that was from just the memories of his kiss!

What if he touched her breasts, slid his fingers…? She didn't know if she was strong enough to survive the experience.

It took her a moment to realise that someone was pounding on her door and she wrinkled her nose. James frequently came by when he was in town and hung out, mostly to avoid their mother nagging him into attending an event. James was as allergic to the social swirl as she was… Was she a bad sister if she pretended not to be here?

She didn't want to talk to anybody. She just wanted to relive Noah's lips on hers, his scent in her nose, the hard muscles she'd felt in his shoulders.

Bang! Bang! Bang!

Bats…

'Who is it?' she demanded in a croaky voice as she pushed herself to her feet.

'Noah.'

The only person she wanted to see and the last person she'd expected. Morgan yanked the door open and there he stood, jacket and tieless, his fist about to connect with the door again.

Morgan put out one finger and pushed his clenched fist down. 'You pounded?'

Noah placed his hands on her hips and without a word pushed her backwards and kicked the door shut behind him.

'Oh, well, just come on in,' Morgan said, trying for sarcastic and hitting breathless.

Noah dropped his hands from her hips and slapped them on his. 'I've been thinking...'

'Did you hurt yourself?' Morgan asked sweetly.

He ignored her. 'On a scale of one to ten, what are the chances of you being in charge of this ball?'

'About...hmm...minus one thousand and fifty-two.'

'Thank God.'

'Why?'

'Because I don't sleep with my clients. Or my colleagues. Ever.'

'You nearly beat down my door to tell me that?'

'Try and keep up, Moreau. I don't sleep with clients.'

Morgan, starting to catch a clue, felt her heart-rate accelerate. 'And since I'm not going to be organising the ball I won't be your client,' she said slowly as she wrapped her head around the implications of those words.

'There you go.' Noah nodded 'I walked away years ago...'

'I know. I was there.'

That was a conversation for another day, and right now she didn't give a foo-foo. She wanted to know if he was here for the same reason she wanted him here. So that they could take that hot kiss they'd shared in the lift to its logical conclusion. And if he was toying with her again she'd have MI Security toss his gorgeous body off the roof.

Noah's eyes glinted blue fire. 'I don't want to spend the next eight years wondering...'

Morgan forced the lust away in order to think. It was hard, but she had to do it. 'You're leaving tomorrow to go back to London?'

'More than likely. There's nothing more I need to do here workwise…at this time.'

'So you are here for one night…one incredible, exceptional, crazy night.' she said, enunciating each word. 'Are we on the same page, here?'

Noah pushed a hand through his messy hair. She could tell it wasn't the first time he'd done that this evening. 'Yeah. Deal?'

Phew! She was going to get lucky! All her little cell protestors threw down their placards, lay down and assumed the 'do me' position. Morgan considered doing the same.

'What do you say, Morgan?'

Yes! Stop talking and take me now, yes! 'Okay, yes, that's a deal.' Morgan started to lift her shirt. She wanted to get naked—*now*.

'Stop. Don't,' Noah said, his voice low and urgent.

Morgan looked at him, fear and fury flashing in her eyes.

Noah took two steps to reach her and clasped her face in his hands. 'Relax, Morgan, I just want to undress you myself. Inch by gorgeous inch.'

'Oh.' Morgan's hands fell to her sides. 'Okay.' She tipped her head back and up, so that she could look into his eyes. 'You think I'm gorgeous?'

'Very—and stop fishing for compliments, Duchess. Try kissing me instead.'

The warmth in his eyes was at odds with his teasing words and Morgan felt her lips tip up in response.

Noah dropped a kiss on her nose before swooping down and covering her mouth with his, his tongue sliding against hers, long and smooth. 'You sure you want to do this, Morgan?' he muttered as his hand palmed her butt.

'Still sure.' Morgan angled her head away so that he could taste her neck, that sensitive spot just under her ear. His broad hand covered her breast and shivers skittered over her skin. Her fingers went to his shirt buttons and soon her hands were on warm male flesh, hot muscle and sexy skin. Her fingers danced over a very impressive six-pack and over the V of hip muscle that descended into his pants.

Noah groaned in the back of his throat as he slowly pulled her T-shirt up her torso, his eyes darkening at the white scraps of lace that covered her full breasts. He pulled her shirt up and over her head and dropped it to the floor, before running a finger along the edge of the lace. 'Pretty.'

Morgan sucked in her breath as his finger touched her hard nipple.

He hooked his hand under the lace and revealed her breast to his sizzling gaze. 'Very pretty indeed.'

His hot mouth covered her as he flipped open her bra and pulled it down her arms. Groaning, he banded his arms around her and, kissing her mouth, walked her backwards to the plump couch, lowering her to the striped fabric when the seat hit the back of her knees. Noah knelt down in front of her and picked up her booted foot, glowering at the knee-high laced boots.

Noah cursed. 'This is going to take far too long.'

'Not so much.' Morgan grinned, reached around to the back of her calf and pulled a zip down the boots. 'Hidden zip.'

'Brilliant.' Noah pulled her boots off impatiently, yanked her pants down her legs, and Morgan giggled when he tossed them over his shoulder. He sat back on his haunches, still dressed only in his suit pants, and looked at her, naked but for a little scrap of lace at the juncture of her thighs. She'd thought she would feel self-conscious, shy, uncomfortable, but how could she feel anything other than sexy and powerful when such a hard-bodied, lusciously masculine man looked at her with pure approval on his rugged face?

Then Morgan saw momentary hesitation in his face, knew that his big brain was trying to crash their party. She was *not*

going to be denied this again… If she had to tie him down—
ooh, that sounded like fun—she was going to have this man
on top of her, around her, inside her.

She leaned forward and placed her hands on his bare
shoulders. 'Stop thinking. I want this. So do you. Tomorrow is another day with another set of rules. Tonight there
is just us…no work, no history, no flaws. Just two people
who want each other. Okay?'

'Yeah.'

Noah nodded and Morgan released her tension in a long
sigh as one hand came up to cover her breast, his thumb idly
brushing her peaked nipple.

'I have a question,' Noah said reverentially, his eyes on
her panties.

Morgan wished he'd shut up and get on with what was
important—i.e. giving her a mind-blowing orgasm—but she
made herself speak. 'Okay…what?'

'Do you still have a Brazilian?'

'Well, soldier, why don't you take a peek?'

Bang! Bang! Bang!

Their heads flew up and turned in unison. Both looked
at the door in utter disbelief.

Noah, his hand in her panties, lifted his eyebrows. 'Expecting someone?'

'Uh—no.' And she wanted them to go away, while she
and Noah got back to what they were doing…which was
him doing her.

And doing her rather well.

Bang! Bang! Bang!

'Morgs, you've got thirty seconds, then I'm using my key.'

'James!' Morgan looked horrified as she pushed Noah
away. 'Clothes—where are my clothes?'

'Scattered,' Noah said as he stood up. 'Get dressed and
I'll delay him.'

'Open the door, Morgan!' James yelled. 'And who is
with you?'

'We're coming!' Morgan yelled back.

'Not in the way we'd hoped,' Noah stated as he reached for his shirt.

'Shut up!' Morgan growled, wiggling into her pants. 'Pass me my bra.'

Noah scooped up her bra, threw it towards her and tucked his shirt into his pants. When she was dressed, he gestured towards the kitchen.

'Got anything alcoholic?' he asked.

Morgan nodded towards an antique drinks cabinet in the corner and flipped open the bolt to her front door.

'James,' she drawled, 'have you ever heard of the concept of calling before you arrive? It's called etiquette. I'm sure Mum tried to teach us some.'

Morgan turned away and walked towards Noah who, being a good Scot, had found her expensive bottle of whisky and was pouring a healthy amount into three glasses.

'Morgan.'

Something in her brother's voice had all the hairs lifting on the back of her neck and arms. She turned around slowly and really looked at her brother. His face was bone-white and there were deep grooves in the lines running down next to his mouth. His eyes, green like hers, were flat and hard in his face.

'What's wrong?' she demanded. 'Is it Mum?'

James lifted up his hands. 'She's okay…really she is, Morgs, but something's happened.'

Morgan sensed Noah's approach and instinctively turned to look at him. He was rolling up the sleeves of his shirt and paused briefly, lifting an eyebrow in James's direction.

'What are you doing here anyway, Fraser?' James scowled.

Morgan figured that James really wouldn't want the answer to that question. Besides, he was a big boy—he could figure it out himself. Instead she gripped the back of one of the kitchen stools and tried to find her voice. 'Mum? What's happened, Jay?'

James gave Noah another tough look before running his hands over his face. 'Mum had an…incident earlier tonight.'

'Define "incident",' Noah said, and all traces of her earlier lover dissipated with those two words. He was in work mode, professional to the core. Serious, smart, and very, very dangerous.

'Jackson was walking Mum through the parking lot of Luigi's—she was meeting Dad for supper—when they were jumped by three guys.'

'Who is Jackson?' Noah grabbed a glass and handed it to Morgan. 'Drink.'

'My mum's long-time bodyguard and driver,' Morgan answered, grateful for something to do with her shaking hand.

Noah passed a whisky to James and gestured for him to carry on.

'Luckily Dad and Henry—Dad's bodyguard—were in the parking lot at the same time and saw what happened. Jackson and Henry reacted quickly—' James released a huff of frustration and sipped his whisky. 'The bodyguards got into it with the kidnappers while Dad picked Mum up— she'd been tossed to the ground in the fight—and bundled her into the car.'

'But not hurt, right?'

'Grazed chin and knees, sprained wrist,' James replied, the muscle in his jaw ticking.

'It's okay, Morgan.' Noah reached over and squeezed her shoulder. 'She's fine. What then?'

'Our guys—especially Henry—are pretty tough, and they managed to subdue two of them. The other got away.' James banged his glass onto the granite counter and splashed whisky. 'Before the police arrived they told them that they were part of a group who were looking to exact retribution for the fact that MI are in the process of reopening an emerald mine in a remote area of north-east Colombia.'

'Why don't they want it reopened?' Morgan asked.

'The mining, trucks and security will interfere with the local drug cartel's transport routes, and with increased population will make the inhabitants less...*reliant* on the generosity of the drug lords. I also suspect they are mining illegally as well,' James replied. 'They said that there are orders out to get MI out of the region.'

'Really blethered on, didn't they?' Noah said, his voice bland.

'Sang like canaries,' James replied. 'Probably because they had a knee in a kidney or a wrist about to be broken.' James folded his arms and rested his bottom against the counter in front of the coffee machine. 'The bottom line is that they want MI out of Colombia and they will do it by...'

Morgan saw his hesitation, the way he looked at her. 'By...?'

'By trying to kidnap someone else. You, me, other executives. I have told the executives in Colombia to be on high alert, and we're doubling their security—and the mine's. But you and I are definite targets. I want protection for you.'

Not again, Morgan thought. She hated having someone follow her around, monitoring her movements...constantly hovering.

'I've called CFT. They will have someone here in two hours. So if you could just stay put until they get here?'

'And Mum? How are we going protect her?' Morgan asked.

'Dad is taking her to the house in the Cayman Islands. You know how secure it is out there.'

'Good. That's good.'

James sent her a direct look. 'Any chance of you joining her there?'

Was he insane? She had jewellery commissions to complete and deliver and—damn it!—with her mother gone someone had to organise the ball. Her mum couldn't do that from the Cayman Islands or anywhere else. She needed to be here—in the city. So who was left to do it? *Me... Damn!*

'I'll take the protection, if you think I must, but I'm staying put.'

James blew air into his cheeks. 'CFT personal protection agents will be here soon. Will you accommodate them?'

What choice did she have? It was at times like these when the reality of how different her life was from that of a normal woman her age became very clear. This was when the fact that she was a Moreau—part of a prominent, hugely wealthy family whose business interests could upset people even a continent away—really smacked her in the face.

That wasn't normal. None of this was normal.

'That's not going to happen.'

Noah made sure that his voice was low, cool and utterly non-negotiable. In unison, James and Morgan turned to him, both pairs of bottle-green eyes surprised and suspicious.

James's eyes hardened a fraction of a second before Morgan's did. He could see that neither of them appreciated him jumping into the conversation but he didn't care. He just folded his arms across his chest and narrowed his own eyes.

'I'm not remotely interested in your opinion,' James told him. 'I'm making arrangements for my sister's protection.'

'So unmake them,' Noah suggested calmly. 'I will act as her personal protection detail.'

'What?'

The siblings' faces registered surprised confusion—and, really, could he blame them? They'd both forgotten that close body protection was what he did, was his business. And wasn't he here for the express purpose of getting his company more MI business? That whole world domination thing?

That was a good reason why he wanted to be the one to protect Morgan, but there were others. Since leaving the unit he'd done lots of close protection before moving into training the new officers. He knew how up close and personal bodyguards had to get to their principals, and there was no way that he was going to allow any CFT hound-dogs that close to Morgan. Fact: the only person that was getting into her personal space in the near future was him.

And, lastly, he wanted the best for Morgan. And he was it. There was a reason why Amanda had offered to double his already stratospheric salary if he stayed with CFT. He was that valuable, that good. Morgan deserved the best, and that was him.

Fact.

'I'm here. I'm already working for you.'

'I didn't realise that sleeping with my sister was part of your duties,' James said, in a very cool, very dangerous voice.

Noah didn't react. Mostly because he felt like punching James on his perfect nose... He didn't like being caught on the back foot, but he had to respect James for calling him on it. If he had a sister he'd do the same. 'Technically, I'm not employed by MI yet—'

'And the chances of you ever getting on the payroll are decreasing rapidly,' James stated.

Damage control, Noah thought, and fast. 'I'm good at what I do, Moreau, and what happened or didn't happen here earlier has nothing to do with that. Morgan and I are both consenting adults and we have an understanding.'

James looked at Morgan. 'Which is...?'

Noah remained silent. Hey, this was *her* brother—if she wanted to explain, she could.

'Well?'

'This has nothing to do with you, big bro,' Morgan stated, lifting her chin.

'You're my baby sister!'

'But I'm not a baby! I can have sex if I want!'

Both James and Noah winced. Noah scratched his forehead and was grateful that *his* brothers didn't require him to monitor *their* social life, because this was the social equivalent of a kick to the groin.

Time to end this conversation, he thought.

'Moving on,' he said briskly, 'and back to the subject at hand. Call Amanda Cope from CFT and ask her who her best bodyguard was—*ever*. I guarantee she'll say me. She hates me, but she's inherently honest. You want and need the best person out there guarding your sister. I'm it and I'm already in place.' It wouldn't hurt to sweeten the pot. 'I'll also give you a fifteen per cent discount on my personal protection fees because I'm doing an analysis on the security for your ball.'

'I don't want you as my bodyguard,' Morgan said.

'Tough,' Noah shot back.

James ignored her and held Noah's stare for thirty seconds before pulling his mobile out of his pocket and scrolling through his contacts. He was actually going to call Amanda! *This could go badly wrong,* Noah thought as James greeted her.

Morgan gripped his wrist and her nails dug into his skin. Even though they were sharp, he still felt heat and lust and attraction rocket up his arm. If he got this right, then acting as her bodyguard was going to be a casual stroll through hell....with a hard-on.

'Noah! Listen to me. I don't want this...*you*!' Morgan hissed.

Noah gently pulled her fingers off him and held her hand in his. 'Shh, I'm trying to listen.'

'I'm going to kill you,' Morgan threatened.

'Later...'

James was speaking. 'I don't need to know why he left, or what you think Auterlochie are doing wrong in the market place, Amanda; this has nothing to do with the rest of your guards or my personal security detail. It's one guy, looking after my sister. I just need to know whether he's good or not.'

When James's frown lifted from a trench to a furrow Noah knew that she had been her customary honest self.

'The best agent you ever had? Well, then...' James disconnected and slapped his mobile into the palm of his hand.

He glared at Noah. 'Fifteen per cent discount on both jobs because you started off by annoying me.'

Ouch.

'Deal,' Noah agreed.

'And keep your hands off my sister,' James growled.

'Basic bodyguarding,' Noah agreed, and he knew that James wasn't sure whether he was messing with him or not. James still looked like a thundercloud so he looked him in the eye. 'I will be completely professional when it comes to Morgan, James. You have my word.'

Besides, her safety depended on it… He couldn't look out for danger if he was eyeing her rack. Or her butt. Or imagining those legs around his hips…

And, although it was a lot less easy to admit, he was grateful for the order to keep his hands off Morgan. She was the type of woman he normally avoided. One of the few women who had caught his interest on more than a physical level. She intrigued him—mentally, emotionally. There was more to her than being the Moreau heiress, the reluctant NYC socialite. And that scared the hell out of him. Besides, he was consumed by his business. He didn't have the time or the energy to give to a woman.

James's shoulders dropped as the tension seeped out of him. Noah knew that James considered his and Morgan's relationship now to be defined, bound by the two contracts he would sign with MI. But to Noah it was written in blood—because he'd given James his word. No agreement written on paper trumped that.

Noah held out his hand and James reluctantly took it. 'Anything happens to Morgan you're a dead man,' James told him.

'Anything happens to Morgan I *will* be a dead man—because that's the only way they'll get to her.'

James's face lightened with appreciation and Noah thought that he might, *maybe*, be back on relatively solid ground with the brother and boss.

'Do either of you care what *I* want or think?' Morgan demanded, her hands on her hips.

Noah shook his head and looked at James. 'Uh…no.'

Noah ducked the glass that she sent flying towards his head and winced when the crystal shattered on the expensive tiles. Maybe he should curb the off-the-cuff honest answers. Good thing she had the aim of a one-eyed toddler or that might have hurt.

And, more importantly, it was a waste of a very fine dram.

CHAPTER FIVE

WASN'T THERE A song about yesterday and troubles seeming so far away? Morgan wondered as she stomped back into her bedroom, kicking her door closed behind her. Yesterday's biggest problems had been how to re-set Mrs Killain's fabulous teardrop diamond earrings into a more contemporary, cleaner setting, whether or not to attend the opening night of the Ballet Belle's new production, and who to take to Merri's wedding.

In one day she'd been slapped with an additional job, an old almost-lover, the attempted kidnapping of her mother, and a new bodyguard whom she wanted to jump.

Bats! On a freaking broomstick!

Right. First things first. Think it through... Her mum's almost-kidnapping. *No, don't think of the 'what ifs'. Push the emotion away...*

Her mum was only superficially hurt, and by now both her parents were in the family jet on their way to a safe place. The house in the Cayman Islands was a well-kept secret and James would have arranged for additional guards for them. Her parents were out of harm's way. That was good news.

Right: problem two. With her mum out of town, someone had to get cracking on organising the Moreau Charity Ball, and it looked as if she was now that someone. How was she going to manage to do that and keep her dyslexia under wraps? The last thing she wanted was to see pitying looks on the faces of Moreau staff…or from anyone else. Unfortunately a lot of people still equated dyslexia with stupidity, and she couldn't just go around announcing, *I'm dyslexic, but my IQ is one hundred and forty-eight*.

No, her dyslexia was *her* issue to deal with, and she didn't require sympathy, pity, or for anyone to make allowances for her. She'd just insist on short reports and plough through them at night…she'd make lists and check and double-check them.

Yay! What joy.

As for her almost-lover and new bodyguard…

She was intensely irritated with Noah on so many different levels that she wasn't sure which one she ranked highest. How dared he and James talk over her head and make arrangements for her safety as if she was a child? Okay, there was a crazy Colombian gang who wanted to use her as a bargaining chip, but Noah could have asked how she felt about him guarding her. She wasn't sure what her answer would have been if he had asked her… *No, I'd rather shag you instead*?

James would have had a coronary on the spot.

Noah irritation number two. How could he switch gears so easily and smoothly? Oh, she was royally ticked that one moment his hand had been tipping her into orgasm and the next he'd been all work—Mr I'll-Protect-Her-and-Give-You-a-Discount!

And on top of that there wasn't any chance of her getting lucky now; she knew that Noah took his duties seriously, and if he wouldn't sleep with her while she'd simply been organising the ball then there was an ice chip's chance in a fat-fryer that—having taken on the role as her bodyguard—he'd even consider picking up where they'd left off earlier.

And, really, did she want to get it on with a man who could flip it on and off with such ease? He had too much control and she too little…where he was concerned.

Well, no more. She was going to stop acting like a tart around him; she'd be cool and calm and collected.

Cool. Calm. Collected. Yep, she could do the three Cs!

'Sulking?' Noah asked from the doorway and she whirled around, her heart slamming against her ribcage. She had shut the door behind her, hadn't she? She was sure she had...

'Heard of knocking?' she demanded, hands on her hips.

Noah crossed one ankle over the other as his shoulder pressed into the doorframe. 'There's broken glass and whisky all over the floor and it's not in my job description to clean up because you lost your temper. Or are you too precious to use a dustpan and broom?'

'Bite me.'

Noah smiled. 'Can't. I promised your brother I wouldn't lay a hand—or lip—on you.'

Morgan felt the bubbles in her blood start to pop.

'You don't have to sound so pleased about it!' Morgan stormed to the doorway and brushed past him, the red mist of temper clouding her vision. What was it about this man that made her long for more? They didn't know each other really, but the fact that he could brush their heat off so easily made her want to throw more than a glass.

Maybe him. Off the twenty-first-floor balcony!

Noah reached out, snagged the waistband of her pants and pulled her to a stop. 'Cool your jets, Morgan, and take a breath.'

'Let. Me. Go,' Morgan muttered through clenched teeth.

'No,' Noah's said.

His fingers were warm against the bare skin of her lower back. She cursed the tremors of attraction that radiated up her spine.

Noah kept his fingers bunched in her pants and moved round so that he was standing, far too close, in front of her. 'Talk.'

More orders? 'Bite me,' she said again

'Stop being a duchess and talk to me. Why are you so annoyed that I am guarding you?'

Morgan folded her arms across her chest to form a barrier between their bodies and glared up at him. 'You didn't want to listen to me when I spoke earlier—why should I bother talking to you now?'

Noah winced. 'Okay, maybe we were a bit heavy-handed.'

'Maybe?'

'Don't push it,' Noah snapped back. 'I wanted to be the one to guard you and I was damned if you were going to talk James out of it.'

Morgan glared at him. 'Because I'm a way to get in with James for you to get more MI business.'

Noah's eyes darkened with fury. 'Stuff the MI business. I did it because no one will protect you as well as I will. Being kidnapped is not a walk down Madison Avenue, Duchess!'

'Uh…'

Noah shoved his hand into his hair and tugged. 'God, you live in this protected little world, kidnapping threats or not. You have no idea what happens to rich people who are 'napped. You want me to go into details?'

Morgan, her temper rapidly subsiding, shook her head.

'So sue me for wanting to keep you safe above wanting to have sex with you!' Noah roared, twin flags of temper staining his cheeks.

He stepped back from her and she could see that he was trying to control his temper. So he had one? Why did that reassure her rather than scare her?

Morgan tipped her head. 'You don't like losing control, do you?'

He lifted a finger and pointed it at her. 'You…you…nobody spikes my temper like you!'

'Ditto,' Morgan replied quietly as green eyes clashed with blue. After a tense, drawn-out silence, Morgan raised her shoulders and spoke again. 'Are you finished yelling at me?'

Noah released a long breath and slapped his hands across his chest. 'Maybe.'

'Okay, then.' Morgan pushed her hair back behind her ears. 'So, I'll go and clean up the broken glass.'

Noah nodded. 'I need to go downstairs for five minutes to pick up my bag and laptop.'

'Well, at least I have a spare bedroom this time.'

Noah rubbed his forehead. 'Does it have an inter-leading door that can stay open?'

Morgan shook her head. 'No.'

'Then we sleep with the doors open.'

'That's not necessary. We have two doormen, and this is one of the most secure buildings in the city.'

'The doors stay open.' Noah walked to the door and when he reached it turned to face her. 'I can't allow myself to be distracted by you, Morgan. Your safety depends on it. So help me out, okay? No propositions, no flirting, no walking around naked.'

There was that arrogance again, and she hated the fact that it turned her on. Determined to show him that he didn't affect her, in any way, she lifted her nose in the air. 'I'll try and restrain myself.'

'You do that, Duchess.'

Noah stood on the balcony in the bright sunshine and looked down into the leafy greenness of Central Park, idly noticing that the park was full of early-morning joggers, cyclists, walkers. Whoever would have thought that Noah Fraser, that angry boy from Glasgow, would be standing here looking at one of the best views in the city. Certainly not him. If he ignored the fact that Morgan was a kidnapping target and he couldn't touch her now, it was one of those stunning spring days.

Spoilt, unfortunately, by his father's voice whining in his ear…on and on and on.

Noah had been sixteen when he'd lost his mother and

taken over the care of his paralysed and violently angry father and his two brothers, six and four years old. And if Michael had been a mean bastard on two legs then he'd become even worse on none.

Noah had cooked, cleaned and cared for his siblings while Michael had cursed God and cursed them. By keeping Michael's attention directed on him, he'd managed to shield the kids from the worst of his verbal and—when he had the opportunity—physical abuse.

Noah had adored those little monsters, and it had nearly killed him when Social Services had moved them into the care of his aunt—his mother's sister. It had been the right thing for them—Michael could have scarred a psychopath—but he'd felt as if his heart had been torn out of his ribcage. Aunt Mary had offered to take him in too, but someone had had to look after Michael; his mam would have turned in her grave if he'd been left on his own.

'You might be poor, Noah, but poor men can act with honour too.'

'What is honour exactly, Mam?'

'It's taking responsibility and keeping your word. Seeking the truth and acting with integrity. Doing the right thing whether people are looking or not. Being better than your circumstances.'

Those words, part of a discussion they'd had a couple of months before her death, had defined the rest of his life.

It was because of those words that he'd endured three years of being belittled, insulted, punched when he was within range, before he'd cracked. It had been the most terrifying moment of his life when he'd come back to himself and realised he was holding...

Don't think about it. Don't remember. Put it back into the cage you keep it in.

He seldom relived the full memory of that horrible day, but every day he recalled how close he'd come to the edge after losing control. The consequences of which would have been far-reaching and...dismal. Catastrophic.

The very next day he'd joined the army—the best decision of his life. Yeah, it had been tough at first, but he'd got three square meals every day and, while he'd been shouted at all the time, he'd realised that it wasn't personal. He'd tolerated it at first and then he'd loved it; it had become, in a way, an inadequate substitution for the family he'd lost.

He'd moved around in the Forces, eventually ending up in the SAS.

Before leaving for Catterick, for his initial training, he'd arranged for a local care-giver to provide Michael with the help he needed: cooking, cleaning and, he'd hoped, occasional bathing. The cost of his care had come out of his meagre army salary, but it had been a small price to pay for his freedom.

He was still paying.

'Your brothers haven't called or visited for over six months.' Michael moaned.

He didn't blame them.

'Useless, both of them. Living with those Robinsons has made them soft... Mike is working as a nancy photographer and Hamish is no better. A bloody chef... Jaysus...and you paid for their education. Waste of money, I tell you. They'll never amount to anything.'

The fact that Mike was working on a respected national newspaper and Hamish was working in a Michelin-starred restaurant as a sous-chef had passed Michael by. With their crazy schedules the brothers didn't spend nearly enough time together, Noah thought. While they emailed and called regularly, they didn't meet often and he missed them.

He had to make more time for them...

'I said I wouldn't take your calls any more if you slag off Hamish and Mike, Michael. Don't do it again,' Noah warned.

He wished he could break the ties with this old man but he was his father. *Family.* Warped, possibly nuts...but you didn't just walk away from your responsibilities. You took what was tossed at you and you dealt with it. But, hell, hadn't he paid enough, done enough, sacrificed enough?

Michael did have one use, though: he was a reminder of how dangerous Noah could be if he lost control. Apart from Michael, the only person who'd managed to push his buttons, to get past the steel lid he kept on his emotions, was that blonde bombshell next door.

And that scared the bejesus out of him. Why her? He'd met a lot of women over the past fifteen years. He'd had successful girls, poor girls, crazy girls and, after he'd finished guarding them, a couple of famous girls.

None of them had made him think of *what ifs* or *maybes*, of moving below the surface stuff of good sex and a couple of laughs. No one except Morgan had ever tempted him to walk into the minefield that was a committed relationship. He'd grown up watching his mother trying to keep her head above water with his crazy, cruel father and he had no intention of being swept away by love and spending the rest of his life trying to get back to shore.

But the fact remained that nobody made him crazy like Morgan Moreau.

Morgan looked up as Noah entered the kitchen via the balcony door. He looked decisive, authoritative, commanding: a natural leader that others looked up to. Dark suit, a white shirt over that broad chest, sombre grey tie hanging loose down his shirt to be tied later.

He also looked freakin' hot!

A shoulder holster held what looked like a very nasty gun...*whoa!*

'When did you get a gun? And from whom?' Morgan demanded, wide eyes on its black matte handle-butt-thingy poking out from the holster.

'It was dropped off early this morning,' Noah replied, heading for the coffee machine and reaching for a cup from the shelf above it. 'Don't worry, I'm licensed to carry a concealed weapon.'

Morgan gripped the back of one of the kitchen counter stools. 'You didn't have one in Cape Town.'

Noah flipped her a look over his shoulder as he tossed sugar into his black coffee. 'Yeah, I did. You just never saw it. Ankle holster when I was wearing jeans. Tucked into the back of my shorts or in my rucksack when we were on the beach. You weren't considered too much of a target so we took the decision not to scare you.'

'Huh.' Morgan wrapped her hands around her now cold coffee cup. Had she been that oblivious? Sure, she'd been nineteen, and blinded by the mammoth crush she'd had on Noah. He could have had a third leg and she would have ignored that too...

So, had anything changed? Morgan wondered. Actually, yes. There was a difference between crushing on him and crushing on his body. This thing between them was purely, utterly, comprehensively physical. *That's my story and I'm sticking to it,* she thought.

'Have they heard anything else about the other kidnappers yet?' she asked. If she knew anything about Noah then she knew that he would be on top of the situation, demanding updates as any came in.

'It's only been twelve hours, Morgan. And they've probably gone underground. New York is a city of eight million people; it's easy to disappear. It'll take time, hard looking and luck to flush them out.'

Morgan sighed and rested her chin in the palm of her hand. 'So, I'm stuck with you for the foreseeable future?'

'Seems like it,' Noah replied equably.

Morgan fiddled with the flat gold chain that rested against her emerald silk top. She'd teamed the shirt with white skinny jeans and black wedges. A black fitted jacket and a scarf would take the outfit from casual to smart. She tapped her finger against her coffee cup and eyed him over the rim. Should she ask this? Hmm, probably not...

What the hey? she thought. *Let's see what he says.*

'So, who's Michael?'

Noah's blue eyes hardened. 'Where did you hear that name?'

'My bedroom window was open; you can hear pretty much everything anyone says out there.'

'I must remember that.' Noah sipped his coffee, leaning against the kitchen counter as he did so. Morgan twisted her lips in annoyance; Noah was an expert in ducking questions he didn't want to answer.

Except that her curiosity was revving in the red zone. There had been something in Noah's voice earlier that she'd never heard before. It had been a combination of resignation, weariness and resentment. A little younger and a lot sad. For a couple of minutes he hadn't been the hard-eyed, hard-assed man who radiated confidence and determination. He'd just sounded like a man with some baggage who desperately wanted to put it in storage.

'And who are Hamish and Mike? Come on—you can tell me...'

'So, what's your schedule like for today?' Noah asked, his expression warning her to back off. Way off.

She wanted to push, to dig a little deeper, a little harder, but it wasn't his grim mouth or ferocious expression that had her hesitating.

It was the misery she saw under the tough-guy expression in his eyes. He didn't intimidate her in the least, didn't scare her one iota, but that flash of desolation had her stopping in her tracks.

'Off-limits subject?'

'Very.'

'Okay.'

His jaw relaxed; his fingers loosened on his coffee cup. 'What are your plans for the day, the week?' he asked again.

'I still have to meet with Cadigan about the security for the hotel, but if you promise to stay in the Moreau building then I won't have to drag you to that.'

'Like you could drag me anywhere,' Morgan scoffed.

A smile touched Noah's lips. 'Want to test that theory?'

He didn't wait for her answer, obviously super-confident that he could and would. Well, he might be stronger than her but he had no idea exactly how stubborn she could be. She'd match her stubbornness against his strength any time.

'Where's your schedule?' he demanded again. 'Diary? Calendar? Or do you have an assistant to keep track of your social life?'

'None of the above. It's all in my head.' She had a diary which she never used, and she didn't need an assistant.

'Publicist? Stylist?'

'Now you're just mocking me.' Morgan sighed and placed her forearms on the table. 'Once a week I call Mum's publicist and find out what functions are on for the next week that I absolutely *have* to attend.'

'How do you know that you've been invited?' Noah asked, pulling out a chair from the table and sitting down. He reached for an apple and crunched into it.

'It sounds ridiculous, I know, but we—the Moreaus— are invited to everything. It's a big social coup to get us to a function…well, maybe not so much my mother; she's a lot more socially active than my dad, James and me.'

Noah looked at his apple, took another bite, chewed and swallowed. 'You guys seem really happy, close…together. A golden family.'

Morgan leaned back and crossed her legs. 'Every family has its own problems, whether they are rich or poor. James spends far too much time alone because he's one of the world's most eligible bachelors. He can't trust a thing that comes out of any girl's mouth because he's convinced that they look at him and see an unlimited credit card, entry into a high social circle and houses all over the world.'

'What should they see?'

A smart, successful man who was lonelier than he needed to be? She wished he'd find someone. She wanted him to be happy. He'd been fabulous growing up...had spent hours—days—years!—helping her to read and write. Holding her when she cried, picking a fight when she needed to work off her frustration. Her older brother, her protector, the best person in her life.

Morgan swallowed and shrugged.

'And you? What's so wrong in your life? You're rich, gorgeous, successful.'

Lonely, isolated, scared that someone will find out that I'm chronically dyslexic and will judge me for it. Terrified to step out of my comfort zone; scared to try and fail... So frightened of disappointing myself and others that I'd rather not try something than run the risk of failing...

Yeah, she was a poster child for a healthy and happy It Girl.

'I have...issues... Don't we all?' See—she could duck the very personal questions too! She twisted the oversized Rolex on her arm and carried on. 'As for my parents—my dad and my mum love each other to death but can't live together long term...'

'But they're trying to revitalise their marriage,' Noah protested. 'She's handing over control to James!'

'James, for all intents and purposes, has been running MI for the past two years. They both pretend that Mum still has her hand in, but in reality James calls the shots and she likes it that way.'

Morgan let out a sound that was half a snort and half a laugh.

'Scenes like yesterday's happen every so often—normally when my mum wants something and doesn't know how else to get it. She wants me involved in MI and she's determined to get me into the fold. Organising the ball is the first step. I guarantee that if I'd refused to do it—as I had intended to—

she would've been back in the city within a week, organising the ball, poking her nose into MI business and driving James crazy. She'd also have been telling me that my dad drove her nuts and there was a reason why they lived apart.'

Morgan scowled at her coffee cup. 'I love my mother dearly, but she's a force of nature and determined to get her own way. If she could find the kidnappers she'd probably say thank you to them for forcing her to leave the country, because now I *have* to organise this damn ball.'

'Harsh,' Noah said, but humour glinted in his eyes. 'Paranoid too. So what's the big deal about this ball? Suck it up and do it.'

Morgan glared at him. 'Easy for you to say. Anyway, back to the original subject…'

'Your social life…or lack of it.'

'Which is about to change because I'm expected to go out and about, promote the ball and get a buzz going. Got a tux?' Morgan demanded.

'Not here.'

'You're going to need one if you intend to accompany me to these functions.'

'And I do.'

'The biggest danger I face there is being bored to death, closely followed by the effects of a rogue margarita or a cheeky cosmopolitan.' Morgan pushed her cup away.

'Listen—and don't shoot the messenger—I need to go as your date,' Noah stated. He lifted a shoulder at the annoyed look on her face. 'Yes, I know what I said…we now have a completely professional relationship. But somehow, miraculously, the kidnapping attempt hasn't hit the papers and the MI PR person and the police want to keep it that way. James has a bodyguard occasionally but you don't. You having one now is going to raise questions that they'd prefer not to answer. So they want us to…*pretend*. James called me this morning and issued the directive.'

Morgan looked at him, caught completely off guard. 'What? You've got to be joking.'

'Trust me, I'd rather just be the bodyguard,' Noah muttered.

Morgan held up her hand. 'So, let me see if I've got this right. We were about to make love, because you weren't—quite—working for MI and I wasn't going to have anything to do with the ball. A one-night deal that worked for both of us which didn't happen because *you* volunteered your close protection services and told me that I am categorically off-limits. And now we have to pretend that we are lovers? Is this a sick joke?'

'Either that or someone has concocted a great way to torture us,' Noah agreed.

Morgan held her head between her hands and closed her eyes. 'This is going to drive me crazy.'

'We can share the padded cell,' Noah agreed.

'Any chance of you resigning?' Morgan lifted her head and looked at him, hope on her face.

'Sorry, Duchess. Not a chance. I'd rather go mad with you than go out of my mind worrying about you if I were off the job. Burying you would also suck.'

Ah, nuts… That was a hard point to argue.

CHAPTER SIX

In her studio Morgan squinted at her computer screen and groaned audibly. She was stuck on the first page of the computerised file that detailed all the steps for organising the Moreau Charity Ball and she was already frustrated. Irritated. And, worse, shaking with fear in her designer shoes.

Date of event determined?
Liaise with banqueting manager at F-G.
Determine specific target audience for personal invites.
Objectives set in accordance to mission statement and vision of MI Foundation.
Complete risk assessment; not only to security of gemstone collection but also to brand and customer perception.

Dear Lord, she thought fifteen minutes later, couldn't they use plain English—and why was it so vague? Where was the 'how to do' part of the list? She hadn't even been aware that the MI Foundation *had* a mission statement, and she'd thought the vision was simple: raise and donate money.

Dammit, *this* was why she shouldn't be in charge of anything more complicated than *See Jane Run*.

Her mother had to be taking a new hormone pill to think

that she could organise the ball—never mind her crazy idea of joining MI as Brand and Image Director.

Morgan swallowed the tears that had gathered in the back of her throat. 'I am not stupid,' she whispered under her breath, glaring at the screen. 'I am not stupid. I am *not* stupid.'

Okay, then, why do I feel so stupid?

Morgan heard the rap on her door and looked up to see Noah through the glass window. She tapped the tip of one index finger with the other, indicating that he should use the finger scanner to enter. Two seconds later the door was opening and Noah, *sans* jacket and tie, entered her studio. She hastily slammed the lid of her laptop closed and inwardly cringed. What could be more mortifying than Noah finding out the scope of her learning problems? There wasn't a lot, she decided as he held the door open and looked at the finger scanner.

'Nifty. A retina scanner would be better, but the fingerprint scanner isn't bad.'

Morgan leaned back in her chair and crossed her legs. 'If the scanner worked then I presume that Security gave you everything you needed to negotiate your way through this super-secure building?'

'Yep.' Noah looked around her studio and she winced at the mess.

On the wooden benches across one wall sat her presses and pliers, mandrels and blocks. Hammers, files, more presses. The wall above it was covered in sketches, some finished, of ring and necklace designs, all of which held the name of the client scribbled across it and the price quoted.

She bit her lip and wondered what he'd think of her studio, with its plants and cosy seating, battered bench and industrial lighting. Yeah, it was eclectic and messy, colourful, but it worked for her. She could sit down at the bench and fall into a creative space that exhilarated her and made time fly. Sometimes the designs changed from the original sketch she'd been working to, but she'd yet to have a client complain of the changes made since they were all, invariably, better for it.

She sighed. Designing jewellery was probably the only aspect of her life that she felt completely confident about.

Noah walked over to the bench and squinted at her sketches. She saw his head pull back and presumed that he was reacting to the prices.

'Can I ask you something jewellery-related?'

Morgan's head shot up—not so much at the question but at the note of tension in his voice.

'Sure.' Oh, yeah, his body was coiled tight, and she narrowed her eyes as he pulled his wallet out from the back pocket of his black pants. He flipped it open, dug in a tight fold and pulled out a silver ring with a red stone. He tossed it to her and she snatched it out of the air.

'What's the stone?'

Before looking at the gem, Morgan looked at the setting. The band was old silver, a delicate swirl of filigree, feminine but with strong lines. Lovely, she thought. Really lovely. Whoever had made the ring was a superb craftsman, she decided as she picked up her loupe and walked over to the window. Holding the ring between two fingers, she lifted the loupe to her eye, angled the ring to the light and the breath caught in her throat. Red beryl, one of her favourite stones; very gorgeous and very rare.

'Bixbite or red beryl. Very rare. Very valuable.'

Noah walked over to her, stared down at the ring and frowned. 'Nah, can't be.'

Morgan arched an eyebrow at him. 'You a gemmologist now, soldier? Trust me on this: it's red beryl, my favourite stone…probably set around nineteen-twenty. It would've been mined from the Wah Wah mountain range in Utah.'

'Huh.'

Morgan frowned when Noah reached out, plucked the ring out of her grip with possessive fingers and put it back into his wallet. 'Where did you get it? And why can't it be valuable?' she asked.

Noah just shrugged and Morgan put her hand on his arm to keep him from turning away. 'Answering my question is my price for the valuation.'

'It was my mother's—passed down from my grandmother. I was given it shortly after she died and I've kept it with me ever since. It would be my lucky charm if I believed in lucky charms,' Noah said, with the reluctance of a child facing a dentist's appointment. 'Her family wasn't…wealthy, so I'm surprised that they possessed something this valuable.'

Forget reluctance. Now he sounded as if he was having root canal without pain relief. Noah did *not* like talking about himself or his family. She wanted to ask how his mother had died—and when—but his expression was forbidding. She wasn't brave enough to go there.

'It's very lovely. And it either belongs on a finger or in a safe, soldier,' Morgan said. His expression begged her to change the subject so she relented. 'How did the meeting go with the Head of Security at the Forrester?'

Noah turned away and walked over to the window, looking down on the busy road beneath them. 'I have some concerns that he needs to address. I'll put them in a report and email it to you.'

Morgan wrinkled her nose. 'Can't you tell me instead?'

'What is it with you and your hatred of reading reports?' Noah asked, resting his butt on the window sill. Sunlight picked up deep golden-brown streaks in his hair and created a bit of an aura around his head. He looked like a rough, tough, gun-toting bad-ass angel.

Morgan clenched her thighs together and ignored the pulsing down below. She really had to get her hormones under control. This was beyond ridiculous.

'Uh…reports. They are just a hassle to read.'

Noah's eyebrows pulled together. 'You don't like reading?'

'Not particularly.'

Noah crossed his legs at the ankles and folded his arms. 'So, what *do* you read? *Tatler* and *Heat*?'

And there he went, making assumptions. 'If I don't like going out in society why would I want to read about it? Actually, *snob*, my favourite authors are Jane Austen and Ernest Hemingway. Harper Lee, John Steinbeck—all the classics.'

'But you just said that you don't like to read.'

Yeah, but not that I don't love books. She did love books— devoured them by the bucket load. Except that along with the paperback she bought the audio book, so that she could read along. Truthfully, she frequently just opted to listen and not read.

Morgan flipped Noah a look and saw that he was looking very confused. Right, time to change the subject before he probed a little deeper. She wasn't ready—probably would never be—to tell him about her dyslexia. It wasn't something she believed he needed to know— now or ever.

'I have a list of this month's events that I need to attend,' Morgan said, picking up the piece of paper she'd printed earlier from the email she'd received from Helen. She walked over to Noah and watched as he speed-read the document. Lucky man.

'Ballet? *Uck.* A ball? Save me… But I can handle the art exhibition; I really like Davie's work.'

'You know Johnno's art?' Morgan asked, surprised.

Noah folded his arms and tipped his head. 'Now who's being a snob? I went to his exhibition in London. Fantastic.'

'Do you have any of his pieces?'

'Duchess, I could only afford to look—not buy.' Noah drawled. 'Maybe one day. Anyway, my partner can't find my tux in my flat. I think it's at the cleaners and has been for the last six months.'

'You left your tux at the cleaners for six months?'

'I've been in and out of the country and I forgot, okay? My tux wasn't high up on my list of priorities. So when do

I need a tux by…?' He looked at the piece of paper she'd handed him. 'Crap! Tonight?'

'Yep.' Morgan laughed at his look of horror.

'Jeez, give me some warning next time.' Noah grumbled.

'Hey, *I'm* the one who has to decide what to wear, do my hair, shoes, jewellery. Make-up. You just have to put on a tux. Big deal,' Morgan shot back. It took work to look like the Moreau heiress people expected to see. A designer dress, stunning salon hair, perfect make-up. The right jewels for the right dress.

'Yeah, but I have to get a tux and get into character…you know…work out how I'm going to pretend to have the hots for you. It's a difficult job, but someone has to do it.'

She was so distracted by the humour dancing in his eyes that it took a while for his words to make sense. When they did she blushed from head to toe and her fist rocketed into his bicep. It made all the impact of a single drop of rain falling in the desert.

'Jerk!'

'Was that supposed to be a punch?' Noah asked, and grinned as she shook her fingers out. '*Wuss*. So, are you going to stay here for the rest of the afternoon while I go and buy myself a tux? Can I trust you to do that?'

Morgan shoved out her lower lip. 'Maybe.'

Noah's face hardened and his mouth flattened. 'You leave this building without me and there will be hell to pay, *Duchess*.'

Morgan pulled in a huge breath. She didn't mind him calling her Duchess, but not in that cold, bossy voice. 'I'm not an idiot, *soldier*. I won't leave until you get back. And if you weren't being such a jerk I'd tell you that if you went across the road to that very famous store over there—' she looked past him and pointed her finger towards the renowned corner shop '—in the men's department there is a salesperson named Norman. In his sixties, bald. Tell him I sent you and he'll sort you out with what you need.'

Morgan was surprised when Noah leaned over and placed his cool lips, very briefly, on her temple. 'Thanks.'

Morgan watched him walk away, and he was at the door before she realised that kissing her was out of bounds too. 'Hey, no kissing!'

Noah tossed her a grin that had her blood pumping. 'Just practising for later. Do some work, Duchess, you have a ball to organise.'

Morgan wrinkled her nose. Sad, but true.

Being a bodyguard pretending to be her latest conquest sucked, Noah thought a couple of hours later in the ballroom of the Park Hyatt, half listening to Morgan as she talked 'ball' to a society matron with a pigeon-egg-sized diamond in her wrinkly cleavage. Doing it with a twitching groin made the situation a thousand times worse.

It was her dress, Noah decided, taking the smallest sip of the glass of whisky he'd been nursing for hours. Moss-green and strapless, it fell from her breasts and skimmed her hips. At first glance it almost seemed demure, slightly bohemian, off-beat. Then she moved and the long slit to one side exposed most of a slim thigh and his blood belted south. That thigh was smooth and silky, and even sexier because nothing covered it except perfect, perfect skin.

Funny and interesting… She was a killer combination. Bright as anything too. She picked up sarcasm, nuances, innuendo and irony, and he could read humour, annoyance and interest as the emotions flickered into her eyes. She'd been fêted all evening and he now realised what she'd meant when she'd said that the Moreaus were welcome everywhere. Conversation stopped when she joined a group, male tongues fell to the floor, women smiled and tried not to look jealous, and she was constantly and persistently asked about the ball.

'How do we get personally invited to the ball?'

'How much do you think we have to bid to secure a ticket?'

'Do you have a theme yet?'

'Do remind your mother that we served together on the blah-blah-blah committee and worked together on the meh-meh-meh project.'

Didn't these people have any pride?

But Morgan just smiled, changed the subject and moved on to another group if the person was too persistent.

'Don't you think so, Noah?' Morgan asked, and Noah sent her a blank look.

Morgan's lips lifted, and he knew by the gleam in her eye that she knew his thoughts were miles away.

'That this year's ball is going to be utterly amazing?' she clarified.

'Uh…yes…'

Wrinkly cleavage leaned across Morgan and showed him far more of what he didn't need to see. 'So, how long have you two been dating?' she demanded.

Oh… Noah looked at Morgan and waited for her to answer.

'We've known each other a long time, Vi,' Morgan said softly, her eyes on his mouth.

The twitch turned to an ache.

'Well, he's a lot better that a lot of those other creatures you've dated, Morgan.'

Morgan's lips lifted with amusement and she tipped her head. 'You don't think he looks too bodyguardish? All "don't mess with me or I'll wipe the floor with your face"?'

'Sitting right here,' Noah reminded them.

'Is that a bad thing?' Vi demanded. 'He *does* have very nice shoulders.'

'Mmm…and a nice butt.'

Noah glared at Morgan and lowered his voice. 'Morgan… enough.' As in *Behave yourself or I'm going to retaliate.*

He knew that she'd got the message because her eyes narrowed at his challenge. Noah looked up at the waiter who had placed the next course in front of her and saw the other plate he held—*his* plate!—wobble as his young knees buck-led under the force of that smile. He couldn't blame him, so he snatched at his plate before the mini-cheese platter ended up in his lap.

Morgan smiled at him before turning to another man on the table. Noah sneaked a look at his watch...it was after eleven already, and people were table-hopping or getting up to dance.

Maybe they could leave soon...

'Morgan, my honey, it's so nice to see you. We don't see enough of your pretty face at these events.'

Noah lifted his eyebrows at the plummy tones and looked at Morgan. The man had his eyes fixed on Morgan's chest and his manicured fingers rested on her shoulder. Noah, re-acting instinctively, slid his arm around the back of Morgan's chair, knocked his hand away and cupped her slim shoulder in his hand. Soft, silky...

Morgan turned slightly, leaned back towards him, and he caught a whiff of her hair: citrus and spice. Lust rock-eted to his groin.

'Morgan...' It was another voice demanding her attention.

Give the girl a break, Noah thought, turning to look up into the face of an elderly gentlemen who looked as if he could do with more than a couple of sessions in the gym and a year on a low-carb diet. Manners pulled them both to their feet and Noah watched as Morgan's knuckles were kissed in an old-fashioned gesture.

'It's so wonderful to have you here at the benefit, Mor-gan, and the room is abuzz with the news that you are taking over the reins of the charity ball from Hannah,' he gushed.

'Well, not quite, Alexander,' Morgan hedged. 'Mum is still in charge.'

'As you know, this ball aims to raise money for scholar-ships for deprived students in the poorer areas of our great city.'

Noah did an inner eye-roll at his pompous words, but Alexander wasn't quite done with the speechmaking.

'Our foundation was a recipient of a portion of the money raised from your ball five years ago, so I thought that you could do a short speech about the ball. In a couple of minutes? Wonderful.'

Smooth, Noah thought, he hadn't given her much chance to refuse.

'And who is your escort, Morgan?' Alexander held out a hand to Noah, which Noah shook. 'Alexander Morton—of Morton's International…banking, dear boy.'

Even when he'd *been* a boy he'd never been anyone's 'dear boy', Noah thought as he shook the soft, fishy hand and resisted the urge to wipe his own on his pants leg.

Morgan made a couple of standard responses to Alexander's queries after her family, but he could hear the tension in her voice, could see it in her suddenly tense jaw.

She was seriously and completely rattled. He wondered why.

Pretend they are naked, Morgan told herself as she gripped the podium and looked out over the expectant faces below. *No, don't think they are naked, you're feeling traumatised enough. They are cabbages…they are dolls…*

They were people waiting for her to fall flat on her face. She wasn't going to disappoint them…

Dear God, she thought, sucking in air, this was her worst nightmare. The room whirled and swirled. She couldn't find the words, didn't know what to say…what was she doing up here? She didn't—couldn't—do speeches, especially unprepared ones.

Her knuckles whitened and she gnawed on her lip as the murmurs from the restless crowd drifted up towards her.

Help. She pulled her tongue down from the top of her mouth and managed to find a few words. 'Um…good evening, ladies and gentlemen.'

Bats! What now? She couldn't think, couldn't find the words... *frozen, there* was the word. She was utterly iced up.

Then Morgan felt movement next to her and a large, familiar hand rested on hers and gently lifted her stiff fingers from the podium.

'Good evening, ladies and gentlemen, my name is James Moreau. Thank you for allowing Morgan and I a few minutes to tell you about the Moreau Charity Ball.'

James... She hadn't even known that he was at the ball tonight. Rescued again. Morgan briefly closed her eyes and felt the panic recede. *Thank you, my darling big brother.*

Morgan squeezed James's hand in gratitude and linked her fingers in his as she listened to his fluid off-the-cuff speech. He soon had his audience laughing and eating out of his hand...the smooth-talking devil.

'I owe you,' she said under cover of the applause. 'I was bulldozed up here.'

'Then bulldoze back, Morgs,' James retorted. 'What would you have done if I wasn't here?'

'I don't have a clue,' Morgan admitted as he led her back into the clapping fray. She tugged her hand out of James's and wiped her glistening forehead with the tips of her fingers. 'I need to visit the ladies' room.'

James gave her a critical look. 'You're as white as a sheet. You need lipstick and a shot of brandy.'

Morgan placed her hand on her sternum as her stomach churned. 'At the very, very least,' she agreed.

On the edge of the dance floor Morgan took the hand that Noah held out and stepped into his arms. He felt solid and strong...and best of all *real*. Just for a moment she wished she could place her head on his shoulder and rest awhile. This was why she hated the social swirl so much; the party-girl cloak she pulled on to get her through evenings like this weighed her down. She felt exhausted and such a fraud.

'So, what was that about?' Noah asked, his voice some-where above her temple.

'What?' It was a stupid question because she immediately knew what he was referring to.

'James rushing to your rescue? I never imagined that you would be at a loss for words. You looked like your knees were knocking together.'

Why did he have to be so perceptive? James had assured her that they'd pulled it off, that most people had thought she was just waiting for him to join her at the podium, but if that was so then why had Noah noticed her nerves? And if he had noticed how scared she was, who else had? Oh, bats, did that mean that everyone was laughing behind her back? Sniggering?

She stepped back, lifted her hands and tossed her head. 'I want to go home now,' she told him, pleased that her voice sounded reasonably steady.

'Why?' Noah demanded.

Because I feel like a fool... 'I have a headache.'

'Not buying it, Duchess.'

Noah placed his hand on her hip, picked up her hand again and pushed her back into the dance. She followed his lead automatically and wished that the floor could swallow her whole. She felt hot with humiliation and cold when she thought about what was being said behind her back.

Morgan made herself meet his far too discerning eyes and didn't realise that her pulse was beating a hard rhythm in the base of her throat.

'Noah, I simply don't care whether you think I am talking rubbish or not. I'm done with this evening, I'm done talk-ing and, frankly, I'm done with you too. I need some space and some time alone.' She shoved a hand into her hair. 'Can you, for once, just act like a bodyguard? Can you stop talk-ing, keep your opinions to yourself and just leave me the hell alone?'

Noah's head jerked back and his implacable remote mask dropped into place. 'Certainly.'

He gestured to the edge of the floor and kept a respectful distance as they walked back to the table. His voice was devoid of emotion when he spoke again. 'If you'll give me a minute, I'll just organise the car.'

Morgan felt a wave of shame as she watched his broad back move away. She'd taken a hunk of his hide because she was feeling vulnerable and mortified. But mostly because she knew that he was strong enough, secure enough, to take it.

It was the perfect end to a long and terrible evening.

'Where's Noah?' Riley asked, dumping her files on the coffee table in Morgan's lounge. Sinking to the silk carpet, Riley took a grateful sip from the glass of white wine Morgan handed her.

After nearly a week of living together, in the non-biblical sense, Noah had finally realised that she was safe alone in the apartment by herself, and every day after work he left her to make use of the state-of-the-art gym and indoor swimming pool within the apartment block, Morgan explained.

'So, how does it feel to be living with a man?' Riley asked, kicking off her heels and crossing her legs.

Morgan sat down on the edge of the couch opposite her and half shrugged. 'Weird, actually.'

'And are you still in separate beds?'

Morgan glared at her. 'What do you think?'

'Judging by that killer look, I'd say your hormones are on a constant low simmer.'

'You should know,' Morgan replied.

As Riley was the only person outside of her family who knew about her dyslexia, Morgan was the only person who knew that Riley had fallen in love with James at first sight and had never quite managed to tumble out of it. She covered her feelings towards him by acting like a diva artist whenever he was around.

'He wants me to do an underwater theme for the windows next month,' Riley grumbled, reading her thoughts.

'Why?'

'Because he's just been scuba diving in Belize and was "blown away" by the coral reefs. I told him that I needed personal experience to do a theme like that.'

Knowing that would never have been the end of their conversation, Morgan tipped her head. 'And he said what in reply?'

'He used that super-sarcastic tone of his and said…' Riley tossed her bright red hair and lowered her voice. '"Then why don't I just take you with me next time?"'

'Jeez, I just wish you and James would get your stuff together, find a room, get it on and then get on with living happily ever after.'

'Like he's ever going to see me as anything other than your best friend.' Riley tapped her nail against her glass. 'Oh, wait—are you talking about us or about you and Noah?'

'Both of us. Although that won't happen to Noah and I.'

'Why not?'

'This thing between us is purely physical, Ri. We don't discuss anything personal.'

'Why not?' Riley repeated.

Morgan shrugged.

'Don't want to venture further down the rabbit hole?' Riley asked.

Morgan looked up at the ceiling.

'I think he might be the one guy who'd understand the dyslexia, Morgs.'

'I doubt it,' Morgan replied, leaning back and putting her feet up on the coffee table. 'He's a perfectionist: highly driven and ambitious. Besides, Noah and I…it would be just about sex—about this crazy chemical reaction we have to each other.'

'You like each other.'

'We don't *know* each other.' Morgan took a huge sip of

wine and rested the glass against her cheek. 'Anyway, I'm not looking for a relationship with Noah. Sex—yes…have you seen that body?'

'Shallow as a puddle.' Riley grinned before leaning back on her hands. 'To be honest, I think you don't tell the guys you date about the dyslexia because you hope they'll bail.'

'Oh, come on!'

'Oh, you *so* do. How many times have you met a nice guy? You date and then you sleep together. Things go really well until he starts picking up that things are a bit off. That you don't write down a message properly or you get the directions to a restaurant wrong. You don't explain and you retreat.'

'I don't do that,' she protested, even though she knew she did.

Riley gave her a hard look. 'Noah isn't like that, Morgan. He wouldn't hold the dyslexia against you.'

'Back away, Ri,' Morgan warned. 'Nobody understands until they have to live with me. You know what I'm like. Sometimes the reading is easy; other days I can barely read my own name. I would drive him crazy in six months. I'm inconsistent, and that's annoying and confusing. Some days I can take on the world; sometimes I can't even read simple instructions. I hate those black holes, and if *I* find them difficult to deal with how would my lover feel?'

'You should at least respect them enough to give them a chance to try.'

'I respect myself too much to be constantly putting my heart out there to possibly be broken,' Morgan retorted.

'Are you feeling comfortable in your little self-protected world?' Riley asked sweetly.

'Yes, thank you very much! The world expects something from "the Moreau heiress" and being chronically dyslexic isn't part of the package.'

Riley mimed playing the violin and Morgan threw a cushion at her head. Riley groaned as it hit her wine glass and wine splashed all over the table.

Noah walked in through the front door as the wine glass fractured and broke. He looked from Riley to the broken glass and back to the spilt wine before finally looking at Morgan. 'Duchess; are you throwing a temper tantrum because another of your subjects has disagreed with you?'

CHAPTER SEVEN

AFTER ORDERING PIZZA from their favourite pizzeria Morgan called James, checked that he was home and told him to come down and share their meal. He arrived with two bottles of her favourite wine: a Merlot from their winery in Stellenbosch.

'One for you and one for Riley, my two favourite wine-o-holics,' he said, depositing them on the kitchen counter. 'Hey, Ri.'

'James.'

James yanked open a drawer and pulled out a corkscrew. 'Started on the designs for my underwater window yet?'

'Yeah, I've scheduled it in for...*never*. Does that work for you?' Riley replied as she opened a cupboard door and took out four glasses.

'You *do* remember that I sign your paycheque, don't you?' James retorted.

'Then fire me; I'll pick up a job with Saks or Bergdorfs with one phone call. And they'll double my salary,' Riley replied in the same genial tone. 'Actually, why don't *you* double my salary and I'll consider staying?'

'Okay, I'll schedule that in for...*never*. Does that work for you?' James dumped some wine into her glass and handed it over. 'Cheers.'

'Bite me.' Riley took the glass and stomped over to the lounge, resuming her seat on the floor next to the coffee table.

Morgan rolled her eyes at Noah, who was sitting at the dining room table, his laptop in front of him, a glass of whisky at his elbow. He was dressed in battered faded jeans and a casual cotton shirt and his feet were bare. Sure, he was a sexy man, but he was also a man who didn't hold a grudge. They'd had a rocky day or two following her outburst at the ball and now they were back to being friends.

But it would be so much more fun if he was hanging around because he wasn't being paid to do so.

'Is anyone doing anything about finding those kidnappers?' she demanded, putting her hands on her hips and glaring at James.

'Only the NYPD, our own security and another private investigation firm I hired to find them. That not enough for you, Your Majesty?' James pushed a glass across the granite counter in her direction.

'Your Majesty? That's even better than Duchess!' Noah smirked.

'Call me that and you're dead,' Morgan warned him. 'Riley and I need to talk about themes for the ball,' she said, hastily changing the subject. 'Would you like to be part of that conversation?'

James and Noah exchanged identical horrified looks. 'Sports channel?'

'Hell, yeah!' Noah agreed, and followed James to the smaller second lounge. It held a large-screen TV and two comfortable couches.

He spoke over his shoulder to Morgan. 'Call me when the pizza arrives. I'll go down and get it. Do *not* leave the apartment.'

'Blah-blah-blah,' Morgan muttered in reply, and pulled her tongue at his back.

'I saw that!' Noah called, without turning around.

Morgan pulled her tongue again at his reply.

'I saw that too.'

Grrr.

* * *

'Treasure ship, masked ball, burlesque, the Russian Court, Vegas,' Morgan listed through mouthfuls of pizza. They were surrounded by files of fabric samples and Riley's rough sketches. Morgan was curled up into the corner of the couch, Riley was still in place on the floor, and James sat in the chair behind her, his long legs on either side of her slim frame. Noah sat in the other chair, a glass of gorgeous red wine on the table next to him.

It could be a group of friends in any other lounge in any other city in the world, just hanging out and eating excellent pizza. It was so normal, and he was still coming to terms with how normal the Moreau siblings could be. Yes, James ran a multi-billion-dollar corporation, and Morgan had an unlimited trust fund, but nobody, seeing them now, would guess that.

'I like the burlesque theme. Bold, opulent, sexy.' Morgan said dreamily. 'We could have various stages scattered throughout the ballroom with different acts to the same singer. Burlesque routines, circus acts, acrobatics…'

'Strippers?' James asked hopefully, and Noah smiled.

Morgan sent him a cold look. 'Would you like me to get disinherited? Or to be dead because our mother has killed me? Anyway, we could have models dressed in corsets and thigh-high stockings and masquerade masks, all wearing Moreau jewellery.'

Noah's head whipped up as her words made sense in his head. 'Not a chance,' Noah told her. 'No live models wearing any jewellery.'

'Why not?' Morgan demanded. 'It would be brilliant…'

'It would be stupid,' Noah replied. 'You're adding a human element that can be exploited; nobody but me and your curator gets access to those jewels.'

'But…' Morgan started to protest.

Noah stared her down. 'My reputation, my rules. Remember?'

'*Arrgh*. We'll discuss it another time,' Morgan said.

She was like a dog with a bone, Noah thought. Stubborn and wilful. Why did that turn him on? Then again, everything about her turned him on.

Riley leaned her head on James's knee and yawned. Noah noticed that James lifted his hand to touch her hair, thought about it and dropped it again. Oh, yeah, there was definitely something brewing with those two. Some day the lid on their self-control would pop and they'd find themselves in a heap of trouble.

Just like he would…

Living with Morgan was killing him. Not sleeping with Morgan made every day a torture. And he knew that she felt exactly the same way. He saw it in the way she looked at him; her eyes would deepen with passion and her breath would catch in her throat and he'd know…just know…that she had them naked and up against the wall. When…*if*…they finally got to do this, New York would experience a quake of significant proportions.

Unfortunately his problems with Morgan went a lot deeper than he'd ever thought possible. Right down to the core of who he was.

He'd never had such a physical reaction to anyone, *ever*. Why it had to be Morgan he had no idea. She could send him from nought to sixty in a heartbeat and have him laughing while she did it. And that was the reason why he had to keep his distance from her—physically, emotionally. He would never give anyone control over him.

She had the ability to make him lose it; definitely in bed, possibly emotionally and, most terrifying of all, in anger. She really knew how to push his buttons. What if they had a fight and he was pushed too far? What would he do? Who would he become? Would he revert to that angry feral boy who'd stood in that grotty kitchen and held a knife to his father's throat? The kid who had watched as droplets of blood beaded on that stubbled neck, enjoyed the sour smell of fear that permeated the air? The Noah who had seriously considered ending it all…the insults, the abuse, the weight of responsibility that had landed on his shoulders?

That person scared him: the uncontrolled, wild, crazy person he could be when he allowed emotion to rule. He was currently locked in a cage and sensible; controlled Noah kept guard over him. And sensible Noah could only do that if he stayed away from emotional complications. Like Morgan.

He couldn't afford to let Morgan in, to allow his guard down, to be the person he could be…

It wasn't going to happen with her or with anyone else.

'What do you think, Noah?' James asked him.

Noah pulled himself back to the conversation. What had they been talking about? Were they still discussing the theme of the ball?

'Burlesque sounds good,' he said lamely.

Morgan laughed as she tossed the crust of her slice of pizza into the empty box. 'Where did you go? We're talking about going home for the wedding. We're leaving in a fortnight.'

Noah sat up, ran a hand over his lower jaw and slapped his brain into gear. 'Back up. Going home? Where? What wedding? Why didn't you tell me about this?'

Morgan pouted. 'I'd hoped this would be over by then.'

'I asked you for a detailed schedule of everything you were committed to in the foreseeable future. Why wasn't this wedding on it?' Noah demanded. How was he supposed to protect her if she didn't keep him informed? Honestly, it was like dealing with an octopus with twenty tentacles.

Riley looked at James. 'I think this is our cue to leave so that they can fight without an audience.'

'I do not fight,' Noah growled. 'I negotiate.'

'No, he orders. He just tells me what to do and expects me to stand there and take it,' Morgan agreed, unfurling her long legs. She stood up, kissed Riley and then James on their cheeks as she said goodnight.

James hugged her, stood back and brushed her hair from her forehead. 'You're my sister, and I know you can be a pain in the butt. Don't make this harder for him than it has to be. Don't forget to tell him about Johnno's exhibition tomorrow night, and the Moreau Polo Cup Challenge on Saturday at Liberty Park. Then we go to the wedding in Stellenbosch in two weeks' time.'

'Got it.' Morgan cut Noah a glance, and when she spoke again her attitude was pure factitiousness. 'Noah, we have an art exhibition tomorrow night, a polo cup on Saturday and a wedding in Stellenbosch in two weeks' time. Put them on the schedule.'

Noah's face promised retaliation. *Bring it on, soldier.*

Noah bade Riley and James goodnight and waited until the door had closed behind them before turning back to Morgan. 'Stellenbosch, South Africa?'

'Yep,' Morgan answered flippantly.

He didn't respond—just waited for a further explanation for why she hadn't thought it was important to fill him in.

Morgan tapped her foot in irritation. 'The kidnappers are in New York. I'm going on the private jet to my home town, where I know everyone, to a wedding that has more security than the Pentagon.'

'Why?'

'Merri, my friend, is marrying into a very influential, very connected political family. Security will be tight.'

'And where will you be staying?'

'At Bon Chance—our house on the family farm. Vineyard.' Morgan picked up the empty pizza boxes and the bottle of wine. 'Grab the glasses, will you?'

'Good plan, since you might throw something when I tell you that I'm coming too.'

Morgan's shoulders stiffened at his sarcasm. 'I told you—it's not necessary. James and Riley will be staying in the house, as well as James's protection people, and the wedding will be secure. The kidnappers are here in New York!'

Noah walked over to the dishwasher, yanked it open and dumped the glasses inside. 'I'm going, Morgan. Until the threat to you is neutralised I'm sticking to you like a shadow. Now, I can either go as your date-cum-bodyguard or just as your bodyguard. I'm equally comfortable with either. Your choice.'

'That might be a bit awkward.'

Awkward... He didn't see why. Morgan turned away and Noah frowned. Strangely it took him a minute to make the connection. 'You've asked someone else to be your date?'

Morgan nodded. 'Yes. '

Noah managed to keep his face implacable but inside he fought the urge to punch his fist into that shiny, fancy fridge. 'Who is he?' he said through gritted teeth.

'A friend. An old friend.'

'That's not all of it,' Noah pushed.

Morgan whirled around. 'Do you want the details? Okay, then! He's an ex-boyfriend who I'm still fond of. He's also a friend of Merri's and we keep in touch. Satisfied?'

'Not by a long shot,' Noah snapped, forcing down the green tide of jealousy swelling up his throat. He made himself stop thinking about Morgan in someone else's arms—dancing, laughing, flirting with another man. This was business... What would he do if it was only business?

He breathed deeply and forced himself to think the problem through. 'If the security at the wedding is as good as you say it is, then I'll deliver you to the wedding and pick you up when you're done.'

Morgan's eyes sparked with anger. 'What if I want to sleep over?'

Was she trying to kill him? Seriously? 'That's not going to happen, Duchess, unless it's with me.'

'Big words from a man who won't even let himself touch me unless he's pretending to be my date!' Morgan hissed.

Give me strength, Noah prayed. 'I gave your brother my word.' He pushed the words out through gritted teeth.

'Well, there's no law that says I have to wait for you, soldier. So if I want to sleep with someone then I will.'

'You bloody well won't!' Noah gripped her arms with his hands. His eyes glittered and he could feel his temper licking the edges of his tongue. 'What would be the point, anyway? You'd be imagining it was me the whole time.'

'You arrogant—' Morgan placed her hands on his chest and shoved.

Annoyed beyond reason, he gripped her shoulders with his big hands and fought the urge to shake her. Instead he slammed his mouth onto hers and yanked her up against his body. He placed one hand low on her back, fingers spread out over her backside, and his other hand held her head in place. Her made-for-sin mouth was hot below his.

Noah could feel her mentally fighting him, her mind cursing him, even though he knew that her body wanted this as much as he did. Pure orneryness kept her mouth clamped shut, and her slim body was rigid with shock. Dropping his hand from her head, he stroked her arm, urging her to relax, and eventually both their tempers ebbed away under the sensual heat they created.

He knew that Morgan was trying to fight the temptation to wind her arms around his neck and fall into his body. It seemed so long since he had touched her, and yet it was like yesterday. She was toned, yet fragile, hot and sexy.

Noah concentrated on applying exactly the right amount of pressure and kept his hands still. He kissed the corner of her mouth and slowly worked his way inwards, nibbling and caressing as he went along. His tongue flicked and retreated, coaxed hers out to play. He sighed in triumph as she groaned and opened her mouth to his. Instantly his tongue accepted her invitation and curled around hers while he pulled her close.

Unable to resist this a moment longer, Morgan threw her arms around his neck and moulded her body against his.

Plunging her fingers in his hair, she wound a calf around his and pressed herself up against his hard frame.

Long, luscious, passion-soaked minutes later Noah knew that he'd reached the point of no return—that if he carried on for another minute he would be lost, doing exactly what he wouldn't allow himself to do. It took every ounce of his legendary self-control to wrench his mouth from hers, to step back, to meet her eyes.

He moved his hand so that he held her jaw, brushed his thumb over her full bottom lip.

Morgan spoke, frustration in her passion-smoked voice. 'You're really stopping?'

He nodded and jammed his hands into the pockets of his jeans so that he didn't reach for her again. 'Really am.'

He watched as Morgan's smoky eyes cleared and confusion replaced heat. 'I don't know why, or how, you can even *start* it. Especially knowing that you're not going to take it further.'

All he knew for sure was that he was a masochist, a glutton for punishment. He could try to explain—temper, jealousy, they were all factors—but his biggest motivator was that at that moment he hadn't been able *not* to kiss her.

Noah watched as the last spark of fight went out of Morgan. She took a step towards him, dropped her head and curled her fingers into his shirt.

'I hate this,' she said in a small voice.

And he hated the thought that he—this crazy situation between them—could make her sound so small, defeated.

He resisted the urge to pull her into his embrace, to soothe her. He didn't do touchy-feely so he just stood there, trying to ignore the surge of protectiveness that threatened to knock his feet from under him.

'Hate what?' he asked quietly.

'This...all of this. The bodyguarding. Being so attracted to you, not being able to touch you, to get it...*you*...out of my system.' Morgan rested her forehead in the middle of his chest. 'It's horrible... I don't like feeling this out of control.'

'I know.'

He had to touch her, so Noah rubbed his hand up and down her spine. It was killing him too. His hand moved up between her shoulder blades onto her neck and under her head. He pulled the hair at the back of her neck and gently tipped her head back.

'I gave my word...it's important to me that I keep it,' he said, looking down into her mesmerising eyes.

'I know. Dammit...I *respect* that. I just don't *like* it!'

Tell him something he didn't know. He didn't consider it a lazy day on the beach either.

Morgan stepped back, wrapped her arms around her waist and tipped her head to one side. 'I wish I could yell at you—scream. I want to act like a diva and fire you and stomp away and throw things.'

'You can if it makes you feel better,' Noah offered on a small smile. He had to hand it to the lass: he never knew what she was going to say or do next—she was *never* predictable.

'Consider yourself yelled at and fired,' Morgan said on a long, tired sigh. She looked at him. 'Any chance of you saving me from the loony bin and actually staying fired?'

Uh, no. That wasn't happening. A cold shower would happen, but him leaving...? 'Nope.'

'Didn't think so,' Morgan grumbled as she left the kitchen.

'This is it.'

Morgan looked out of the window of the cab and frowned when she didn't see the swish art gallery she'd expected to see. She looked across the road but there was nothing in the immediate vicinity except a closed dry cleaners and a rather grubby-looking diner. The other side of the street held a pawn shop and a strip club.

Where were they?

'Are you sure this is three-six-two?' Morgan asked.

Dark eyes glared at her from the front seat of the cab. 'You said six-three-two, lady. Three-six-two is uptown.'

Morgan closed her eyes at his harsh voice.

'Take it easy, buddy,' Noah said in a calm voice.

'She said six-three-two,' the cabbie insisted.

'You'll still get paid, so relax.' Noah laid a hand on her knee. 'Where's the invite, Morgan? Let's check the address.'

Morgan felt heat infuse her cheeks and rise up her neck and was grateful for the early evening shadows in the cab. She flipped open her clutch bag and pulled out the invitation. She glanced at the numbers and thrust the invitation towards the taxi driver.

'Six-three-two,' she muttered.

The driver glanced down at the invitation and shook his head in disgust. 'Jeez, lady, whassa matter wi' you? This says two-three-six!'

'Back off, man, she made a mistake,' Noah said in a hard, cold voice, and with a final huff the driver whirled around in his seat, slammed the car into gear and abruptly pulled off into the traffic.

Morgan licked her lips and waited for Noah's probing questions as they retraced their route. How was she going to talk her way out of this?

'Sorry.'

Noah shrugged and leaned back in his seat. 'You're tired...we both are. Mistakes are easy to make. Ignore him.'

Noah looked out of the window and Morgan glanced at his masculine profile. That was it? Where were the questions, the demands for an explanation, the mockery for making such a basic silly mistake? Why didn't he follow up on the cab driver's question, probe a little deeper?

Did he know and not care? Did he suspect and was distancing himself from the problem? Was he just simply not curious or, even scarier, didn't he give a hoot?

At the gallery a little while later, Morgan was still thinking of his non-reaction in the taxi and how she'd managed to dodge the explanation bullet. She stepped away from the group of people who were talking around her, looking past Johnno Davie at Noah, who was standing in front of one of Johnno's massive paintings. It was one of the few non-abstract paintings on display: a nude on a bed in a symphony of gold and cream, with hints of blush. It didn't need the tag *Sophie—Naked and Relaxed*; anyone with half a brain could tell exactly what Sophie had been up to before Johnno had decided to capture her on canvas.

Morgan wondered if Sophie knew that her…*ahem*…satisfaction was part of Johnno's latest collection.

Morgan lifted her glass of wine to her lips and watched Noah as he stared at the canvas. He was perfectly dressed for an art exhibition in NYC: dark jeans, a white button-down shirt and a black jacket.

Noah's immense self-control scared her—she admitted it. He'd been as swept away by their kiss last night as she had and yet he'd managed to pull back, to step away. She thought that she could be naked and he could be inside her, a fraction off orgasm, and if he decided to jam on the brakes he would. Oh, Morgan knew that he was self-motivated and determined, and that he kept his own counsel—that his natural way of interacting with people was to be brief and succinct, focusing on practicality above emotion—but even so sometimes she thought that there was another Noah trying to escape. A Noah who was a little more relaxed, a little impulsive—someone who was desperate to have a good time—but every time that Noah stepped over the line he got slapped back into his cage.

It was almost as if Noah was scared to let himself feel…

What had happened to him that had made him wary of… of…*himself*, really?

Morgan stared at his broad back as she walked over to him. She playfully nudged his shoulder with hers. 'I'm sorry about the confusion with the address earlier. I got the numbers mixed up.'

'Mmm…as I said, it happens.'

Morgan folded her arms across her raspberry-coloured poncho dress. It was a favourite of hers, with a one-shoulder neckline with a batwing sleeve. The dress fell to mid-thigh and she wore it with nude spiked heels and long, dangly earrings made from garnets.

'Listen, I need to say something. I'm sorry…about that kiss last night.' Noah held his hands in the pockets of his jeans and straightened his arms. 'I shouldn't have…'

'Here we go again… Noah, for goodness' sake, we are adults! We shared a kiss, and if you didn't have the control of a Tibetan monk we would've done much more.'

Noah glanced around as her voice lifted in frustration. '*Inside* voice, dammit!'

'What *is* the problem? And don't give me that garbage about not being professional and the promise you made to my brother.'

'Why don't you talk louder? I don't think the people at the far end of the gallery heard you,' Noah muttered as he gripped her arm and pulled her closer to the painting. 'And I *did* make a promise to your brother…'

Morgan turned her back to the room and looked at the painting. 'The old promise-to-my-brother excuse.' Morgan lifted up her arms and then fisted her hands. 'You know what…? Forget it! I've never chased after a man in my life and I am *not* starting with you!'

Noah muttered an expletive and raked his hand through his hair. 'Morgan…no, don't walk away.' He waited a beat before talking again. 'I've worked really hard to establish my business and, no matter how stupid you think it is, people *will* look to see how I conduct myself with you and they *will* judge that. I need to be seen to be professional and competent.'

Anyone would think she was asking him to do her in Central Park as Saturday afternoon entertainment. She saw him fiddle with his collar… He did that, she realised with a flash of insight, when he was feeling uncomfortable or when he was hedging. Or flat-out lying.

'That might be part of it but it's not the whole truth. The important truth.' Morgan looked him in the eye. When his eyes slid right she knew she had him and he knew that she had him. So he did what all men did when they were caught out: he changed the subject.

'Okay, say we have this hot fling. And afterwards, Duchess, what then?'

Morgan frowned and lowered the glass she'd raised to her lips. 'What do you mean?'

'We scratch this itch and then what happens? What are you expecting?'

Morgan took a sip of wine and considered his question. What did she expect? What *could* she expect?

What could she give?

After a moment's thought she came to the only logical, practical conclusion she could. 'I don't expect anything, Noah. You don't seem to be the type who needs or, frankly, wants a relationship, so if we did find ourselves in bed I'd expect nothing, because I know that you have nothing to give me.'

Besides, I'm too scared to take the chance of loving someone, being found unworthy, getting my teeth kicked in.

'You make me sound like a robot,' Noah muttered.

Morgan suspected that if he opened those cage doors he'd be anything but robotic—he'd be fearless and passionate and unstoppable. But right now he did have elements of the mechanical about him. Except when he was kissing her...

Morgan reached out and tapped his chest with one French manicured finger. 'You need to have some fun, Fraser. Lighten up.' Maybe they both did. 'The world won't fall on your head, you know.'

'You sound just like Chris. And my brothers.'

Whoa....stop the presses! Noah Fraser had volunteered some personal information! 'You have brothers?'

'Well, despite what you think, I wasn't cloned in a Petri dish,' Noah said, his tone grumpy.

'Younger? Older? Where are they? What do they do? Are they married?'

'Jeez, mention one little thing and I get a million questions.' Noah stopped a waiter, asked for a mineral water and rolled his eyes at her obviously curious face. 'Two much younger brothers, twenty-three and twenty-one. A sous chef at a London Michelin-starred restaurant and a freelance photographer who sells to several national newspapers. Neither are married and they both live in London. Satisfied?'

'Not nearly. Are they also buttoned-down, controlled and restrained?'

Noah took his mineral water from the tray presented to him. He looked past her shoulder to a place that was somewhere in the past. 'No, I stood as a shield so that they didn't turn out like me.'

And what on earth did he mean by *that*? Morgan opened her mouth to ask but he gestured to the painting and forced a small smile onto his face. 'It looks like a multiple to me.'

It took Morgan a minute to catch up, and when she did she cocked her head. 'Maybe it was a really good piece of chocolate.'

'Dream on,' Noah scoffed, before he fell serious. 'I have to admit I love this painting. I'd buy it in a heartbeat if I had enough cash floating around.'

Morgan leaned forward and peered at the tiny, tiny price in the corner of the tag. Holy bats…that was a lot of money—even for her. Morgan stepped back and looked at the painting again…she agreed with Noah. It was a sensational piece of art: fluid, sexy, happy. She could see it on the wall above her bed…

Sophie had had a really fine time, Morgan thought on a smile. But maybe it was time to give her a bit of privacy and get her out of the gallery.

'Let's go home,' Morgan said impulsively.

Noah looked at her, surprised. 'It's not even eight-thirty yet. And we were going to that cocktail party at the Hyatt.'

'I just want to go home, have a long bath and an early night. I want to drop the cloak. I need to be me tonight.'

'Sorry?'

Morgan waved his questions away. 'Ignore me. So, what do you think?'

'Hell, no, I *want* to stick around and make small talk with people I don't know.'

Morgan laughed at his sarcasm, handed her glass over to a passing waiter and inclined her head towards Johnno. 'I just need a quick word with the artist.'

'I'll be waiting at the door. Make it quick, Duchess.'

CHAPTER EIGHT

BACK IN MORGAN'S apartment, Noah glanced to the other side of the couch and smiled when he saw that Morgan had shuffled down, her head on a cushion, eyes closed and her sock-covered feet touching his thigh. Noah placed his beer on the side table and glanced at his watch; it was just past nine-thirty.

Standing up, he walked over to her and gently removed the earphones she'd plugged into her ears earlier. Her hand still loosely clutched her iPad and he pulled that away too. She liked listening to music while she read, she'd told him earlier, and wasn't that keen on TV, so he was welcome to watch what he liked.

Noah heard sound coming from the earphones and lifted one bud up to his ear. Instead of music, a low, melodious voice filled his ear. Frowning, he tapped the tablet and quickly realised that Morgan was listening to an audiobook, Ken Follet's *Pillars of the Earth*—a book he'd read years ago and thoroughly loved.

Noah had barely any time to react as Morgan launched up and tried to whip the tablet from his grasp. Her fingers skimmed the tablet as he moved it out of her reach.

'What the hell are you doing?' she demanded. 'Give it back!'

'Calm down, Duchess. Anyone would think you're hiding something here.' He grinned. 'Erotica? How to be an It Girl manuals?'

Morgan just glared at him, reared up and tried to take the device again.

'Oooh, temper. Now, I definitely know you're hiding something!'

'Stop being an ass! Give. It. Back!' Morgan shouted.

'Nah...I want to see what you're hiding. Bad music? Sappy movies? Your addiction to Angry Birds? Badly written cowboy books?'

'Noah!'

Noah tapped the menu and scrolled through her books. Frowning, he looked at the books on the device—there were many, and they covered a wide range of genres and subjects. But they were all audiobooks. He scrolled up, backwards, checked her files, and eventually realised that there wasn't a single e-book anywhere on the device.

'Only audiobooks, Morgs? Are you too lazy to read?'

He saw the colour seep from her face and her eyes fill with hurt. He frowned, knowing that he had misstepped badly, but he wasn't sure why his comment had had such an effect on her.

'Just give it back, Fraser,' Morgan said in a small voice.

Pride and defiance now flashed in her eyes, but underneath he could still sense her embarrassment and her vulnerability.

'My reading habits have nothing to do with you.'

'Reports are a hassle to read.'

'Can you give me a verbal report instead?'

He rubbed his jaw. Could it be...was it possible...that Morgan couldn't read? No, come on...*everyone* could read in this day and age, right? And she was so smart. There had to be another explanation.

Morgan sat back down on the couch and stared at the floor. Instinctively he balanced himself on his haunches and pushed her hair behind her ears, gently stroking the tender skin behind her ear.

'Do you have a problem with reading?'

She didn't reply and wouldn't meet his eyes. He hated to ask but he needed to know. 'Can you read…at all?'

Morgan jolted up and looked at him, her eyes wide and horrified. 'Of course I can read! Not well or fast, but I can read!' She stumbled to her feet, walked across the carpet and turned to look at him, her expression belligerent. 'Go on—say it. I dare you.'

'What?' Noah asked, genuinely confused.

Morgan placed a hand on her cocked hip and lifted her chin. 'I've heard them all, Noah—all the wisecracks, all the jokes. *She's got the looks and she's got money—what does she need a brain for? She's so thick that she'd get trapped on an escalator if the power went out. Quickest way to drown her? Put a mirror on the bottom of the pool—*'

'That's enough. Stop.' Noah held up his hand and kept his voice even. Who had said such brutal things about her? Whoever it was deserved a kick up the ass. It would be his pleasure to do it. 'Come and sit down, lass,' he said eventually, his voice gentle.

Noah waited until Morgan had perched on the edge of the couch, her bottom lip between her teeth. He resumed his position on his haunches in front of her.

'I'm not going to make fun of you, Morgan, but I do need to understand.' Noah rested his hand on her knee. 'Dyslexia?'

Morgan sighed. 'Chronic.' She glared at him again. 'But know this: I am *not* stupid, Noah. I have an exceedingly high IQ. I am *not* a dumb blonde.'

'Anyone with half a brain can see that.' Of course she wasn't stupid. She had the vocabulary of a Scrabble master and a brain that could tie him up in knots. 'You're probably one of the smartest women I know.' He ran a finger down her chest, skimming over her T-shirt between her breasts. 'This body is a work of art, but this—' he lifted his hand

and gently tapped her temple with his finger '—what's in here scares the daylights out of me.'

Morgan's eyes lightened in pleasure and a whole lot of relief. He smiled as a peachy blush spread over her cheekbones.

'It's just another part of you and you have absolutely nothing to be ashamed of. So, who was the loser?'

'The loser?'

'The guy who threw those comments at you. Name? Address? Name of the cemetery you want his dead body dumped at…'

Morgan's small smile disappeared quickly. She stared at her hands. 'First lover—a couple of months after you. I convinced myself that I loved him. He told me that I couldn't take a joke. He was verbally abusive but I gave him the ammunition to hurt me. Since then I've kept the dyslexia to myself.'

Noah uttered an obscenity and rubbed his hand over his face. 'Seriously, Morgs. Give me his name and I can cause him a world of pain.'

Morgan placed the tips of her fingers on his cheek. 'I appreciate the offer, but he's not worth the jail sentence.'

'You're no fun,' he complained mildly. She thought he was joking yet he'd happily use some of his nastiest unarmed combat skills on any man who so much as looked at Morgan the wrong way.

Noah sighed, looked at the shelves and shelves of books lining the walls surrounding them. How hard it must be to look at them but not be able to use them. 'So tell me about the paperbacks, Morgan.'

'I have a print copy for every audiobook I have. I used to try and read along, but the narrators read too fast so the words swim and dance and I get a cracking headache by page five.'

Noah unfurled his long length and sat down on the couch next to her. 'You don't need to keep it a secret, Morgan.'

Morgan dipped her head so her forehead touched his collarbone. 'Yeah, I kind of do.' She snuggled closer to him and his arm went around her slim back as he leant back against the couch. 'I'm not just a little dyslexic, Noah, I'm really bad. And some days I'm terrible.'

'Is that why you were so reluctant to organise the ball?'

'Yeah. It's too important for me to fail at it…and I don't want to disappoint my mum. It's hard, trying to live up to the Moreau name. The family are all terribly well educated— they all have two degrees; my dad has three—and I scraped through college by the skin of my teeth, taking twice the amount of time anyone else did.'

'You just told me that you are not stupid,' Noah pointed out. 'Surely they know that too? And as educated people don't you think that they admire you for trying something outside of your comfort zone? I know I do, and I only have one degree.'

'They keep telling me that. Maybe I'm just scared of disappointing myself.' Morgan tipped her head back to look at him. 'What do you have a degree in?'

'Business and history,' he admitted reluctantly. 'Love history. It's still my favourite subject.'

Morgan sighed happily. 'Then I must show you some of the old diaries from the first Moreau prospectors—the brothers who discovered the mines. They were wacky and colourful and quite unethical.'

'I'd love to read them.' Noah gently pulled her ponytail. 'You look exhausted, Duchess. Why don't you go to bed?'

'I'm tired, but I probably won't sleep,' Morgan admitted. 'My brain is whirling.'

'You need something to de-stress you.'

He stood up, scanned the bookshelves and found what he was looking for. Yanking the book from the shelf, he sat down again, stretched out his legs and tucked Morgan back into his side.

'If I remember correctly, you were just about to start chapter six.'

Morgan's eyes were as big as saucers. 'You're going to read to me?'

Her eyes filled with emotion and Noah winced. Oh, jeez, maybe he'd insulted her by offering to read to her. Maybe she hadn't heard a thing he'd said earlier about how smart he thought she was...

'I'm sorry. Look, it's not because I don't think you're... Bad idea, huh?'

Morgan's fingers on his lips dried up his words. 'No, it's probably the sweetest thing any man has ever done for me.'

Noah grimaced. 'Sweet, huh?'

'Yeah—very, very sweet.'

Noah pulled another face. 'Yuck, that's not how any ex-Special Forces soldier would like to hear himself described. Now, will you please shut up? I'm trying to read here...'

Noah handed Morgan a glass of champagne and, from behind his dark sunglasses, cast a look down her long, long legs. Every other woman at the Moreau Polo Cup Challenge was dressed to the nines, but Morgan, in tailored white shorts that ended at mid-thigh, and a white and green gypsy top revealing her shoulders and messy hair, looked every cent of the millions of dollars she was supposed to be worth.

Earlier, just because he was curious, he'd timed her to see how long she took to get ready. Ten minutes. He'd known women who took ten minutes to put on mascara. He really, really liked the fact that she didn't fuss.

And that she still managed to look super-hot.

'Do you ride?' Morgan nodded to the field and the charging, sweaty thoroughbred horses.

Noah snorted. 'Not many stables where I grew up.'

'Where *did* you grow up, Noah?' Morgan asked.

Well, he'd cracked the door open... Noah sighed, thought about ducking her question, remembered that she'd shared her biggest secret with him and told himself not to be a jerk. 'I grew up in Glasgow, in a bad part of town.'

Morgan kept her eyes on the field. 'Did you have a tough childhood?'

'Yeah.'

And that was all he was prepared to say. Besides, it was all such a long time ago. He was with a gorgeous girl at a fancy event and he didn't want those memories to corrode his enjoyment of this stunning spring day.

'So, tell me about your date for the wedding,' he said casually.

Noah frowned as a tall, slim Spaniard in a white polo shirt and jodhpurs streaked with dirt leaned over the fence, placed his hands on Morgan's shoulders, kissed her on both cheeks and then lightly on the mouth. Morgan laughed, patted his cheek, and conversed with him in passable Spanish. Their conversation ended with another flurry of cheek-kisses and, *dammit*, another brush of her mouth.

Noah resisted the urge to reach for his gun.

'Friend of yours?' Noah asked, unaware of the bite in his voice.

'Juan Carlos. Playboy. Polo player. He taught me to tango,' Morgan said in a dreamy voice.

'That had better be all he taught you,' Noah said in a low mutter.

Morgan's mouth twitched. 'A *duchess* never tells. Andrew—how *are* you?'

Kiss, kiss…flirt, flirt…

Noah looked at his water and wished he could ask for a whisky as she dived into conversation with yet another polo player who'd ambled up to greet her. She would drive any sane man to drink, Noah decided as a bead of sweat ran down his spine.

He wanted to remove his navy linen jacket but he wouldn't. He didn't want to raise questions about why he was wearing a sidearm to one of the most elite social events in the city. He was on constant alert at functions like these;

there was no security, people came and went, and anything could happen.

Unfortunately no one was close to finding the kidnappers and the tensions at the mine remained unresolved; in fact they had just got worse, and they'd all been warned to be on high alert.

James had flown out to Colombia to try and resolve the dispute, and a posse of CFT personnel were guarding his back. That was why James wasn't at the Polo Challenge and why Morgan would be handing out the prizes to the polo players—and no doubt kissing eight or more fit, rich, polo-playing numbskulls.

Oh, joy of joys.

Polo Boy number two walked away and Morgan pushed her glasses up into her hair and fanned her programme close to her face. 'What were we talking about?'

'Your date for the wedding.'

He caught the tiny wince. 'Oh…him.'

'Yeah, *him*. Want to come clean, Morgs?' Noah asked, a smile hiking up the corner of his lips.

Morgan placed her champagne glass on a tall table and sighed. 'I lied. I was trying to wind you up—'

'You succeeded,' Noah mumbled, thinking that it was the thought of her sleeping with someone else that had ignited his temper and led to the urge to kiss her, brand her, possess her. 'So, he's fictional?'

Morgan scuffed the grass with the tip of one of her apple-green wedges. 'Mmm.'

Noah slowly pushed his shades up into his hair and looked down into her face, idly thinking that he loved the handful of freckles on her nose that make-up never quite seemed to cover. 'Do you lie often?'

'No. Only when I'm pushed beyond reason.'

'I'm very reasonable.' Noah protested.

'Pfft.' Morgan rolled her eyes.

Noah rested his forearms on the fence. 'I've been thinking about something you said the other night at the art exhibition.'

'What did I say?'

'You said something about the cloak you'd like to drop... what did you mean by that?'

Morgan took a little while to answer. When she did her voice was softer, vulnerable. 'Don't we all have cloaks or armour that we drag on to protect us from the circumstances we find ourselves in? Something we do, or say, a way that we act to get us through whatever it is making us feel uncomfortable? A cloak that covers all our insecurities, the real us that we don't want people to see?'

Noah gave her words some thought. 'Your flirty, charming party-girl persona...that's your cloak? The bright, bubbly, charming flirt? The real you is quieter, more introspective... dreamier.'

Morgan cocked her thumb and extended her index finger. 'There you go. And you only know that because we've been living in each other's pockets. And your implacable and remote face that discourages all conversation is yours. Your can't-touch-me mask is supposed to discourage anyone from wanting to dig deeper, to get to know you a bit better.'

Noah couldn't help wincing. He did do that—did keep everyone at an emotional distance.

He rubbed his hand across his face. 'You've come closer than anyone—ever.' He caught the flash of fear in her eyes, saw her take the tiniest step backwards. 'And that makes you uncomfortable,' he added.

'Wary.' Morgan looked out at the busy field. 'We can hurt each other... No, let me rephrase that. You can hurt me...if we ever change from friends to lovers.'

'*If* we change—and I'll try not to, Morgan—you have to know that I wouldn't be able to promise you for ever. All I can say is that I would be monogamous, that I'd treat you well as long as it lasted—be it a week or months. But at some point our paths would split and I'd be back in London, doing what I do.'

'I know.'

'If you want more from me than a fun time in bed then maybe we should just quit while we're ahead. Stay as *Duchess* and *Soldier*.' Noah folded his arms and hoped she couldn't see how much he hoped that she didn't choose option B. Because that would, well...*suck*. 'So, what's it to be?'

Morgan played with the emerald and diamond studs in her ears. 'I'm probably going to regret this, but we do have unfinished business between us.' She sent him a coy look and the humour was back in her eyes. 'By the way, are you into threesomes?'

If he'd had anything in his mouth he would have sprayed her, or choked. As it was, he felt he had to pick his jaw up from the floor. 'What the...? Who? What? Are you being serious?'

'Well, by the time this situation is resolved my friend Sophie from the gallery will be sharing my bedroom. I thought I should warn you.'

Noah felt his heart slow down to a gallop as her words started to make sense. 'Morgan, you nearly gave me a heart attack! You bought Johnno Davie's painting?'

'I did.' Morgan smiled. 'It'll be delivered when the exhibition is over.'

They turned as someone called her name.

'Ooh, I'm being summoned. I need to go and hand out the prizes and flirt with the players.'

Noah couldn't help the possessive hand he put on her back, the growl in his voice. 'Keep it to a minimum, sweetheart. Remember that I'm armed and dangerous. I'd hate to have to shoot one of them.'

Morgan touched her lips to his cheek and whispered in his ear. 'Just to be clear, soldier, Sophie is the closest you are ever going to get to a threesome that involves me.'

He could live with that. Heck, he was happy fantasising about a 'onesome' with her.

A few days later Noah heard the lobby phone chime and got up from the dining table where he had been working on staff scheduling—his normal Auterlochie work hadn't stopped, so he worked from Morgan's dining room table or the MI conference room. He picked up the phone.

'Hey, Patrick.'

He'd become good friends with the doormen—both ex-cops, with excellent service records—and Patrick's voice boomed in his ear.

'I have Miss Riley here, plus two guys carrying mannequins and stuff. Can I send them up?'

'What? Hold on, let me take a look.' Noah walked backed to his laptop and pulled up the live feed from the lobby. Patching into the apartment building's security feed had been his first task when he'd moved into the apartment weeks ago. True enough, there was Riley, chatting to two young guys holding two life-size mannequins.

Why was Riley bringing mannequins up to the apartment? He wasn't sure he wanted to know.

He went back to the phone and thought for a minute. The situation in Colombia had descended into near anarchy and threats were flying. Hannah and Jedd were still not allowed to leave their house in the Cayman Islands. He'd spent twenty minutes on the phone with James earlier that day and they'd agreed that Morgan should curtail her social obligations. So now he had to try and keep her in the apartment as much as possible…which would be a butt-pain, because resisting the urge to haul her off to bed was now on a par with him splitting the atom.

'Put Riley, the mannequins and the bags into the lifts and send the men home. I'll help her unload on this side,' Noah told Patrick, and went back to his laptop.

When the doors had closed on Riley and her plastic companions, he called to Morgan.

'Hey, Riley will be here in twenty seconds with some life-size dolls. Why?'

'Yay!' Morgan said, coming from the bedroom and towel-drying her wet hair. She draped her towel over the back of the couch and Noah fought the urge to ask her to put it back in the bathroom. He was obsessively neat, courtesy of the army, and she was a slob. Her untidiness drove him nuts.

Noah opened the front door, and walked over to the lift. As the doors opened he grabbed one mannequin and tucked it under his arm. 'Friends of yours, Ri?'

'Ha-ha.'

Riley handed him a duffel bag and he walked back to the apartment and dumped them in the hallway. He went back for the second dummy and Riley followed him, carrying the second smaller bag.

He watched, amused, as Morgan and Riley sat the mannequins—expensive ones, with arm and leg joints—on the colourful couches. Morgan squealed and immediately reached for the duffel bags. Thinking that they probably needed alcohol for whatever they were up to, he went into the kitchen and opened a bottle of wine. When he returned with two glasses in hand his eyes widened at the rainbow-hued lingerie now scattered over the coffee table. No, not lingerie…sexy-as-sin burlesque costumes. Beaded and decorated corsets with fluffy skirts and feathers. And there were some without skirts, skimpy, with oversized clips to attach to stockings.

His mind instinctively imagined Morgan in one of those outfits and he cursed when his pants stirred. High heels, stockings… He thought of the survival courses he'd taken in the SAS. Nothing sexy about those…

Thoughts of sex bolted away and his heart ran cold as Morgan picked up a duffel bag and a treasure trove of jewellery rained down on the table. Emeralds, rubies, diamonds, gold…so much gold. Pearls, sapphires… If Morgan had liberated the MI jewellery collection from the walk-in safe on the fourth floor—and he knew she had access to do that—he was going to freakin' kill her. Slowly, and with much pleasure.

'Oh, my, look at his face.' Morgan chuckled as she held Riley's arm and doubled over with mirth. 'Quick, grab your mobile and snap a pic. We'll call it *Nervous Noah*.'

'In a moment you are going to be *Mortuary Morgan*,' Noah replied as he approached them. He handed over the wine and picked up a necklace with a canary-egg-size diamond hanging off a gold clasp. He examined the stone, didn't see the deep sparkle and reflections a diamond that size should have and his blood pressure dropped. 'Paste. You nearly gave me a heart attack!'

Morgan grinned. 'They are all paste, and it's fantastic that we have them to play with.'

Noah held up his hand. 'I think *I* need wine for this…hold on.' He went back to the kitchen, brought another glass and the bottle back and perched on the arm of the chair. 'Now, what are you doing, exactly?'

Morgan crossed her legs Indian-style and with her wet hair and make-up-free face she looked a teenager. Like she had when she was nineteen, when she'd stolen his breath from his lungs. Nothing much had changed there, Noah thought.

'Okay, so you said that we can't have live models showing off the collection…'

'Categorically not,' Noah said.

'So, Riley and I want to place mannequins on round plinths throughout the ballroom, each of them in a gold burlesque birdcage *à la Moulin Rouge*. We'll put them in provocative poses—on swings, bending over, et cetera. The mannequins will all be dressed in burlesque costumes— sexy corsets and stockings, high heels and masks.' Morgan picked up a handful of lace and stockings. 'The great thing is that we have paste copies of all the jewellery collection and Riley has the mannequins, so we can experiment before we make a final decision.'

'Why?' Noah asked.

Morgan, who was examining a pearl necklace, frowned up at him. 'Why what?'

'Why do you have paste copies of the jewellery collection?' Noah asked patiently.

'Oh…a Great-Something Moreau needed to raise some cash to buy another mine and he handed over the collection as collateral. He didn't want it known that he was cash-strapped, so before he did that he had paste copies made of the jewellery. He got the jewels back but ever since, whenever the family acquired a new piece, a copy was made. Riley and I played with these as kids.'

'Huh. So they are exact replicas?'

'Absolutely.' Riley draped a long string of pearls around her neck. 'So what do you think of our birdcage idea, Noah? Can the real jewels be secured?'

Noah thought for a minute. 'I want an area between the guests and the cages, about a foot and a half, where we can put a pressure plate so that if anyone steps up to a mannequin it'll trigger a silent alarm.'

Morgan looked at Riley. 'We can do that.'

'I want in on the design of the birdcages. I want to put laser beams between the rods, so that if anyone breaks the beam it'll trigger an alarm.'

Morgan lifted a bustier of white silk embossed with silver beads and waved his security issues away in order to play with the colourful garments and the fake bling.

'Okay… Look at this one, Ri! Such a gorgeous red, with black inserts, and the feathers make a teeny-tiny skirt. If we teamed it with those striped thigh-highs…dynamite! Let's dress a mannequin in an outfit, choose the corresponding jewellery and mask, photograph it and do the next one. And where on earth did you find all these outfits?'

'A burlesque show that lasted six weeks on Broadway.

Apparently the costumes were fabby, the performers not so good.'

Noah put his wine down, stood up and picked up a mannequin, looking it over.

'What on earth are you doing, Noah?' Morgan asked.

'Seeing where we can place a motion sensor so if the jewels are moved once they've been put in place it will trigger—'

'A silent alarm.' Morgan and Riley chorused.

'Smartasses.' Noah dropped the mannequin and thought that he badly needed some testosterone before he started to grow breasts. 'I'm going to watch some manly sports on ESPN. Have fun playing with your grown-up Barbies, girls.'

Noah's hand drifted over Morgan's hair as he passed her. He wasn't sure if she noticed because she was frantically scrabbling through the piles of multi-coloured, beaded and luscious garments to look for…who knew what?

Concentrating on sport was a nightmare when he couldn't stop imagining Morgan in a tiny black and red corset sparkling with diamond-like beads, black striped thigh-high stockings, red 'screw me' heels and an elaborate Mardi Gras mask…straddling his hips, his hands on the smooth, warm, bare flesh above those heart attack-inducing stockings…

He dropped his head back against the arm of the couch and adjusted his jeans. Could a man die from lack of sex and frustration? He was convinced that it was a distinct possibility.

CHAPTER NINE

MORGAN KNOCKED ONCE on the conference door and popped her head in. Noah, on a video conference, flicked a glance at her, smiled, and looked back at his screen.

'I sent off the quote for that corporate security analysis in Hungary, Chris. I think we might—'

Morgan leaned her shoulder into the doorframe and waited for him to finish his conversation. Look at him—so sexy with his tousled hair and wire-rimmed reading glasses. Morgan felt the usual rush of lust, quickly followed by the warm and fuzzies. She suspected if they ever got to have sex he'd be an amazing lover: sweet and tender, hot and fast, slow but hot... She suspected that, like the many facets of his personality, the variations to his lovemaking would be endless. But right now she loved talking to him over the first cup of coffee in the morning, over a glass of wine at night, arguing about the fact that she was the untidiest person he'd ever met. She couldn't imagine him not being in her life and knew, with or without sex, that she could, if she wasn't very, very careful, fall chaotically, crazily in love with him.

She couldn't, shouldn't...wouldn't. Some day soon the situation with the Colombian mine would be sorted out and he'd go back to London, to his life and business there.

'Hey, what's up?' Noah asked, pulling his glasses off his face and resting his forearms on the table. A cup of cold coffee, his mobile and his wallet were placed in a neat row on the other side of his laptop and his sidearm was snug against his shoulder.

Morgan placed her hands behind her back. 'It must be really difficult, trying to run your business from here, Noah.'

Noah looked around. 'It's not so bad. I'm plugged into the server at work—it's practically the same as if I was working in my office and Chris in his. The only difference is arguing face to face instead of over Skype.'

'Well, I'm still sorry if guarding me is an inconvenience.'

'Better than the alternative of you being kidnapped. Or dead.' Noah placed his arms behind his head. 'How was your day? Still battling with the Barnado piece? Has she settled on a design yet?'

She was currently dealing with an ultra-picky client with the concentration span of a cricket. 'Nope. I've been wading through cost projections for the ball and my eyes are crossing.'

'Need some help?' Noah asked.

He asked it in the same voice he used when he wanted to know whether she wanted coffee. As if she was so very normal…and to Noah she was. Her dyslexia was just another part of her—like her untidiness or her freckles.

'Morgs, do you need help?'

Noah repeating his question pulled her back.

'I'll make time if you need me to.'

'No, I'm good. I heard from James; we'll be flying out at five tomorrow afternoon and we'll be in Cape Town mid Friday morning. I told Merri about you. She said that it's a garden wedding and one more person won't make a difference, so she's insisting that you attend with me.'

Noah raked his hand through his hair. 'If the security seems okay then I'm quite happy to leave you there, Morgan. I really don't feel like attending another stuffy function, talking to people I have nothing in common with.'

Morgan walked over to him, laid a hand on his arm and felt his warm skin beneath her fingers. He'd rolled up the sleeves on his casual duck egg blue button-down shirt and she could feel the raised veins in his arms. 'It won't be like that, I promise. Merri is a hoot—stunningly beautiful, but utterly laid back. And the rest of my good, solidly normal friends will be there… Ellie, Jess, Clem and their men. You'll like them.'

'Jeez, Morgan, I don't know.'

'Please, Noah?'

'Does anyone ever say no to you when you flutter your eyelashes and do your Puss-in-Boots look?'

Morgan's lips twitched at the corners. 'Not often, no.'

'Didn't think so. Do I have to wear the tux again?'

'It's a garden wedding. No tux needed.'

'Finally a sensible bride.' Noah glanced at his watch. 'Are you ready to go home?'

Morgan shook her head to clear it. 'Actually, I wanted to tell you that I need to go into Moreau's Gems to see a customer. He's demanding a second opinion on a valuation Carl has given him and insists on getting one from a Moreau. Idiot. He made a scene earlier, and Carl made an arrangement for me to meet him after-hours—which is now.'

Noah frowned. 'Is that normal? Meeting clients after-hours?'

Morgan shrugged. 'Yeah, we meet with clients at the time that suits them, not us. Anyway, he's there now and waiting for us.'

'Security?'

'They aren't allowed to leave until Carl does,' Morgan said, cocking her head at them. 'It's a client, Noah, and it happens all the time. Fifteen minutes, in and out, and then we can order Thai for supper.'

Morgan saw the look he sent to his screen and the frustration that flashed in his eyes. 'I can ask one of the security officers from the lobby to see me there and back if you're busy. Fifteen minutes, tops.'

Noah seemed to be considering the option for a minute,

but he eventually stood up and pulled on his jacket. 'Nope. Let me just send an email delaying my next conference call and I'll come down with you.'

He bent over the screen and his hands flew over the keyboard. He hit 'enter' and picked up his mobile and wallet. Then his eyes met hers and her heart spluttered, misfired and coughed to life again.

Morgan held her breath as his strong hands encircled her jaw and throat and watched wide-eyed as he tipped his head and his lips hovered just above hers. She saw something in his eyes that she hadn't noticed before: something soft, almost tender. Morgan gripped his wrists with her hands and kept her eyes locked on his, waiting for him to swoop down and claim her lips in a kiss that she knew would blow her socks off.

She wanted to sink slowly into the hot whirlpool of his mouth. He would be more delicious than she remembered, far tastier than her imagination suggested. Noah caressed the side of her neck and she inhaled the intoxicating scent of his skin. If she moved a fraction closer she would feel the thrust of her breasts against his chest...their skin would only be separated by his shirt and her silk T-shirt.

Worse than the thumping lust that pooled between her legs, the rapid beat of her heart, was the thought that she was one step closer to losing her heart. It was slipping further away from her and she knew that if she allowed it to fall out of her hand it would be his for ever.

Noah stepped back, but his big hand still grasped the side of her neck and his thumb touched her jaw and tipped her head up.

He muttered an obscenity and her eyes widened.

'One of these days—hours—minutes—I'm not going to be able to step away from you.' Noah moved back and gestured towards the door. 'Let's get this done. I've still got work to do tonight.'

So did she—really important work, Morgan thought, troubled.

Like figuring out how to ensure she didn't fall in love with him.

Morgan had gone somewhere in her head, Noah thought as they hit the pavement outside MI headquarters and moved into the busy end-of-day crowds, and he had no idea where. He'd almost kissed her and then she'd got this weird look on her face and wondered off to a place where he couldn't reach her.

Maybe she was thinking about the design she was battling with, or the ball; he knew how much she had on her plate at the moment and was surprised at how well she was coping. The dyslexia popped up now and again, but he knew that it was nothing that she couldn't handle. It got worse if she rushed or was stressed, and he'd worked out that if he distracted her she frequently relaxed and could then read whatever she'd been stuck on before. He was also beginning to believe that her dyslexia was directly related to her confidence and her happiness; if she was relaxed she had far fewer problems than she did if she was stressed.

He knew that sex would be a brilliant distraction… *Promise to James, promise to James.*

The Moreau's Gems door was locked so Noah knocked. Morgan shook her head at him and pressed a discreet button on the side of the door. He heard a click and frowned when the door popped open.

'There are cameras inside Carl's office; they can see who is at the door,' Morgan said, grinning at his obvious paranoia.

'Where's the guard?' Noah asked as he pushed Morgan inside.

'Probably making coffee. I don't know, Noah! Jeez!' Morgan said. 'Come on, Carl will be in his office.'

Noah made sure the door was locked behind him and looked around. His Spidey Sense was going nutso. It was the same feeling he'd had numerous times in the army, when he'd known things were going to go to hell in a handbasket.

Cold shivers ran down his spine and he instinctively *knew* that he'd just walked them into a heap of trouble. He placed a protective arm around Morgan's waist and pretended to nuzzle her ear.

'If I call you Duchess, you drop like a stone to the floor,' he said, in a low voice that only she could hear.

Morgan—funny girl—rolled her eyes at him as they approached the main counter holding a precious display of some of the world's best gems set in amazing designs. He withdrew his gun and Morgan's eyes widened.

'What the heck are you doing? Put that away. It'll go off and you'll hurt someone!'

Seriously? He was a highly trained operative and if he made it 'go off' then he'd damn well be intending to hurt someone. *Honestly—civilians!*

He made the mistake of sending her a pointed look and out of the corner of his eye saw movement. The next minute a boot connected with his wrist and his gun went flying. Where had he come from? he thought as he dodged a knife-swipe at his belly. He heard Morgan's whimper, ignored it, saw an opening and ploughed his fist into a throat. His attacker crumpled.

Then all hell broke loose.

Noah yelled at Morgan to move and shoved her out of the way as he bulleted over a counter and slammed into the space behind—where a suited thug waited for the opportunity to gut him like a fish. Noah waited for the attack, grabbed the arm attached to the knife, broke his ulna and launched his elbow into a temple. Out of the corner of his eye he saw another shadow and his foot flew out and connected with the chin of another knife-wielding lout who'd come to his friend's aid. It just glanced off a granite face and he came at him again.

The fight was a blur of motion…kick, punch, kick from

both of them. Noah knew that he couldn't worry or even think about Morgan just yet—not while he had to contend with this better-trained and skilled attacker. Noah bounced on his toes, waited for his opening and hooked a fist into his sternum, following up with a well-placed kick to his groin. Just because he was angry, he picked the guy up and tossed him into a counter. Glass and jewellery flew out of the case.

Whoops!

'Stop.'

The voice came from behind him and every muscle in Noah's body contracted. He wiped his bleeding mouth with his hand before slowly turning around. Fear turned to terror as he let his eyes drift down and saw the thick forearm crushing Morgan's windpipe and the knife at her throat. This man was tall, better-dressed, and had a scar that went from the corner of his mouth to his temple. His eyes would have been better suited to a snake. This was someone to be feared, he realised. No conscience, no empathy, just sheer evil intention.

Kidnapper number four. Noah swore as he walked around the annihilated counter and into the centre of the room.

'I'm going to walk her out of here and neither of you will get hurt.'

Moron, Noah thought. 'Do I look like I mind getting hurt? Let her go and *you* won't get hurt.'

A reptile smile to go with the reptile eyes. Noah expected to see a forked tongue at any moment. He flicked his glance to Morgan, who was looking at him, her gaze steady. Good girl—she wasn't panicking. He was close to it, he thought, as a drop of blood rolled down her neck and soaked into her T-shirt.

He'd cut her...

He was going to kill him for that.

'What do you want?' Noah demanded.

'Her, of course. Negotiations will be so much easier in Colombia if we have a bargaining chip.'

Noah shook his head. 'That's not going to happen. Where are the store employees?'

Snake-eyes shrugged. 'In the back. They might need medical care; we had to *persuade* them to call Miss Moreau down.'

Persuade as in beat the crap out of them to make them obey.

'We've been watching you for weeks—waiting for an opportunity. We couldn't afford to wait any more so we set a trap and you walked straight into it.'

Tell me about it. If one of his employees had done the same they'd be fired. He'd been distracted...by Morgan. *Maybe you shouldn't guard someone you want to sleep with...do you think, soldier?*

'I'm going to rip you apart,' Noah said.

And he would. That was a promise. Nobody threatened Morgan...ever.

'You okay there, Duchess?'

On cue she dropped like a stone, pulling Snake-eyes off-balance. Noah became a blur of speed, motion and deadly intent as he kicked the knife out of his hand and followed up with a lightning-fast punch to his stomach. Air whooshed out of his opponent as he sank to his knees.

Just to make sure that he had the upper hand, Noah wound his forearm around his neck and considered doing the specialised jerk that would send him into the ever after.

'You think you can put your grubby hands on my woman? Put a knife to her throat? Cut her?' he demanded, his voice rough.

He heard a faint gurgling and Morgan's desperate pleas from the other end of the long tunnel he was in. He continued to threaten his captor, tightening his grip with every word he spoke.

Morgan's hand smacking his head jerked him toward reality.

'The guy is turning blue! Let him go! You're going to kill him!'

Noah looked up at her, ignored her tear-filled eyes and shrugged. 'He hurt you. No one hurts you and gets away with it. You're bleeding.'

'It's a scratch, Noah. Look—the police are here. Let them take care of him.' Morgan slapped his head again. 'Let him go! *Now!* Please, Noah. Don't do this.'

Noah released the pressure and heard a couple of deep, rattling and relieved gurgles from his captor.

Noah felt sanity flowing back into him and withdrew his arm. He flipped the sleazoid over and smacked his head into the floor. *Oops...*

'Open the door, Duchess. And please tell them that I am one of the good guys and not to shoot me.'

Noah opened the door to Morgan's apartment and his hand on her back urged her into her home. She headed straight for her squishy couch and sank down onto the edge, staring at the multi-coloured Persian rug below her feet.

He was coming off the adrenalin high and was starting to feel every punch and kick he'd taken. He yanked his tie up and over his head and dropped it, very unusually for him, on the back of the couch. His lip was still bleeding and under the butterfly bandage the cut on his cheek was telling him—loudly—that it was there. His knuckles were bruised and bloody.

But Morgan was fine...mostly. Her neck was bruised from having that muscled arm applied to it, and there was a small nick on her neck from the knife. He kept looking at her to check that she hadn't developed another injury the EMTs might have overlooked.

'Sore?' Noah demanded when she touched her fingers to her throat.

'Mmm.' Morgan looked up at Noah's ravaged face and managed a smile. 'I'm fine, I promise.'

Noah crouched on his heels in front of her and rested his forehead on her knee. 'I thought I'd lost you, Morgan.'

Morgan lifted her hand to touch his cheek, letting her fingertips flutter just beneath the cut on his cheekbone. 'You're too good to lose anyone.'

'I was going to kill him,' Noah said. 'I lost control... *again.*'

'What do you mean?' She touched the deep frown between his brows. 'Noah? What's wrong?'

'Apart from the fact that you were nearly kidnapped and killed? That my heart stopped when I saw that knife to your neck?'

Morgan's eyes widened as his voice became louder with every word.

'That I nearly lost you and I can't lose anyone—ever again?'

'Okay, Noah, calm down.'

'I nearly got you killed in there because I wasn't concentrating!'

'Stop shouting! I'm pretty sure that people can hear you in the lobby.'

'You! Nearly! Died!'

Morgan shook her head. 'Yet here I still sit—alive, but starting to think that you're one crazy man. You were there. You saved me,' Morgan said, her eyes on his mouth. 'My real-life hero.'

'Don't call me that! It should never have happened,' Noah stated, his voice full of disgust. 'I walked you into an ambush...what was I thinking?'

'Stop beating yourself up... Oh, wait—someone already did that today.' Morgan's eyes and twitching mouth invited him to find his sense of humour.

'Ha-ha.'

Noah looked up into her beautiful eyes. His gaze travelled over her face and he winced at the small cut on her neck, the faint bruises on her throat. He'd already forgotten that his cheekbone was cut, that his bottom lip was split and puffy, that his body was battered and bruised.

She was okay. That was all that mattered. Life was too short and he knew that he could not go a minute more without making love to her. He needed her, craved her…emotions he found difficult to admit to. But he'd come so close to losing his life. And—far more scarily—her life.

Life, he decided, was too sweet to waste another minute denying himself the pleasure of making her his.

Noah's eyes darkened with passion and he couldn't resist any longer. When his lips met hers his tongue delved and danced and she responded, and he felt awed by the pent-up longing in her kiss. Unaware that his kisses were just as demanding, as urgent, he sucked in his breath when Morgan's hands moved to the bottom of his shirt, tugging it out of his jeans. Desperate to feel his flesh on hers, he moaned his frustration and resented the brief separation from her body as he stepped away from her to pull his shirt over his head.

Morgan leaned forward and ran her lips across his chest, stopping to flick her tongue over his nipple, to rub her cheek on his chest hair. Noah flipped open her shirt buttons and pulled the fabric apart, revealing her lacy pink bra and luscious chest to his gaze. She was so feminine, he thought. From her sense of humour to her resilience, her long legs and bold eyes, the texture and smell of her skin, she embodied all the traits that he'd spent his adult life looking for.

He finally—*finally!*—had his hands on her, and his imagination had fallen far short of the reality of how life-affirming touching her was. This time there would be no stopping him—stopping them. He needed her, had to have her, to be in her, around her, sharing this experience with her.

Noah felt Morgan's body soften, surrendering to the moment and to him. He bumbled through removing her clothes—suave he was *not*!—but eventually she lay back on the cushions, gloriously, stunningly naked except for the tiny scrap of flimsy lace that covered her crotch. He kept his eyes on her, planning which part of her luscious skin he'd suck on first—hard pink nipple, soft inner thigh?—as he quickly shed the rest of his clothing while Morgan watched him through heavy, half-closed eyes.

On a muttered curse, he reached for his discarded pants and pulled his wallet out of his back pocket. Scattering cards and cash, he found the condom he had taken to carrying around with him and ripped the top open with his teeth. He dropped the condom onto the table and he saw that Morgan was neither surprised nor shocked when he grabbed the flimsy material of her panties and snapped the thin bands that held the triangle in place. Her hand reached out to encircle his erection and he immediately rubbed himself against her most secret places, asking for her permission to enter. He wanted to take his time, to adore every inch of her body, but he'd waited for so long—weeks, years!

His fingers and his mouth followed where his erection had been, and under his touch Morgan surrendered, dissolved, just as he'd known she would. He knew the exact moment to pull back, when she could tolerate no more, so he lifted his head to adore her breasts with his mouth, tongue and lips.

Morgan patted the table, found the condom and stretched down to close her fingers around him. He relished the sound of her breathing, heavy in the quietness of the evening. The latex whispered over him, her fingers making the prosaic action the most erotic sexual play. Green eyes clashed with blue as she tugged him towards her, and he felt as if he'd come home when her softness wrapped around his solidity and enclosed him in her wet warmth. Noah slid one hand under her hip and the other cradled her head into his neck as he both encouraged her to ride with him and promised protection from the storm to follow. They were together.

Noah moved within her and Morgan followed. He demanded and Morgan responded. Deeper, longer, higher, faster. She met him stroke for stroke, matching his passion, glorying in her power. Then she shuddered, splintered. and through the swells of her climax Noah fractured with her.

It was heaven. It was home.

Emotionally, physically depleted, Noah pushed his face into Morgan's neck, breathed, sighed, and for the first time in far too long relaxed completely.

She was safe and she was his. Finally.

CHAPTER TEN

STELLENBOSCH, WESTERN CAPE. Home, Morgan thought as she flopped back onto the mattress of the canopied bed and groaned in delight. This was her favourite place in the entire world; the Bon Chance Wine Estate nestled into the mountains that embraced the family wine farm. This was where, as a child, she'd run wild with Riley and the children of the workers, all of them barefoot and dirty, their faces smeared with the juice of the mulberries they'd picked off the trees in the orchards, their pockets filled with the biscuits or mini-cakes Mariah, the cook, had tucked into their pockets.

On arrival, the kitchen had been the first place she'd headed to and there she'd been, her hair grey and her caramel face wrinkled, but her eyes shining with love.

After Mariah had met Noah and hugged James and Riley, and they'd all had a cup of her thick and strong stove-percolated coffee, she'd ushered them off to their rooms to freshen up—but not before tucking a large biscuit into Morgan's hand.

Morgan sat up, sat cross-legged on the bed under the antique wooden canopy and reached for the biscuit she'd placed on the side table.

'Are you going to share that?' Noah asked from where he stood in her open doorway.

Morgan waved him in as she bit down. 'No,' she said as the taste of vanilla and warm butter exploded on her tongue.

Noah walked in, took the biscuit from her hand and snapped it in half. He ignored her vociferous protests and popped it into his mouth. 'Damn it, that's good,' he said, after swallowing.

'Wait until you taste her pan-fried trout with almonds. That's on the menu for tonight.'

Noah walked over to the wooden sash window, placed his hands on the windowsill and looked out. 'It's so beautiful here, Morgan,' he stated quietly. 'The vines, the mountains…'

Morgan climbed off the bed and joined him at the window. 'Isn't it? This, more than any other place on earth, is my home. It's where we mostly grew up. A Moreau forefather bought this place in the late eighteen-hundreds, with the profits out of the first diamond mine they worked, but the house and winery date back to the beginning of the century.'

'The house is fantastic. From the moment you drive through those gates and up the oak-lined driveway you know that you are entering a place that's imbued with history. The white gables, the exposed wooden beams, the wooden floors. And, God, the furniture.'

Morgan looked amused. 'You've been around wealth before, soldier, why are you sounding so impressed?'

Noah gave her cheek the gentlest of flicks. 'I'm not impressed by wealth and you know it. It's the…*history*—the idea that your great-great-grandmother ate at that same table in the dining room that we will eat at tonight. It's the continuity of family…'

'Tell me about yours, Noah. Your family.'

Noah shook his head and his eyes hardened. 'The only thing to tell is that they are nothing like yours. Socially, economically, mentally…the other end of the spectrum' Noah looked around and raised his eye at the very luscious wooden canopy bed. 'And that is one heck of a bed. One might say that it is fit for a duchess.'

'If you play your cards right I might invite you into it.' Morgan batted her eyelashes at him.

'If you play your cards right I might say yes.' Noah batted his eyelashes back.

Morgan laughed and he grinned.

Noah stepped up to her, rested his temple against hers, his hands loose on her hips. 'James said that we're having a wine-tasting in the cellar in fifteen minutes, and as much as I want you I also want to take my time with you. Every waking moment during that interminable flight I spent planning what I intend to do with you...to you.'

Morgan licked her bottom lip as her hands drifted down over his stomach. 'Bet I could make a case for quick and fast now.'

Noah looked tempted, then swatted her on the backside before he walked away to the door. He gestured her through it 'Stop leading me into temptation and show me Bon Chance.'

Morgan grinned as she drifted past him in a cloud of mischief and expensive perfume. 'So you're admitting that I *can* lead you into temptation?'

'You know that you can,' Noah muttered, and placed his hand on her lower back to push her away from the bedrooms and towards the magnificent yellow wood staircase. 'Behave, Duchess.'

'But I'd so much rather *mis*behave...'

Noah hooked his arm around her neck and placed his hand over her mouth. 'Man, you're a pain in the ass.'

Morgan giggled as she placed her butt on the banister and slid down the stairs, landing on her feet in the hall. It was good to be home. And it was fabulous to be home with Noah.

Noah pushed open the massive oak door to Bon Chance and ushered Morgan through it, his hand on the centre of her back. She inhaled his sexy aftershave and held his arm as she slipped her sky-high open heels off her feet.

'I love this dress,' Noah stated, pulling the fabric of the

top layer of blush-pink silk organza between his finger and thumb and rubbing. The mini under-dress was a patchwork of different pinks...V neckline, black trim. She liked it, but judging by the gleam in Noah's eyes he couldn't wait to get her out of it.

Morgan tossed her clutch bag on the hall table, placed her hands on her back and stretched, pushing out her chest. She grinned when his eyes dropped and stayed on her chest.

Sometimes being a girl was the best fun ever—especially when you had a super-starry, sexy soldier looking at you with lust in his eyes.

'So, my friends weren't so bad, were they? You spent a lot of time talking to Jack and Luke,' Morgan commented.

Noah pulled his eyes up to her face. 'Uh...Jack knows my brother Mike. Journalist and photographer.'

'Small world.' Morgan glanced into the formal lounge. 'Do you want a nightcap? My dad likes a drop of Macallan every night.'

'My favourite whisky. Sounds good.'

Morgan walked in her bare feet into the lounge, shut the French doors behind her and opened a cabinet, revealing tumblers and a couple of bottles of whisky. 'There's an iPod on the shelf over there—do you want to choose some music?'

Morgan sighed when Sarah McLachlan's voice filled the room. Taking a glass over to Noah, she pressed the drink into his hand. She was about to step back when Noah's arms snaked around her waist and pulled her to him.

'No, stay here. Dance with me again.'

Morgan swayed on the spot with him and then took the glass out of his hand and took a sip. Anyone would think that she had never danced with a man before, yet never had she been so aroused this quickly. Standing up on her toes, she grazed his chin with her lips and slowly kissed his mouth. The music vibrated with desire, with love lost and found.

She heard the bang of crystal hitting wood and felt one of Noah's hands on her bottom, the other on the side of her face. Tongues tangled and hands rubbed at the restrictive barrier of clothing as the plaintive music faded into white noise. She groaned in the back of her throat as hearts clashed and tongues collided, stroked, duelled. One song drifted into another and Morgan murmured her dismay as Noah lifted his head and rested his forehead on hers. He tangled his fist in her hair and tipped her head up so that he could look into her sparkling eyes.

'I need you, Morgan. I know we shouldn't keep doing this…I promised your brother…'

'You saved my life. Trust me, you are James's new best friend—'

'But I still need you. Want you.'

'Then take me,' she whispered.

Her eyes drifted closed and her lips parted as she tipped her head to allow him access to her neck, to the very sensitive spot in the hollow of her throat. He pushed his hand up under her dress and lifted it. Easily, quickly, he found her nipple with his thumb. Morgan groaned, desperately wanting his lips and mouth to continue the exquisite torture. She slid her hand over his hip and stretched her hand so that she barely brushed his erection. It was a faint touch, but Morgan felt the electricity power through him. She felt strong and powerful, and she increased the pressure of her touch and had Noah moaning aloud.

Fumbling with the buttons on his shirt, Morgan eventually pulled the fabric apart and spread her hands over his chest, exploring his defined pecs and his washboard stomach. Pushing the shirt off his shoulders, she touched his collarbone with her tongue and inhaled the scent of his masculine skin.

'You're killing me here, lass. If you carry on like that it's not going to be slow and it's not going to be pretty.' Noah muttered.

'I never asked for either.'

Noah's hand skimmed her thigh and moved across her pelvis. His thumb rested on her mound and she groaned when it drifted lower, yelped when he hit the spot.

'It would be easier if we just got naked,' Noah replied, spinning her around and looking for the zip that held her dress together. Morgan felt cool air on her back and sighed when Noah's hot mouth touched her spine as her dress dropped. His big hands reached around to clasp her breasts and his fingers pulled her nipples into rock-hard points.

This was better than she could have imagined. Noah unclasped her bra and it fell to the floor in a pretty puddle of pink froth, and then her panties were pushed down her legs and she stood naked, her back to his chest, his lips on her neck.

'You're so beautiful.'

Noah turned her around and watched her with lowered lust-filled eyes as he dropped his hands to undo his belt. Morgan gripped the back of the antique couch and licked her lips as he pushed his pants down his legs, standing in front of her in a pair of plain black tight trunks, strained by his very impressive erection.

Two seconds later his trunks were on the floor, his hands were under her thighs and he was lifting her up, his penis probing her slick, wet folds. He held her eyes as he surged into her. He was hard and wonderful and her body shuddered.

'So wet...so warm.'

Morgan moaned as she linked her arms around his strong neck. Her clitoris brushed against his groin as he pulled her even closer and she moaned and tipped her head back. She ground herself into him as Noah looked for and found her mouth. His tongue swirled and slid as he pumped his hips. Morgan groaned as she felt the fierce upward swing of concentrated pleasure...reaching out for that dizzying release... She lifted her hips and mashed herself against him.

'Take it, baby. Use it,' Noah said, his voice low and intense in her ear. 'Use me! Take it all.'

She was all feeling, all concentrated pleasure, as she did

what he said. She bucked and pumped, sinking into him and then using her hands against the couch to push up and away from him so that she could crash down on him again. Power and release built as her body became a vessel of shimmying, sensational pleasure.

Reaching, reaching, and then bursting, flying, Morgan flung her arms around Noah's neck and held on as she split into a thousand pieces and was tacked back together with fairy dust. Somewhere, somehow, she knew that Noah had followed her over the edge; she could hear him panting in her ear, could feel the aftershocks rippling through his muscles, the slight softening of his erection inside her.

Morgan lost track of time; she wasn't sure how long she sat there, half supported by the couch, half by Noah's bulging-with-muscles arms. But eventually Noah slid out of her and held her as her feet touched the floor, holding her arm to make sure that she was steady.

Noah brushed her hair back from her face. 'You okay?'

'Good. Really, really good,' Morgan said on a yawn. 'Boneless.'

Noah picked up his pants, stepped into them and tucked himself away as he did up the fly. 'Let's get you dressed and into bed.'

Noah picked up her dress and she shimmied it over her head. Picking up their underwear, he shoved it into his pockets and picked up his shoes. Taking Morgan's hand, he pulled her towards the French doors.

'Upstairs.'

'I don't think I have the energy to climb those stairs.' Morgan looked at the stairs doubtfully. 'I'm utterly exhausted.'

Noah bent his knees, grabbed her around the thighs and tossed her over his shoulder. Morgan squealed and laughed and slapped his back. 'I was joking, Noah! Put me down.'

'I live to serve, Duchess. Stop wriggling or I will drop you on your imperial ass.'

* * *

Morgan woke up late and rolled over in her massive bed, looking for Noah. Not finding any part of his masculine bod in her bed, she sat up and scowled. He'd sneaked out, the rat, after a night spent exploring her in the most intimate ways possible. He'd reached for her time and time again and they had only drifted off to sleep when the sun had started to yawn, allowing its weak early-morning rays to drift over the mountain.

Being with him had been—bar none and by far—the best sex of her life. The sexy, slightly stand-offish soldier was an amazing lover: demanding, adoring, creative. He hadn't allowed her to feel any modesty and had encouraged her to be forthright and honest. She'd felt comfortable telling him what she liked and didn't like him doing.

There hadn't been any 'getting to know you' or 'wanting to impress you' sex. It had been down and dirty—more like 'I want to know how far I can push you' sex.

More like the type of sex people had when they had known each other a while and were really comfortable in bed together. Weird and astonishing for their first few times together.

Morgan glanced at the clock. It was just past nine and, while she could easily roll over and go back to sleep, she wanted to be with Noah, here in her most favourite spot in the world.

Morgan pushed back the covers and padded over to the en-suite bathroom. Hearing muted voices in the passage-way, she cocked her head. Riley and…her brother? What was James doing on this side of the passage? His room and study were on the other wing of the house—to the right of the staircase and not to the left.

Curious, she padded on tiptoe to the door and cracked it open. Her eyes widened as she saw James, still dressed in the pants he'd worn to the wedding and with his smart grey shirt bunched in his hand.

'If you say it was a mistake, I swear I'll stab you with…
something,' Riley hissed.

'Dammit, Riley, you are like my—'

Morgan put her hand against her mouth to stifle her laughter as Riley, obviously naked beneath a silky short robe,
plastered her mouth against James's and slapped her hands
on his butt. She kissed him thoroughly and with some skill,
Morgan noticed, and when they came up for air James looked
shell-shocked.

'You didn't say that when you were moaning my name
in the throes of passion last night.'

'Ri—okay. But—'

'I am not your sister or your friend. And I'm done pining
away for you. You have ten seconds to decide if you want
to explore this heat we have always had or whether you are
walking away for good. But you should know that if you
walk that's it. You don't get a second chance.'

'Riley, I—'

'Ten seconds, nine, eight, seven—'

'It's not that easy.'

Yes, it is, you ass! Morgan wanted to shout. *She's the best
thing that ever happened to you!*

'Six, five, four, three…'

Morgan bit her lip as her best friend counted down and
her stupid brother just stared at her with miserable eyes.
Morgan closed her own eyes at the immense pain she saw
in Riley's before the door closed in James's face.

Morgan fought the urge to step into the passage and slap
some sense into James. She knew it wouldn't help. James
was as stubborn as she was—maybe more. She couldn't help
him see what was right in front of his face; couldn't force
him to feel love when he didn't.

Morgan watched him walk down the passage and then
glanced to Riley's closed door. To knock or not to knock?
Normally she would just barge in there and offer comfort,
curse her brother just to make Riley smile. But she suspected

that this went too deep, meant too much, and her gut instinct was to leave Riley alone. She would reach out when she could and when she was ready to.

In the meantime she had her own six-foot-three man to find.

Morgan, dressed in a very brief pair of faded denim shorts, flip-flops and a tank top—early autumn in South Africa still spiked the temperatures to boiling—took the cup of coffee Mariah poured her and with a muffin in her hand walked out through the back door of the house. Mariah had said that she'd seen Noah walk in the direction of the southside vines and the dam, and that was nearly an hour ago.

Morgan, munching on her cheese and spinach muffin and sipping her coffee, tipped her face to the sun and pulled in deep breaths of fresh mountain air. She wished that they weren't flying out later tonight, that she and Noah could hang out here a bit longer. There was no security threat, no pollution, no crazy traffic, no boring functions to attend, no ball to organise. It was impossible, but it was a lovely dream to indulge in as she looked for her lover-slash-bodyguard.

Morgan dusted her hands against the seat of her pants to get rid of the crumbs and waved to some labourers working the vines.

And there he was, Morgan thought, sitting on the edge of the dam, his arms loosely linked around his knees, his dark hair glinting in the sun. He hadn't shaved and his stubble gave him a rugged look that had her mouth watering. Warmth pooled between her legs as she remembered the feel of those back muscles that red T-shirt covered, the hard butt underneath his cotton shorts. He was beautiful: masculine grace wrapping a fantastically loyal spirit and a sharp brain.

Morgan approached him quietly, covered his eyes with her hands and whispered in his ear. 'Guess who?'

Noah didn't say anything. He just pulled her hands down

and held her arms so that she was plastered against his back, her head next to his, her breasts mashed into his chest.

'You okay, Noah?' she asked quietly. 'What's going on in that head of yours, soldier?'

A part of him—a big part of him—wished he could open up, just release all this churned-up emotion inside him. He wanted to tell her that he couldn't decide whether he regretted sleeping with her or not…that being with her had been everything he'd dreamt of and more and also, on the other hand, his biggest nightmare. He'd lost himself in her body, had adored every minute of her, and he mourned his lack of self-control as he'd lost himself in her. He wanted to tell her that when she'd drifted off in the early hours of this morning he'd just lain next to her and watched her breathe.

She'd decimated him with her soft lips, her whispered moans, her delicate hands on his not-so-delicate body. She'd touched his heart with her murmurs of delight, her whispers of gratitude at the way he made her feel, and his heart had swelled when he'd heard his name on her lips as he tipped her over into orgasm time and time again.

But on the flipside of the coin he hadn't even started to think what effect sleeping with her would have on his job, on his ability to keep her safe. They'd caught four more kidnappers but another gang could be contracted tomorrow. Until the situation in Colombia was definitively resolved she wouldn't be completely safe, so he would remain in place as her bodyguard. Would thoughts of what they did to and with each other distract him if something else happened? Would he be less sharp, less aware, less able to say no to her when she wanted to do something or be somewhere that could place her in danger?

Morgan pulled her hands out of his grasp and sat down beside him on the grassy bank, staring at the water. Now and again the water rippled as a trout broke the surface to look for food. In another life he could imagine being here with Morgan, casting a fly while she lazed on the bank, a glass of wine in her hand.

Noah leaned back on his hands and looked past the dam to the vines in their perfect rows, and from there to the purple-blue mountain looming over the farm. 'It's such a stunning place, Morgs. I can't understand why you're in New York when you can be here.'

'Clients, mostly. But I should take more time to come back here.' Morgan pushed her hair behind her ears. Then she placed her palm on Noah's thigh, gently squeezed and lifted it again. 'Please don't regret what happened between us, Noah. It was too good for regrets.'

'It's so complicated, Morgan,' he said in a gruff voice.

'I think you make it a great deal more complicated than it is,' Morgan replied. 'We're friends who have shared our bodies. We had a great deal of fun, and if we do it again we'll have fun again.'

Noah frowned. 'So, you're not looking forward? Expecting anything from me?'

Morgan crossed her legs, picked a blade of grass and ran it through her fingers. 'I was talking to Riley about this a little while ago, and spending more time with you has just reinforced my opinion that I'm not cut out to be with someone long-term.'

Noah frowned, utterly confused. 'Why not?'

'I've shielded you from my dyslexia—shielded you from what I go through on a daily basis. I shield everyone. I never read the news; I watch it. I try to avoid writing anything down because my handwriting looks like a chicken's scrawl and I can't spell. At all. I don't drive unless I know exactly where I am and the route I'm travelling, and I never drive in New York or any other city.'

'Okay.'

'On the few occasions I do write something on the computer I call Riley to check the spelling.'

'Um…spellcheck?' Noah volunteered.

'It doesn't help if you don't recognise the word, Noah.'

Oh, flip. He hadn't thought of that.

'Look, I've done tons of research on dyslexia and there are a couple of things I can't wrap my head around. Both of them involve a steady relationship. One is that if I get involved then I can't do it halfway. I'd want the whole bang-shoot. Marriage, kids…everything. Having kids is a risk, because dyslexia is hereditary and I couldn't bear it if my husband blamed me for his child struggling at school. The other is that one day, as hard as I will try to prevent it, my partner will feel frustrated with me and then disappointed. Quickly followed by him thinking that, despite how hard we've tried, something is lacking. In me.'

Noah stared at her profile for a long, long time before pulling in a deep breath. He looked for the right words but only two hovered on his tongue. 'Horse crap, Morgan.'

'Excuse me?' she gasped, shocked.

'That is the biggest load of self-indulgent horse crap I've ever heard—' Noah cursed as his mobile disturbed the country silence of the morning. He pulled out his mobile, checked the display and frowned. 'Sorry, it's my father's carer. I need to take this.'

As the feminine Scottish lilt travelled across the miles, giving him news he didn't want to hear, Noah felt the world shift under his feet. He dropped the phone to the grass and bent his head as he struggled to make sense of her words.

Fell out of his wheelchair. Hit his head. Bleeding on the brain. Dead…

'Noah?'

He felt Morgan's cool hand on his cheek.

'Hon, what's happened?'

'He's dead. He's finally dead.' Noah heard the words but his brain had no connection to the words his tongue was speaking. 'I thought I'd be happier.'

'Who's dead, Noah?'

'My father.' He ran his hand over his face. 'I have to go

to Scotland. I have to tell my brothers. Man, can't we just go back to our conversation? I want to tell you why I thought you were talking rubbish. It doesn't have to be like that…'

The trees were dancing and the water in the dam was rising and falling. What was happening to him?

Morgan gripped his hands. 'Just breathe, Noah. In and out.'

'So many times I wished he was dead, and now he is and I don't know what to feel.' Noah stared at the sky. 'I need to go, Morgan. I need to tell my brothers.'

He heard his irrational gabbling and felt embarrassed. He never gabbled…wasn't irrational.

'You will tell them, Noah. Just breathe for now, take in the news, stop thinking and let yourself feel.'

Noah shook his head and jumped to his feet. *Hell, no!* The last thing he wanted or needed to do was feel.

Morgan followed him up, placed her hands on his chest and looked up into his ravaged face. 'Noah, stop. Listen to me—no, don't push past me! You're as white as a sheet. *Listen* to me!'

Noah forced himself to concentrate on her words.

'I'm going to walk away and you are going to sit down and take it in. Take a deep breath and look around. You've just heard that your father is dead. Take a moment. Feel. Cry. Do what you need to do. There's going to be a time when you need to be strong, and the next fifteen minutes, half an hour—the rest of the day if that's what you need—isn't that time.' Morgan touched his cheek with her fingers. 'Take the time, Noah. Please.'

Noah saw the sympathy in her eyes and bit his lip, fighting the emotion that was threatening to crash over him. If she had let him walk, do what he needed to do, he could have pushed it away, but if he had to stay here then he didn't want her seeing the mess he would probably dissolve into. The anger, the regret, the swamping, swamping guilt.

'Go.' Noah muttered the word, shoving his hand into his hair. 'Go now.'

Morgan nodded once, then bent down, quickly scooped up his mobile and tucked it into her pocket. He watched her walk away and it was only when she was out of sight that he allowed the first hot, angry, guilty wave of emotion to crash over him.

CHAPTER ELEVEN

MORGAN WALKED FROM the galley area of the jet and sat down next to Noah, who was staring out at the solid black expanse that was the African continent below them. She pressed a whisky into his hand and put her temple on his shoulder. 'How are you doing, soldier?'

Noah took a sip, shuddered, and gestured to the window. 'I never realised how dark Africa really is. You hardly ever see lights.'

So, not ready to talk, then.

'Just miles and miles of nothingness,' Morgan agreed, tucking her feet up under her. She'd shed her shoes earlier and she reached for the soft blanket that she'd put on the chairs opposite them and pulled it over her knees.

'Cold?' Noah asked, slipping his arm around her and pulling her closer.

'A little.'

Noah kissed her hair before taking another sip of his whisky. 'I never expected you to commandeer the family jet to take me to London, Morgan.'

'It was James's suggestion, Noah. I'm sorry we couldn't leave earlier, but they were doing some maintenance on it.' Morgan replied.

James had been quick to offer the use of the plane, saying that the jet could turn around in London and come back to pick them up. So they'd return to New York a day later? The world wouldn't stop. Morgan knew that there was a reason why she adored her brother. It made it hard to remain annoyed with him over the hurting-Riley issue.

'It's an expensive exercise, Morgan. I could've just caught a normal flight. And I didn't expect you to come with me. I was going to send another operative to guard you while I was away.'

'I don't want to train someone else,' Morgan joked, and then sighed at his worried eyes and his serious face. 'Noah, relax. We're hugely rich and we can afford to send the jet anywhere we want, whenever we want. We wanted to get you to London in the quickest, most comfortable way possible. I wanted to be with you because I don't think that anybody should be alone at a time like this.'

Noah kissed her head again. 'I'm not used to people doing stuff for me.'

'Yeah, I realised that. Talking of which, James contacted Chris and gave him a heads-up. He'll meet you at the airport with another guard for me and I'll let you do what you need to do. I'd like to stay with you, but that might not be what you want.'

Noah was silent for a long time and Morgan subdued her pang of disappointment. Of course he didn't want to have to worry about her at a time like this... Yeah, they had slept together, but that didn't mean he wanted her to invade his emotional space.

'When you're done—when the funeral is over—the jet will take us back to New York. That's if you're coming back with me.'

Noah rubbed his eyes. 'It's so difficult to think. To decide what to do next.'

Morgan placed her hand on his thigh and left it there. 'I know... Well, I don't know, but I can imagine.'

'My brothers—'

Morgan remembered the comment he'd made at the art

exhibition. 'As much as you want to, you can't shield them from this, Noah.'

'Yeah.' Noah turned his head to look out of the window again into the black nothingness.

She'd never known anyone who needed someone to release what was obviously years of pent-up emotion more than he did. She knew that there was a huge and possibly tragic story here—that Noah was dealing with far more than just—*just!*—the death of his dad. Morgan wished she could shake it out of him, but she also suspected that she was the last person he'd allow to peek into his soul.

He saw himself as the protector, the guardian, but he didn't realise that in order to give you had to be able to receive. That you had to be strong enough—physically, mentally, *emotionally*—to do that. She worried about him... worried that as soon as the plane landed he would be all business in a 'let's-get-this-done-and-sorted' mode. She didn't know much about death but she knew that he had to grieve, had to mourn. He couldn't keep tamping down his emotion because one day he would erupt and splatter.

But this wasn't her party and she couldn't make him cry if she wanted to. All she could do was to be here, offering her unconditional support.

'We were raised in a bad area of Glasgow,' Noah said, his accent broad and his voice low.

He was still staring out of the window and Morgan didn't move a muscle, scared that he'd stop talking if she reacted at all. 'My father was frequently out of work. He had few skills and no desire to get any more. He lived off the dole and drank most of it away. My mum took whatever work she could find and kept him under control—mostly. He was an angry man and liked being that way.'

Morgan pushed her shoulder into his, pushed her fingers into his hand and kept her silence.

'My mum wanted to move out; she could get a job in her brother's inn in Kelso. He didn't want to move but she finally persuaded him to visit with her. They borrowed a car and my brothers and I stayed behind—I can't remember why. My father wasn't an experienced driver and it was wet and they spun off the road. Mum was killed instantly. Michael was paralysed from the waist down.'

Michael, he called his father Michael. Not Dad—just Michael.

'Long story short: he became our worst nightmare. Anger turned to rage, rage to violence, and if you think a man can't be physically violent confined to a wheelchair then you should've seen him. I watched my brothers become walking robots, scared to move—to breathe—and I called Social Services, They arranged for them to go and live with my aunt—my mum's sister.'

'And you?'

'Somebody had to stay and look after him. I lasted three years,' Noah said. 'I was nineteen when I joined up.'

'What happened that made you leave?' Morgan asked, because she knew that something major had happened. Noah, being Noah, with his unquestionable loyalty, would have had to have an excellent reason to walk away.

Still looking out of the window, he said, 'I said he was abusive and he was. Verbally, physically… But that day had been a quiet day—no drama from him. He'd actually been behaving himself. I walked past him and saw this cold look in his eye, and then his fist flew out and he punched me in my…you know…'

Morgan's eyes widened but she kept her voice even. 'Groin?'

'Yeah. I just reacted. We were in the kitchen and…I don't know what happened but I lost time. When I came back I was holding a knife to his throat and he was begging me not to kill him. I wanted to; it would've been so easy.'

'But you didn't.'

'No, I walked away, made arrangements for his care and joined the army. I left him alone.'

Morgan turned to face him, lifted up her hand and touched his chin, forcing him to look at her. 'You spent three years in a horrid situation with an abusive father. You earned the right to walk away, Noah. Knowing you, you've probably supported him financially all this time.'

'Yes, I have—but you don't understand!' Noah sounded agitated. 'I nearly *killed* him, Morgan!'

Morgan raised her eyebrows. 'But you *didn't*, Noah! He was an abusive father who inflicted violence on you. He sucker-punched you—in a man's most vulnerable place!— and it was the straw that broke your back. I'm surprised that you *didn't* kill him, Noah.'

'You don't understand! I lost control! Like I nearly did the other day.'

'Oh, Noah, millions of men would think that you showed immense control by *not* killing him! And you were nowhere near losing control last week.'

Noah looked at her with wide shocked eyes and she could see him trying to process her words. 'Have you ever spoken to anyone about this? Chris? Your brothers? A psychologist?'

Noah shook his head.

She was the only person that knew his secret? How could that be? 'Maybe you should. Maybe they can convince you that you were just a boy, trying to survive and doing the best you could in a dreadful situation.'

Noah closed his eyes and rested his head on hers. 'I'm so tired, Morgs.'

Morgan pushed his hair off his forehead. 'Then why don't you rest awhile? Push the seat back and try and sleep, okay?' Morgan pulled the lever on his seat and watched as he stretched out. She passed him a pillow, pulled another blanket over him, before flipping her seat back and lying so that she faced him. Holding his hand, she watched as he drifted off to sleep.

'Morgs?'

'Yes?'

He yawned and his voice was thick with sleep when he spoke again. 'Stay with me, okay? I'd like you there…at the funeral and when I tell my brothers.'

'I'll be there,' Morgan whispered, and watched him while he slept.

Noah was as jittery as a crack addict desperate for a fix. He stood in front of one of the many houses in the grimy brick block and placed his hand on the incongruous red railing—and quickly lifted it when he felt the sticky gunge on his skin. Wiping his palm on his jeans, he played with the keys in his hand.

He hadn't been back to the house he'd been raised in in nearly fifteen years and he didn't want to go inside now. He just wanted to put this entire nightmare behind him. But before he could he had to bury his father tomorrow and clean out his house today. Postponing wasn't an option, because his brothers were flying in later and would insist on helping him. Their aunt's house was their real home, and he didn't want them to see the reality of how their parents had lived.

He didn't want Morgan seeing it either, but she wouldn't be dissuaded from accompanying him. He'd pleaded for her to stay in the hotel room, had offered another bodyguard for the day so that she could spend the day sightseeing, but she'd refused.

She was coming with him and he'd have to deal with it, she'd stated, calmly and resolutely. Nobody should have to clear out their parents' house alone.

He wasn't sure whether to be grateful or to strangle her. He looked over to her, dressed as he was in old jeans and a casual sweater. But she still looked out of place in this place of dank and dark buildings covered in grime and graffiti.

Over the past day or so Morgan's presence had kept him centred, grounded, able to go through the steps of organising the funeral, notifying the few relatives they had left, and that hard conversation with his brothers, who'd taken the news rather prosaically. He couldn't judge them for their lack of grief; they'd had minimal contact with Michael for most of their lives and didn't have a personal relationship with him. He also knew that their offer to come to the funeral was more to support him than to say goodbye to their father.

Yesterday, after a long, cold, tough day, he'd lost himself in Morgan's body, stepping away from the memories of the past and the reality of his father's passing and losing himself in her smooth skin, her frantic gasps, her warm, wet heat. And when guilt had welled up and threatened to consume him whole, when he'd felt like punching a fist through a wall, her words, spoken quietly but with such truth, drifted through his head.

'*Millions of men would think that you showed immense control by* not *killing him. You were just a boy, trying to survive and doing the best you could in a dreadful situation.*'

Morgan. She was becoming as necessary to him as breathing and he either wanted to beg her never to leave him or he wanted to run as far and as fast away from her as possible.

Noah saw movement across the road and caught the eye of the obvious leader of a gang of teens across the road. He gave them a don't-mess-with-me stare. They ducked their heads and moved off and Noah sighed. *There but for the grace of God go I*, he'd thought, on more than one occasion.

'Let's go in, Noah, it's cold out here,' Morgan suggested, her hand on his back.

Noah shook himself out of his trance and walked up the cracked steps into the mouldy building. He shuddered as he breathed in the smell of decaying food and despair.

He automatically turned to the door on the left and his hand shook as he tried to place the key in the lock. He didn't know why they bothered with locking up; he knew that one solid kick would have the door flying open. When he couldn't make the connection between key and lock he considered it a viable option.

Morgan took the key from his hand, jabbed it in the lock

and pushed open the door. She stepped inside and Noah wanted to warn her not to…that his father was unstable, volatile, capricious.

No, his father was dead. Noah bit his bottom lip, looked around and swore. Nothing had changed; the old blue couch was just paler and grubbier, the furniture that much more battered. And, man, it was messy. His father had always been a slob but Noah had paid for a cleaner, for someone to look after him.

'How did he live like this?' Noah whispered. 'If the carer didn't clean, then did she feed him, look after him?'

Guilt threatened to buckle his knees, sink him to the floor.

Morgan tossed him a glance and immediately went to the old fridge, yanked it open. She pulled back at the smell but pointed out the milk, the cheese. Slamming the door shut, she pulled open the freezer section and nodded.

'There are quite a few homemade meals in here, Noah, and lots of dirty dishes in the sink. He was eating. And, look, there's a note on the fridge, saying that the carer was going on holiday. She got back the day he died. I think.'

'Thank you.' Noah looked down as he kicked a half-empty bottle of whisky at his feet. So the drinking hadn't stopped.

He couldn't do this with her here… Couldn't handle seeing his classy NYC girl in a smelly flat filled with dirty dishes and soiled clothes and windows covered with soot and grime. Couldn't handle the pity he thought he saw in her eyes. He wanted to cry but he couldn't do that with her— couldn't let her see him at his weakest.

'Morgan, please leave.'

Morgan looked at him with huge eyes. 'I don't want to. I don't want you to do this on your own. Let me stay, please.'

Noah dropped his head and felt the walls of the room closing in on him. He desperately wanted to be alone, wanted some time to himself, to sort through the emotion to find the truth of what he was feeling. He knew it was time to pull away from her now, to find some distance. He wanted to take back his life, his mind, his control. He wanted to stand alone, as he always had. He needed to know that he could, that he didn't need that gorgeous blonde in his life, standing in his corner.

Why had he even explained his past to Morgan? Where had that crazy impulse come from? Being side-winded after hearing that Michael was dead? Now he felt as if he was standing in front of her, his chest cracked open, and inviting her to wreak havoc. By allowing her inside he'd handed her his pistol and invited her to shoot him in the heart.

He was the closest he'd ever come to falling over that long cliff into love, and he couldn't help thinking whether he would be feeling the same way if his father hadn't died— if his feelings for her didn't seem deeper because there was so much emotion swirling around him.

He just wanted to step away from this freakin' soul-searching and get on an even keel again. He wanted to feel normal.

Morgan folded her arms across her chest. 'Talk to me, Noah. Please.'

'You're not going to like what I say,' he warned her.

'Talk to me anyway,' Morgan said, perching her butt on the side of the rickety dining room table. She stood in nearly the same place as he had when he'd taken a knife to his father's throat...

He stared at the old television screen. 'My parents are both dead and I should feel free. Except that I don't.'

'Why not?'

'Because you're here.'

'Do you want to explain that?'

Noah shoved his hand into his hair and tugged. 'I don't want you to think that just because you're here we have something serious happening. I don't want you thinking that we're in some sort of relationship...'

'We are. If nothing else, we are friends.'

'Friends?'

Noah snorted, thinking that by allowing her to come with him he'd tied himself to Morgan, bound himself into some sort of relationship. He was furious that she'd pricked through his self-sufficiency and made him rely on her.

He looked around the room and felt anger whirl and swirl. 'I left this place fifteen years ago and I swore that I would never feel vulnerable again. I vowed, after walking away from him, that I'd never feel weak again.'

Yet here he was, shortly before burying the person who'd taught him that lesson, putting himself in the same position. With her.

He was such a fool. He couldn't, *wouldn't* ever rely on someone else again...and this touchy-feely crap he had going on with Morgan stopped now.

'I don't want you here. I want you gone.'

Had he actually voiced those words? He must have because her head jerked back in shock and all colour drained from her face.

'Noah...'

'This—you and I—it stops. Right now.'

'You're tired and upset and not thinking straight,' Morgan said after a moment, and he could see that she was trying to keep calm, desperately looking to keep the conversation, the situation, rational.

In normal circumstances her words might have jerked him back to sanity, but nothing about standing in his father's filthy house, being bombarded with ugly memories and emotions, was normal. If he wasn't in such a turbulent mood he'd readily admit that when it came to him she generally knew exactly what to say. How to make him laugh, think, want her with every breath he took.

He didn't *want* to want her like this; didn't want to deal with the tender emotions only she could pull to the surface. Didn't want to deal with anything right now...

'Why don't I give you some space?' Morgan sucked in her cheeks. 'I'll wait for you outside.'

Morgan turned to walk to the door but his harsh voice had her stopping just before she reached it. 'No. I don't want you to wait. I don't want this—you—any more.'

He saw, maybe felt the shudder that rocketed through her, saw her head fall. He fought the urge to go to her, to soothe, to protect. The child in him protested that *he'd* never been soothed, protected.

'I never promised you anything and I always said that I would leave.'

Morgan finally turned around, lifted her head and gave him a withering look. 'Stop acting like an ass, Noah. I understand that this has been a rough time for you, but don't take your anger out on the people who love you.'

Noah leaned backed and stretched out his feet. 'So now you *love* me?'

Morgan's eyes froze. 'I'm not even going to dignify that with a reply. You're angry and hurt and acting like a jerk. You're just going through the stages of grief—albeit quicker than most. First shock, you skipped denial. and now you're feeling angry.'

'No, you're looking for an excuse because you don't want to hear what I'm saying.'

'Which is exactly what, Noah? Put your cards on the table, Fraser.'

Well, okay, then. 'I don't want you in my life any more.'

'That's not how you felt this morning, last night, twenty minutes ago.'

That was the truth.

'It's how I feel now. I don't like feeling this connected to someone—feeling like my heart wants to explode with joy just because you're in the room. I want to feel normal again—me again… Not a twisted-with-emotion sap.' Noah ground the words out, forcing them around his reluctant tongue. 'I don't want to love you! And I certainly don't need you. I was perfectly fine on my own.'

He hadn't been, his heart shouted, but he shut out its screams.

Morgan shook her head, blinked away the emotion in her eyes and bit her bottom lip. He felt lower than an amoeba infected with anthrax. What was wrong with him? He was tossing away the best thing in his life...*ever*.

'Well, that was very clear.'

Morgan lifted her chin and he had to admire her courage.

'Well, screw you and your lousy, spiteful, wimpy attitude.' She grabbed her bag off the table and yanked it over her shoulder. 'I'm going back to the hotel.'

Noah watched her take a couple of steps before remembering that she was still a target, Glasgow or not. 'You can't leave by yourself!' he shouted.

Morgan bared her teeth at him and he was quite sure that her eyes were glowing red. He couldn't blame her.

'Watch me. I'd rather be kidnapped by rabid Colombians than spend one more minute with you!'

Noah stood up, pulled out his mobile and nodded, his face grim. 'That's easy to make happen.' Pushing buttons, he held it up to his ear, and his voice was rough when he spoke. 'Amanda?' He waited a minute before speaking again. 'Listen, I know that we've had our problems but do you have any agents in Glasgow who can take over Morgan Moreau's protection detail?' He waited a beat and spoke again. 'No, I need him now. Like within the next half-hour...hour. You have? Great.'

Noah rattled off the address and bit his lip. 'Thanks. Amanda. I think the threat level to her has mostly been neutralised. but tell him that if anything happens to her—if she breaks even a fingernail—he's dead.'

Noah disconnected the call and slapped his mobile against the palm of his hand. He looked at Morgan, whose eyes were wide with shock, humiliation and hurt. He wanted to take her in his arms, apologise, but he knew that the smarter course of action would be to walk away from her while he still could. While his heart was still his and not walking around in her hands.

'Your wish is my command, Duchess,' he said with a mocking bow.

Now he just had to keep himself from hitting redial, cancelling the new bodyguard, gathering Morgan up and keeping her for ever.

It was the longest, quietest, hardest, most excruciating wait of his life, and when she walked out to the car with a kid who looked as if he should still be in school he stood in his old house, sank to the couch and, for the first time in fifteen years, cried.

CHAPTER TWELVE

A WEEK LATER Riley walked into Morgan's studio, two cups in her hand, and Morgan sighed at the green logo of the twin-tailed mermaid on the cup. It was a mega hazelnut-flavoured latte, her favourite, and she needed it—along with Prozac and probably a padded cell.

'Hey, I was just about to buzz you,' Morgan said. 'I need help.'

'Okay.' Riley took a seat on the stool next to her at the workbench. 'You look like hell. Still crying?'

Morgan took a deep breath and nodded. 'Yeah. You?'

'Mmm… What a pair we are. You've heard the news?'

'That James is on his way back from Colombia and a deal is imminent?'

'Yeah.'

Morgan sighed and pointed out a word on her computer screen. 'What's this word?'

Riley bent down and peered over her shoulder. 'Vichyssoise.'

'Jeez, I can't read in English and they throw French words in,' Morgan grumbled. 'Do you have some time? Can you go through this menu for the ball with me?'

'Sure.'

She and Riley spent the next fifteen minutes discussing the ball, finalising the menu and the entertainment, the decorations and the ticket sales—which were going through the roof.

'We also need to approve the design of the mannequin cages and we need Noah's input there.'

Morgan stared at her fingers. 'Feel free to call him. I won't.'

She felt the tears in the back of her throat. His words from a week ago still bounced around her skull.

'I don't want you here any more.'

He'd preferred to face his demons alone than have her around. What did that say about her? She could understand him dumping her when they got back to New York, when he got bored with the sex, but she'd seen how much pain he'd been in, how he'd been struggling to deal with the memories of his past, and she'd thought that he'd want her there—that he wouldn't want to go through that alone.

But, no, Noah hadn't wanted her around.

All her life she'd tried to be good enough—for her family, for herself. She knew that she didn't always reach the standard she'd set for herself, and mostly she was okay with that. But to be told, during such a sad time, that she wasn't wanted or needed had lashed her soul.

She simply wasn't good enough...

'Horse crap, Morgan.'

She heard Noah's words spoken at Bon Chance as clear as day and actually looked around for the source of that statement. When Riley didn't react she looked inside herself and heard the phrase again.

'The biggest, load of self-indulgent horse crap.'

Morgan almost laughed as emotion swelled inside her. She wasn't sure where it came from, what its source was, but she recognised the power of it, saw the pure truth for the first time in a week, months—her entire life.

'Bats on a freakin' broomstick,' she muttered.

'Pardon?' Riley looked up and frowned.

Morgan looked at her best friend and put her hand over

her mouth in surprised shock. 'What happened with Noah wasn't about me…it was about *him*.'

'Okay, I have no idea what you're talking about,' Riley complained.

'Him kicking me into touch wasn't about me—wasn't about me not being good enough. I just assumed it was because I always assume the worst about myself. I keep saying that it's hard for people to deal with my dyslexia. but in truth I've never come to terms with it. And because of that I assume that everything is about me. My habitual reaction is to think that I'm not good enough, to think the worst of myself.'

Riley leaned back and clapped a slow beat. 'Well, glory hallelujah, the child has seen the light.'

Morgan stood up and paced the area in front of Riley. 'He told me what the problem was but I didn't listen. He said that he didn't like feeling so connected to me—something about his heart and feeling joy when I was around. That around me emotion twisted him up.' Morgan pointed her finger at Riley. '*He's* the one who's scared, who doesn't know what to do with me. He felt insecure and emotional and… Damn it, I'm going to smack him into next year!'

Riley smiled. 'I'd like to see you try.'

'He was hurting and not knowing why he was grieving for his father—the man was a waste of oxygen by all accounts—he didn't know how to channel his emotion and he lashed out. He needed me, but he was scared to need me. Everyone else he needed had either left him or let him down. He had to push me away to protect himself.'

'Look at you—you're a female Dr Phil.' Riley crossed her legs. 'So, what are you going to do, Morgs?'

'Go to him, of course. I might understand better, but I'm still mad that he kicked me into touch.' Morgan smiled grimly. 'Oh, I'm *so* going to kick some gorgeous SAS ass.'

Riley nodded. 'That's my girl.'

* * *

Back in London, in his favourite pub, Noah took a listless sip of his beer and looked up as his brothers sat down on the bar stools on either side of him. It seemed that Chris, who was outside taking a call, felt he needed reinforcements for the lecture he intended to dole out. *Wuss.*

Noah sent a look to the door and thought that he could get by Chris if he wanted to. He'd taken on a room full of Colombian thugs—nearly killing one in the process—and won.

Yeah, run away from this conversation like a coward, Fraser—like you did from Morgan. Just to add to the long list of things he'd done lately that he wasn't proud of.

Hamish slapped him on the back and placed their orders for drinks. 'So, let me see if Chris has the story straight. You still haven't spoken to Morgan and apologised?'

No small talk, no lead-up just...*pow!* 'Essentially.'

'You really are a git, big bro',' said Mike, lifting his glass and toasting him. 'Though admittedly it *is* nice to see that you have clay feet. But dumping Morgan...' Mike leaned forward and frowned at him. 'Did you get punched in the head? In other words, *are you freaking insane?*'

Noah lifted his hand to protest and saw that Chris had joined his merry group. 'Thanks,' he said, sarcastically. 'Did they need to know?'

'Sure they need to see their control freak big brother unhinged,' Chris said on a smile.

'I am *not* unhinged,' Noah said through gritted teeth. Miserable and dejected, but still clear-thinking.

'Mmm, that's why you're the model of efficiency at work. *Not.*'

'You talk like a teenage girl,' Noah muttered.

'You're acting like one,' Chris countered.

'And I am not unhinged! Unhinged was what I felt like when I saw that knife to her neck. When I contemplated what life would be without her...' He hadn't meant to add that.

'You're living a life without her,' Mike pointed out. 'And how's *that* working out for you?'

'Shut up, Oprah.'

Bloody awful, but the point was… What was the point? All he knew was that he was scared to love her, scared to lose her, and scared to live this half-life without her in it. He just wanted to go back to his life as it had been before he met her, when he'd been heartless and independent and unemotional.

When life had been easy and uncomplicated. It hadn't quite worked out that way. Yet.

And he really didn't want to have this conversation with his brothers and Chris. There was nothing wrong, in his opinion, with those old-fashioned men-to-men conversations, where they didn't discuss emotions at all. But, no, he had to be saddled with three touchy-feely, new age guys who thought it was perfectly reasonable to discuss his broken heart.

'The least you can do is talk to her,' Hamish suggested.

'Back off,' he growled into his beer.

'Either that or go to my bothy in the Highlands and lick you wounds in private,' Chris suggested.

'Will any of you follow me there and carry on bleating in my ear?' Noah demanded.

They looked at each other, shook their heads. 'Not for a day or two at least.'

'Sold.' Noah slapped his hands on the bar. It was exactly what he needed: time and solitude to think, recover and relive his time with Morgan.

No, that wasn't right. To *get over* Morgan. Because that was what he had to do, the sensible thing to do.

Ten days from that momentous day—the one that had ended with Noah kicking her out of her life—and she was back in Scotland, Morgan thought, her hands on the wheel of the rental car. She was driving in a country halfway across the world.

James had worked out an agreement at the mine that was complicated and confusing, and the details of which she cared absolutely nothing about. What was important was that everyone was thoroughly convinced that the threat to their well-being was neutralised and her mother and father had come out of hiding thoroughly sick of each other. Her father had disappeared on a trip to investigate a mine in Botswana and her mother had started poking her nose into MI business and, more annoyingly, ball business. Situation normal there.

James and Riley were either snipping at each other, ignoring each other or avoiding each other. Situation... She didn't even know how to categorise their situation...crazy?

The CFT guards—even more robotic than Noah—had gone back to being robotic with someone else and her apartment had become her own again.

Situation so very *not* normal there.

She hated it. She hated the silence and the fact that there was no one to drink wine with, chat with, curl up around at night, make sweet love to in the morning.

She missed him. With every breath she took. But more than anything else she was so steel-meltingly angry with him that he'd just walked away—because she couldn't concentrate on a thing and because her stress levels were stratospheric.

She couldn't design, couldn't make decisions on the ball, couldn't eat, couldn't sleep.

She had a business to run, an important social event to organise, and after she'd given him many, *many* pieces of her mind she'd put him aside and resume her life—go back to normal. She was not going to beg, to tell him she loved him, adored his body, loved his generous, protective spirit. She wouldn't tell him that she'd fallen in love with him eight years ago and never really stopped. *Dammit*.

Morgan felt the familiar cocktail of love and misery and anger churn in her stomach. How dared he throw comments mentioning joy and love at her head and then kick her out of his life? He was the most courageous man she knew except when it came to loving—*keeping!*—her. Well, she wasn't just going to lie down and accept it...

Telling him where to get off and that she was worth taking a chance on were the *only* reasons she was on this godforsaken road in the middle of the Scottish Highlands, probably lost. Again.

Okay, depending on how wretched he was, she might let it slip that she missed him and that she loved him—maybe. Probably.

Morgan yawned and shoved her exhaustion away. She'd landed at Heathrow yesterday, threatened Chris with dismemberment if he didn't tell her where he was and nearly bitten his head off when he'd offered to take her to the bothy close to Auterlochie. She could find it herself, she'd stated grandly, and now she wished she'd taken him up on his offer. Because this place was desolate, and it was getting dark, and there were scary cows with big horns that glared at her from the side of the road.

As night and the temperature fell Morgan saw the glimmer of a stone cottage off the road and wondered if this could possibly be the bothy Noah sometimes escaped to. There were no lights on in the house, and there wasn't any sign of the deep green Land Rover Chris said he used up here.

There was only one way to find out, she thought, bunching her much hated map in her hand and storming up to the front door. After knocking and getting no response she found the door opened to her touch, and she looked around a large room: kitchen at one end, lounge at the other. Through the closed door she presumed there was a bedroom and bathroom. There were battered couches, one that held a jersey draped over its arm. Morgan picked it up and sighed when she inhaled Noah's familiar scent.

The cabin was also ridiculously tidy, and she knew she was in the right place.

She loved him...but she was going to kill him when she

saw him. For making her fall in love with him, for making her chase after him, for being a totally stupid, pathetically scared of commitment, moron *man*.

'What? Not naked this time?' Noah said from the door-way.

Morgan dropped the shirt and whipped around. Her heart bounced and then settled as her eyes drifted over him in the half-light of the cottage.

Kill him…slowly…

'Can you put some lights on?' Morgan asked politely.

'Why?'

'So that I can see your face when I scream at you.'

Morgan blinked as he flicked the switch on the wall next to the door.

Noah walked into the room and shoved his hands into his jeans pockets. Morgan cocked her head at him and saw that there were blue shadows under his eyes and his mouth looked grim. Tense. Possibly scared.

Good. He should be.

'You don't seem very surprised to see me,' Morgan said.

'Chris gave me a heads-up that you were on your way but I expected you hours ago. I was out looking for you. What happened? Did you get lost?'

With that comment he lit the fuse to her temper. 'Of *course* I got lost, you idiot! Lots and lots of times! I forgot to check if there was a GPS when I hired the car! I have dyslexia and I can't read a damn map at the best of times. When I'm sad and stressed and heartbroken and miserable and depressed it's near impossible!'

She scrunched the map into a ball and launched it at his head.

'Tell me how you really feel, Morgs.' Noah struggled to keep his grin from forming.

Morgan looked at him, hurt and shocked. 'You think this is a joke? That the pain you've caused me is funny? I've been travelling for days so that you can *laugh* at me?'

Noah scrubbed his hands over his face. 'No—God, no! Sorry. I didn't mean that. I'm just amazed that you are here; you nearly missed me. I was going to leave in the morning. I'm really, really happy that you *are* here.'

Morgan gave him a stony look. 'Sure you are.. Look, this is stupid. I'm probably very stupid… I'll just go.'

Noah moved to stand in front of the door. 'You're not going anywhere, and you are definitely not driving anywhere in the dark. You might end up in a loch.'

Morgan tried to push him out of the way but she couldn't move his bulk. 'You lost the right to tell me what to do, to protect me, when you kicked me out of your life and sicced those CFT agents on me!'

'I intend to protect you for the rest of your life, if you'll let me.'

Everything in Morgan's body tensed as she looked up into his gorgeous face. The humour had fled and his eyes were deep and serious and radiating truth. And love. And hope. Her heart lurched.

'Come and sit down, Morgan. Please.'

Okay, maybe she could just hear him out…just a little. Morgan allowed Noah to take her hand and she perched on the edge of a couch. Noah pulled the battered coffee table closer to the couch and sat on it, facing her.

'I was—*am*—happy to see you, When I couldn't find you…I thought you'd plunged off the road or crashed somewhere. I was considering calling out a search party when I saw your car pull in here. I belted back here, just so relieved that you are okay.'

'Uh-huh.'

'Secondly, I was planning to leave tomorrow. I was going to go home.'

'Back to London.'

'Back to *you*. You are my home, Morgan. You're the place where I want to be.' Noah touched her hand with his fingers. 'I've spent the last week trying to convince myself that I'm

better on my own, that I can live without you, that I'm independent and a hard-ass and I don't need anyone. And I don't
need *anyone*, Morgs. I just need you. I love you. More than
I can express and much more than you will ever know,' he
added, his voice saturated with emotion.

'But you sent me away!' Morgan's fist rocketed into his
shoulder. 'I loved you, but you sent me away like I was
nothing!'

'I sent you away because you were *everything* and I was
scared.' Noah gripped her fist and kissed her knuckles. 'I'm
stupid when it comes to you—haven't you realised that yet?
Do you want me to grovel?'

Morgan sniffed as her head and her heart started pounding with the warm fairy dust sparkles of happiness. 'I can't
imagine you grovelling well.'

'True.' Noah kissed her knuckles again and held her eyes.
'I'm sorry that I acted like a jerk.'

'I've been miserable without you. I can't do anything
without you,' Morgan grumbled, her fingers on his cheek.

'I know.'

'No, you don't understand. The dyslexia has been really
bad—'

'Babe, it's not that. I've also been less than useless at the
office…why do you think Chris sent me up here? I couldn't
think, hold a reasonable conversation, I forgot meetings and
stopped midway through my sentences. I couldn't function
without you.' Noah's other hand clasped her face and his
thumb drifted over her cheekbone. 'It has nothing to do with
the dyslexia and everything to do with the fact that you and
I are better together than we are apart.'

'So it seems.'

'Do you remember what you said at Bon Chance? Just
before I heard about Michael?'

Morgan nodded.

'I want the whole bang-shoot too—with you. I don't care
how many dyslexic kids we have because they will be *our*

kids and they will be brilliant in their own ways—just as you are. I will never think anything is lacking in you, or them. Yeah, I'll get frustrated with you—as you will with me— but it will never be caused by your dyslexia. And I will love you, hard, often, passionately, for ever.'

'Oh, Noah. I love you too.' But Morgan thought she should issue one more threat before she allowed pure happiness to envelop her. 'I came here to kick your ass.'

'I'd much prefer to kiss yours.' Noah's curved lips drifted down to hers. Before they touched, he spoke again. 'I don't suppose you packed any of those burlesque corsets, did you? I've been having a few fantasies about them...'

Morgan smiled against his mouth. 'No, you're going to have to earn a corset. You can start by kissing me, soldier.'

'With all my pleasure, Duchess.'

EPILOGUE

Four months later...

IN A CROWD of three thousand people Morgan knew exactly whose hand touched her back—recognised the gentleness in his strong touch. Morgan lifted her solid black mask and smiled at Noah, who'd refused her entreaties to wear a costume as befitting a 1920s burlesque-themed ball or a mask. Then again, nobody could quite pull off a tuxedo like her soldier.

Well, a tuxedo jacket. The lower half of his tuxedo consisted of a kilt in the Fraser tartan, complete with furry sporran.

Noah could pull off a kilt too. Not that she would ever tell him that—she was having far too much fun teasing him about his 'Scottish skirt'.

And naked... Actually nobody could pull off naked as well as Noah could, and as soon as she was done with the ball they were headed for Stellenbosch, where she intended to devote her considerable energies to keeping him naked as much as possible.

Noah placed both his arms around her and held her as they stared down at the crowds below them. The ballroom glittered and heaved with colour, laughter rose and fell, and champagne and other fine spirits flowed. Couples whirled around the dance floor and other guests stood in front of the birdcages and looked at the beautiful pieces of jewellery art.

'Why are you hiding up here on this little balcony by yourself?' Noah asked.

'I just need a break,' Morgan answered. 'Isn't it spectacular, Noah?'

'It is, and you should be proud of yourself. You did this, Duchess. This is all yours and it's fabulous.'

'Well, mine and Ri's. We work well together.'

Morgan rested her head on his chest and stroked his hand with her fingertips. 'By the way, Mum has agreed to using some of the money raised tonight to make a hefty donation to that dyslexic foundation I visited the other day. They want me to sit on their board.'

'Are you going to tell them—tell people about your dyslexia?' Noah asked, turning her to face him.

'I thought…maybe. What do you think?'

'I think that you—apart from the fact that you are the untidiest person alive—are awe-inspiring.' Noah kissed her nose. 'I have something for you.'

'You do? Will I like it?'

Noah looked uncharacteristically serious. 'I hope so. Buying a gift for the Diamond Queen's daughter is a nightmare of epic proportions, and everyone I've spoken to has a different idea about what you like. Riley says one thing, James another—mostly just to take the opposite view to Riley, I think.'

'I have to do something about those two, and soon,' Morgan muttered, her eyes narrowing.

'Hey, concentrate! We're talking about your present. And the angst I've gone through to get it.'

Morgan grinned. 'Sorry. So, what did I do to deserve a present?'

Noah tipped his head in thought. 'Well, you do this little thing with your tongue…'

Morgan blushed. 'Noah! *Jeez!*'

Noah touched her cheek with the back of his knuckle. 'I love you with everything I have and the last months have been crazy exciting.'

'Do you miss London? Your brothers? You've uprooted your life…' Morgan said, a little worried. He'd made huge changes to his life to be with her and she needed to know that he had no regrets.

'We've expanded Auterlochie by opening another branch in the city, and I've moved into a gorgeous flat with a woman who says she loves me and gives me frequent sex. Such a hard thing to do…' Noah said, his eyes laughing at her fears.

Morgan rolled her eyes. *Okay, then.* 'So, about my present…what did you buy me?'

'Not so much buy as…' Noah pulled a box out of his pocket and handed it over. 'We talked about getting married at some point and I wanted to make it official. I know it's not the fanciest or the biggest or the—'

'Shut up, No,' Morgan said, flipping open the lid. Inside, cleaned and sparkling, sat his mother's red beryl ring—the one she hadn't seen since that day in the studio.

Morgan swallowed and put her hand on her chest as she stared at the box in her hand.

He could have had a ring designed by Carl, bought her the flashiest diamond and got down on one knee in front of all these people and proposed, but nothing, Morgan knew, would have had a greater emotional impact on her than receiving his beloved mother's ring.

Morgan pulled it out and handed it back to him.

'You don't want it?' he asked quietly, disappointment in his eyes and voice.

Morgan shook her head, her eyes welling. 'I want you to put it on me. And as you do it,' she added, as Noah picked up her hand and held her ring finger, 'I want to tell you that I'm honoured to wear this ring and that, like her, I will always love you.'

Noah kissed her lips and held her against him, and she felt warm and protected and so very, very loved in his arms.

After a long, emotion-soaked moment he whispered in her ear. 'I'm loving your dress, Duchess.'

She grinned and curtsied. 'Merci."

She'd had a steam punk green and black corset designed for the evening and teamed it with a black tulle and organza skirt that rode low on her hips and exposed a strip of her belly. It had been worth every penny to see Noah's eyes bug when he'd first caught sight of it.

'I can't wait to get you alone,' Noah said, nuzzling her neck. 'I'm going to have so much fun taking it off you.'

Morgan bent her knees, dipped her hand under his kilt and touched his warm thigh. Her eyes sparkled as she looked up into his face. 'And I'm going to have lots of fun taking *your* skirt off you.'

'It's a kilt!' Noah howled for the umpteenth time that night. 'Respect the kilt!'

Morgan grinned, knowing that her happiness was echoed in his eyes. 'I deeply respect what's under the—'

'Don't say skirt.'

Noah captured her face in his hands and kissed her lips as her hand danced up his thigh.

'Duchess?'

'Yes, soldier?'

'Behave.'

Morgan's eyes laughed at him. 'Absolutely...*not*.'

* * * * *

DEFYING HER
DESERT DUTY

ANNIE WEST

With profound thanks to
Vanessa, Sharon, Karen and Kandy
for all your support.

CHAPTER ONE

HE WAS watching her.

Still.

Soraya's nape prickled. A ripple of hot sensation skated down her arms. She fought the need to look up, knowing what she'd see.

The man in the shadows.

Big. Dark. Broad-shouldered in his leather jacket, the hard lines of his face a study in masculine strength. His upper face was in shadow yet every time she looked across the dimly lit bar there was no doubt his gaze was fixed on her. She felt the intensity of that look in her sizzling blood. And in the curious breathless catch in her throat.

His interest unsettled Soraya. She leaned closer to her group: Raoul and Jean Paul debating politics while Michelle and Marie talked fashion. Raoul roped a negligent arm around her shoulders. Instantly she stiffened, then forced herself to relax, reminding herself it was just a friendly gesture.

Soraya loved Paris's casual lifestyle, but still hadn't overcome her reserve. You could take the girl out of Bakhara but Bakhara still lingered in the girl. Her lips twisted. She'd no need of the chaperone her father had wanted to send.

Movement caught her eye and despite her intentions she turned.

He hadn't moved; he still leaned back just beyond the flickering light of the candle on his table. But now he looked up at a leggy blonde in a red satin mini-dress. The woman leaned in, her low-cut neckline a blatant invitation.

Soraya snapped her head back to her friends, ignoring the way Raoul tightened his hold.

Zahir sank back in his chair and cradled his drink, its cool condensation a respite from the heat. A heat that owed nothing to the close atmosphere of the nightclub and everything to the woman on the other side of the room.

What the devil had he walked into?

Simple, Hussein had said. Straightforward.

Zahir shook his head. Every sense screamed 'alert'. Every instinct warned of trouble.

Still he remained. He had no choice. Now he'd found her, he couldn't leave.

He tipped his head back so the ice slid into his mouth. He crunched it hard, as if the shock of cold might restore his equanimity.

It would take more than ice to counteract his tension.

In other circumstances he might have taken up the invitation of the voluptuous Swedish girl in the short dress. He enjoyed life's pleasures—in his down time.

Never at the expense of his duty.

Tonight was duty, responsibility, obligation.

Yet it was something more too. Something…unfamiliar, evoked by sloe-dark eyes and a full Cupid's bow mouth. By the woman hanging on the words of a scrawny intellectual pontificating as if he had any idea how to run a country!

Zahir snorted and put down his glass.

Whatever it was he felt, he didn't like it. It was a complication he didn't need. Zahir had spent a lifetime learning how to cut through complications.

Over the years he'd learned to curb his impatience. Now he mostly used a statesman's skills: negotiation and discretion. But he'd trained as a warrior from birth. He was still technically head of the Emir's bodyguard, a position that gave opportunities for the satisfaction of hard, physical combat. The clash of one man against another.

He surveyed the *poseur* who was boasting of his intellect and pulling the woman in the dark dress close. The Frenchman's hand hovered near her bare arm. Zahir's fist tightened.

He'd like to get his hands on that buffoon and give him a short, sharp lesson in the real meaning of power.

The intensity of his bloodlust brought him up short.

Premonition skittered like icy fingers down his spine.

This mission was a mistake. He felt it in his bones.

Soraya moved back as far as Raoul's encircling arms allowed.

It was ridiculously late and she'd rather be home in bed. Except her flatmate Lisle had finally made peace with her boyfriend and Soraya knew they needed privacy, even if it meant staying out till dawn. Lisle had been a good friend and friendship was something precious to her.

But she'd made a mistake, finally agreeing to dance with Raoul. She frowned and shifted his straying hand.

Usually Soraya didn't make such mistakes. Keeping her distance from men came naturally. She'd acted out of character, spooked by the need to escape the stranger's unnerving stare. It had made her feel…heated. Aware.

Yet even now she felt his gaze like a brand on her back, her bare arms, her cheeks.

What did he *want*? She wasn't eye-catching. Her dress was modest—positively maidenly, Lisle would say.

Soraya wanted to march across the room and demand he stop it. But this was Paris. Men stared at women all the time. It was a national pastime.

Raoul's marauding hand cut her line of thought and she stiffened. Enough was enough. 'Stop it! Move your hand or—'

'The lady is ready for a change, I believe.' The voice, a deep burr, curled around her like a caress, but there was no mistaking its steely undertone.

Raoul stumbled to a halt then stepped back abruptly as a

large hand removed his arm from Soraya's waist. His eyes flared as he drew himself up. Yet, tall as he was, the stranger topped him easily.

Raoul spluttered as he was shouldered aside. Soraya felt the tensile strength in the intruder's big body as he clasped her in a waltz hold and swung her away.

Torn between relief at being rid of Raoul's octopus hands and stomach-dipping shock at the newcomer's actions, protest froze in Soraya's throat.

It was *him*, the man who'd watched her all evening.

Suddenly he was so near, his breath feathered her forehead, the heat of his body warmed hers and his big hands grasped her so easily it was obvious he was used to being close to a woman.

Soraya shivered as an unfamiliar sensation swirled deep. Not trepidation. Not indignation. But something that tied her thoughts in knots and prompted her to fall in step unthinkingly as he moved to the slow tune.

'Now just you wait—' Over the stranger's shoulder she saw Raoul's face, red with indignation, his fist raised. Soraya's eyes widened. Could he be violent?

'Raoul! No! That's enough.'

'Excuse me a moment.' The stranger released her, swung round to confront Raoul and said something under his breath that made the graduate student pale and falter back a pace.

Then, before she had time to question, he turned back, gathered her to him and swung her across the dance floor.

It was an impressive example of a male staking his territory. But Soraya didn't appreciate being swept away without so much as a by-your-leave.

Even if he had rescued her from Raoul's pawing.

'There's no need for this.' She'd rather just get off the dance floor. But he gave no indication he'd heard.

It chagrined her that her feet automatically followed his lead. She'd never followed *any* man, except her beloved father!

She could wrench herself from his arms and off the dance

floor, but she shied from making more of a scene unless absolutely necessary.

Besides, she was curious.

'What makes you think I want to dance with you?' She jutted her chin defiantly to counteract the strange, breathy quality of her voice.

The movement was a mistake. With her face tilted, her gaze collided with sizzling dark-emerald fire. Shock jolted her and only quick reflexes kept her from stumbling.

His eyes were heavy-lidded, almost lazy. Yet there was nothing lazy about his rapier-sharp scrutiny. She sucked in a breath as it roved her face.

His features were compelling. Strong, with an earthy stamp of male sexuality that melded with sharp cheekbones, a determined jaw and a long blade of a nose to create a breathtaking whole. His skin was dark gold, eyes rayed with the tiny lines that spoke of hours spent outdoors. She couldn't believe they were smile lines. Not on this man who surveyed her so grimly.

Soraya blinked and tore her gaze away, disturbed to find her pulse skittering faster.

'You weren't *enjoying* your dance with him?' He shrugged and she knew in that moment that, despite his perfect French, he wasn't local. There was none of the Gallic insouciance in that movement. Instead she read the fluid yet deliberate action of a man who had more on his mind than a little light flirtation.

He moved with a lithe grace yet every action, from the way he held her hand to the light clasp of his other palm at her waist, was carefully controlled.

For all his agility he was a big man, all hard-packed muscle, iron-hard sinew and bone. Formidable.

Suddenly she felt…trapped, at risk. Ridiculous, since she was in full public view with her friends close by.

Desperately she sucked in a deep breath and sought out her companions. They watched, rapt, elbows on the table and mouths moving as if they'd never seen anything more fascinating than Soraya dancing, and with a stranger. As her eyes met Raoul's, he flushed and moved closer to Marie.

'That's not the point.'

'So you don't disagree. He was annoying you.' His voice was low yet she had an inkling he worked to keep his tone easy.

'I don't need a protector!' Soraya prided herself on her independence.

'Then why didn't you stop him grabbing at you?' There was no mistaking the thread of anger in that deep voice, or the quiver of repressed power that rippled through him in a rolling tide.

It was her turn to shrug.

What was there to say? That despite the freedom of studying abroad she wasn't used to dealing with groping hands? She usually kept a discreet distance from male colleagues. Soraya had perfected the art of blending into a crowd and avoiding individual male attention. Tonight was the first time she'd ever danced with a man.

No way was she confessing that! It was the norm for a well-brought-up girl in Bakhara. Here it would make her seem like a freak.

As would the fact she preferred it that way. She had no interest in a love affair.

'Nothing to say?'

'What I do is none of your business.'

At her words his lips firmed, deep lines bracketing a mobile mouth that revealed tension despite his air of command. One sleek black eyebrow climbed towards close-cropped dark hair.

That superior look would goad any woman's patience.

The music finished and they slowed to a stop.

'Thank you for the dance.' Formal politeness barely masked her annoyance. How dared he suggest she should be thankful to him?

She turned and took a step away, only to find his hold tightening at her waist. Long fingers and a broad palm seared through the soft fabric of her dress, warming her in a way that suddenly seemed too intimate.

The music resumed and with a swift movement he tugged her close so she stumbled against a hard wall of hot muscle.

'What the—?'

'What if I choose to make it my business?' His breath was warm on her face. Those straight eyebrows arrowed down in a scowl that accentuated the intensity of his blazing green stare.

It was as if he memorised everything, from her too-short nose and plain brown eyes to the wisps of hair escaping her once-neat chignon.

The intensity of that look dazed her. 'Sorry?'

'You heard me, princess. Don't play games.'

'Play games?' She shook her head, her jaw clenching in indignation. She planted her hands against his upper arms, trying to prise herself free, and felt only unyielding steel. 'I've done nothing! It's you playing games. Sitting there all night, just watching me.'

Her eyes met his again and her chest tightened at the simmering heat she saw there. Her skin tingled all over.

'You wanted me to do more than watch?' His words were a whispered thread of frayed velvet. 'Is that why you cosied up to your friend over there—to trigger a response?'

'No!' Soraya rocked back on her heels, but his arm at her waist, like a rope of steel, lashed her to him.

For an instant she read something in his gaze, something half-hidden that both disturbed and fascinated.

Then she came to her senses. With a swift, well-executed movement she ground her stiletto heel onto his instep with all her weight.

A moment later she was free. His hand fell away and with it the warmth at her waist she'd almost grown used to.

She strode from the dance floor, head up and shoulders back. A woman in control.

But at the back of her mind lingered the image of his face when she'd fought to break free. There'd been no flicker of pain in his eyes, no hint of a wince on his face, despite what must have been piercing agony.

What sort of man trained himself not to react to pain?

The question unnerved her.

So did the realisation she was only free because he'd *chosen* to release her.

Holding her in his arms had been a mistake.

Zahir grimaced and ruthlessly shoved aside any analysis of *why* it was a mistake.

No need to go there. All that mattered was that she was trouble with a capital T.

He'd known it when he'd arrived at her apartment and found, not the respectable accommodation he'd expected, but a love nest for an almost-naked couple. Clearly they'd tumbled out of bed only because his insistent ringing of the bell had threatened to attract the neighbours.

His assessment had been reinforced when he'd finally tracked her to this seedy club. True, she didn't flaunt herself half-naked like some women. But that dress, the colour of ripe plums, clung lovingly to curves designed to snare a man's attention. Its skirt flirted and flounced around shapely legs when she moved. It slithered enticingly under a man's palm, making him itch to explore further.

Zahir swallowed a curse as his palms tingled.

This wasn't about what she made him feel.

He wasn't in the business of feeling *anything* for her.

Except disgust that she'd played Hussein for a fool. Look at the way she'd snuggled up to that turkey with the ridiculously sculpted excuse for a beard!

He stifled a low growl of anger.

No, she was *not* what he'd been led to believe. And he didn't just mean the fact that the old photo he'd been given showed the round, almost chubby face of an innocent. The woman tonight had the cheekbones, sexy curves and full, pouting lips of a born seductress. And those shoes—spangled four-inch stilettos that screamed *'take me...now!'*.

Heat pooled low. Disgust, he assured himself.

The one time she'd impressed was when she'd stood up to him. Few people dared do that.

The look in her eye when she'd used that damned spike heel had, for a moment, arrested him. And the way she'd strode back across the dance floor, with the grace and hauteur of an empress, had made him want to applaud.

At least she had guts. She was no push-over.

The determined click of feminine heels snared his attention and he straightened from the wall.

Instantly the rhythm of those footsteps slowed and a disturbing fire sparked in his blood. He'd felt it each time her eyes collided with his.

Hell! Now he felt it from her mere glance.

A volatile mixture of fury, guilt and some other darker emotion surged to the surface.

This was *not* the way it should be. Zahir refused to countenance it.

He swung round to face her across the foyer of the nightclub. At this hour even the bouncer had deserted his post. They were alone.

'You! What are you doing here?' Her hand crept to her throat, then, as if recognising that for a sign of weakness, she dropped it to her side and lifted her chin. Subtly she widened her stance. What, did she mean to kick him in the groin if he tried to approach her?

It would do her no good, of course. Overpowering her would be a moment's work.

But that wasn't an option. Despite her flaws, she would be treated with respect. That was why he'd waited till they had privacy to approach her.

He ignored that ill-advised, inexplicable impulse to approach her on the dance floor.

'We need to talk.'

But already she was shaking her head. Flyaway strands of dark chocolate tresses swirled around her slender throat.

Zahir forced his focus to her eyes. Dark as ebony, they held his unflinchingly. He gave her full marks for bravado.

'We have nothing to discuss.' Her gaze skated across his shoulders, his chest and back up again. 'If you don't leave me alone I'll—'

'What? Call out for lover-boy to rescue you?' He crossed his arms over his chest and saw her gaze follow the movement. The low simmer of heat in his veins became a sizzle, igniting a temper he'd almost forgotten he had.

What was it about this woman that got under his skin? It was unheard of.

'No.' She took a mobile phone from her purse and flipped it open. 'I'll call the police.'

'Not a wise move, princess.'

'*Don't* call me that!' She quivered with outrage, her mouth a pout of wrathful indignation.

Too late, Zahir realised why he'd baited her.

Not because she deserved it.

Not because he was naturally crass.

But because he wanted her to look at him, respond to him, as she had on the dance floor. There, despite her defiant words, her body had melted against his just for a moment in an unspoken invitation as old as time.

Hell and damnation!

What was he playing at?

'Forgive me, Ms Karim.' Carefully he blanked his expression, speaking in the modulated tones he used when brokering a particularly difficult negotiation.

'You know my name!' She stumbled back a half-step, alarm in her eyes.

Registering her fear, Zahir tasted self-disgust on his tongue. Nothing he'd done tonight had gone as intended. Where was his professionalism, his years of experience handling the most difficult and delicate missions?

'You have nothing to fear.' He spread his palms in an open gesture.

But she backed up another step, groping behind her for the door into the bar. 'I don't hold conversations with strange men in places like this.' Her gesture encompassed the empty foyer.

Zahir drew a deep breath. 'Not even a man who comes direct from your bridegroom?'

CHAPTER TWO

SORAYA froze, muscles cramping in shock as that one word reverberated through her stunned brain.

Bridegroom...

No, no! Not yet. Not now. She wasn't ready.

Her heart rose in her throat, clogging her airways, lurching out of kilter. Her senses swam. It couldn't be. She had months yet here in Paris—hadn't she?

Soraya staggered back till the hand behind her met a solid surface. Fingers splayed, she pressed into the wall, needing its support.

Through hazy vision she registered abrupt movement: the stranger striding across the small space, arm raised as if to reach for her.

She stiffened and he slammed to a halt, his hand dropping. This close she should be able to read his expression but in the dim light his features looked like they'd been carved from harsh stone, betraying nothing. His eyes blazed, but with what she couldn't discern.

At least he didn't touch her again.

She didn't want his hand on her. She didn't like the curious heat that stirred when he did.

She dragged in a deep breath, then another, trying to calm her racing pulse. With him so close, watching like an eagle sighting its prey, it was impossible. She had nowhere to retreat to. And even if she did she knew he'd follow.

He had the grim, resolute aura of a man who finished what he started.

Her heart give a little jagged thump and she forced herself to stand tall. Even in her new shoes she still had to tilt her head to meet his gaze. He was big—broad across the shoulder and tall. Yet his physical size was only part of the impact. There was something in his eyes...

Soraya jerked her gaze away.

'You've come from Bakhara?' Her voice was husky.

'I have.'

She opened her mouth to ask if he'd come direct from *him*, but the words disintegrated in her dry mouth. It was stupid, but for as long as she didn't say the words she could almost pretend it wasn't true.

Yet even in denial Soraya couldn't pretend this was a mistake. The man before her wasn't the sort to make mistakes. That poised, lethal stillness spoke a language all its own. There'd be no errors with this man. She shivered, cold to the bones.

'And you are?' Soraya forced herself to speak.

One slashing black eyebrow rose, as if he recognised her question for the delay tactic it was.

'My name is Zahir Adnan El Hashem.' He sketched an elegant bow that confirmed his story more definitively than any words. It proclaimed him totally at home with the formal etiquette of the royal court.

In jeans, boots and black leather, the movement should have looked out of place, but somehow the casual western clothes only reinforced his hard strength and unyielding posture. And made her think of formidable desert fighters.

Soraya swallowed hard, her flesh chilling.

She'd heard of Zahir El Hashem. Who in Bakhara hadn't? He was the Emir's right-hand man. A force to be reckoned with: a renowned warrior and, according to her father, a man fast developing a reputation in the region as a canny but well-regarded diplomat.

Her fingers threaded into a taut knot.

She'd thought he'd be older, given his reputation. But what made her tense was the fact that the Emir had sent *him*, his most trusted royal advisor. A man rumoured to be as close to the Emir as family. A man known not for kindness but for his uncompromising strength. A man who'd have no compunction about hauling home an unwilling bride.

Her heart sank.

It was true, then. Absolutely, irrefutably true.

Her future had caught up with her.

The future she'd hoped might never eventuate.

'And you are Soraya Karim.'

It wasn't a question. He knew exactly who she was.

And hated her for it, she realised with a flash of disturbing insight as something flickered in the sea-green depths of those remarkable eyes.

No, not hatred. Something else.

Finally she found her voice, no matter that it was raspy with shock. 'Why seek me out here? It's hardly a suitable time to meet.'

His other eyebrow rose and heat flooded her cheeks. He knew she was prevaricating. Did he realise she'd do almost anything not to hear the news he brought?

'What I have to say is important.'

'I have no doubt.' She dragged her hand from the supporting wall and made a show of flicking shut her phone and putting it away. 'But surely we could discuss it tomorrow at a civilised time?' She was putting off the inevitable and probably sounding like a spoiled brat in the bargain. But she couldn't help it. Her blood chilled at the thought of what he'd come all this way to tell her.

'It's already tomorrow.'

And he wasn't going anywhere. His stance said it all.

'You have no interest in my message?' He paused, his eyes boring into her as if looking for something he couldn't find. 'You're not concerned with the possibility that I bring bad news?' His face remained unreadable but there was no mistaking the sharp edge to his voice.

The phone clattered to the floor from Soraya's nerveless fingers.

'My father?' Her hand shot to her mouth, pressing against trembling lips.

'No!' Colour deepened the razor-sharp line of his cheekbones. He shook his head emphatically. 'No. Your father is well. I'm sorry. I shouldn't have—'

'If not my father, then—?'

An abrupt gesture stopped her words. 'My apologies, Ms Karim. I should not have mentioned the possibility. It was thoughtless of me. Let me assure you, everyone close to you is well.'

Close to her. That included the man who'd sent him.

Suddenly, looking into the stormy depths of Zahir El Hashem's eyes, Soraya realised why he'd pushed her. How unnatural of any woman not to be concerned that sudden news might bring bad tidings about the man she was supposed to spend the rest of her life with.

Guilt hit her. How unnatural *was* she? Surely she cared about him? He deserved no less. Yet these last months she'd almost fooled herself into believing that future might never come to pass.

No wonder his emissary looked at her so searchingly. Had her response, or lack of it, given her away?

'I'm glad to hear it,' she murmured, ducking her head to cover the confusion she felt. At her feet lay her phone. She bent to retrieve it only to find her hand meeting his as he scooped the phone up.

His hand was hard, callused, broad of palm and long-fingered. The hand of a man who, despite his familiarity with the royal court, did far more with his days than consider protocol.

The touch of his flesh, warm and so different from her own, made her retreat instinctively, her breath sucking in on a gasp.

Or was it the memory of that same hand holding her tight against him on the dance floor? Fire snaked through her veins, making her aware of him as *male*.

'Your phone.'

'Thank you.' She kept her eyes averted, not wanting to face his searching stare again.

'Again, I apologise for my clumsiness. For letting you fear—'

'It's all right. No harm done.' Soraya shook her head, wishing it was the case, when all she could think of was that her reaction betrayed her as thoughtless, ungrateful, not deserving the good fortune she'd so enjoyed.

Worse, it was proof positive the doubts she'd begun to harbour had matured into far more than vague dissatisfaction and pie-in-the-sky wishing.

'Come,' he said, his voice brusque. 'We can't discuss this here.'

Reluctantly Soraya raised her head, taking in the deserted foyer, the muffled music from the club and the mingled scents of cigarette smoke, perfume and sweat.

He was right. She needed to hear the details.

She nodded, exhaustion engulfing her. It was the exhaustion a cornered animal must feel, facing its predator at the end of a long hunt from which there was no escape.

She felt spent. Vulnerable.

Soraya straightened her shoulders. 'Of course.'

He ushered her out and she felt the warmth of his hand at her back, close but not touching. Something in the quiver of tension between them told her he wouldn't touch her again. She was grateful for it.

Fingers of pale grey spread across the dawn sky, vying with the streetlights in the deserted alley. She looked around for a long, dark, official-looking vehicle. The place was deserted but for a big motorbike in the shadows.

Where to? She couldn't take him home; not with Lisle

and her boyfriend there. The place was roomy but the walls were thin.

'This way.' He ushered her towards the main road then down another side street with a sureness that told her he knew exactly where he was going.

She supposed she should have asked for proof of identity before following him. But she dismissed the thought as another delaying tactic. There was no doubt in her mind that he was who he said.

Besides, she felt like she'd gone three rounds in a boxing ring already. And this had only just started! How would she cope?

A shudder rippled down her spine.

A moment later weighted warmth encompassed her. She faltered to a stop. Around her shoulders swung a man's heavy leather jacket, lined with soft fabric that held the heat of his body and the clean fragrance of male skin.

Soraya's nostrils flared as her senses dipped and whirled, dizzy with the invasion of her space and the onslaught of unfamiliar reactions.

'You were cold.' His words were clipped. In the gloom his face was unreadable, but his stance proclaimed his distance, mental as well as physical.

He stood tall, the dark fabric of his T-shirt skimming a torso taut with leashed energy. His hands curled and the muscles in his arms bunched, revealing the blatant power his jacket had concealed. Resolutely she stopped her eyes skimming lower to those long denim-clad legs.

He looked potent. *Dangerous*.

'Thank you.' Soraya forced her gaze away, down the street that had begun to stir with carriers hefting boxes. A street market was beginning to take shape.

Relief welled. Surrounded by other people, surely the unfamiliar sensations she felt alone with him would dissipate? She'd been like a cat on burning sand for hours, all because of him.

She dragged his jacket in around her shoulders, telling herself the shock of news from Bakhara unnerved her. Her sense of unreality had nothing to do with the man so stonily silent beside her.

Zahir shortened his pace to match hers. She had long legs but those heels weren't made for cobblestones. They slowed her walk to a provocative hip-tilting sway far slower than his usual stride.

Resolutely he kept his eyes fixed ahead, not on her undulating walk.

Heat seared his throat and tightened his belly. How could he have been so stupid? So thoughtless? The look on her face when she'd thought he brought bad news about her father had punched a fist of guilt right through his belly.

Damn him for a blundering fool!

All because he'd judged her and found her wanting. Because she wasn't eager to hear the news from Hussein. Because she didn't care what tidings he brought if they interfered with her night out.

Because she wasn't the woman he'd presumed her to be, a woman worthy of Hussein.

Not when she spent the night snuggling up to another man, dancing with him, bewitching him with those enormous, lustrous eyes. Letting him paw her as if he owned her.

Zahir cupped the back of his neck, massaging it to ease the tension there.

Resolutely he shoved aside the whisper of suspicion that he'd have welcomed the chance to keep her in his own arms, feel her lush body pressed close.

This wasn't about him.

It was about her.

And the man to whom he owed everything.

'Thank you.' Soraya hugged the jacket close as he stood aside, holding open the door to a brightly lit café.

Entering, she felt she'd strayed back in time a century.

Wooden booths lined the walls, topped with mirrors etched in lush *art nouveau* designs. There were brass fittings of an earlier age, burnished and welcoming, and posters from a time when women wore corsets and men sported boaters or top hats.

But the whoosh of the gleaming coffee machine was modern, as was the sultry smile the petite, female *barista* bestowed on Zahir.

Something tweaked tight in Soraya's stomach. A thread of annoyance.

No wonder he was so sure of himself. He must take feminine adulation as his due.

Not this female.

Her heels clacked across the black-and-white tiled floor, giving the pretence of a confidence she didn't feel. Her legs shook and each step was an effort.

Sliding into a cushioned seat she focused on the café rather than the man who sat down opposite her.

If she'd had to guess she'd have said he'd favour a place that was sleek, dark and anonymous. Somewhere edgy, like him. Not a café that was traditional and comforting with its beautiful fittings and aura of quiet bustle.

A waitress had followed them to their table, her eyes on Zahir as they ordered.

He was worth looking at, Soraya grudgingly admitted, averting her gaze from his hard, sculpted jaw with its intriguing hint of morning shadow.

'You've come all the way from Bakhara,' she said flatly when they were alone. 'Why?'

She needed to hear it spelled out, even though there was only one reason he could be here.

'I come with a message from the Emir.'

Soraya nodded, swallowing a lump in her dry throat. Tension drilled down her spine. 'And?'

'The Emir sends greetings and enquires after your well-being.'

She speared him with a look. An enquiry after her health?

That could have been done through her father, who updated the Emir on her progress. Suddenly she was impatient to hear the worst. The delay notched her tension higher.

'I'm well.' She kept her tone even, despite the fact she couldn't seem to catch her breath. 'And the Emir? I hope he is in good health.'

'The Emir is in excellent health.' It was the expected response in the polite give-and-take of formal courtesy.

The sort of courtesy that had been so completely lacking in her dealings with this man.

Soraya's heart pulsed quicker as she recalled those overpowering emotions—the fury and indignation, the compulsion to know more, the feel of his gaze on her. The blast of untrammelled awareness when he'd held her.

She blinked and looked away.

Silence thickened, broken only by the eager waitress returning with their coffees: espresso for him, *café crème* for her. Automatically her hands wrapped round the oversized cup and she tilted her head, inhaling the steamy scent of hot cream and fragrant coffee.

'The Emir also sent me with news.'

Soraya nodded and lifted the cup to her lips, needing its heat. Even draped in his jacket she was cold. Cold with a chill that had nothing to do with the room temperature and everything to do with the creeping frost that crackled through her senses. The chill of foreboding.

'He asks that you accompany me to Bakhara. It's time for your wedding.'

Her slim fingers cupped the bowl of milky coffee so tightly Zahir saw them whiten. She didn't look up, but kept her eyes fixed on her drink. Following her gaze, he saw the creamy liquid ripple dangerously as her hands shook.

Instinct bade him reach out before she spilled the hot coffee and burned her hands.

Sense made him keep his hands to himself.

Bad enough that he knew the feel of her in his arms. Worse that he'd wanted…

No! He thrust the insidious thought aside.

Tiredness was to blame. The freedom of travelling the open road on his bike was what he'd needed after weeks locked in diplomatic negotiation on Hussein's behalf. But it had been a long journey.

As for the hum of awareness deep in his belly—it was a while since he'd shared his bed. That was all.

'I see.' Still she didn't look up. Nor did she drink. Instead she slowly lowered the coffee to the table, her hands still clamped round it as if for warmth.

Zahir frowned.

'Are you all right?' The words were tugged from his lips before he realised it.

Her mouth quirked up in a lopsided smile that somehow lacked humour. 'Perfectly, thank you.'

She lifted her head slowly, as if it was an effort.

Yet when her eyes met his he read nothing in them but a slight shimmer, as if the coffee's steam had made her eyes water. They were remarkable eyes. In the gloom of the club he'd thought them ebony. Here in the light he realised they were a dark, velvety brown, rich with a smattering of lighter specks, like gold dust.

Zahir sat back abruptly and lifted his espresso. Pungent and rich, the liquid seared his mouth and cleared his head.

'The Emir has set a date for the wedding?' Her voice was cool and crisp, yet he sensed strain there. Just as he saw strain in the rigid set of her neck and shoulders.

He shrugged. 'No date was mentioned to me.' As if Hussein would consult him on the minor details of his nuptials! That was what wedding planners were for. No doubt there were hordes of them, eager to have a hand in what would be the wedding of the decade.

'But…' She frowned and caught her bottom lip between her teeth. Resolutely he shifted his gaze from her lush mouth and turned to survey the café. It was doing a roaring trade in early-morning coffees for the market workers eager for a take-away caffeine fix. Yet here at the rear Zahir and his companion were totally alone.

'The Emir wants me to return?'

Hadn't he just said so? Zahir turned and found himself drowning in dark eyes that, if he didn't know better, he'd say held fear.

Nonsense. What was there to fear? Any woman would be ecstatic with the news he'd come to take her back to marry the Emir of Bakhara. If Hussein's character weren't enough to attract any woman, his personal wealth, not to mention his position of supreme authority, were bonuses few women could resist.

Soraya Karim had nothing to fear and everything to gain.

'He does.'

Zahir watched her shift in her seat. Her shoulders straightened, banishing the hint of a slump. Her chin lifted and her posture morphed into one of cool composure. Like the woman who'd stalked away from him in the club.

His heart gave a kick of appreciation and the dormant fire in his veins smouldered anew.

Hell! Since when had any woman had such an effect on him? Not even his last lover, naked and eager in his bed, would have garnered such an instantaneous response.

He rubbed his hand across his jaw, noting the stubble he hadn't bothered to remove. Lack of sleep was the problem. He'd been awake for thirty-six hours—eager to get here and get this over quickly so he could return to the new challenge that awaited him.

His reactions were haywire.

'The Emir has asked me to escort you home.' He curved his mouth in a reassuring smile and reined in his impatience—as if he had nothing better to do with his time than act as her minder on the trip from Paris to Bakhara.

Yet he couldn't begrudge Hussein this favour. Soraya Karim

would soon be his bride—of course he wanted her kept safe on the journey.

A pity no-one had thought to keep an eye on her while she partied in Paris!

'I thank the Emir for his kindness in providing an escort.' Her smile didn't reach her eyes. 'However, it would have been helpful if you'd contacted me before you arrived. That would have given me time to prepare.'

Zahir frowned at the hint of disapproval in her carefully polite tone.

What was there to prepare? Surely, as an eager bride, she'd jump at the chance to return to Bakhara and the opulent bridal gifts Hussein would shower upon her.

After years of delay Hussein was finally ready to proceed with the wedding. His chosen bride should be grinning with delight.

Instead she surveyed Zahir coolly.

'I'm here to assist. You can leave the details to me.' Winding up the lease on her apartment and organising a team of removalists would be the work of a few phone calls.

She nodded. 'I'm obliged to you. However, I prefer to make my own arrangements.' She paused. 'When is the Emir expecting me?'

'I've organised a flight tomorrow night. The royal jet will fly us back.' A day to complete his nursemaid duties and deliver her safely to Hussein. Then Zahir could make his way to his new post. He'd been itching to get to it for weeks.

'The Emir expects me *tomorrow*?' Her face leached of colour, leaving her looking unexpectedly fragile.

Zahir opened his mouth then shut it again.

This wasn't going to plan. He'd envisaged her eager to return to Bakhara and embrace her new life as wife of the country's ruler. He'd expected excitement, gratitude, even.

Instead she looked horrified.

A thread of curiosity curled within him till he blanked it out. He wasn't interested in understanding Soraya Karim, es-

pecially as he had a fair idea he wouldn't like what he found
on closer inspection. He prized loyalty above all things and
Hussein deserved better than a fiancée who couldn't be trusted
to keep away from other men.

'There's a problem with tomorrow?' He didn't bother to
hide his disapproval.

His nostrils flared with distaste as he wondered if she
needed extra time to say goodbye to that lanky fool from the
nightclub. Surely she wouldn't delay her departure for *him*?
Or had he been a ploy? Perhaps she'd been trying to make the
handsome blond guy at their table jealous.

He'd observed the covetous glances she'd attracted in that
bar. Anger stirred at the notion she'd played fast and loose with
Hussein's trust.

'No, tomorrow's not convenient.' Just that. No explanations,
no apologies, just a shimmer of defiance in those fine eyes and
a hint of mulish wilfulness in her down-turned mouth.

Despite himself, Zahir felt a spark of appreciation for the
way she stonewalled him. The negotiators this last week could
have done with some of her spunk. They might have come out
of the joint-venture deal with a better share of the profits.

But that didn't negate the fact that she disrupted his plans.
True, Hussein hadn't specified a date for his bride's return, but
Zahir wanted to conclude this task and move on to his new role.
He hadn't been so eager for anything in years.

'And when will it be *convenient*?'

Colour rose in her cheeks and her lips parted as if to protest
his curt tone. Zahir's pulse missed a beat and heat combusted
deep in his belly as he watched her mouth turn from sulky to
an enticing O. With his jacket pulled around her shoulders and
her hair coming down in soft curling tresses, she looked inviting, available, *tempting*.

Not like the fiancée of his mentor and best friend.

Her eyes widened as if she read his response despite the
savage control he exerted to keep it hidden.

The tension between them notched higher. It trembled in the

air, a pressure that had more do with his reaction to her than with the subject under discussion.

This couldn't be!

It *wouldn't* be.

By hook or by crook he'd have her back in Bakhara, safe with her fiancé and out of his life, before her feet could touch the ground.

CHAPTER THREE

SORAYA knew disapproval when she saw it.

Despite his almost expressionless face, that flat, accusing stare said everything his words didn't.

If it hadn't been imprinted on her so early perhaps she'd never have recognised it. But nothing, not time or distance, could erase the memory of her father's relatives whispering and tutting over the sordid details of her mother's misdemeanours—or their certainty that, if unchecked, Soraya would go the same way to ruin. Even the servants gossiped in delighted condemnation.

Stifling the urge to lash out, Soraya withdrew into herself. What did she care if the Emir's lackey didn't approve of her? Even if, far from being a lackey he was one of the most powerful men in the country?

She had more on her mind than winning his approval. His news changed her life.

'Give me tomorrow,' she said, her voice husky with tension that threatened to choke her. 'Then I'll have a better idea.'

How long to pack her gear, say her goodbyes and, above all, get her research in some sort of order? She feared however long it took wouldn't be enough.

Anxiety welled and she beat it back. Time enough to give in to fear when she was alone. She refused to let this man see her weak.

Abruptly she stood. He rose too, dwarfing the booth and

crowding her space. Instantly she was transported to the club where his touch had sapped common sense. Where just for a moment she'd wanted to lean close to his powerful frame rather than escape his hold. Fear closed around her.

'I want to go home.' Even to her own ears her voice held a betraying wobble. Paris had become her home, a haven where she'd been able to spread her wings and enjoy a measure of freedom for the first time. The idea of returning to Bakhara, to marriage…

'I'll see you back.' Already he was ushering her through the café, one hand hovering near her elbow as if to ensure she didn't do a runner. He dropped payment on the counter where the waitress beamed her approval.

What was wrong with the girl? Couldn't she see he was the sort of bad-tempered, take-charge brute who'd make any woman's life a misery?

Clearly not. The waitress's gaze followed him longingly, needling Soraya's temper.

'Thank you but I can make my own way.'

To her chagrin he was already hailing a taxi—a miracle at this time of the morning. It was daylight but the city was just stirring. Before she could reiterate her point he was opening the door for her then climbing in the other side.

'I said—'

Her words disintegrated as he gave her address to the driver. Her heart thudded and she sank back in her corner.

Of course he knew her address. How else would he have located her? But the thought of Zahir El Hashem shouldering his way into her cosy flat sent disquiet scudding through her. Instinct warned her to keep her distance.

She didn't want him near her.

The fact that he sat as far from her as the wide back seat allowed should have pleased her. Instead it struck her as insulting. He didn't have to make such a conspicuous issue of keeping his distance, so grimly silent.

What she'd done to annoy him, she had no idea. *He* was the

one whose behaviour was questionable, following her every move in the nightclub. What was that about?

Fifteen minutes later they stood on the pavement before her building. He'd overridden her assurance that he needn't see her to the entrance, just as he'd paid the taxi fare as she fumbled for cash. Polite gestures no doubt but he insidiously invaded her space, encroaching on her claim to be an independent woman.

Never before had that claim seemed so precious.

Her heart plunged as she thought of what lay ahead.

A promise to keep.

A duty to perform.

A *lifetime* of it.

So much for the tantalising sense of freedom she'd only just found. The dreams she'd dared to harbour. She'd been mad to let herself imagine a future of her own making.

'Here. Thank you.' She tugged his jacket off her shoulders. Instantly she missed its heavy, comforting warmth and, she realised with horror, its subtle spicy scent. The scent of *him*.

She looked into his shadowed face, unable to read his expression. But there was no mistaking the care he took not to touch her as he took the jacket from her hands. As if she might contaminate him!

Why had she, even for a moment, worried what he thought of her? She'd long ago learned to rise above what others thought, what they expected. Only by being true to herself and those she cared for had she found strength.

'Goodbye. Thank you for seeing me home.' What did it matter if her voice was stilted with indignation? She inclined her head stiffly and turned, unlocking the door.

'It's no trouble.' His deep voice rumbled, low and soft as a zephyr of hot desert wind, across her nape. Too late she realised she *felt* his warm breath, a caress on her bare skin as she stepped into the foyer and he followed.

Soraya slammed to a halt and felt the heat of his big frame behind her. Static electricity sparked and rippled across her flesh. It dismayed her. She'd never known anything like it.

But, she rationalised, till tonight she'd never been so close to a man other than her father.

Would she feel this strange surge of power in the air and across her skin when she went to the Emir?

Despite the heat of Zahir's body Soraya shivered.

'I'll see you to your apartment.'

Flattening her lips at his assumption she couldn't look after herself in her own building, she strode across the foyer. No point arguing. She had as much chance of budging him as of moving the Eiffel Tower.

But she refused to share the miniscule lift. The thought of being cocooned with him in that cramped space sent a spasm of horror through her. She'd rather take the five flights of stairs, even if her new shoes *were* pinching.

Soraya was ridiculously breathless when she reached her floor. She shoved her key in the door and turned to face him.

He wasn't even breathing quickly after their rapid ascent. Nor did he feel that strange under-the-skin restlessness that so unnerved her. That was clear from his impassive face. He looked solid and immoveable. Nothing pierced his control.

'Here.' He held out a thick cream card. On one side was a mobile-phone number. No name, nothing else. On the other he'd scrawled in bold, slashing strokes the name of a hotel she knew by reputation only. 'Call me if you need anything. I'll make all the necessary arrangements.'

No point in assuring him again she'd do her own organizing; it would be a waste of breath. He had the look of a man who heard what he chose to hear. She'd sort out the details later when she wasn't so weary.

'Thank you,' she murmured, resolutely hauling her gaze from his clear-eyed stare. 'Good night.'

Behind her she pushed open the door to the apartment.

'Is that you, Soraya?' From inside, Lisle's husky voice shattered the stilted silence. 'We're in the bedroom. Come in and join us.'

A stifled noise made her look up. Zahir El Hashem looked

for once shaken out of his complacency. His eyes were wide and his mouth slack. He blinked and opened his mouth as if to speak but Soraya had had enough.

She stepped through the door and swung it closed. For the length of five heartbeats she stood, her back pressed against the door, waiting for his imperious summons, for there was no doubt he'd been about to speak.

Instead there was silence. Even through the door she sensed his presence, like a disapproving thundercloud. Her skin prickled as if she'd touched a live wire and her pulse pattered out of sync.

'Soraya? Julie's here too. Come on in.'

'Coming,' she croaked, knowing she had no hope of escaping Lisle or her sister. Julie must have stopped by to see how things were with her twin as soon as Lisle's boyfriend had left.

Girly gossip wasn't what Soraya needed but at least it would take her mind off the news she'd just received: that her wonderful adventure in Paris was over and she was returning home to fulfil the duty she'd been bound to from the age of fourteen. The duty she'd become accustomed to thinking was in some far-off future that became less real with every passing year.

Yet as she snicked the bolt shut and scooped up Lisle's carelessly discarded camisole, Soraya was surprised to realise it was Zahir El Hashem's strong features that filled her mind. Not those of her betrothed.

Zahir stared at the door, one hand still raised as if to stop it shutting. Or force it open.

Shock held him rigid. It wasn't a familiar feeling. He was a man of some experience. Little surprised him. To be at a loss because she'd been invited to make up a threesome with the lovers he'd seen last night should be impossible.

Yet he rocked back on his feet, his gut clenching as if he'd caught a hammer blow to the belly. Searing bile snaked through his system.

Despite what he'd seen earlier, he'd almost convinced himself he'd been mistaken about Soraya. That the woman who carried herself with such poise and grace, yet with that intriguing shadow of anxiety in her eyes, was special. When he'd relaxed his guard he'd liked her, despite his doubts.

Stupid wishful thinking!

Had she deliberately sidetracked him?

Valiantly he'd tried to keep his eyes off the syncopated sway of her pert backside as she climbed the stairs in precarious heels. Even when he'd managed not to look he'd imagined the slip of soft fabric across warm, rounded flesh. His palms had tingled with remembered heat.

Anger welled. His hands fisted and his jaw ached as he clenched his teeth against the need to bellow out her name.

She'd played him for a fool. Tried to con him.

He felt…gutted.

He slumped against the door, hand splayed against it for support, recalling that discarded scrap of lingerie casually discarded just inside the door.

He'd spoiled her fun at the club and, he realised now, with the news she had to return to Bakhara where her every move would be scrutinised. Was she even now hauling that slinky dress over her head to join her friends in a little early-morning debauchery?

Nausea writhed.

Breathing heavily, Zahir sought calm.

Could he have misread what he'd seen and heard? He had so little evidence. Was he wrong to assume the worst? It was tempting to hope so.

Till he realised how much he *wanted* to be wrong. Fear feathered his backbone as he registered the sense almost of longing within him.

From the first his instinct had screamed a warning about Soraya Karim: she was dangerous. She tested his control to the limit and messed with his judgement.

He couldn't let her undermine his duty too.

Zahir sighed and scrubbed his hand over gritty eyes, suddenly more tired than he could remember. How could he break it to Hussein that the woman he planned to marry might not be fit for the honour?

'I'm sorry, madam. I'm afraid the guest you enquired about isn't available.'

'Not in or not available?' Soraya tamped down the steaming anger that had been simmering for hours. 'It's important I see him as soon as possible.'

'Excuse me a moment while I check.' The receptionist turned to confer with a colleague, leaving Soraya free to focus on her surroundings.

The foyer was luxurious in the bred-in-the-bone way you'd expect of one of Paris's grandest hotels. From the crimson carpet leading in from the cobblestoned pavement to the discreetly helpful staff, exquisite antiques and massive Venetian glass chandeliers, the placed screamed money, but in the most hushed and refined tones. The guests, whether wearing couture, business suits or staggeringly mismatched casuals, took the opulence in their stride, as only the super-wealthy could.

Soraya in her workaday jeans, T-shirt and loose jacket had never felt so out of place. Her family, one of the oldest in Bakhara, was comfortably off but had never aspired to this sort of rarefied luxury.

Even her shoes, her one pretension to elegance, had been snaffled in a miraculous end-of-sale bargain.

She stood taller. None of that mattered. All that mattered was seeing *him*. A tremor of repressed fury skated down her spine. Hadn't he promised her a day to get her bearings and then contact him? He'd had no right...

'I'm sorry for the delay, madam.' The receptionist was back. 'I'm able to tell you the guest you asked for has left strict instructions not to be disturbed.'

Soraya's lips compressed. That was why he hadn't answered his phone for the past two hours and she'd finally had to leave her work and come here in person. As if she didn't have more important things to concern her!

Why give her his phone number if he was going to be in-communicado for hours?

An image flashed into her brain of the waitress at the café melting at the sight of his blatant masculinity.

Was that why he couldn't be disturbed? Some assignation with an adoring woman?

'Thank you.' Her voice was crisp. 'In that case I'll wait till he *is* available.'

With a humph of disgust, Soraya stepped away from the desk.

Zahir El Hashem would soon discover she was no pushover.

In the early hours of this morning she'd been numb with the shock of his news, so dizzy with it she'd let him take charge. Now she'd had time to absorb the fact that she had no choice but to face her future head-on. That didn't stop the regrets, the anxiety, the downright fear. But she had to be strong if she was to survive the ordeal ahead. At the moment that meant teaching Zahir she wasn't some lackey to be ordered about at his convenience.

She was, like it or not, his Emir's future queen and a woman in her own right.

Soraya stalked across the room, oblivious now to its refined opulence, and plonked herself down on a plump sofa. She un-zipped her laptop case and switched on the computer.

She'd rather be angry than fearful. And better than either was to immerse herself in something she really cared about. Two minutes later she was focused on her report, seeking an elusive error in the heat-transfer calculations.

Soraya didn't know what finally tugged her attention from the latest projections, but something made her look up, a sixth sense that sliced through her absorption.

A cluster of men in dark suits stood on the far side of the lobby. She recognised one as a senior French politician, his face familiar from news reports. But it was the tallest of the group who drew her frowning attention. His skin was burnished a dark honey gold, his features arresting.

Abruptly he looked up, his eyes locking instantly with hers. Shock danced down her spine at the impact.

Just like before.

The world had fallen away when he'd looked at her last night too.

Her hands jerked on the laptop keys. From the corner of her vision she saw a stream of extra rows appear in the carefully constructed table of technical analysis. Yet she couldn't drag her eyes from his.

In leather and denim he'd been a virile bad boy with an undeniable aura of danger.

Today, in exquisite tailoring and with an air of urbane assurance, he looked like he'd stepped from the ranks of the world's power brokers.

Who *was* Zahir El Hashem? Politician or heavy? Sophisticate or rogue?

Why did locking eyes with him make Soraya's heart thud to a discordant beat that stirred unfamiliar sensations?

She jerked her gaze away, blindly hit 'save' on her document and fumbled to shut down the laptop.

She'd had no sleep and she was stressed; no wonder she imagined things. There'd been no instantaneous pulse of connection between them. She'd simply imagined its heavy weight constricting her lungs and drawing her belly tight.

Shoving her laptop into its case she looked up to see him striding towards her.

Trepidation struck her. An awareness that, despite his elegant apparel and their rarefied surroundings, there was an elemental toughness about him she'd do well to remember. Only last night she'd recognised the desert warrior in him. Now as he approached Soraya knew she hadn't imagined the subtle scent of danger clinging to him.

'What's wrong? Why are you here?' His low voice drew the

fine hairs on her nape to prickling attention even as dark heat pooled low inside. It only fuelled her anger.

She refused to feel fear…or anything else for him.

'To see you, of course,' she hissed, jerking to her feet and wishing she was taller so he couldn't loom quite so effectively over her.

His narrowed eyes surveyed the room quickly and comprehensively. It was the sort of look she'd seen bodyguards use, searching for threat.

She'd give him threat!

'We had an agreement.' This time she kept her voice low and even. 'You broke it.'

His dark eyebrows climbed high but he gave no other reaction. 'Come.' He gestured for her to precede him.

Instantly Soraya shifted her weight, widening her stance a fraction as if to plant herself more firmly. She had no intention of meekly following him anywhere.

'I think not. We can talk here.'

Something flickered in those deeply hooded eyes. Something that might have been surprise or annoyance. Frankly, she didn't care. Instinct told her not to be alone with him. She knew next to nothing about him and looking at that granite-carved jaw, she wouldn't put it past him to try coercion.

'This is not the place for our conversation. This is a delicate matter and the person I represent—'

'Would perfectly understand my preference for meeting you here, rather than in a private room.'

He said nothing, just surveyed her with a look that was impossible to interpret. A look that seemed to take in everything from her too-fast breathing to the laptop she clutched like a shield to her chest.

Finally he nodded. 'Of course. If that is what you wish.' He turned and indicated a couple of chairs grouped at the rear of the room. 'Though perhaps we could go some place where we're less likely to be overheard.'

He had a point. Soraya nodded stiffly and let him usher her across the room.

Zahir frowned as he followed her. That instant surge of adrenalin in his blood, the momentary fear that something was wrong, had undermined his calm. All because she'd come looking for him when it was the last thing he'd expected.

It was absurd. Clearly she was in no danger. Panic was a weakness he didn't indulge in. Yet his pulse thundered in his ears as he watched her thread her way across the room.

He didn't like her, didn't approve of her, so why the instant, gut-deep need to protect that had made him hurry to her? He wanted to put it down to duty honed by years of training, but it wasn't that. From the first she'd stirred instincts and feelings that discomfited him. However much he fought it he felt... connected to her. Ever since that first, blinding moment of recognition.

She settled on a gilded sofa and made a production of crossing those long legs. As he seated himself opposite her, Zahir forced his gaze from the way the soft denim clung to each dip and curve.

'You wanted to see me?'

'Not really, but I had little choice.' Her neat white teeth snapped off each word. 'You weren't answering your phone.'

Ah. That was why she was in a temper. When she'd wrecked his plans to return to Bakhara today he'd used the extra time to fit in some meetings. Clearly she expected him to be at her beck and call like some underling.

'As you saw, I had business to conduct.' He refused to apologise for not being available at her whim. 'How can I assist you?'

Her eyes flashed ebony fire. 'By keeping your word.'

Zahir stiffened. 'That is not in question.' Did she have any concept of the insult she offered him?

'Isn't it?' She leaned forward and her scent insinuated itself into his nostrils. Light and delicate, like a field of mountain flowers awakening to the day's first sun. It had haunted him all day, a sense memory he'd tried to forget. 'We agreed you'd give me today to get organised yet my flatmate rang me at five this afternoon because a team of removalists had turned up wanting to pack my belongings.'

Zahir settled back in his seat and inclined his head. 'We agreed that you'd have today. We also agreed that I'd take care of the arrangements. I've done so. You've had your day to organise yourself.'

Colour mounted her cheeks and her eyes glittered with temper. Women could be so predictable when they didn't get what they wanted. He waited for a blast of ungoverned rage.

It didn't come.

Instead she sat back against the silk brocade of her seat.

'You don't approve of me, do you?' Her voice was coolly measured. 'Is that what this is about? Is that why you're being so high-handed?'

Momentarily he was thrown by her directness. He encountered it so rarely since he'd moved into the diplomatic sphere. It was the sort of tactic he used himself to great effect when others preferred to circle the truth. Cutting through the niceties to the heart of the matter was sometimes the most effective way forward.

He hadn't expected it from her.

Unwilling admiration stirred.

'My opinion of you is not in question, Ms Karim. My role is simply to facilitate your safe arrival to Bakhara.'

'Don't give me that! You're more than a courier.' She nodded to where he'd stood saying farewell to his guests. 'That's clear from the leaders who came here to meet you. You're trying to railroad me for your own reasons.'

She was clever too. Obviously she'd recognised the man tipped to become the next French foreign minister.

But what disturbed him was her accusation he was pushing her to hurry because it suited him.

He should have contacted Hussein this morning and voiced his concerns about Soraya Karim. But he'd baulked at the notion. That sort of conversation had to take place man-to-man, not long distance. It had the added advantage that Zahir could then walk away from her and concentrate on the work he'd been preparing for all his life.

'What is it about Paris that keeps you delaying? What's more important than your promise to marry?'

The colour faded from her cheeks and for a second he saw something flicker in the rich depths of her pansy-dark eyes. Something that looked like genuine pain. It surprised him for it seemed at odds with his image of a selfish pleasure-seeking woman.

'I have things to wrap up before I go.'

Things or relationships? His jaw tightened.

'Surely it won't take more than a day to say goodbye to your special *friends*.' He nodded curtly to her laptop. 'And no doubt you'll stay in contact.' Was she the sort who suffered withdrawal if disconnected from social media?

Her smooth forehead puckered then she shrugged. 'I have some work to finish too.'

Soraya almost laughed aloud as a flash of disbelief widened his eyes. Clearly he thought her some dilettante who used university as an excuse for a holiday in Paris.

He recovered quickly. 'It's summer. University break.'

'Have you heard of summer school? Between semesters?'

'I applaud your diligence.' But his tone belied his words. 'Are you saying you have to be here to complete your work? Surely alternative arrangements can be made?'

Circumstances being the fact that she was expected to return home meekly and marry a man, a virtual stranger, more than thirty years her senior.

Cold wrapped itself around Soraya's chest and seeped into bones that seemed suddenly brittle and aged. She drew a deep breath, willing away the panic that threatened whenever she thought too far ahead.

That was the problem; she'd forgotten to think ahead. For too long she'd assumed the future was nebulous and unreal. From the moment at fourteen, when her father had explained the honour bestowed on their family by the Emir's interest in her, through every year when Emir Hussein had remained a distant yet benign figure.

At fourteen the betrothal had been exciting, like something from an age-old tale. Later it had grown less and less real, especially when her fiancé had shown little interest beyond polite responses to her father's updates on her wellbeing and educational progress.

Now it was suddenly all too real.

'It's not just the work,' she blurted out. 'I'd planned to be here longer and I want to make the most of my time in France.'

'I'm sure you're doing just that.' His lips twisted.

She ignored his disapproval. 'I can finish up some of my work elsewhere, but not all of it.' She gestured to the laptop. 'Besides, I don't want a direct flight to Bakhara.'

His only response was to lift his eyebrows, stoking her impatience.

'I intend to travel overland. In all these months I haven't been out of Paris and I want to see more of the country before I return.'

And store up some precious memories—of her last days of freedom. It wasn't too much to ask. Once she returned she'd be the woman the Emir and his people expected. She'd marry a man renowned for his devotion to duty and her life would be circumscribed by that.

She needed this time, just a little time, to adjust to the fact that her life as an individual was ending. The alternative, to return immediately, stifled the breath in her lungs and sent panic shuddering through her.

'That's not possible. The Emir is expecting you.'

She nodded, glad now that she'd found the courage to do what she'd never done before and call the Bakhari Palace, giving her name and asking for the Emir. It had been surprisingly easy.

'Yes, he is.' For the first time she smiled. 'I spoke to him today. He thinks it's a wonderful idea that I take my time and soak up some of the sights along the way. He agrees it will be educational for me to get a better understanding of other places and people, not just Paris.'

It had felt odd talking to the man who for so long had been a distant figure and who soon would be her husband.

Zahir's stunned expression would have pleased her if she'd wanted to score points off this man who always seemed so sure of himself. But she had more important concerns.

'I've got till the end of the month.' That would give her the breathing space she so desperately needed. There was only one problem, but right now it should be the least of her worries. She squared her shoulders and met his eyes. 'The Emir's only stipulation was that you accompany me.'

CHAPTER FOUR

'I KNOW it's not what you planned, Zahir, but I see huge benefits in this trip. Soraya was very convincing.'

Zahir gritted his teeth. He just bet she had been. He heard the smile in Hussein's tone even over the phone. No doubt she'd employed her soft, sultry voice to best advantage in her long-distance call to Bakhara.

'But a week is more than enough, isn't it? The sooner she returns the better, surely?'

'It will be a big change for her,' Hussein answered slowly. 'Living as my wife in the palace. Meeting VIPs, playing a role in diplomatic functions. Plus there's the work that will be expected of her with our own people. She'll be an advocate for many who, for whatever reason, are daunted by approaching their ruler directly. Giving her a chance to mix with as wide a range of people as possible can only be an advantage.'

He paused. 'That's one of the reasons I supported her studying in Paris. She needs to broaden her horizons, ready for her future role.'

Zahir stared unseeingly at the lights of Paris. His heart sank. Not just because Hussein supported Soraya's plan to delay her return. Far worse was the burden of suspicion she wasn't fit to be his mentor's bride.

He thrust a hand through his hair. How could he disabuse Hussein?

How could he not?

He'd do anything to save Hussein pain. The older man was more than a father to him. Friend, mentor, hero, he'd shown Zahir care, regard and even love when no one else had. He'd brought him up more like a son than a charity case. A not-quite-orphan shouldn't have warranted the Emir's personal attention.

Zahir owed him everything: his place in the world, his education, his self-respect, even his life.

He was caught between shattering Hussein's illusions about his bride and letting her dupe him.

His belly churned. 'Hussein, I—'

'I know you're disappointed, Zahir. You're eager to take up the post of provincial governor.'

A sliver of guilt carved its way through Zahir's gut. 'You know me too well.'

Hussein's chuckle was like the man himself, warm and compelling. 'How could I not? You're the son I never had.'

Something rose in Zahir's chest, a welling sensation that tightened his lungs and choked his vocal chords. Despite their closeness, the regard between him and Hussein was rarely spoken. Bakhari males left emotion to their womenfolk, focusing instead on masculine concerns such as pride, duty and honour.

'You make it sound like your time has past. You're in your late fifties, not your dotage. You've got plenty of time to father a son. A whole family.'

And, with a young, sexy bride, nothing was more likely.

Out of nowhere Zahir glimpsed an image of Hussein holding Soraya close, pulling her to him and letting his hands slip over the curve of her hip, the soft fabric of her dress enhancing the femininity of her shapely figure.

He swallowed hard as a jagged spike of pain skewered him. His breath shallowed and he turned to stride down the length of the suite, fighting sudden nausea.

He was tired of being cooped up. He longed for the clean air of the desert, the wide sky studded with diamond-bright stars. *The total absence of Soraya Karim.*

'Well, time will tell,' was all Hussein said. 'But as for the governorship...'

'That doesn't matter.' Zahir splayed a hand against one wall and stared out at the glittering spectacle of the Eiffel Tower sparkling with a million electric lights. He'd trade it in a second for the light of the moon over the desert, highlighting dunes and silhouetting proud, ancient citadels.

'Of course it matters. You'll be the best governor the place has had.'

Silence engulfed them. No doubt Hussein, like himself, was remembering the long period when Bakhara's largest province had been ruled by a ruthless, decadent and utterly unscrupulous tribal leader. A man who'd tried many years before to increase his prestige by backing a coup to unseat Hussein.

Zahir's father.

His biological father, never his *real* father.

It sickened Zahir that he shared the blood of a traitor, a man who'd clung to his position only because of Hussein's forgiveness and the fact that removing him would have caused more unrest at a dangerous, volatile time.

'Your faith in me means everything.' Zahir bowed his head. It was the closest he'd ever come to expressing aloud his devotion to the man who'd rescued him, ragged, neglected and virtually feral at the age of four from his father's palace.

Rather than speak it, Zahir had spent a lifetime demonstrating his loyalty, his regard, his love.

'As does yours, Zahir.' Hussein's tone held a husky warmth that spoke far more than words. 'As for the governorship—it will be there waiting for you. I think my bride isn't the only one who'll benefit from a break. You've pushed yourself hard lately. Take your time and relax. Who knows?' He chortled. 'You might even enjoy the novelty of a vacation.'

Zahir opened his mouth to say he didn't need a vacation. He thrived on responsibility, challenge, pressure. The prospect of managing the vast province held an allure he couldn't put in words. To have total responsibility, rather than be another's aide: it had captured his interest from the moment Hussein had broached it.

'It's not simply the time away.' Zahir paused, wondering how to continue. He wasn't used to being at a loss for words.

'Go on.'

He drew a difficult breath and wished his concerns were about something as simple as the next bilateral trade agreement or progress on a major public-works programme.

'Your fiancée. She's not what I expected.'

Silence. Zahir knew Hussein valued his opinion on so many difficult issues. He'd even trusted him with his life. But this was different.

'I see.'

Zahir shook his head. Hussein *didn't* see. That was the problem. He'd left Soraya to her own devices in Paris, believing she was worthy of his trust.

'I'm not sure she's…quite the woman you expect.'

'Taken you by surprise, has she?' Hussein's chuckle was rich.

Zahir's hand clenched in a taut fist. 'You could say that.' No, he mustn't hide the truth any longer. 'I'm afraid she may not be the right woman for you.'

Hell! He'd give anything not to have to break this news. Hussein deserved better, so much better than a party girl who shared her sexual favours freely.

'Your concern does you credit, Zahir. But I know more of Soraya than you think. I know she's exactly the woman I need.' When he spoke again his words silenced Zahir's protests. 'We will talk on your return. In the meantime, know that I believe in her as I believe in you, Zahir. I trust you both.'

'What are you doing here?' The words shot out of Soraya's mouth before she could stop them. She wasn't used to opening her door to find six-foot-something of male leaning indolently against the doorjamb.

Her heart leapt up against her throat and she felt light-headed at the impact of him.

He was so close she recognised the clean, spicy scent of his skin. It reminded her of the strange sensations she'd experienced when he'd held her in his arms and she'd felt...

'Good morning, Soraya. It's good to see you looking well.' He straightened but only so he could loom imposingly.

'How did you get into the building?' She sounded absurdly breathless given the fact she'd expected to meet him downstairs in ten minutes. But, she was learning that meeting this man head-on was marginally easier if one was prepared.

His gaze raked her face. Heat combusted and spread under her skin.

Who was she kidding? There was nothing easy about this. She only wished she understood what it was about him that screwed her tension up to such dangerous levels.

He shrugged and she couldn't help but follow the movement of his broad shoulders beneath the pale, exquisitely laundered shirt. Casual, expensive elegance; that was the theme of the day. Scrupulously shaved jaw and a heavy yet discreet watch she was sure she recognised from one of Lisle's fashion magazines.

'One of the tenants let me in when she saw me waiting outside.' His glimmer of a smile drew the tightness in her belly even harder.

Soraya breathed deep. Of course it had been a woman. Had she taken one look at Zahir's compelling face and melted deep inside the way Soraya had in the nightclub?

She stiffened her spine.

'I'd expected to meet you at the car.'

'And I thought you might appreciate help with your luggage.' The hint of a smile had vanished and his eyes held that hard glitter she knew masked disapproval.

She forced down the churlish impulse to refuse. The way he took control so smoothly exacerbated her deepest fears about giving up her independence, reminding her that, once married, she would be bound to honour and, above all, obey. She repressed a quiver of apprehension and looked away.

'Thank you. That's very kind.' She stepped aside and invited him in.

'No farewell party?' He looked past her to the neat sitting room and the small, empty corridor.

'No.' She'd said her goodbyes earlier. Parting with Lisle in particular had been difficult. She'd had no intention of doing that under Zahir's assessing gaze.

Despite their different backgrounds, Soraya and Lisle had forged far more than a casual friendship. For the first time Soraya had glimpsed what it might be like to have a sister. Outgoing where Soraya was reserved, flamboyant rather than contained, funny, warm and impulsive—Lisle had been a revelation to a woman who'd spent her life in cloistered, sedate, correct social circles. Lisle was a whirlwind, ripping into Soraya's quiet life and setting it on a new path. One that had opened her eyes to all the world could offer a woman with her life ahead of her.

Except that now those possibilities crumbled to nothing. Soraya's future was set, had been since she was fourteen. It was too late to change it now.

'Soraya?'

She blinked and looked up to find him closer. For a split second she'd have said she read concern in his hooded eyes. She blinked again and the mirage was gone.

'Here.' She gestured to the case behind her in the hallway.

'That's all?' He looked past her as if to locate a secret stash of luggage.

'That's all. Your removalists were very efficient. My books and other bits and pieces are already on their way to Bakhara.' Her voice dropped to a husky note. She really had to pull herself together.

Despite the claustrophobic sense of the future smothering her, she knew the man she'd agreed to marry had reputedly been a devoted husband to his now-dead first wife. He was decent, generous and honourable.

That was more than many women could say.

It would have to be enough. It wasn't as if she was eager to seek out love. She knew what a devastating emotion that was.

As for her tentative dreams—instead she'd have to put her energies into the goals that had enticed her when she had been a starry-eyed teen: being a queen who made a real difference to her people. Being a good wife. At least with her qualifications she could be the former.

'I'll just get my shoulder bag.'

Thirty seconds later she was in her room, hugging close the oversized bag she'd haggled for in the markets two weeks ago. Only it wasn't her room any more. Stripped of her possessions, it was an empty shell. Not the place she'd been so happy.

Stupid to be sentimental about it.

There was no point dwelling on what was past. She'd learned that as a child, bereft and confused.

She turned and found Zahir in the doorway, his gaze, as ever, fixed on her. A subterranean tremor quaked through her, threatening to destabilise the control she fought so valiantly to maintain.

Turning quickly, she scooped up her laptop.

'I'm ready.'

The Loire River snaked below them like a bright pewter ribbon. Studded along its banks and beyond were neat towns, a patchwork of farms and a scattering of chateaux.

But Zahir's attention wasn't on the view, even when the chopper swooped low over quaint towns or stately homes.

It was the woman next to him who riveted Zahir's thoughts and his gaze. Uptight from the moment he turned up at her door, she'd grown coolly distant when he'd informed her they wouldn't travel by car as she'd planned.

She seemed to think he'd countermanded the idea out of a need to take control!

He huffed silently to himself. He had no need to prove his authority.

What he had was a burning need *not* to be cooped up alone with Soraya for the time it would take to drive to their destination.

Zahir couldn't pinpoint what it was about her that made him edgy—it was more than his qualms about her unsuitability as Hussein's bride.

Yet as they headed south-west from Paris he hadn't been able to drag his attention from her. He'd read her initial nerves, watched as she gradually relaxed and began to talk with the pilot. Initially dour, the pilot now chatted easily, flattered no doubt by her questions on everything from pilot training to wind speed and the local topography.

She was a woman who could charm a man with ease.

'You're enjoying the trip?' Zahir found himself asking. He suppressed the suspicion that he'd spoken only to break the camaraderie building between the other two.

'Absolutely.' There was a breathy quality to her voice that told him she was smiling even though she faced away, peering at the view. 'I love seeing everything laid out like this. It's fantastic.'

'I'm glad you like it.'

'Thank you for organising it.' She swung round and the pleasure on her face arrested him. It lit her from within, making her eyes glow and her face come alive.

Something inside Zahir shuddered into being: a recognition, a sense almost of rightness, he couldn't explain.

He'd seen her angry, defiant, exhausted. He'd seen her furious and frigidly cool but, he realised, he'd never seen her happy.

Maybe it would have been better to travel by car after all. *Safer.*

'You've never been in a helicopter before?' It was easier to talk than dwell on the impact of that knockout grin.

She shook her head and a tendril of dark hair slipped free of the knot at the back of her head and coiled down past her breast.

Involuntarily his fingers twitched, as if needing to feel its softness.

The preternatural feeling of recognition grew to something like déjà vu: as if Zahir had been with her before, had watched her joyous smile and felt that deep-down explosion of blistering heat. He could envisage her pulling her hair free of its pins so it swung in a seductive silk curtain, inviting his touch.

'No, I've never flown in a helicopter before. Isn't it terrific? I love the feeling when we swoop low then rise up high again.'

On cue the pilot angled the chopper down to circle a bluff crowned by a half-ruined tower then lifted them back up.

A throaty gurgle escaped her lips. 'Like that. Thanks, Marc.'

The pilot nodded silently and Zahir knew a moment's searing discomfort. As if the easy friendliness between the two had the power to annoy him.

The notion was absurd.

'I can't wait to try it again. I've decided I like air travel after all.' She turned away to watch as they passed over a field of sunflowers, head bent as if utterly absorbed.

'You didn't enjoy it before?'

'My only other flight was on the jet from Bakhara to Paris, so I couldn't be sure.'

Zahir sat back in his seat, processing that. 'You'd never been on a flight before then?' He'd imagined her spending holidays at foreign resorts then shopping till she dropped in the expensive boutiques of various capital cities.

She shook her head and he watched, transfixed by the wistful smile that shaped her face as she half-turned. 'I'd never been out of Bakhara before.'

No wonder Hussein had seen benefit in her studying abroad. No wonder he thought exposure to other places and people would do her good.

Bakhara was no longer the feudal state it had been till recently. The wife of the country's ruler would need polish, poise and some exposure to the wider world.

A pity her exposure hadn't been more carefully supervised.

Zahir frowned. Had she been wild for the hedonistic pleasures Paris offered or had she been seduced by them? He
remembered the husky voice inviting her to bed the other morning, and the blatant lust in that pseudo-intellectual's face at
the club. There'd be no shortage of people eager to introduce
Soraya to life's seamier pleasures.

Heat trickled through his belly. What had Hussein been
thinking, letting her loose in Paris without a chaperone?
Without someone to guide and protect her, had she been easy
prey?

Yet, even as he thought it, Zahir *knew* he was wrong. Soraya
Karim was no easy victim. Beneath the feminine sway of hips
and that delicious pout of a mouth was a will of iron. Look at
how she'd managed to get her own way over delaying her return to Bakhara. Whatever she'd done, she'd done with her
eyes wide-open.

The heat in his gut twisted in a sickening swirl.

He vowed he at least wouldn't succumb to her blandish-
ments.

Ahead Soraya glimpsed spires amidst a dark swathe of
green. As they approached, her breath hitched at the sheer
fairy-tale beauty of the chateau below them. Pale grey, almost
white in the bright sunlight, it boasted an abundance of tow-
ers capped with conical slate roofs. The windows were large
and mullioned, reflecting the sun glinting off the moat that
surrounded it. An arched bridge led across to vast lawns and
ornamental gardens. The whole was enclosed by a forest that
isolated it from everything else. Like an enchanted world.

She sighed. It was so beautiful, so different from anything
she'd seen either in Paris or at home. No wonder Lisle had told
her she couldn't miss the Loire Valley! She'd said it would appeal to the dreamer in her.

Just the place for Prince Charming to appear and spirit her
away on his milk-white stallion.

Her smile twisted. She wasn't in the market for a rescuing

prince. She'd never yearned for romance, not after weathering the destructive aftermath of her parents' disastrous love match.

Besides, one prince was enough in any girl's life.

More than enough.

She wrapped her arms around herself as a chill invaded her bones.

Try as she might, nothing could take her mind off the fact that in a few short weeks she'd be at the Emir's court, preparing for her wedding—to give herself to a stranger.

Dread carved a hollow in her chest, leaving a yawning hole where she'd once nurtured fledgling dreams. Not earth-shattering dreams, just the chance to make her own choices. To build a career she loved and live as she chose.

Right now they seemed as likely as flying to the moon.

It was only as the thud of the helicopter's rotors died that she realised they'd landed. Bewildered, she looked out to see they were between the forest and the river. In front of them rose the exquisite chateau she'd admired from the air.

Soraya tried to dredge up her enthusiasm for the fanciful architecture, the elegant embellishments, the beautiful symmetry. But the cold, hard fact of her looming future marred her appreciation.

She fumbled for her seatbelt, annoyed with herself. She should be making the most of every moment, of each new place and experience. Yet here she was doing what she'd vowed not to do—dwelling on what she couldn't change.

'Let me.' Zahir's warm fingers tangled with hers and she stiffened.

There had to be a scientific explanation for the pulse of energy that sparked under her skin whenever he touched her. Once it had been surprising—twice, too much of a coincidence. Now she found it…disturbing.

'Thank you.' She scrambled out of the door before he could come around and help. Her knees felt ridiculously weak but she put that down to the after-effects of her first chopper flight.

She went forward to thank Marc. He'd been friendly and so patient with her questions.

She'd barely thanked him when Zahir loomed beside her.

'This way.' He didn't touch her again but with him so close she found herself cutting short her goodbyes and preceding him to the chateau.

'I think you'll like this,' he said as they crunched up the white gravel path. 'There's swimming, tennis, archery, riding— all the usual—and the restaurant has a couple of Michelin stars, of course.'

Of course.

'The day spa is renowned and you have a reservation there in—' he glanced at his watch '—forty minutes.'

Soraya shifted her stare from the opulent chateau to the man striding at her side.

'We're staying *here*?' She'd thought they'd stopped to get a better look since she'd wanted to visit the region.

'You don't approve?' He slashed a sideways glance at her then away, never slowing his pace. The set of his shoulders and the clench of his solid jaw spoke of impatience. Or was it anger?

From the very first, disapproval had emanated from him in waves. She was tired of it.

Soraya shook her head. 'No, it's not that.' She just wasn't accustomed to such grandeur; it made her uncomfortable. But, she reminded herself, she'd have to get used to it soon. The Emir of Bakhara was one of the wealthiest men in the world. 'I'm sure it will be…lovely.'

Zahir must have picked up her cautious tone for he stopped, blocking her path. 'If you have a problem, tell me.' His eyes iced over, chilling her anew. 'I'd rather know now than have you running to the Emir and bothering him with your complaints when he's busy.'

Soraya's head jerked back as if he'd slapped her.

The Emir hadn't minded her calling. In fact, he'd sounded pleased she'd rung and surprisingly delighted with her plan for a slow route home.

Nor had she any need to explain herself to Zahir El Hashem. Whatever it was that twisted him in knots wasn't her concern.

She met his glacial stare with what she hoped was casual disdain. 'As you pointed out a few days ago, the Emir is my future husband. I will call him if I wish.'

No need to say she had no intention of making further calls. She refused to let the man looming like a thundercloud think he could bully her. She stepped forward, intending to brush by him, but he didn't budge, just stood before her, blocking her way—unless she chose to scramble through the rose bushes edging the path. He seemed all solid muscle and bone—broad enough to blot out the chateau with those shoulders and towering over her even though she wore her heels.

'One thing you should know.' His voice was soft, a low, lethal growl that sent primitive fear scudding down her spine. 'You betray him and you answer to me.'

Soraya's head shot up, her eyes clashing with his.

Gone was the coolness, the icy detachment. He was all heat and fury. She felt it sizzle around her like a force-field, drawing her in, trapping her. The air between them zapped and crackled with the emotion radiating from him.

For the first time Soraya saw *him*—not the polished, unreadable veneer of a man who hid his true thoughts behind impenetrable barriers.

She'd wondered what lay behind that façade. Now she had a glimpse and was stunned by what she discovered.

For all his appearance of detachment, and despite his reputation as a diplomatic trouble shooter, Zahir El Hashem was a man of passion and volcanic temper. He *cared* about the Emir, and not just as the man who paid his salary.

Prickles of heat broke out across her flesh as she met his glare and refused to back away.

'Your sentiment does you proud,' she said when finally she found her voice. 'But your judgement is seriously flawed if you think I intend to betray him.'

That was just it. She wasn't the sort to blithely walk away from a promise, even a promise given so young.

Her past had moulded her into a woman who understood the value of honour. And the destructive force of betrayal. Besides, she couldn't disappoint her father, who saw this as her bright, wonderful future. Nor could she betray the Emir, the man who'd given her back what she'd almost lost. She owed him so much.

No matter which way she looked at it, she was shackled to her destiny.

'Now,' she continued, her voice husky with weariness, 'please step out of my way. I want to go to my room.'

CHAPTER FIVE

It wasn't guilt Zahir felt.

He'd been right to warn her. Let her know he was watching her. That he had Hussein's back covered.

Zahir had willingly put himself between Hussein and danger in the past. It was what he'd trained to do. What he was proud to do. Dealing with an unfaithful woman was nothing compared to facing down a would-be assassin.

Yet something niggled at him. Something was *wrong*.

Gut instinct warned he'd missed something. That he didn't have the full picture—till he reminded himself he wasn't the sort to be swayed by a show of bravado and a flicker of pain in eyes like bruised pansies.

Yet he found himself pushing open the door to the hotel's plush day spa. It reeked of perfume, hothouse orchids and flushed female flesh.

'Can I help you, *monsieur*?' A pretty redhead looked up from the reception desk.

'Yes, I'm looking for Mademoiselle Karim.'

'Karim?' The woman frowned and turned to her computer. 'Ah, I thought I recognised the name. That booking was cancelled this morning.'

'Cancelled?' He'd made no such cancellation.

The redhead nodded. 'That's right. Mademoiselle rang from her room. She'd changed her mind and...' She looked up to find the plate-glass door to the spa swinging closed.

Twenty minutes later Zahir was on the road. At least he knew he wasn't chasing a runaway; her luggage was in her suite. Even her beloved laptop.

Only Soraya was missing.

He cursed himself and accelerated too soon out of a sweeping bend in the road.

How had he let her slip away? Why hadn't he confirmed she was set for a day's pampering rather than assuming it, before settling down with his own laptop?

Because he'd been too eager to put distance between them.

Whether pensive or defiant or giving him the cold shoulder, Soraya Karim tugged at something hot and hungry deep inside him.

Something he had no business feeling for the woman who, rightly or wrongly, was to marry Hussein.

That was the hell of it.

Why her?

He had his choice of women now he was *someone*. His mouth twisted in a smile of derision, remembering his youth, when lack of status had lost him the woman he'd fallen for so desperately. He'd thought his heart broken.

Of course he'd survived. As for his heart—he harboured no fantasies now about love. He never let women close to him emotionally. They barely caused a ripple in his life.

Until Soraya Karim.

Tension crawled through him. He'd had to force himself to give her space. Had he provided her with an opportunity to take off and meet a lover?

His only clues were the details of the car the concierge had organised for her and the map he'd provided—a map on which he'd marked the places Soraya had queried: a couple of chateaux, an old house and what turned out to be a nuclear power-plant. That last had to be a mistake. He mentally crossed it off his list and accelerated down a straight stretch of road, his mouth set.

* * *

It was late when he tracked her down.

A familiar, husky voice caught Zahir's ear. He slammed to a halt at the base of the stone stairs in the old house-cum-museum. Swinging his head round, he saw her.

She was safe.

Relief hit him so hard his knees weakened for a moment. An instant later fury descended, swirling through him like a desert storm.

Hussein trusted him to keep her safe yet he'd let her slip away. For the first time ever Zahir had let emotion interfere with his judgement, with his duty.

Inevitably she was talking with a man, her head bent close.

Zahir pushed away from the stairs, outrage pounding through him that he'd let himself worry about her. Then his mind processed what he saw and he stopped again, frowning.

This was no assignation. The man had stooped shoulders and greying hair. Beside him was a trim woman in her late sixties, smiling benignly as Soraya and her male companion discussed…mechanical gears?

Zahir moved to one side and saw what fixed their attention— a display of machinery. His frown deepened as he flashed a glance around the cellar of the old house.

All around were models of half-familiar machines. A whirligig that looked like the precursor to a helicopter. A model of a tilting bridge. A contraption for hauling water uphill by turning a huge screw.

It hit Zahir then that he'd been right: he *didn't* understand Soraya. He'd missed something vital.

He intended to find out what it was.

'Ah, we mustn't keep you any longer. Thank you for your time, my dear. I've enjoyed our chat.' There was a twinkle in the old man's eyes as he looked past her and up.

Soraya's nape prickled and the hairs on her arms rose as if someone had walked over her grave.

Slowly she turned. Her gaze hit a broad chest in a snowy

shirt then climbed past a strong, sun-burnished throat to a familiar, rock-hard jaw, firm, sculpted lips, lean cheeks and eyes
of dazzling emerald.

Heat snaked from her chest to her abdomen, circling there
as he held her eyes.

'Hello, Soraya. You take some tracking down.'

Behind her she was aware of the older couple moving away
and knew regret. She'd so enjoyed their discussion. Now her
day of freedom was over. Was it imagination or did the sunlight dim, as if obscured by sudden cloud?

'Then why did you bother? I'm perfectly capable of looking
after myself.' Anger bit deep that she'd not been allowed even
a day of freedom. Was this what it would be like in Bakhara?
No time to herself? Always watched? Silently she railed against
the future she couldn't change.

'So I'm discovering.' Instead of the scowl she anticipated
she read only curiosity in his gaze. 'Shall we?' He gestured
towards the door that led into the garden.

Reluctantly she led the way. There was no point continuing
with her plans to see the rest of the estate now he was here. He'd
have some reason why she had to return to the chateau-hotel.

Choosing a seat at a shaded courtyard table, Soraya slipped
her sunglasses on. She needed all the protection she could get
against his piercing scrutiny.

Zahir didn't say anything, simply ordered iced water and
coffee then lounged, one arm slung along the back of his chair
as if totally relaxed, watching her.

Soraya's blood tingled in response to that look.

It was almost a relief when their order came. Surely now
he'd break the brooding suspense to berate her for leaving and
not telling him her plans?

She stiffened her spine in readiness and lifted her glass of
chilled water.

'Tell me about yourself,' he said at last, and her hand jerked
so she almost spilled the drink down her dress. It was the last
thing she'd expected him to say.

'Why?' Sourness tinged her response. 'I'm just the package you need to courier to Bakhara, remember?'

Slowly he shook his head, his eyes never leaving hers. He held her pinioned just with the force of that look. Her limbs felt heavy as if invisibly weighted.

How could he *do* that?

A flutter of apprehension stirred. No other man had the power to make her feel anything like it.

'You're far more than that and you know it, Soraya.'

Her brow puckered. There was something in his tone she couldn't fathom. A keen edge that matched the coil of tension swirling its way down to the pit of her stomach.

'I thought you were here to whisk me back to the hotel.' He said nothing. 'Why *are* you here, then?' After his threat back at the chateau, she'd put nothing past him.

'Hussein entrusted me with your safety. You're my responsibility till you return to Bakhara and—'

'I'm perfectly capable. I don't need to be watched over.' Indignation welled.

'Be that as it may, I was concerned when I found you gone. You're in unfamiliar territory, alone, when by your own admission you have limited experience of foreign travel. I needed to make sure you were all right.'

His voice rang with sincerity and abruptly Soraya's bubble of anger punctured. He was doing his job. It wasn't his fault it felt like he was her own personal gaoler. As for his disapproval— she saw no evidence of it now.

'Why did you come *here*?' He reached for his coffee.

'You make it sound as if Amboise is an unusual choice. It's a quaint old town with a chateau, cliff dwellings—'

'Not the town. *Here*.' His gesture encompassed both the old house and the sweep of park-like gardens she'd yet to explore. 'It's pleasant, but it doesn't match the opulence of the royal chateaux.'

'And, of course, I should be interested in opulence, is that it?' What did he think, that she'd somehow snaffled the Emir for his wealth?

Was that why Zahir had installed her in that beautiful, luxurious hotel that, to her overwrought nerves, felt ridiculously like a gilded prison?

'That's just it.' He leaned forward. 'I don't know what interests you.' His gaze dropped from her face. 'Apart from shoes with more sex appeal than substance.'

A flush rose from the vicinity of her ankles where the scarlet straps of her wedge-heeled espadrilles ended in saucy bows. Heat flooded up her thighs, through her body and scorched its way to her cheeks.

Because he thought her shoes sexy.

Her heart gave an odd little flutter.

Why did that observation sound like an admission of some sort? And why did it unsettle her so?

Zahir lifted his espresso but he didn't look away. Soraya gulped down some icy water, hoping to ease the rush of blood under her skin.

'Clos Lucé is where Leonardo da Vinci lived the final years of his life.'

'I thought he was Italian?'

'He was, but the King of France thought him so special he offered him a home.' She nodded to the open window above them. 'He slept in that room.'

'So you're a fan of his art?'

She shrugged. 'I never saw the Mona Lisa in Paris. There were too many other things to do.'

Zahir's eyebrows rose. 'Hussein mentioned you were studying art history in Paris.'

'I was.' Her chin tilted higher, on the defensive now.

Zahir said nothing but his silence told her he was waiting. For long moments she held his gaze, then she shrugged. What was the point in prevaricating?

'It wasn't my idea, it was my father's. He thought an understanding of art would be useful given my...future. A sort of wider cultural education.' What he hadn't said, of course, was that studying art was more genteel, more suitable for a lady. Not that he'd ever say that out loud.

Soraya smiled. Her dad had never quite understood her interest in the unfeminine sciences, but he was her staunchest ally against the traditionalists who'd looked down their noses at her chosen path. They'd seen her lack of interest in the usual female occupations as dangerous—a possible sign she was like her unnatural mother.

Her smile faded.

'Soraya?'

She looked up to find Zahir's eyes narrowing. 'Sorry?'

'You didn't enjoy the course?'

'No, I did. It's not what I would have chosen myself but it was interesting.' She paused, relishing the warmth of the filtered sunlight and the gentle bird calls, the sense, illusory as it was, of freedom.

'I should have made an effort to see his art. He was gifted in so many fields. Did you *see* the models of his inventions?' That had been such fun, especially when she'd met two amateur inventors eager to discuss them.

'I saw them.' His voice told her Leonardo's breakthroughs were mildly interesting to him, no more.

'Where do you think the world would be without people like that, finding new ways to solve problems?'

'What, like that multi-barrelled gun to mow down as many people as possible at a time?'

Soraya found herself smiling ruefully into eyes that had lost their hard edge and crinkled appealingly at the corners. That hint of amusement eased the hard lines of Zahir's face, making him more relaxed, not the stern figure of the last few days.

She'd thought him in his mid-thirties. Now she reassessed. He was younger than she'd assumed.

'It takes the gloss off his "man of the arts" image, doesn't it? But he was working on what people wanted.'

'You could say that about nuclear weapons.'

'True. It's the age-old issue, isn't it? What people do with what scientists invent.'

'That's what interests you? Science?' His eyes widened a fraction.

'Careful, Zahir. You're not in danger of typecasting me because I'm female, are you?' She'd come up against enough raised eyebrows in Bakhara for her supposedly unconventional interests. Inevitably she felt disappointment stir. 'Women aren't all interested in the same things. We're as varied as men.'

'So I'm learning.'

Soraya raised her eyebrows. Her guess was he expected women to focus on luxury and be dependent on men to make the decisions. No wonder they had been at loggerheads.

'If you weren't so interested in art history, why were you concerned to finish your project before you left?'

She sat back in her chair, surveying him carefully. 'You are sharp, aren't you?'

'I could say the same about you.' This time she caught it—a tiny flash of appreciation in his eyes. She felt an answering flicker of pleasure. 'Are you going to tell me what you were doing or is it a secret?'

'No secret. I just took more than one class.'

He said nothing, simply put down his cup and waited, as if he had all the time in the world and nothing more important to do than listen. Yet that stiff, judgemental attitude was missing. What had changed?

'Not really a class, actually. A job.'

'You *worked*?'

She couldn't help it. A gurgle of laughter escaped at his astonished expression. 'Is that so hard to believe?' She held up her hand. 'No, don't answer. I can guess—you thought I pretended to study but secretly majored in shopping.'

A twist of his lips told her she was on the right track. Despite her amusement, annoyance stirred.

'I'm rather fond of shopping, actually. Paris is a real treat for that—everything from haute couture to street markets.'

Soraya looked down at her shoes, but instead of remembering her thrill at getting such a bargain it was a different thrill entirely that rippled through her. Had she imagined the heat in Zahir's stare? He'd made her feel *sexy* with that casual reference to her footwear.

Her skin tingled and her blood throbbed with that weird, unfamiliar blast of heat. Unfamiliar till three days ago, that was. Till Zahir had singled her out in that bar.

She lifted her head.

'That night in the bar. Why did you stare at me like that?'

Zahir read the curiosity in her gaze and knew he'd seriously underestimated her. She had a sharp intellect as well as a strong streak of independence—characteristics he admired.

Yet he hadn't wanted to like her since the moment he'd seen her with another man. Had he let that blind him to other aspects of her character? Had he rushed to judgement?

'I was assessing the situation. You wouldn't have liked me interrupting your night out.'

Her head tilted to one side. Her brow wrinkled and her mouth pouted in a moue of concentration.

Zahir's breathing shallowed as he stared at those lush lips. He dragged his gaze to her dark eyes.

'No, that's not right.' She shook her head. 'You had no compunction about interrupting my night out. Once you decided to make your move, that was it.'

If he'd decided to 'make his move', that night would have ended very differently.

The thought exploded out of nowhere as he imagined doing what he'd been tempted to do on the dance floor—not release her, as she'd demanded, but sling her over his shoulder and carry her somewhere private where he could ravage her sultry mouth and possess her seductive body with the thorough attention they deserved.

A flash of incendiary heat roared through Zahir's veins, tightening his body to instant, painful readiness. His hand clenched so hard on the tiny coffee cup, he feared he'd break the handle. With stiff fingers he released it and slid his hand from the table.

With one casual remark she'd accelerated his pulse from zero to the speed of sound in an instant. It was unprecedented. It was *dangerous*.

'Zahir?' Dark eyes searched his. This time the throb of electricity between them was more than sexual. It struck right at his core, as if she could do the impossible and delve into his psyche. 'Why did you watch me like that?'

She was persistent. And naïve, he realised with shock, if she really had to ask. If she had any sense, she'd leave such questions safely unspoken. Was she more naïve than he'd assumed? The notion disturbed him.

Or was this a double bluff from a woman who knew her sexual power and was trying to toy with him?

Resentment surfaced. He was no woman's pawn.

'I assumed you wouldn't want me approaching the table and discussing your business in front of everyone.'

He saw from her frown she wasn't satisfied with his answer.

'But you sat there for *ages*.'

Silently he held her gaze. He had no intention of pandering to her ego by explaining a response that shouldn't be: his instant, logic-destroying attraction to Hussein's chosen bride.

Damn it. Why couldn't Hussein have sent someone else—a whole team of someone elses—to bring his fiancée home?

His heart plunged. The answer was easy. Because Zahir was the one Hussein trusted above all.

Shame drenched him.

Abruptly he shoved his chair back across the gravel and shot to his feet.

'Did you want to see the grounds?'

'You don't need to stay. I'll meet you back at the hotel.' From the corner of his eye he saw her spring to her feet. Eager for more sightseeing? Or for another chance to escape his vigilance?

For the first time in years Zahir felt unsure. Usually instinct combined with thorough research gave him all the certainty he needed. With Soraya he'd skipped the research, believing this a quick, simple task. As for instinct... He firmed his lips against a bitter laugh. He no longer trusted his instincts where she was concerned.

'I have no other pressing business.' He slipped some cash under his cup and gestured for her to lead the way, ignoring the flash of dismay in her dark eyes. 'I'm curious to see what the place has to offer.' Especially if it meant getting to know the real Soraya Karim.

CHAPTER SIX

SORAYA told herself she was disappointed he didn't give her the choice to explore alone. Yet disappointment didn't explain the curling awareness in the pit of her stomach, nor the tingle of heat between her shoulder blades where his gaze rested as she led the way down the path beside the wide sweep of lawn.

They stopped at a model of a spiral blade for a flying machine, big enough for a person to stand beneath and turn the handle to make it rotate.

'It's more elegant than the modern design.' She tried hard to focus on the model rather than the man beside her. Her nostrils twitched appreciatively at the scent of his warm skin with a hint of desert spice. She'd carried that scent on her own skin after wearing his jacket. It disturbed her how much she relished it.

'Personally I don't care how it looks,' he drawled. 'So long as it keeps me in the air. I'd rather a modern chopper that works than one that looks elegant.'

Soraya huffed with amusement and looked up at the sail turning above her head. She didn't want to relax with Zahir, for there was an undercurrent between them that unsettled her. These tiny hints of dry humour appealed to her too much. It was far easier not to like him.

'That's my line. I'm supposed to be the one focused on functionality.'

She smiled as a big family group arrived with children eager to experiment, then she led the way downhill to where more models of inventions studded the wooded grounds.

'Because you're a scientist?'

'Engineer. I qualified before I left Bakhara.' She flashed a look over her shoulder but no hint of surprise marred those indecently attractive features.

Swiftly she looked away, stopping before a model of a paddle-wheel boat and pretending to survey it closely.

The other group caught up with them again and children of all ages swarmed over the model, while some tiny tots crouched by the stream, playing a complicated game with sticks and leaves.

'That explains why you asked for directions to a power plant.' Zahir's words drew her attention.

'Sorry?'

'The concierge showed me the places you were interested in seeing.'

'Oh.' She'd forgotten to ask how he'd found her. Zahir must have searched for hours, yet instead of being angry he'd shown only curiosity. Every time she thought she had him pegged, he surprised her again.

'I visited a chateau instead. Far more *opulent* and appealing than a utilitarian power station.'

His chuckle surprised her, sneaking across her skin like a caress. A traitorous part of her enjoyed sharing a joke with him, wanted to see him smile at her.

Abruptly she turned and moved away down the path. She couldn't remember ever being so responsive to a man.

Or was it simply that she'd never spent time alone with such an attractive man? Had lack of exposure made her susceptible? She'd had no trouble keeping her head around her colleagues. But from the moment her gaze had locked with Zahir's she'd felt a zap of high-voltage connection. She couldn't shake it and that made her nervous.

'Somehow I suspect that's not why you changed your mind about visiting it.'

'It's not a state-of-the-art facility so I didn't bother.' Especially as nuclear power wasn't her field.

Not that she'd *have* a field once she became wife to the Emir.

'Is what you were doing in Paris? Engineering?'

'Yes. I was lucky enough to land work as assistant in a research project. Mainly I was just calculating data.'

'You must be good to be taken on.'

His simple statement warmed her. In the Women's University in Bakhara there'd been few interested in engineering. Most people viewed her choice as a misguided attempt to prove herself in a male domain. Or proof that she was unfeminine. Many in Bakhara clung to tradition.

'My professor recommended me. She thought even if I was in Paris for the cultural experience it would be a crime not to take advantage of the opportunity.'

'She was right. Opportunities are there to be grabbed. Did you enjoy the work?'

'Loved it! The team was excellent and I learned so much. I—' She looked down at her hands, clenched too tight before her.

'You...?'

She shook her head. What was the point of saying she'd planned to take part in the project's next phase—that the team leader had asked her to take on more responsibility? That she'd begun to see a future for herself that had nothing to do with a royal marriage and everything to do with her own interests and professional skills?

Ruthlessly she cut off the regrets that churned under the surface. No point going there.

'Look at this.' She quickened her pace to circle a large wooden shell. 'An early model for a war tank. Who'd have thought it?'

Zahir watched her duck her head and step up into the structure. A flash of shapely legs drew his eye but he managed not to stare. Her dress was light and summery rather than revealing, but the way she filled it in all the right places would be pure distraction to any red-blooded man.

Soraya was a captivating mix. She made a show of keeping him at arm's length but regularly forgot and relaxed into unguarded moments. She was intelligent and sexy, a woman he enjoyed crossing swords with.

Until he remembered pleasure was an emotion he shouldn't feel around Hussein's fiancée.

Yet that didn't prevent him wondering what she'd been going to say. She didn't hide her emotions as well as she imagined and he had no doubt she'd changed the subject rather than pursue a line of thought that bothered her. Something about the team she worked with in Paris.

'Your friends at the club the other night—are they engineers too?'

'Sorry?' She looked up, her eyes wide as if surprised at the change of subject.

'The guy you danced with. Does he work on the same project?'

Was it imagination or did her lips tighten?

'No. They're from the university but not in my field.'

Zahir waited for her to elaborate but she said nothing.

'So you don't have a passion for engineering in common?'

'Who? Me and Raoul? Hardly.' She stepped down, pretending not to notice the arm he extended to steady her.

'What do you have in common? You seemed *very* close.'

Her head jerked up and her eyes clashed with his. Sparks of sensation flared and burst across his skin like a brush fire igniting from a summer-lightning strike. It disturbed him that he'd never known such a reaction to a woman. Even in the throes of first and only love, it had taken more than a look to set his blood simmering.

'That's none of your business.' Soraya's breathing shallowed. Zahir became tantalisingly aware of her breasts' jagged rise and fall as she struggled to remain calm.

'It is, when I'm taking you home to marry Hussein.' He let

the words crash out, harsh and honest, as if saying them would break the strange spell she wove around him.

Something had to.

Her eyes rounded and her mouth formed an 'O' of shock. Finally she found her voice.

'Is that what you were doing all that time? Spying on me?' Her voice rose in outrage.

Zahir said nothing. He'd had no plan that night other than to track her down and tell her about Hussein's request that she return. It had been the shock of seeing her. The shock of recognition that had rooted him to the spot. As if he *knew* her, not as the subject of his next mission, but as someone intrinsically important to *himself.*

For once he hadn't known how to proceed. Not when his overwhelming impulse had been to ignore his mission and stake a personal claim on her.

Guilt pooled in his belly. No wonder he'd made a hash of everything that night.

'I don't spy,' Zahir said at last. 'But I won't shy from telling Hussein anything I feel he should know.'

'Like the fact that I had the temerity to *dance* with a man in a public place?' She shook her head. 'What century did you crawl out of, Zahir?'

'If it was only dances, I'm sure Hussein won't be concerned.' He paused, telling himself his urgent need to know was pure altruism. A favour to a friend. 'Is that all there was, Soraya?'

Colour seeped across her cheekbones and her eyes snapped a warning. 'My personal life is just that. Personal. If the Emir has questions, he can ask me himself.'

Her chin jutted belligerently as she faced him toe-to-toe. He applauded her backbone. Few men in Bakhara or elsewhere would have stood up to him this way.

'What about your friend's invitation when you got home?' The words slipped out before he could reconsider. 'She asked you to join her and her lover in bed. Does your bridegroom have a right to know if you make a habit of sharing so *intimately* with your flatmate?'

Her head jerked back, her cheeks leaching of colour as she goggled up at him.

He opened his mouth to speak again—to say what, he didn't know—when her laughter erupted. It had a ragged, raw quality that spoke of disbelief, amusement and something else that made him wish he'd kept his mouth shut.

'You heard that?' She shook her head, wiping her eyes. 'Then it's a shame you didn't hear Lisle mention her twin sister was visiting and they were in her room having a catch-up since her boyfriend had left.' Her hand dropped and her eyes sizzled defiantly.

'Don't presume to judge me by the standards of others. Or are they your standards, Zahir?' She raised a hand when he'd have spoken. 'No, don't tell me. Contrary to your lurid imaginings, I didn't lead a life of debauchery in Paris, nor did I develop a taste for threesomes.'

It was the truth. He read it in every outraged bone in her stiffly held body. In the shock shadowing her eyes and the distaste twisting her full lips.

More than that, he felt it deep within, a truth he'd deliberately ignored.

Why? Why draw conclusions on such flimsy evidence when he'd spent a lifetime learning balanced judgement?

Because he'd needed a reason not to like her.

Because from the instant he'd clapped eyes on her he'd felt an attraction so strong he'd sought any excuse to pretend it didn't exist. It had rocked his world, as if the earth's tectonic plates had shifted beneath his feet.

Because distrusting her gave him a reason not to acknowledge that inexplicable attraction. He'd hidden behind it rather than face the truth.

'Do you always leap to conclusions about people?'

'No.' He shook his head. 'Never.'

'Just with me?' Her sceptical look froze as she read his face.

'Yes.' Shame burned him. Soraya was right. He'd taken one look at her and his judgement, his brain, had shut down. 'I'm sorry, Soraya.' He held her gaze, restraining himself against the impulse to step forward and comfort her. As if she'd welcome his touch! 'That was crass of me, as well as wrong. I apologise unreservedly. The accusation was unworthy of you.'

'So now you pretend to know me? That's rich.'

'I don't know you. That's why I'm here now, because I want to understand you.'

'To spy for the Emir.'

'No!' What a mess he'd made of this. No one would ever believe him the same man who brokered multinational deals on a regular basis.

'Then why?' The anger had gone from her eyes, replaced by a searching curiosity as strong as his own.

Zahir drew in a fortifying breath. He owed her the truth, no matter how vulnerable it made him.

'For myself. Because I need to.'

Her eyes widened and his heart crashed faster as he read comprehension in her eyes. Soraya stared so hard she didn't even seem to notice the straggling group of families pass by— adults, a couple of teenagers and younger children.

'No,' she said at last. 'I don't want you here.'

'Soraya, I'm truly sorry. I—'

'It's not because of what you…assumed about me. I'd just rather be alone.' Zahir's stomach knotted as he read awareness in her dark gaze and a flicker of fear.

He should be relieved one of them was behaving wisely.

She turned away. 'I'll see you back at the hotel.'

Zahir knew it was the right thing to do. Some things were better hidden and never acknowledged. Yet not following her took far more will-power than it should.

He stood, watching her go, until a curve in the path brought the family group back in view. He saw two empty prams and one of the toddlers holding the hand of an older child.

Frowning, he surveyed the group, checking his recollection from when their paths had crossed before.

His heart kicked up a pace as adrenalin surged. He wasn't mistaken: the group wasn't complete. It was the sort of detail he'd been trained to notice. He breathed deep, double-checking.

The toddler in the yellow T-shirt was missing.

Even as the thought formed in his head, Zahir loped onto the track, cutting across Soraya's path.

'Zahir, I'd really rather—'

He quickened his pace, away from the families and back in the direction they'd come. The area was lightly forested and open enough to see for some way. Unless the child was down near the tempting little rivulets that meandered through the grounds.

Zahir's neck prickled as he jogged forward.

'Zahir?' She must have followed him.

Then he saw it: a flare of sunshine-yellow in the shadows. *In the glinting water.* His heart seemed to judder to a stop mid-beat even as he broke into a run.

'Here,' he called over his shoulder. 'Ambulance!' He didn't pause to see if she caught the phone he tossed.

'Soraya? Are you okay?'

She looked up, tugged from her thoughts by Zahir's rich baritone. Around them the discreet chatter of the hotel restaurant resurfaced, the sense of being with others, even if in a secluded corner of the great gilded dining salon. The sky glowed with the sun's last syrupy, pink light as indigo darkness closed in from the forest, cutting off the chateau from the outside world.

It was peaceful and pleasant. So different from the scene branded on her brain. The toddler's face, that awful waxen colour. The screams of his mother. The dreadful, wrenching terror that had reduced everything to slow motion.

Even now the remembered scent of fear clogged her nostrils, vying with the rich scents of their superb meal.

'I'm fine. Thank you.' She cast Zahir a perfunctory smile and lifted a morsel of fish to her mouth. Yet her limbs still felt ridiculously shaky. As if she'd run for her life that day, not simply called the medics and corralled the toddler's family while Zahir had saved his life.

She hadn't even realised there *was* an emergency. She'd been so absorbed, thinking about Zahir, how he'd insulted her then apologised so gravely she'd had no choice but to believe he regretted it. Especially when his eyes mirrored her own deep confusion. She'd struggled to grasp what had happened even as Zahir hauled the boy from the creek and puffed air into his little lungs.

Her knife and fork clattered onto her plate.

'Thank heaven you were there today. If you hadn't been, if you hadn't noticed he was missing—'

'There's no point dwelling on "what ifs". The child is safe.' Zahir reached across the table as if to take her hand where it clenched in a tense fist on the linen cloth. At the last moment he reached instead for his water.

Soraya knew she should be glad he didn't invade her personal space. Yet that didn't douse her longing for the comfort of his touch. Despite the long soak in her suite's oversized bath, she still felt chilled by the afternoon's events. Zahir's hand would be warm, solid and real.

'I know,' she murmured. 'I can't help it. I keep going over it again and again in my head.' She drew a shuddery breath and reached for her glass.

'It was a shock. That's a natural reaction.' There was understanding in his voice.

'*You* weren't shocked.' She bit her lip. 'I'm sorry. I didn't mean for that to sound like an accusation.'

'I understand.' The ghost of a smile softened his mouth and that invisible thread of connection between them twanged tighter, dragging at her internal muscles. 'Don't worry, I was running on adrenalin too. It's just that I've been in emergency situations before. Too often.'

That glimmer of a smile died, obliterated by a sudden harshness that transformed his features. It reminded her that she knew next to nothing about this man with whom she would spend the next few weeks—more, since he was the Emir's right-hand man. In Bakhara their paths would cross regularly.

'Tell me. Please.' Her words escaped without conscious thought and she met his surprised gaze. 'It's none of my business I know. I just…' Soraya bit her lip, not understanding her compulsion to know him. It had nothing to do with prurient curiosity and everything to do with the awareness that had shimmered so strongly between them this afternoon. From the first it had been there. He'd all but acknowledged it himself today.

She needed to know what it was.

'I don't *understand* you.' The words tumbled from her lips. 'And this afternoon…'

How did she explain something fundamental had shifted today when they'd shared laughter and she'd glimpsed a man who appealed far too much, when he'd apologised so sincerely she'd felt his shame and then when he'd saved that child? He wasn't the cold, arrogant man she'd tried to cast him. He was so much more.

She sensed it was dangerous to like Zahir too much. She'd felt safe in her indignation. Yet she couldn't keep pretending he was her unfeeling enemy. It just didn't ring true.

'If it had been left to his family he'd have drowned. They wouldn't have realised till too late.' The words burst out. 'If I'd been there without you, as I said I wanted, I wouldn't have been able to save him either. Only *you*—'

'Don't beat yourself up, Soraya.' His voice was calm, mellow and reassuring. 'You did wonderfully, keeping everyone in order till the medics came.'

Strong fingers covered hers and instantly heat seeped back along her veins.

She'd been right. There was magic in Zahir's touch. This time she wasn't going to question it or pull away.

A sense of wellbeing grew, a glow that wasn't simply the

physical warmth of flesh touching flesh. She looked from their joined hands then up into eyes that had darkened to the colour of the encircling forest.

'I want to understand.' Though she wasn't sure what exactly she needed to know. It was all tangled together—today's events and the enigma of Zahir's true personality. This...*something* between them. The unsettling realisation she didn't understand herself as well as she'd thought.

Absently he rubbed his thumb over her hand and some of the tightness in her belly unravelled. Her rigid shoulders dropped a fraction.

'There's not much to understand. I've seen violence in my life, too often. I learned to react quickly. Even as a child.'

'So young?' At her query his mouth twisted and he looked down at their joined hands.

'One of my first memories is of blood pooling across a stone floor and wondering why the man with the funny stare didn't move before the red stained his clothes.'

'Oh, Zahir.' Her free hand closed over his as he held her. 'I'm so sorry.'

He shrugged. 'It was no one I knew. Just one of my father's cronies.' He spoke with such matter-of-fact coolness it sent a tiny quiver through her. 'He'd had too much to drink and was unsteady on his feet. When he fell, he cracked his skull.'

'How old were you?'

'Three, perhaps. Maybe four.'

'That's dreadful.' Something deep inside twisted. He'd been so young. So vulnerable. What had his life been like that he'd come across such a scene?

'I remember my father stumbling across the room, cursing about the mess. And making myself scarce. I was good at that.' His mouth was a flat line, no trace of insouciance now.

Soraya felt him stiffen under her touch and wondered what he was remembering. The look on his face as much as his words told her it hadn't been pleasant. What had his mother been doing while her son had watched that horrible scene?

'There were other…incidents too. Enough to learn how swift and unpredictable violence can be.' His gaze fixed on a point beyond her but she wondered if what he saw was far beyond the walls of the hotel. 'It was useful training, in a way. It meant I was always half-prepared.'

Soraya blinked and stared. Zahir painted a picture that, despite the lack of detail, horrified her. A childhood where the most valuable lesson learned was a readiness to confront violence.

'It sounds like your childhood was eventful.'

Swiftly he turned his gaze on her and she caught a flicker of amusement in his eyes. 'Obviously Hussein knows what he's doing, choosing you as his wife. That's a diplomatic response if ever I heard one.'

He looked down and frowned as if registering for the first time their linked hands. Abruptly he drew his away, leaving her oddly bereft.

She laced her fingers together and slipped her hands into her lap. They still held the imprint of his, hard and comforting against hers.

'My early childhood was a disaster, but I survived. Then I joined the royal household. I was safe, well-fed, educated, comfortable. But I trained with the warriors. I saw my share of accidents and wounds. I could diagnose a dislocation, a broken bone or sprain by the age of twelve.'

'That must have been tough.'

'I loved it.' Zahir's sudden grin took her by surprise and she sat back, her pulse thudding an uneven response to the sheer glory of it.

Oh my. Oh. My!

It was the second time she'd glimpsed the man behind the wall of steel. The first, when he'd threatened her with such fervour if she ever injured the Emir. And now a look of such unadulterated joy it was like swallowing sunshine, just seeing it. It took Soraya a moment to find her voice.

'Why did you love it?'

He picked up his cutlery but didn't move to eat. 'I belonged,' he said at last. 'That became my world.'

Soraya frowned, more curious than ever for details. But she had no right to push for what was clearly private and difficult territory. As it was, she sensed Zahir had revealed more than he usually deigned to share.

'Eventually I joined the Emir's bodyguard, even led it. So you see I've had lots of opportunities to deal with crises.' His smile now was more restrained, a polite curve of the lips only, not that blinding flash of pleasure that had thwacked her senses into overdrive.

'But no one would want to harm the Emir.' She, more than most of his subjects, had cause to know what a generous and honourable man he was.

Zahir shook his head. 'There is always the possibility—from someone who seeks fame through a violent act, to someone disturbed or ruthless. There have been times when noticing a small detail, or sensing something amiss, made all the difference.'

Soraya slid her hands up to rub her arms. 'Like noticing that boy wasn't with his family.'

Zahir nodded. 'I was trained to register the smallest details. To take note and act quickly when necessary.'

'No one asked you to monitor them.'

His straight shoulders lifted. 'You don't entirely switch off even when you're no longer on close personal protection duty. I haven't done that for years but the skills stay with you.'

'Just as well.'

He shot her a quick glance but she felt its intensity to the tips of her toes.

'Eat, Soraya. It's over. The child is safe and the family reunited. There's nothing to worry about.'

She picked up her cutlery and made a show of eating her meal, as he did. But her niggle of anxiety grew rather than faded with the knowledge she'd gained.

It had all been easier when she could write Zahir off as bossy, arrogant and interfering. Before he'd revealed a humanity and tenderness that made a mockery of her easy assumptions. He'd thought badly of her, but his apology had been genuine and his contrition real. She'd seen the shame and regret in his eyes. And at least he'd been up-front with her.

She recalled him, his clothes plastered to his tall body, cradling the toddler and crooning to him once he had begun to breathe again. He hadn't turned a hair when the child vomited comprehensively and begun to cry. He'd been patience itself with both the boy and his distraught mother, managing to calm them both and monitoring them till professional help had arrived.

The sight of the small child held so easily and safely against Zahir's powerful frame ignited a blast of emotions Soraya couldn't label, but felt to her core.

Nor had he been eager for acknowledgement. As soon as the child was with medical staff he'd taken Soraya's trembling hand, offered his best wishes to the group and led her away for a restorative coffee. He hadn't turned a hair at the stares he'd received with his muddied trousers and his wet shirt clinging to his powerful torso. He'd been solicitous of *her*, as if she'd been the one injured.

Zahir was quietly competent, caring, strong when she was weak.

And he…appealed to her.

He appealed too much for a woman who wasn't interested in men. Who'd seen the pitfalls of romance and decided early not to go there. That had been one of the reasons she'd agreed to her royal betrothal—the belief that an arranged marriage to an honourable man was safer than a so-called love match.

She'd never been romantically interested in any man. Given her background, maybe she'd even worked a little too hard to avoid such temptation.

Why then did Zahir fascinate her so? Why did she need to understand him?

Because she wasn't as self-sufficient as she'd thought?

Because, perhaps, she was susceptible to the charm of a strong, handsome man? A man who hid surprising gentleness and a mile-wide streak of heroism behind a cool façade?

CHAPTER SEVEN

TWO DAYS later Soraya and Zahir returned to the hotel to find a familiar family group in the car park.

'Mademoiselle Karim!' a teenage girl called out. Soraya remembered her; she'd been pale and distraught, blaming herself for her little brother's accident.

'Lucie, how are you? How is your brother?' Soraya smiled as she neared the group, pleasure filling her as she saw the little boy safe in his mother's arms.

'Recovered fully, as you see.' The older woman smiled tentatively before glancing at her husband, clearly uncomfortable beside her. 'We came to thank you both.' Her gaze rested on Zahir. 'Without you…'

'Without them he would have died,' her husband said, his voice harsh. 'Because you couldn't watch him.'

Soraya stiffened, stunned at the venom in his tone.

'In my experience,' said a firm baritone beside her, 'a man casts blame when he holds himself responsible but hasn't the guts to acknowledge it.' Zahir stood so close she felt the fury emanating from him. 'It's a father's duty to protect his family.'

The bristling man before them seemed to deflate. Enough to reveal the hollowed eyes and pallor of a man still working through shock.

'It's very hot out here,' Soraya said quickly. 'Why don't we go inside for a cool drink?' She smiled at the children. 'Or ice-cream? They have terrific ice-cream here.'

* * *

It was a relief to escape outside again with the children. Despite Soraya's calming presence and his own tight control, Zahir could barely stomach being with a man who refused to accept responsibility for his son's safety and blamed his womenfolk for his shortcomings.

'Well done!' Zahir congratulated one of the girls on her archery skills. 'You hit the target this time. Now, try it again, but don't forget to hold the bow this way.' He leaned in to demonstrate.

He glanced at the window where Soraya sat with their older guests, her smile warm. The mother had relaxed enough to relinquish the toddler into Soraya's arms and she bounced him on her knees. Even the woman's husband had unwound enough to nod at something she said.

Zahir's dislike for the man would have stifled the atmosphere. The child's father had struck his personal sore spot: neglectful fathers topped his list of dislikes.

He shook his head as he helped one of the children aim her bow.

Soraya had marshalled the group before he'd even got a grip on his anger. She'd charmed them all, reassured them and acted as hostess as if born to it. He remembered how she'd organised the crowd at the accident. Without her it would have been mayhem.

Her skills would make her perfect in the role of Hussein's queen. She was gracious, charming and able to put people at ease in difficult circumstances.

Hussein had chosen his bride well. Socially accomplished, quick thinking and feisty enough to hint at a passionate nature. She would make a fine wife: an asset in public and the sort of spouse a man rejoiced to come home to at the end of a long day.

The realisation should have reassured him that his mission to return her to Bakhara was important. But it brought no pleasure.

Just a twist in his gut that felt horribly like envy.

* * *

'You've got an ice-cream addiction, Soraya.'

'*I* have?' She looked at the remains of the double-scoop pistachio-and-coffee ice-cream he held and shook her head. 'I don't hear you complaining.'

Zahir shrugged and she averted her eyes lest they cling too long to the movement of his broad shoulders. She'd discovered a weakness for Zahir's wide, straight shoulders and rare, spectacular smile.

She looked instead around the stone-built town. Its square was hung with flags for Bastille Day and lights in the plane trees had just been turned on. In the background a small but enthusiastic band entertained onlookers.

'I'm just keeping you company.' Zahir's deep voice tickled her senses. 'Being a good companion.'

As he had been ever since Amboise. It was as if his accusation and apology, not to mention the crisis there, had cleared the air between them. No word of reproach or disapproval passed his lips. Nor—and she told herself she was relieved by it—did he refer to the shimmering attraction between them.

She'd begun to wonder if, after all, it was one-sided. Who wouldn't be star-struck by a man like Zahir? Even if his attention was for her as bride to his mentor.

'Watch out!' She saw the football before Zahir yet he managed to whip around and stop its wayward trajectory. He kicked it up, bouncing it easily off his knees and feet as he scanned the playing field beside the river.

A grinning boy waved and Zahir kicked the ball straight to him.

'You play football?'

'I used to. When I was young.'

'Me too.'

'Why aren't I surprised?' A slow grin spread across his face and Soraya wondered if she'd ever be able to see it without her pulse stuttering out of control.

'What else did you do when you were young?' They'd been

careful to avoid personal topics. They discussed France and the places they saw, or politics and books.

The one subject they never touched on was Bakhara.

'I rode. I discovered chess. I learned to fight.'

Soraya laughed. 'Of course. You sound like a traditional Bakhari male.'

'I *am* a traditional Bakhari male.'

She shook her head. A traditionalist wouldn't have let her drive his precious car, or listen attentively to a woman explaining the principles of geothermal power.

'What did you do when you were young?'

'Learn to cook, keep house and embroider.' She sighed, remembering hours of dutiful boredom. 'And sneaked out to play football.'

'And dreamed of marrying a handsome prince?'

'No!' The word shot out sharply. 'Never that.'

Zahir watched her intently. 'Marrying Hussein isn't the fulfilment of a lifelong ambition? I thought little girls fixated on a glamorous marriage.'

Soraya lifted her ice-cream, hoping the cherry flavour would counteract the sour tang on her tongue. 'Other little girls maybe. Marriage was never my dream.'

'But things are different now.'

'Oh yes, they're different now.' Bitterness welled, and with it anger at the limitations placed on her life by her engagement. 'Can we not talk about it now? I'd rather concentrate on this.' She waved a hand to encompass the crowd and the holiday atmosphere.

'Besides—' she nodded in the direction of the playing field '—I think you're wanted.'

The football sailed through the air to land near Zahir. The same grinning teenager waved for him to join the impromptu game.

Zahir shook his head. 'I can't leave you.'

'Of course you can. I'm perfectly fine.' She reached to pull his jacket off one shoulder then stopped as a sizzle of fire shot through her fingertips. Beneath her touch his muscles stiffened. His eyes darkened and her breath snagged as heat pulsed between them.

Just one touch did that.

'Go,' she said hoarsely, her hand dropping. 'Please.' She needed time alone to regroup. So much for her innocent belief that things were easier between them. On the surface their relationship was pleasant, friendly, even. But beneath the surface lurked emotions she didn't want to stir.

'If you wish.' He stripped his jacket off and handed it to her. 'Unless you'd prefer to play?'

That made her smile. 'It's you they want. Go.' Studiously she ignored the warmth of his jacket over her arm. She made a production of waving him off then leaned against a tree, watching him lope down to the field.

It didn't surprise her that he sided with the younger players who seemed outclassed by their more experienced rivals. Soraya had seen him with children before. He was a natural, treating them as equals, yet with a patience that made him a good teacher and role model.

She watched him sprint across the field, take the ball almost to the goal and deftly avoid several tackles till a boy of thirteen or so had time to join him. Zahir passed him the ball, then applauded as the boy's shot at goal missed by a whisker.

Pride surfaced. She *liked* Zahir, admired him. She wondered what he'd be like with his own children. She guessed he'd be fiercely loyal and supportive, a true friend. He'd be the same with the woman he loved.

Soraya caught the direction of her thoughts and slammed them shut with a gasp of horror.

Fixing her gaze on the river glinting beyond the playing field, she focused on the last few licks of her ice-cream and the sound of music filling the dusk.

A tentative voice intruded. 'Would you care to dance?' The man's smile was open and the hand he extended marked by hard work. She guessed he was a farmer with his craggy, sun-bronzed face. The music beckoned.

Why not? She'd promised herself she'd make the most of these last precious days of freedom. Placing Zahir's jacket and her bag of purchases on a nearby seat, Soraya took the stranger's hand.

Zahir felt like a kid again, light-hearted and spontaneous. He was even showing off for the girl in the floaty, floral dress standing in the shade at the edge of the square, as if he had nothing more on his mind than making the most of the day.

He couldn't remember the last time he'd felt this way. As if life was simple and full of pleasure, rather than a complicated series of manoeuvres to be plotted carefully, a contest to be won. More and more he felt it, the infectious joy of being with Soraya. As if weighty matters of state weren't the be-all and end-all of his existence. As if, imperceptibly, his priorities had changed.

The sensation was alluring. Like Soraya.

He glanced up, expecting to see her there, watching, but she'd gone. She was fine, he told himself. She'd be in the square, tasting local delicacies or chatting with someone. But a few minutes later he excused himself and jogged over to where he'd left her.

His jacket lay folded on a chair beside her cloth bag that was filled to the brim with her haul of goodies from the market stalls. He turned and surveyed the crowd. Sure enough, there she was, smiling as she danced with a husky young man. Her joy was infectious, even from this distance, and he wished it was him holding her as they danced over the cobblestones.

But discretion was the better part of valour. Holding Soraya would be inviting trouble. Instead he folded his arms and watched as the sky darkened and the woman who filled his thoughts moved from partner to partner.

* * *

'Time to stop?' Zahir's words interrupted her partner's thanks as the music ended. Soraya swung round, breathing heavily after that last mad polka. In the dim light Zahir loomed. Was that disapproval in his voice? His face was set in harsh lines she hadn't seen in days.

Instantly resentment stirred. And disappointment. She'd thought they were past the disapproval.

'Why?' She tucked a strand of hair behind her ear then crossed her arms defensively. 'Because I'm too boisterous? Because it's not the behaviour of a soon-to-be-queen?' His gaze bored into hers and, despite her annoyance, secret heat flared. The heat a woman felt for a man. 'Surely you don't think I'm flirting?'

'Nothing like that. You've been dancing nonstop and I thought you needed a rest.' His eyes skimmed the rapid rise of her breasts before he looked away.

'Sorry.' She ducked her head. 'I thought you were taking me to task.'

'Not surprising, given the way I jumped down your throat initially.'

Surprised, Soraya looked up. One thing about Zahir, he didn't hide from the facts. Even reminders of his mistakes. He wasn't like anyone else she knew. Or maybe it was her feelings for him that were unique.

'Dance with me?' The moment she said it she realised how much she wanted to.

'Surely you've had enough. Let me buy you a cold drink while we wait for the fireworks.'

Soraya shook her head. She wanted Zahir to hold her. She'd spent a lifetime doing the right thing, was facing a future of duty, and for this day wanted something for herself.

'Please, Zahir? Just one dance? It's Bastille Day, after all.' She held out her arms and after a long moment he took her in his arms, holding her gently and not too close. Even so her senses clamoured in delight as the music struck up and they moved together.

'You're not French. Bastille Day means nothing to you.'

'You're wrong.' She fought to keep her voice even when her bloodstream bubbled with pleasure. 'It's about liberty. There's nothing more important than freedom.'

Zahir heard the edge in her voice and tried to read her face in the darkness. She was like fluid quicksilver in his arms. He had to make an effort not to drag her close. Instead he focused on her words.

'Liberty? You speak as if it's threatened.'

She didn't answer for a moment. 'This is *my* time,' she said eventually. 'When I reach Bakhara I won't be able to do as I want or make my own choices. I'll be constrained.'

Because she'd be Hussein's bride.

'You don't sound enthusiastic.'

This time her silence was even longer. 'It's a great honour to be chosen as the Emir's bride.'

Yet he heard no pleasure in her voice. Or was it that he didn't want to hear it? Damn him for his jealousy.

'You're right,' he said at last. 'Your life will be restricted.' Hadn't his own become tightly constrained by duty, loyalty and the demands placed on it? Maybe that explained his dizzying sense of freedom with Soraya. This was a vacation from a life of responsibilities. Yet he couldn't help suspecting the wonder of it would continue if he had Soraya by his side, always. 'But there will be benefits. Hussein is a good man. He'll look after you.'

Though he shied from the thought of them together.

The music ended and they stopped moving in the shadows at the edge of the square. He told himself to let her go but didn't move. Nor did she.

'I know he is,' she said quietly. 'But it's an enormous step, giving up the life I know.'

Zahir breathed deep, dizzy with her sweet, fresh scent, revelling in the feel of her in his arms.

'Would you ever consider not going through with it?'

His hoarse words seemed over-loud in the charged silence.

Appalled, he wished he could retract them. What sort of mad, wishful thinking was that?

'Why would I do that?'

He told himself this was just a hypothetical discussion. 'If you fell for someone else.' Yet he held his breath as he waited for her answer, his pulse drumming in his ears.

'Imagine the fallout.' Her head drooped towards his chest so that he looked down on her vulnerable nape. He gathered her in to him. Just to comfort her, he assured himself. Yet his arms moulded to her as if they belonged.

She sighed. 'The scandal would be enormous, especially after my mother.'

'Your mother?'

'She disgraced herself and the family and my dad bore the brunt of disapproval for not vilifying her. Poor Dad, I couldn't do that to him. His business would be ruined and he'd be an outcast.'

And so would she, Zahir reminded himself. A man who truly cared for her wouldn't do that to her.

'Anyway, I'm pretty sure it's against the law to break a contract with the nation's ruler.' Her laugh was hollow. 'Besides.' She lifted her head and looked him straight in the eye. 'What man would dare steal the Emir's bride? He'd be punished, surely?'

Soraya's upturned face was beautiful, her eyes almost beseeching, and Zahir knew a crazy urge to kiss her till the world faded and all that was left was them.

'He'd lose all claim to honour or loyalty to the crown,' Zahir said slowly, feeling the full weight of such a prospect. He'd made honour and loyalty his life. 'He'd never be able to hold his head up again. He'd be stripped of official titles and positions and the council of elders would banish him from Bakhara.' He drew a deep breath. 'Hussein could never call him friend again.'

'As I thought.' Her hands dropped and she stepped abruptly out of his hold. 'No man would even consider it.'

CHAPTER EIGHT

IT WASN'T working.

Zahir hefted in a determined breath and thrust off from the end of the pool, forcing his burning lungs and overworked body into another lap.

No matter how hard he pushed himself, he couldn't strip her from his mind. Soraya was there constantly.

He was at the end of his tether. Sleep grew elusive. His attempts to focus on the future and the governorship which would be his greatest challenge to date faded into the background. Soraya took centre stage.

He'd thought to change her mind about taking a slow route back to Bakhara since their time together was fraught with perilous undercurrents.

She'd said she wanted to see the countryside and he'd given it to her. They stayed in a friend's manor house in the Perigord, surrounded by walnut groves, tiny villages and winding narrow roads. No boutiques. No nightclubs.

Soraya loved it.

So much for his plans to convince her to cut short their stay and head for the bright lights! She found everything fascinating; from the stone-building styles to the local accent and the people they met. Even the limestone caves with their prehistoric paintings captured her interest.

Her delight in it all, her vivid joy in each moment, made

every experience fresh and new to him too. He was rediscovering simple pleasures.

Yet there was nothing simple or innocent about his feelings for her.

Zahir hauled himself from the water. It was still early and he was taking the chopper to Paris. Ostensibly it was a meeting that called him. In reality, it was as an excuse to absent himself from Soraya.

He enjoyed being with her too much. He found himself opening up to her. He'd even told her about his childhood, something he never shared. More than that, he felt emotions stirring that he had no business feeling. For years he'd locked emotions behind a wall of steel. Now it seemed there were fissures in the barricade he'd built around himself. He was a different man from the one who'd met her in Paris. He *felt* more, experienced more, cared more.

Zahir was halfway to the house when he saw the garage door open. He frowned. The old estate manager wouldn't be up at dawn working, but with the owners in Paris, who else could it be?

One step into the building and he knew.

The breath sucked from his lungs as he saw her on her back beneath an old four-wheel drive; neat sneakers, white socks and the most mouth-watering legs he'd ever seen.

With those light summer dresses she wore he'd had ample opportunity to recognise Soraya had world-class legs. But her clothes were always modest. Now for the first time his gaze trawled up past her knees to smooth, slim thighs that made him think of cool sheets and a hot woman, of passion and endless hours of erotic pleasure.

Humming off-key, Soraya wasn't sure at first, but she thought she heard swearing, low-voiced and urgent. She paused and wiped her brow with a grimy hand.

A stream of whispered words vied with the early-morning birdsong.

Her skin prickled as she realised she wasn't alone. An instant later she scooted out from beneath the vehicle.

Long legs were braced wide before her. Bare, sinewy feet. Powerfully muscled thighs in sodden board shorts. A towel clutched in one large, white-knuckled hand.

Soraya's throat dried as she yanked her gaze higher, skimming over a washboard abdomen, wide pectoral muscles and straight shoulders. Higher, till she got lost in green eyes turned dark and smoky in the early-morning light.

Her heart jumped and she sat up quickly.

'Zahir.' Her voice was breathless and high. She swallowed and tried again, ignoring the feverish pleasure that surged at the sound of his name on her lips. Ever since the Bastille Day celebrations she'd been ultra-aware of him.

Who was she kidding? She'd been aware of him from the start, only in the beginning she'd been able to hide behind dislike.

'You surprised me.' Great. Now her conversation had dried up with her brain.

Despite the affinity she felt for Zahir and her pleasure in his company, she grew more on edge daily.

It was as if another woman inhabited her body. A woman with desires and needs utterly foreign to her. A woman whose eyes followed this man's every move. Whose breasts were swollen and tender with longing for his touch. Who felt hunger curl hard in her belly just at the sound of his deep voice.

Maybe the critics of her childhood were right. Maybe after all she was doomed to follow in her mother's footsteps—unable to resist the lure of a handsome man. Perhaps her father's protectiveness had been well-founded, and her own innate caution, her wariness of intimacy, had been more valid than she'd realised.

At twenty-four she'd begun to think herself completely immune to the male sex, for none had ever stirred her blood.

Now she knew better.

Whatever it was she felt for Zahir, it wasn't immunity. It was wild and strong, exciting and frightening. Worse, it wasn't just because of his looks. She enjoyed his dry humour, his intelligence, the fact that he was a decent man who took his responsibilities seriously. He was marvellous with kids and patient with a woman spooked by her looming future.

'What are you wearing?' His voice was husky.

She glanced down, then hurriedly folded her legs close, wrapping her arms around them.

'I didn't have any shorts so I cut off some jeans. It's too hot for them here.'

She'd made a mess of the job. Sewing had never been her forte, to the dismay of her female relatives who'd spent so many hours trying to interest her in embroidery and a dozen other housewifely skills. She couldn't even hack the legs off her old jeans in a straight line!

Zahir's dark eyebrows crunched together. 'That doesn't explain why you're down in the dirt.'

Ridiculously his words reminded her of the scolds she'd received from aunts about unladylike behaviour. For a moment the old guilt rose: about the fact she was her mother's daughter. That she was impulsive and strong-willed. That she didn't fit the mould.

Soraya lifted her chin. 'I'm tinkering with the car. Hortense had trouble with it and I thought I'd take a look.'

'Hortense?' Zahir rubbed his chin ruminatively and Soraya almost thought she heard the whisper of early-morning bristles against his hand. His chin was shadowed, accentuating the proud angle of his jaw.

'The housekeeper,' Soraya explained. 'She can take another vehicle.' She waved towards the new models filling the rest of the garage. 'But she's used to this one.'

'You don't have to do that. You're a guest.'

'But I *enjoy* it.' Soraya braced herself for a look of dismay or disapproval.

Instead she was rewarded with a grin that kicked her pulse to top speed.

'Better you than me, Soraya. Horses, people or computers I'll willingly spend hours with. But the underside of a chassis? You can have it and welcome.'

Warmth curled round Soraya's heart and squeezed hard. Zahir's eyes danced and she felt her mouth tilt in an answering smile.

'Yet you drive like a professional.' She loved sitting beside Zahir as he drove them through the countryside. He was competent; not afraid of speed, but she'd never felt in safer hands.

'That's because I *am* a professional. I was trained by the best. Defensive driving, off-road navigation and dune-driving for starters.'

He slung his towel casually over one shoulder, not bothering to wipe away the stray droplets of water that ran from his hair down his collarbone. Soraya followed their progress over his burnished flesh and found herself clasping her hands together far too tightly.

'I can strip down a motor and get it back together in record time,' he continued, oblivious to her stare. 'But that doesn't mean I'd do it for fun.'

'What *do* you do for fun? How do you relax?'

Zahir's easy smile faded.

'You must do something to unwind,' she persevered.

'I find ways.' His voice dropped so low it plucked at her nerve ends and made her tremble.

Green fire blazed beneath his now-hooded lids and Soraya felt an answering conflagration start somewhere in her midriff. As his eyes held hers that ball of heat plunged down to her pelvis. The thud of her heartbeat swelled to a roar that clogged her senses.

Women, she realised. He relaxed with *women*.

The sexual awareness in his stare was so blatant even someone as inexperienced as she couldn't miss it.

But he wasn't thinking about other women now.

Zahir was looking at *her*.

That look was a caress, trailing across her skin and drawing every muscle and nerve ending into singing life.

Soraya revelled in it. Gone in an instant was a lifetime's caution, obliterated by a welling force so elemental it muted any opposition.

Suddenly that tension, the unspoken awareness they'd tried to pretend didn't exist, was back full force. Soraya had tried to convince herself she'd imagined it. Now she saw it in Zahir's intense look. Its impact dragged the air from her lungs.

Did she look at him the same way?

The air between them shimmered as if with heat haze. Honeyed warmth pooled low between her legs and a strange lethargy stole through her.

If Zahir were to close the space between them and reach out his hand she'd welcome his touch.

She *willed* him to do it.

His eyes dropped to her mouth and her lips throbbed as if in response to the brush of his mouth against hers.

What would his kiss be like? Urgent and fiery or slow and sensuous?

Soraya's eyelids drooped as if weighted. Her lips opened, ripe for his. Her hands slipped from where they'd looped around her legs. Her chest rose as a fractured breath became a sigh of expectation.

Zahir stepped close, so close she felt a drop of pool water land on her ankle. She looked up, stretching her neck to hold his gaze.

Did she imagine a tremor pass through his solid frame?

'I…' He speared a hand through his hair. 'I have a meeting in Paris,' he said finally, his voice harsh. 'I won't be back for dinner. Don't wait up for me.'

A moment later he was gone.

A day alone had done nothing to douse the flare of sexual excitement smouldering within her.

Soraya was honest enough not to pretend it was anything

else that made her skin seem too tight for her body and her
pulse points ache with longing.

It was an awful irony that now, mere weeks from going to
the man she had to marry, she was finally experiencing sexual
desire. A desire she'd believed herself immune to.

That didn't mean she had to give in to it. She'd busied herself, thinking if she kept herself occupied every minute of every
day until her return to Bakhara she'd conquer this yearning.

It hadn't worked so far—despite tuning the four-wheel drive
till it purred, putting in hours on the laptop finishing her report,
catching up on emails, driving to a local market and stocking
up on so much mouth-watering fresh produce poor Hortense
had been cooking all afternoon.

Now, as the day drew to a close and Zahir hadn't returned,
Soraya knew she couldn't settle with a book or film.

What better time to face what she'd been putting off ever
since they'd arrived?

She took a deep breath and walked down the first step into
the outdoor pool. The water was like warm silk on her feet and
ankles, yet goose bumps broke out on Soraya's flesh.

Another step and she tried to concentrate on how the underwater lights made the depths look appealing, the blue and gold
key-pattern mosaic that ran the sides of the pool.

Her pulse revved as she moved deeper. But her hand was
firm on the sun-warmed flagstone at the pool edge. She had
nothing to fear, she reminded herself.

Only the fear she'd never been able to conquer.

Her brain filled with the image of that toddler, ghastly pale
as Zahir hauled him from the stream. Her stomach twisted and
terror was sharp metal on her tongue.

Had she looked like that the day she'd almost drowned?

This time she was determined to conquer her phobia.

Finally she reached a point where she couldn't proceed without submerging. Her heart hammered but she made herself turn
and grip the edge with both trembling hands.

Her legs stretched out, weightless behind her. Soraya was

torn between a thrill of exhilaration that she'd ventured so far beyond her comfort zone, and crawling horror at what might happen next.

Experimentally she kicked her legs. It was easier than she'd expected. But how to coordinate arms and legs? Better to concentrate on floating.

It took a while but finally she let go with one arm. If she could just relax enough she was sure she could float. Everyone said it was so easy. Daringly, she let her body stretch out, till she gripped the edge by her fingertips. See? It wasn't so hard. Tomorrow she'd go to the shallow end and try it without holding on. She'd...

'Soraya?' Out of the dusk a figure loomed.

She opened her mouth to reply and swallowed water. Shock swamped her. She scrabbled for the edge, one arm flailing even as she went under.

Panic welled, fed by the taste of treated water in her mouth and nostrils. Shock gave way to fear and she thrashed for the surface.

Till strong arms hauled her up, holding her tight.

She clawed at wide shoulders, desperate for the feel of solid bone and flesh beneath her fingers. Precious oxygen filled her lungs and she gulped it down in great, gasping breaths.

'It's okay, Soraya. You're all right. You're safe. I've got you.' Zahir's voice, like dark treacle, seeped past the panic, finally slowing her frantic heartbeat.

Eyes smarting, she wrapped her arms tight round his neck, burying her face against Zahir's slick skin. He felt warm and solid and so very, very safe.

'But who's got you?' she gasped. 'The water's too deep to stand.' Her lips moved against his skin and she tasted male spice and salt, but she couldn't bring herself to lift her head away.

'I've got us both. Don't worry.'

She registered his big hands splayed warm around her ribs. His legs moved against hers, slowly kicking as he kept them afloat.

'You're sure?' She hated how unsteady she sounded.

'Positive.'

A moment later she felt the tiled steps beneath her feet. His hand uncurled hers from their vice-like grip of his neck and placed it on the warm flagstone at the pool's edge.

'You're safe now. Absolutely.'

Yet it wasn't the stairs beneath her feet that convinced her. It was Zahir's strong, hard form flush against hers.

She'd assumed the next time they met she'd feel awkward, remembering the sizzle of sexual awareness that had charged the atmosphere back in the garage. But embarrassment was obliterated by relief.

'Thank you.' She couldn't seem to let him go, but clung to him with her other arm, her heart galloping. He seemed to understand, for he didn't release her.

'You don't swim?' His eyes held hers.

She shook her head. 'No,' she croaked.

'And you were in the pool because…?'

'I was teaching myself to float.' Her mouth wobbled in a parody of a smile. 'Or trying to.' She clamped her lips shut, not wanting to go further. Yet his constant, silent regard finally dragged the truth from her. 'I'm scared of the water.'

She waited for his look of surprise but it didn't come. He merely nodded his head. 'Sensible of you. I would be too if I couldn't swim.'

A ribbon of heat unfurled within her at Zahir's easy acceptance and matter-of-fact tone. No condescension, no disbelief. He said nothing more, just held her safe as the water lapped around them and Soraya was grateful for his silent support.

'It was the boy,' she finally said, needing to explain. 'Seeing him almost die because he couldn't save himself.' She yanked in a breath. 'I saw him and felt…'

She looked away. What had she felt? Horror, déjà vu, fear. *And more.*

'I felt ashamed I'd never conquered my fear and learned to swim. I don't want to be that helpless.'

Zahir's fingers tightened on her. 'Why are you so scared of the water?'

'I almost drowned as a child. I was playing in the shallows. I thought my mother was watching me but she was…busy.'

Soraya pulled in a searing breath. Her mother had gone to her lover, the man she had eventually ran away with, presumably thinking Soraya wouldn't venture deep.

Somehow through the years the two events had become entangled in her brain—the loss of her mother and her brush with death. As a child she'd almost believed she'd somehow driven her mother to leave with her near-drowning. Of course she knew better now, but the result was a dread of water she'd never been able to overcome.

Zahir's broad palm slid up her back then down again in a gesture of silent comfort that unstrung more of the tension still threading her body.

'What happened in Amboise must have brought it all back for you. No wonder you were white as a sheet.'

Soraya shrugged stiffly. 'It was…horrible. But it made me realise I couldn't go on pretending this fear doesn't matter. I have to do something about it.'

Strong fingers took her chin and lifted it till she was staring into eyes dark as the night closing in around them.

'Promise me you won't do it alone.' Though soft, Zahir's voice had a rough edge that abraded her senses.

'But I—'

'I'll teach you to swim, Soraya. Just promise me you won't try it alone.'

Her heart pounded as his gaze held hers. Soraya's insides melted at the banked heat she saw there.

'I promise.'

'Good.' He nodded and took her hand in his. 'We'll start now.'

'Now?' Her eyes rounded.

'No time like the present. Besides, we don't want tonight's episode to compound your fear, do we?'

It already had, but she bit down on the admission. The thought of going further into the depths horrified her.

Zahir's fingers threaded between hers, his strength and heat melding with hers.

'Trust me, Soraya?'

Her gaze roved his serious, almost grim face. She took in the lines of strength and character carved beside his mouth. There was determination in that solid jaw, arrogance in those aristocratic cheekbones and imperious nose, and a question in his clear gaze.

She thought of all she knew of him. He was capable, dependable and kind. How could she not trust him?

'Yes,' she said finally, and let him draw her into the water.

'Tilt your head back into the water further.'

Soraya did as he bid and Zahir was amazed anew that this was the same woman who a short time ago had been thrashing in panic half a metre from the edge of the pool. Now she floated on her back, his hands beneath her, the safeguard she needed to be confident in the water.

It humbled him that she trusted him so implicitly. Particularly since trust hadn't come easily to her. Initially they'd been like wary, armed combatants in an uneasy truce because of his early misjudgements of her.

Recently that wariness had blossomed into something akin to friendship, or at least understanding.

Except when his libido escaped his constraints and reminded him she was the most seductively attractive woman he'd ever known. Dancing with her in a public square had tested his limits. But this... Even dressed in a tank top and cut-offs rather than a skimpy bikini, she fired his blood.

'Why didn't you wear a swimsuit?' He asked, trying to take his mind off the sensual promise of her body spread before him.

He felt like a sultan offered a feast for the senses. But he had to deny himself and keep his touch brisk and businesslike. He couldn't betray her trust.

'I don't own one.' She darted a look at him then away. 'There's no point when I'd never use it.'

Zahir refrained from pointing out many women wore bikinis that never got wet. They were for display, to show off ripe female curves to best advantage.

The more he knew Soraya the more he understood she was unique. Her shame at not overcoming her fear had surprised him. Her determination to beat it rather than live with what she saw as weakness appealed. She was some woman.

He applauded her pride and perseverance. She had such heart—as much as any warrior he'd known.

Yet her bravery had run close to stupidity tonight. In an instant she'd shattered the hard-won calm he'd spent all day working to achieve. What if he hadn't come down to the pool for a swim? What if she'd drowned here alone? Anger and fear vied for dominance.

'What were you doing in the deep end?' Despite his best efforts his voice had a raw edge.

'I knew if I was in the shallows I wouldn't push myself. I had to face the danger.'

Hot shivers rippled through Zahir's belly. 'Just don't do it again, *ever*, without me.'

She drove him crazy. Pride, fear and desire made for a combustible mix. How much longer could he keep a lid on them all?

'I've already promised I won't.' She looked at him solemnly and his heart kicked against his ribs. 'But I need to learn fast. You won't always be around to help me.'

Of course he wouldn't. He'd be managing Bakhara's largest province and Soraya would be…with Hussein.

Clammy sweat broke out on Zahir's skin and sick dread churned his stomach. He tried so hard to be honourable in thought as well as deed, but lately it was more than he could do.

It was a constant battle to rein in his imagination. As for concentrating on teaching her to relax in the water—it took every ounce of determination to focus.

'Try kicking again but keep your legs straight.'

She did as instructed and together they moved down the pool. 'I'm moving! I'm swimming!'

The delighted look she sent him drove a shaft of pure pleasure through his chest.

It was more reward than he deserved.

Even as he smiled back, his body tensed.

Her long hair, unbound for the first time, spread in a cloud of dark satin. Like mermaid's tresses it caressed his hands, arms and belly as he walked with her. He'd never imagined it was so long. Now he couldn't help but wonder what it would be like rippling down her naked back and breasts as he made love to her.

Unable to take any more, he slipped his hands from beneath her and moved just far enough away to avoid contact. They were in the shallow end and she was in no danger.

Excited at her success, she didn't notice his withdrawal. Her face glowed with effervescent joy.

A man would have to be made of desert stone not to respond to Soraya.

Despite his reputation as a hard warrior, Zahir was made of all-too-human flesh. If only he *were* stone!

How could he hold out against a woman who appealed to him on a level no woman ever had? Not even the girl he'd been head over heels in love with as a youth.

'Zahir? What's wrong?' She was standing, water sluicing down the black top that clung like a second skin.

He shook his head. 'Nothing's wrong.' He turned away. 'That's enough now. We'll continue tomorrow and you can learn to float face-down, ready to swim properly.'

'Really?' She caught his hand and stopped him moving away. 'You think I'm ready?'

Reluctantly he turned and looked down into a face that to his dazzled eyes seemed flawless. Excitement shone in her eyes and her smile wrapped around his heart.

He wasn't aware of reaching out but found his hand cupping

her jaw. Her satiny skin was smooth and sleek to the touch. Her pulse trembled against his fingertips.

Something deep inside, something stronger than logic or caution, roared into life.

Her eyes were wide as she swayed towards him, her lips parting. To warn him off?

It was too late.

His lips met hers and the world collapsed around them.

CHAPTER NINE

Soraya had imagined his kiss so often. She'd even dreamed of it. The reality obliterated her imaginings as a tidal wave would the ripple of a single stone.

Zahir's broad hands cradled her face, his touch tender yet strong as he held her head just so and angled his own for better access.

His questing tongue slicked her lips, parted them, and she shuddered in great racking waves as sensation exploded within her. Zahir devoured her, invited her, stole her breath with his audacious demands, yet even while plundering rapaciously offered back such sweet, poignant pleasure Soraya was lost.

The fresh taste of his breath was in her mouth. It was the most delicious flavour in the world—spice and salt and the mystery that was maleness. His scent filled her nostrils. His hard body was muscled and intriguing, his heart thundering with hers. His wet skin burned, branding her through her clothes, making her breasts tingle and a curl of indescribable tension twist deep and low.

Instinctively she grabbed his shoulders, swaying as her limbs melted, and the world became a place she didn't recognise.

Nothing had prepared her for the vital life force throbbing through them as if they were one. Or the need spiralling out of control and the sheer wanton delight of being in his arms. Every sense was hyper-alert. Even the softly eddying water was a silken caress drawing her deeper into sensual overload.

She'd never felt more frail, more delicately feminine than now, with his heavy-muscled thighs braced wide around her, his hands trapping her, and his mouth seducing her with sheer, carnal pleasure.

Yet she'd never felt stronger. As if power sizzled and sparked in her blood. As if she could lay mountains low with a single flick of her fingers.

His kiss shattered her and rebuilt her at the same time.

Her hands slid from his shoulders to the back of his neck, up through his damp hair and he growled low in the back of his throat. It was a sound of approval, of male possession, and she revelled in it. Revelled in the power that she, even with her inexperience, had over this man who haunted her thoughts and dreams.

His tongue slid against hers, demanding a response, and she gave it, tentatively at first, then wholeheartedly, lost in the wonder of this heady world of passion.

Her whole body ached, throbbed for Zahir. Only him. She wanted to climb up his tall frame and meld herself against him. She *needed* with a desperation she'd never experienced or thought to know.

Even the rough pressure of his chest expanding against hers incited a thrill.

Soraya pressed closer, needy as never before. She loved the feel of his body, the unfamiliar outline of muscle, bone and sinew. The tickle of his hairy legs against hers. Lifting herself higher into his hold, her hips tilted against him and she registered the solid proof of his arousal.

At the feel of him, hot and heavy just *there* against her, she stilled. A frayed thread of common sense told her to move away, yet some older, sense-deep feminine instinct urged her closer.

Soraya was swaying nearer when firm hands grabbed her upper arms. An instant later she gulped huge drafts of air into oxygen-starved lungs as he put her from him. But nothing made up for the loss of Zahir's mouth on hers, or his body against hers.

Hungrily she eyed his reddened lips. They were drawn flat now, matching the horizontal lines furrowing his brow.

Yet his eyes didn't match his scowl. His eyes were smoky-dark and held a hint of the same shock she felt.

Soraya loved his eyes, she realised. From the first when they'd watched her so intently she'd felt a sizzle of awareness. Even when he'd looked askance at her, Zahir's eyes had fascinated. Now they shared the secret she felt: the secret turmoil of amazing emotions and sensations.

The secret his grim face denied.

'I'm sorry.' His voice was harsh and unrecognisable. 'That shouldn't have happened.'

His gaze left hers to fix on something over her shoulder. As if he couldn't bear to see her. Or as if he couldn't face what he read in her face.

It was the first time he'd ever avoided her gaze.

Soraya felt something crumble inside.

She gulped down a shaky breath and searched for control. Her heart pounded and she had the shakes so badly she wasn't sure she could stand without his support.

'But you can't pretend it didn't happen.' The words emerged breathless and uneven.

She didn't understand what made her say it till he yanked his gaze back to hers and heat exploded inside.

That's why. Because you want to feel it again—what Zahir makes you feel.

Because you want him to admit he feels it too.

But Zahir shook his head, thrusting her further away.

'It was *wrong.*' The last word was dragged from him as if from a tortured soul and she felt his pain as hers. His hands dropped and he stepped back, as if unable to remain within touching distance.

As if she tainted him.

Of course it was wrong. Soraya understood that all too well. To desire her husband-to-be's most trusted advisor was disastrous. Unthinkable!

Yet it felt so right. When it was just she and Zahir, it felt incredible.

'Zahir. Please, I…'

She didn't know what she was going to say. Only knew she couldn't bear the pain she read on his proud features. That she had to ease it somehow.

Yet he didn't give her the chance. Before the words had left her mouth he'd vaulted from the pool, every line of his athlete's body taut with rejection.

He didn't say a word as he strode away.

Sunlight flooded the dining room as Soraya lingered over a very late breakfast. She'd fallen asleep at dawn and couldn't summon the energy to go out, despite the glorious day.

What had she done?

Her flesh prickled whenever she thought of last night's kiss. The way Zahir's body and hers had fused together, driven by a force so potent she'd had no chance of overcoming it.

Or had she?

She shivered and rubbed her hands up her arms.

Her life had been shaped by the mother who'd left when she was six. Her mother had flitted from one affair to another. First to Soraya's father, then to a string of handsome men till her untimely death.

Maybe it was a response to the negativity of those who expected her to turn out like her mum, but Soraya had never sought male attention. She'd happily accepted her beloved father's over-protective ways and steered clear of men.

She'd told herself love was a weakness and desire—

She pushed her untasted breakfast away.

Desire had been a mere word. Safe in the knowledge she'd never experienced it, Soraya had supposed she never would. Until Zahir had caught her in his stormy gaze and nothing had been the same. It was as if he'd branded her as his that night and nothing, not logic or the threat of approaching marriage, could change that.

Her heart dipped.

Was she too destined to make a fool of herself, of honour and duty, for an attractive man?

It didn't matter that duty led her down a path she shrank from. She'd committed to her fate. She couldn't change it. Soraya pressed a hand to her forehead, as if to still her whirling thoughts.

She should be ashamed she'd kissed Zahir and wanted more.

Yes, she felt guilt and horror at what she'd done. Yet that wasn't all. Last night had felt *right*, as if she and Zahir were *meant*. No matter how she castigated herself she couldn't regret that kiss. It was emblazoned in her soul. A single point of perfect happiness.

It did no good to tell herself it was more than sex. That she'd begun to fall for the proud, caring, fascinating man she'd come to know. That just made the situation more impossible.

'Mademoiselle?' Soraya looked up to see the housekeeper in the doorway. 'Monsieur El Hashem sent this for you.'

'Thank you, Hortense.' Puzzled, she took the shopping bag from her hand. Inside Soraya discovered silky material in swirling aquamarine and turquoise.

'*Monsieur* said he'd be waiting for you in the pool.'

'The pool?' Soraya's head shot up, tension crackling through her.

Hortense nodded and tsked as she collected Soraya's still-laden breakfast plate. 'That's right. He said you had a lesson.'

It was foolhardy, Zahir knew. Being alone with her, his hands on her body, would be purest temptation. Yet he'd promised to teach her to swim.

The memory of Soraya flailing in the water, panicking and possibly drowning but for his intervention, froze his veins with a glacial chill. He had to know she'd be safe.

Besides, it would be cowardly to back out. A woman with so much heart and character deserved his respect.

She didn't deserve his tongue in her mouth and his erection

surging between her legs—no matter how much he wanted her. She mightn't be a complete innocent but he'd taken her by surprise with his ardour. He'd felt her shock and tried to pull back. Instead he'd succumbed to pleasure so intense it was like a drug.

Sweat broke out on his brow as Zahir relived the intense pleasure of last night's kiss. The taste of her so deliciously enticing. The feel of her siren's body against his. That mix of sweet tenderness and fiery wanton that had blown him away.

The wanting had been bad enough before he'd touched her. After last night it would be pure torment, knowing paradise was so close yet so far beyond his reach.

A sound made him look up. Soraya walked towards the pool, closely wrapped in a voluminous towelling robe despite the heat. Even seeing her bundled up sent his pulse soaring. Her hair, almost to her waist, trailed over one shoulder like an invitation to touch. Even her bare feet were enticing.

Zahir swallowed a knot of tension.

This would be his penance. Every second would be torture but he deserved it, and worse.

She was Hussein's woman. He'd known it and still hadn't stopped. Now he would face his punishment though it would be the most difficult thing he'd ever done.

She stopped by the pool, eyes wary.

'Are you sure you want to do this?'

'I promised I would teach you to swim. I never go back on a promise.' Yet just watching her played havoc with his breathing. A tremor quivered through his limbs as he met her doubtful gaze.

'I apologise for my behaviour last night.' The words spilled from stiff lips. 'I have no excuse. But, believe me, it won't happen again.'

She met his eyes and for an insane moment he felt a thud of connection between them. It made no difference. It *couldn't* make a difference.

'I'm sorry too,' she murmured, her gaze dipping. 'Last night... It wasn't just you. It was me too.'

Zahir didn't need to be reminded of how she'd undone him with her sweet responsiveness. He shook his head. He knew exactly where the guilt lay.

'I'm responsible for you.'

'For my safety. That's all.' Her eyes sparkled with a militant light but he forbore to argue.

'Thank you for the swimsuit,' she said at last, not quite meeting his gaze. 'You must have been out early.'

He hadn't been to bed, had spent the night alternately berating himself and reliving the guilty pleasure he'd sworn to put behind him.

Zahir remained silent as she fumbled with the tie at her waist and let the robe fall away.

The air sucked from his lungs in a rush as she turned.

She looked like a mermaid, indecently alluring even in the most modest one-piece outfit he could find. He'd been right about her size—too right. The stretch fabric clung like a lover's caress, making his fingers itch as he remembered the feel of her beneath his hands.

She was all enticing curves and supple limbs. The fall of her hair in thick, waving tresses accentuated her femininity, appealing to some primal male part of him that relished each difference between them. Heat roared through him in an out-of-control rush and he fought to retain his composure.

Deliberately he looked at his watch. 'We've just time for another lesson before we leave.'

She faltered at the edge of the pool. 'Leave?'

Zahir nodded and beckoned her down the steps. 'Yes. I've arranged the next leg of our journey. You wanted to see France and you can't do that while we're isolated here.'

He looked away before he could read her reaction. It didn't matter what she said; the decision was made. Immersion in rural quiet had thrown them together. What they needed now was people, cities, action. Anything to keep them occupied and stop him dwelling on Soraya Karim and what she did to him.

Half an hour later Soraya was flushed with excitement and pleasure at what she'd achieved. Even her distress and embarrassment had ebbed to a dull, gnawing ache. For Zahir was utterly businesslike, intent only on her progress.

It was as if last night hadn't happened, except for the jerk of electricity, as if from a live wire, whenever they touched.

Now, breathless, she sank back against the end of the pool, watching as Zahir hauled himself out.

The play of bunching muscles across his back and arms mesmerised her. He really was the most remarkable-looking man. She could watch him for hours. Every movement was graceful despite the raw power he so carefully leashed.

'What's that mark? The one along your side?'

As he turned, his brows jammed together as if he was displeased she'd ended their unspoken agreement to avoid personal topics.

'I've been a warrior all my life. I have scars. It comes with the territory.' He shrugged and reached for his towel.

Soraya noticed then that the dark golden skin of his back was smooth and unblemished. The old scars were on his chest and arms. The marks of a warrior.

Something, a little frisson of feminine excitement, tingled through her, making her frown. It wasn't that she relished the idea of combat, but at a deep, primitive level there was something thrilling about the idea of a strong man prepared to defend what he believed in.

'But that one's different.' She pointed to a white pucker of flesh at his side. It was none of her business but she couldn't stifle the need to know more about him. Surely her question was innocuous?

Sighing, he rubbed the towel over his face. 'A bullet caught me.'

Soraya's breath hitched in a hiss of dismay. Her heart hammered at the thought of Zahir in a gun's sights.

'It's okay, Soraya.' He must have read her horror, for his severe expression eased. 'It was just a flesh wound and a bit of a knick to one rib.'

Just a knick…

'How did it happen?' Prying or not, she couldn't leave it there.

'I used to lead the Emir's personal protection unit, remember? I came between him and someone who intended harm.'

Soraya clung to the side of the pool as weakness invaded her limbs. Zahir had put himself in front of the Emir. Taken a bullet meant for him!

Slowly she shook her head. 'I can't comprehend how you could do that. Put yourself in danger that way.'

'Can't you?' Eyes of vivid emerald caught and held hers. 'Isn't there anyone you'd risk yourself for?'

Before she could answer he went on, 'It was my job. What I'd signed on to do. More than that, Hussein is far more than an employer to me.'

The ripple of emotion across his stern features surprised her. 'Hussein was the one who rescued me from my father's palace when I was just a child. As supreme leader he forced my father's hand into letting me go. Not that my father was bothered about keeping me.' Zahir's austerely sculpted lips curled in a smile that held no humour. It sent a terrible chill prickling down Soraya's spine. What did he mean, his father hadn't been bothered about keeping him?

'Hussein has been father and friend to me. Mentor and role model. I don't just owe him my job, but my life. If I'd stayed in my father's palace I've no doubt I'd have died from neglect.'

The quiet certainty in Zahir's calm tone turned Soraya's blood cold. He'd said his early years were eventful but she'd had no idea.

'What about your mother?'

Absently he swiped his towel over his shoulders. 'I never knew her. She died when I was tiny. So there was no-one to care that I ran feral, barely surviving. No-one to care that my father never legally acknowledged me as his.'

'Zahir!' Having grown up with at least one loving parent, Soraya found the picture he painted appalling. She could barely imagine being so alone.

He shrugged. 'They weren't married. She was one of his mistresses. A dancing girl. Why should he stir himself over a brat who wasn't even legitimately his?' His tone was blank, as if his father's rejection didn't bother him.

How could that be? Soraya knew too well the weight a parent's rejection. She'd carried it ever since she was six. What hidden scars burdened Zahir? It must have been doubly painful for him not to have either parent there for him when he was young.

She'd seen behind Zahir's mask of calm. She knew beyond the formidable control was a man of powerful emotions and blazing passion. A man who felt deeply.

The memory of that man sent heat spiralling in that secret feminine place.

'Hussein gave me a home.' Zahir's voice deepened to that low burr that brushed the back of her neck into tingling heat. 'He cared about me, raised me, made me who I am. I owe him everything, especially loyalty.' Zahir paced the edge of the pool towards her, his words ringing between them, deliberate and measured.

'I could never betray him.'

He was reminding her why there could never be anything between them, despite the shimmering heat that charged the air and the growing sense of a bond between them. Zahir was a man of honour and loyalty. How much more loyal could you get than to offer your life to save another?

No wonder he'd looked sick last night as he'd turned from her. By kissing her, he'd betrayed the man he'd admired all his life.

Against that, the guilt that hounded her paled. To her the Emir was a distant benefactor. How much worse this all was for Zahir, who knew and loved him.

Her heart twisted for Zahir. For the pain he'd borne in the past. For the hurt she'd unwittingly caused him.

And for herself, trapped between duty and desire, with no way out. Her throat closed convulsively. Was that all the future held? Duty?

Once she'd believed it would be enough. She'd thought emotional independence was all she needed.

Then recently she'd begun to imagine a future other than the one mapped out for her—a future of her own making, where she could pursue the half-formed hopes and dreams she'd dared to dream in Paris. Of a career, a future that was about *her* needs and interests, not the nation's.

Now even that seemed unreal, unsatisfactory, a poor facsimile of a *real* future. For the first time in her life Soraya caught a glimpse of what life might be like with more than solely career or duty to fill it. With a man she cared for, a man who made her blood spark and her soul take flight. A man like Zahir...

Like a tidal wave, realisation crashed down on her. She grabbed for the edge of the pool, desperate for support as her world reeled.

'Time to move. We're leaving here, and remember you need to pack.' Zahir turned his back rather than let his gaze run over her again.

The swimming lesson had been as testing as he'd feared. Even the mention of what he owed Hussein only succeeded in racheting up the level of sick guilt in his belly. It did nothing to drive out his fascination with Soraya. It was as if she'd got under his skin, like a desert sandstorm infiltrating every defence.

What *was* it about Soraya? Even in the throes of first love he hadn't felt so...saturated by his feelings. They impinged on every thought after years of him bottling them up. He was aware of her as if she was part of him. Nor was it simple sexual awareness. If only it were that!

He slung the towel round his neck then shot a glance over her shoulder.

She hadn't moved. She stood, hands braced on the flagstones at the edge of the pool, head bent as if winded.

'Soraya?' Concern spiked. He turned back to her. She didn't look up, and he saw her breasts rise and fall quickly as if she'd just swum a sprint. He yanked his gaze higher and realised her face was pale.

He'd thought it impossible to feel more guilt, but he'd been wrong. The way she stood, as if absorbing a body blow, told him she battled pain. Because of him? His chest constricted hard.

Disregarding his resolution not to touch her again, he extended his hand. 'Come on, princess. It's time we left.'

'I told you before—*don't* call me that!'

Zahir's blood frosted as she looked up and he read the haunted depths of her eyes. The slight shadows that spoke of a sleepless night were more pronounced in her milky-white face. Her skin looked drawn too tight. Even her lush mouth seemed pinched.

'Soraya?' His scalp itched with warning. Something was very wrong. 'What is it?'

She shook her head and looked away.

'Sorry,' she mumbled. 'It's nothing. I overreacted.'

Zahir's brow knotted. Even in the face of his blatant disapproval she'd stood defiant and proud. Yet now she looked as if the merest breeze would knock her down.

'Because I called you princess?'

She gave no response, ignoring his hand and clambering stiffly from the pool. Yet even in the sun she shivered, and he draped his towel around her. It said something about her state of mind that she stood meekly while he wrapped it close, rubbing her arms through the towelling.

'Soraya?' She met his gaze but her eyes had a dazed, blind look that worried him. 'What is it?'

'Nothing. I'm fine.' He refused to move away. Finally she spoke again. 'My mother used to call me that, you know.' Her lips stretched in a parody of a smile. 'When I was tiny I even used to believe I was a little princess. At least that I was *her* princess.'

The towel slipped and she clutched it close.

'It just goes to show how gullible children are, doesn't it?' Her voice rang hollow. 'I wasn't special enough to make her stay when her latest lover called. She left me behind then without a second thought.'

A shudder racked her and Zahir had to fight the need to tug her close and wrap himself around her. She looked…fragile.

But a moment later Soraya recovered. She straightened, pushing her shoulders back in that familiar way and turned to survey the pool.

'The last time she called me that was the day I almost drowned. I was wading in a pool and I was sure she was still there, watching me. I didn't find out till later that was the day she'd left us to go to her lover.'

His heart wrenched at the pain he read in her taut features. At the hurt she battled even to think of venturing into water again. He'd believed her strong and determined but he hadn't known the half of it.

'I should have remembered that lesson,' she murmured.

'What lesson?'

'Never to expect too much.' Her expression held infinite sadness as she turned and walked away.

Zahir felt as if someone had taken a knife to his belly and gutted him.

CHAPTER TEN

Soraya leaned on the railing of the giant motor cruiser and took in the brilliant cluster of lights that was Monte Carlo. Even the water was gold and silver, reflecting the illuminated city climbing the hills.

All around her was luxury. From the multi-million-dollar vessels crammed into the marina to the exclusive party she'd left on the other deck.

Was this what her life would be like as the Emir's wife? A world of untold wealth and privilege?

Fervently she wished she could be thrilled by the prospect. Another woman might have found nothing but pleasure in the comforts of extreme wealth but Soraya had so much on her mind, they left her unmoved. They were comforts Zahir took for granted, fitting easily into this rarefied world of diplomats, royalty and celebrities.

He might have been a bodyguard once, and a lost soul as a child, but he'd moved on. He was strong, confident, a man sure of himself and his purpose, with nothing to prove.

Her heart squeezed haphazardly as she thought of her weeks with Zahir. Despite the caution they exercised, she'd slipped further under his spell.

Riding horses in the Camargue, eating heavenly bouillabaisse in a tiny waterfront restaurant, even visiting lavender fields and a perfume factory; Soraya couldn't have asked for a better companion. He'd been pleasant, amusing and caring.

Yet he scrupulously kept a telling distance between them. He hadn't touched her again. Even during her swimming lessons, and he insisted on those daily. He supervised, instructed and encouraged but kept to the side of the pool.

How she missed his touch! His strong arms around her.

A sigh shuddered through her.

She couldn't ask for more. Briefly she'd been angry at his unswerving loyalty to the Emir, for it meant there was no chance for *them*. But there *was* no 'them'. There were too many obstacles against it. Besides, Zahir's loyalty was part of what made him the man he was.

All she could do was store up memories against a future when he must be a stranger to her. That was what she'd done, gathered memories, as if they could comfort her when she gave herself to another man.

She'd railed at a fate that bound her to a marriage she didn't want. How much worse now when, too late, she'd discovered what it was to care deeply? *For the wrong man.*

Pain tore through her and she gripped the railing harder. She wanted...

No! She couldn't allow herself to go there.

That morning of her second swimming lesson Zahir had thought her upset because he'd called her 'princess'.

It was true the casual endearment had evoked painful memories. But the real anguish had come from the realization that she, who'd thought herself immune from love, had fallen for a man who could never be hers.

She was head over heels in love with Zahir.

The knowledge made her body sing with excitement and her soul shrivel. It was wonderful, delicious and terrible. A blessing that was a curse.

Travelling with him was torture and pleasure combined. Maybe if he felt nothing for her it would be easier, but his punctilious distance told her he felt something for her too. That knowledge kept her on a knife edge of torment, trawling back through conversations, seeking proof of his feelings. Like

Bastille Day, when he'd asked about the possibility of her loving someone other than her betrothed.

If only circumstances had been different.

'Soraya. What are you doing down here when the party's in full swing upstairs?'

Zahir halted several paces away. His eyes ate her up; she was luscious in a long dress of dusky rose. A gown that was innocently demure by the standards of the scantily dressed socialites at the party. Yet it skimmed her body in a way that reminded him too clearly of the hour-glass figure that tempted him during each day's swimming lesson.

Heat clutched deep in his belly.

Her scent, wildflowers rather than hothouse exotics, teased his nostrils. Her hair, held back by jewelled clips, cascaded down her back in a ripple of thick silk.

More than one man had cast covetous eyes on her tonight and Zahir had been busy staking a possessive claim on her to prevent any untoward advances.

Staking a claim on behalf of Hussein, he reminded himself.

She half-turned but didn't meet his eyes. 'I wanted some peace and quiet.'

At her words he stiffened. He'd seen her excited, happy, indignant and angry, but never listless.

There'd been inevitable tension after their kiss. But he'd worked hard not to let her see that taste of her had driven him to the brink of endurance. For her part, Soraya had thrown herself into sightseeing with a fervour that gave no hint she wanted anything else.

At first he'd wondered if she was a little too enthusiastic, then chided himself. It wasn't that he *wanted* her pining for what could never be.

'You're not enjoying yourself?' Tonight he'd sought safety in numbers. This exclusive society party had seemed a perfect alternative to a night alone with Soraya and the terrible gnawing tension within.

Beautiful women with come-hither eyes and smiles that

promised pleasure were here tonight in droves. Yet none had drawn a second glance from him.

Not one could hold a candle to Soraya for beauty or character. She was gentle—despite her bravado in standing up for herself—capable, caring, inquisitive and deeply fascinating. Her fierce independence, her determination and natural exuberance, entranced him. With her he'd felt more than he had in a decade and a half. It was like emerging from a grey half-life into a world of sunshine and colour.

'The party is amazing. Thank you for bringing me.' Yet she didn't sound as enthusiastic as when she discussed her research project. 'So many interesting people. So many celebrities. And I've never seen so much bling in my life.'

'But?'

She shook her head and those long tresses slid and curled around her slim back. Was it ridiculous to resent the fact she wore her hair down tonight? He hated the way men looked at her, imagining that bountiful hair loose around her shoulders as she made love.

He knew they did. Any man would.

He did. God help him!

'But it's only days till our flight from Rome to Bakhara.' Her husky words drew his belly tight. 'It's crept up on me and I needed time to digest it.'

She was going home to marry the finest man he knew.

Zahir ignored the wave of nausea that passed through him at the thought.

'I know Hussein is looking forward to seeing you.' If Hussein had any idea of the lovely woman she'd become, he'd be eager for her arrival.

Soraya bowed her head as if in assent. But her grip on the railing reminded him of a falcon's claws clamped hard and sharp on a leather glove.

'Soraya?' He took a pace towards her then, realising, stopped. '*Are* you all right?'

'Of course.' She tilted her chin up as she stared across the shimmering brightness. 'What could be wrong?'

Something was. He'd come to recognise the way she angled that neat chin as a defence mechanism.

He reminded himself his duty was simply to return her safe to Bakhara, not delve into her thoughts and fears.

Yet telling himself couldn't make it so. Nor could he banish the suspicion he knew *exactly* what was wrong. That, despite her proud front, Soraya felt as he did. That they'd circled an unspoken truth for weeks.

'Tell me!'

Perhaps the harshness in his voice surprised her for she turned her head, eyes wide and it was there again, that jangle along the senses as if lightning had sparked between them.

Damn it. He shouldn't feel this. He shouldn't feel anything except impersonal concern for her wellbeing.

Yet what he felt was personal. Far too personal.

Did she feel it too? Was that why she whipped her head round so fast?

'Soraya. Please.' It was no good telling himself this was merely a job. It had ceased to be 'just a job' the moment he had seen her in that Paris nightclub.

'I don't want to go back,' she said at last. 'I don't want...' Her voice dipped and she swallowed convulsively. That single movement spoke of a vulnerability that tugged at something in his very core. Something he couldn't name.

He found himself behind her, not touching, but mirroring her body with his as if to protect her. He couldn't keep back.

'What don't you want, Soraya?' His breath held.

A deep breath lifted her narrow shoulders. 'I don't want to marry the Emir.'

Like the boom of a bomb blast, her words rocked him back on his heels.

Elation ripped through him, a momentary inward cry of delight, till he smothered it, using every particle of will-power left to him.

It was on the tip of his tongue to ask why she didn't want to marry Hussein. But he wouldn't let the words come. He knew what he wanted her answer to be and he couldn't let either of them go there.

To betray Hussein would make him no better than his traitor father. And it would bring her nothing but shame and public disgrace.

His body snapped taut almost to breaking point. His chest rose and fell hard as he dragged in one sharp breath after another. Silence welled. One wrong word could shatter the world in a way that could never be repaired. The air around them strung close with tension.

'Why marry him then?' He told himself it was time to remind them both that this was what she really wanted. She'd just temporarily lost sight of the fact.

'Because I promised,' she whispered. 'It's arranged.'

'And you can't go back on your word.' It wasn't a question, it was recognition that she, like him, had standards to live by. Zahir had never broken a vow. He knew the value of a promise—particularly a promise given to the man who'd made him who he was today.

If only that reminder could strengthen him now! Temptation was here before him, made flesh in a way that threatened everything he knew of himself.

'That's right. It's my duty to marry him.'

Duty. Another word that ruled Zahir's world.

Wasn't it duty that kept him standing here, his body a mere hand span from hers? That tiny distance represented a yawning chasm, cleaved by his conscience. No matter what he wanted, duty kept her safe from his touch.

Yet it didn't prevent him feeling her heat, scenting her skin and hair, hearing her shaky little inhalations of breath. Almost, he embraced her. He remembered the imprint of her soft body against his and his will-power frayed.

'I promised him and my father. I owe them so much and it's what they both want.'

But not what she wanted.

'Did your father coerce you into it?' The suspicion drove bile to the back of Zahir's throat. Hussein would never do such a thing, but perhaps her father would.

'No.' Her voice rang true. 'My father is a dear man. He would never force me.'

'Then why did you agree?' Zahir hated the plea that broke his voice, but he was past dissembling.

She turned around and suddenly they were just a kiss apart. He ordered himself to move back but his feet wouldn't obey. He shoved his hands deep in his trouser pockets rather than be tempted to touch.

Her beautiful oval face tilted up towards his.

'I was fourteen, Zahir.'

'So young?' He frowned. Despite the old customs of his people, such an early betrothal was no longer the norm.

What had Hussein been thinking? Zahir's heart skipped at the unpalatable suspicion Hussein had been attracted to a girl barely in her teens. But their long engagement countered that idea.

The arrangement was odd. Why hadn't Hussein chosen a woman closer to his own age? Why wait ten years to marry?

Unless the betrothal had been hastily arranged?

The constitution stipulated the Emir of Bakhara had to be married, a family man with the prospect of heirs. Fortunately for Hussein a formal betrothal was as binding as marriage and there'd been no-one eager to hurry him into a second marriage when his beloved first wife had died. Had he chosen an early betrothal to keep the balance of power while he came to terms with his widower status?

'And you wanted to be queen.'

Soraya shook her head. Traditional Bakhari chandelier earrings scintillated at her ear lobes, drawing his eye to her delicate ears and slender throat.

Zahir clenched his hands tight in his pockets rather than reach out and stroke that delicate skin.

'No,' she said slowly. 'Not particularly, though the royal glamour was very exciting. But after a while I saw possibilities. As the Emir's consort I could be useful. Help our people. Devote myself to good works.' Her mouth twisted wryly as if mocking her earlier self.

'There's nothing wrong with that.' It sounded laudable, if distant from a flesh-and-blood marriage.

'Of course there's not.' Abruptly she looked away. 'That's exactly what I tell myself now when I try to imagine the future.'

A future when she would be Hussein's bride. In Hussein's arms.

'So why agree to the marriage?' Zahir's voice was rough. 'For the money? The prestige?'

'Zahir!'

Her shock made him look down, to discover he held her arms in a vice-like grip. Instantly he eased his hold.

'I'm sorry.' Yet he couldn't let her go. The touch of her soft flesh made him war with himself. 'Why, Soraya?'

'Because he saved my father's life.' Her eyes were dark pools of stormy emotion that dragged him down. A self-destructive part of him wanted to dive into those depths and never surface again.

'How?'

It shouldn't surprise him. He had first-hand knowledge of Hussein's generous spirit. Not only had Hussein saved Zahir as a child, he'd never held his father's treachery against him, measuring him against his own deeds rather than the taint of his blood kin.

'My father had a kidney disease,' Soraya responded. 'He needed a transplant, but you know how long the waiting list is for donors.'

Zahir nodded. Organ donation was still new in Bakhara and convincing people to join a donor registry was an uphill battle.

'He would have died while waiting for a transplant.' A tremor passed through her. 'I was too young to donate to him, and he wouldn't give his permission for me to do it.'

ANNIE WEST

Of course she'd wanted to do it. Why wasn't he surprised?

'But the Emir said he owed my father his throne and his life. Apparently years ago there'd been an uprising by several tribal leaders. They'd tried to unseat the Emir and put one of their own in his place.'

Zahir stiffened. 'I know. My father was one of them.' The words scalded his tongue.

'He was?' Her eyes roved his face as if searching for something. 'You're not very like him, are you?'

'What do you mean?' Even now his skin crawled at the knowledge that man's blood ran in his veins. 'You didn't know him.'

'I know *you*, Zahir.' The way she spoke his name was like a caress.

He was so besotted he was hearing things now. He should step back but couldn't shift his feet. As for lifting his hold on her arms—it was impossible!

'I know you're a man of honour. A man who takes his responsibilities seriously.' Her lips curved in a wistful smile. 'I also know you'd never neglect a child of yours.'

'Of course not.' His lips thinned as he thought of the work still to be done to protect the rights of children, and others needing help, in his province.

'Of course not.' She twisted her hands and suddenly it was she holding him, her fingers on his soft yet strong. Ripples of illicit pleasure radiated from her touch.

'I saw you with that toddler. You didn't just save him, you cradled him and comforted him till his mother was calm enough to hold him. Then you made sure all the others were okay too, especially the teenager who blamed herself for not noticing he'd gone. You were gentle and understanding.'

'Anyone would do the same.' His voice was threadbare, stretched tight by the feel of Soraya holding him so tenderly. How he'd longed for her touch.

He should move away.

'Not everyone. Especially when the child was promptly sick

everywhere.' Her smile as she met his eyes was beguiling. He felt its impact deep in his diaphragm. 'You're a natural with kids. You'd be wonderful with your own.'

Suddenly he didn't need to break her hold. She did it, wrapping her arms around herself, as if chilled despite the balmy evening.

He wanted to comfort her, knowing from her stricken expression she felt pain. But he didn't trust himself to hold her then let her go.

'Anyway,' she said briskly, looking at a point near his shoulder. 'When the uprising occurred, my father sided with the Emir. In fact, he was with him when the palace was stormed. He was injured protecting the Emir and apparently it was the sight of blood drawn in the royal council-room that shocked the more sensible leaders into negotiation. The Emir always said my dad saved his life as well as the peace of the nation.'

'I've heard the story. But I hadn't realised that was your father.'

Soraya lifted her shoulders. 'It was a long time ago and I don't think either of them like to talk about it. Later, when my father got sick, the Emir did something truly extraordinary.' Her pale face lifted and he saw a genuine smile there, like a beacon in the shadows. 'He gave a kidney to save my father.'

'I had no idea.' Zahir was stunned. It must have happened the year he'd been sent to study in the USA. 'They kept it very quiet. I've heard nothing about it.'

No wonder. For a nation's ruler to risk his wellbeing like that was almost incomprehensible. Zahir could think of no other who would do it. But Hussein was in a class of his own.

'It's easy to thank someone, but to repay a debt like that...' Soraya shook her head.

'He's a special man.' Zahir had known that since he was four.

'Yes.' Her dark eyes clung to his. 'He is. So when he asked for marriage, my father was thrilled. He knew I'd be marrying the very best of men.'

Zahir nodded, unable to fault her father's logic, even though

thinking of her with Hussein made hot pincers tear at his in-
nards.

'So you see,' she added in a low voice that tugged at him, 'I
have every reason to marry him and none to refuse.'

'Except you don't love him.'

Her eyes widened but the surprise on her face was nothing
to his own. Since when had romantic love featured as even a
passing fantasy in his thoughts?

He knew all about dynastic marriages. He'd make one himself one day. He'd tasted love at nineteen and thought his life
blighted when his beloved's father had deemed him, the bastard son of a traitor, not a worthy son-in-law. From that day
he'd devoted himself to proving himself better and stronger
than all his peers.

'No.' Soraya didn't meet his eyes. 'I don't love him.'

Her words hung like a benediction in the air. Zahir's heart
felt full.

'But he's a good man. A decent man,' she murmured. 'I
owe him my father's life. Without the Emir I would have lost
him years ago.'

'So you're repaying the debt.'

She nodded and Zahir had to quell the impatient urge to
say the debt had been cancelled with Hussein's actions. It was
Hussein who'd owed Soraya's father. But there was no point.
He read determination in her fine features. Besides, how could
he urge her to go against her conscience?

He could offer her no alternative. Not when he was bound
by every tie of loyalty, duty and love to deliver her to Hussein.
Not when the alternative would make her a social pariah, an
outcast even to her family.

'What of your own dreams? Your aspirations?' The words
spilled from him. He'd heard enough about her work to know
she needed more from life. The idea of her as no more than a
prop to grace Hussein's regal table and be by his side at official
functions seemed a travesty. Soraya had so much more to offer.

'My dreams have changed.' Again that small, wistful smile.

'When I was young I had grandiose dreams of helping the nation. Now I...'

She shook her head. 'Now I have the qualifications to do something really useful for our people. I'm hoping the Emir will let me use those skills to support some innovation. We have the resources, and know how in Bakhara to bring power to the outlying regions, for a start.'

'Is that all you want? The good of others?'

Something flared in her eyes, an emotion almost too painful to watch.

'In Paris I'd begun to dream of a different future,' she murmured. 'Where *I* got to choose for myself. I'd follow my career, spread my wings, make my own mistakes.' Her lips twisted. 'I learned how much fun it was to make friends with other women, not because they were from the right families or because we studied together, but because we clicked. I discovered a weakness for philosophical debate and pop music and fantastic shoes.' She lifted her shoulders. 'Nothing earth-shattering or important. Nothing worth pining over.'

Except it was important to her: the right to choose her own path. She'd said as much in his arms on Bastille Day—that there was nothing as important as freedom. He ached at the thought of what she would give up.

'What about you, Zahir? What do you dream of?'

His dreams? Why did they seem less vivid than before?

'Hussein is making me governor of our largest province. It's the province my father misruled as a despot and it will be my job to make it flourish and prosper.'

He waited for the pleasure he usually experienced as he thought of the challenge ahead. The satisfaction of knowing he'd be redressing the depredations of his father.

Nothing came. Not even pride at the fact Hussein valued and trusted him with this important role.

Instead his eyes locked on Soraya's and something swelled between them. An understanding, an emotion he didn't dare name. His body was aflame and the need to touch her again was a compulsion.

Abruptly Zahir stepped back. He kept moving, needing distance before he forgot sense.

He ignored the over-bright shimmer in her eyes and the down-turned curve of her lips as she watched him go. 'I need to talk to our host,' he said.

'Zahir?' He stopped, heart hammering at the sound of his name on her lips.

'Yes?'

'I'm doing the right thing. Aren't I?'

His head whipped round and again that thwack to the solar plexus hit him when her eyes met his.

He breathed deep and searched for the right answer.

He could find none that would satisfy both conscience and desire.

'You're doing the honourable thing.' His voice rang hollow in the silence.

As he forced himself to walk away, he knew for the first time in his life that honour wasn't enough.

CHAPTER ELEVEN

Soraya paced the luxury hotel-suite, ignoring the view of a quaint Roman square as the sky morphed from peach and bronze to shades of violet and indigo.

Once she'd have watched enthralled, thrilled by the vibrant, fascinating city of Rome. She'd have revelled in today's sightseeing, the historic sites, the curious byways and above all the people, so full of life and energy.

Yet the city had passed in a blur, overshadowed by the fact this was the end.

The end of her freedom.

The end of her time with Zahir.

Her heart shuddered to a halt then picked up again unsteadily.

Rome was their last stop. Tomorrow they'd board a royal jet that would take them to Bakhara.

Desperation was a coiling queasiness in her stomach, a rusty taste on her tongue, as if she'd drawn blood when she bit her lip.

Tomorrow she'd face the man who would become her husband. She was no nearer finding the equanimity she needed for that than when Zahir had broken the news.

Zahir.

She clutched at a velvet curtain for support, reliving the delicious feel of his hair in her hands as they kissed.

That kiss had blasted away the convenient platitudes she'd

hidden behind. It had revealed in shocking, glorious detail how much she wanted him. How much she needed him.

Heat consumed her. Was she so like her mother? So weak in the face of sexual desire? In the face of love?

Yet this didn't feel like weakness. It felt like strength, light and honesty. A heady euphoria edged with terrible fear that it could never be.

She'd tried to convince herself she couldn't be in love with anyone so aloof and bossy. But the frightening man she'd met in Paris wasn't the real Zahir.

Zahir was proud and inclined to take the lead, but he wasn't a bully. He went out of his way to visit places she had her heart set on, patiently waiting as she combed markets, hunting gifts for her dad and Lisle. He took pleasure in the same things she did, chatting to farmers about the harvest, playing with the local kids. He was warm-hearted and caring. A man generous with his time.

He'd continued her lessons daily till she could swim unaided, determined she'd be safe in the water. He'd stuck to his promise despite the strain of those lessons.

Zahir was excellent company, even if he kept a conspicuous distance from her.

How she craved his touch. His affection.

He felt something for her, she knew it. It was there in his carefully blanked expression and in the fierce, possessive light in his eyes when she caught him off guard.

The memory of that look melted her bones.

She loved him. Yet they couldn't be together. The thought scooped a gaping hole inside her chest.

She was destined for the man who'd given her back her father when she'd been about to lose him. Who'd given her years she'd feared she'd never have. Who'd honoured her with his proposal. By all accounts he'd been a faithful and caring husband to his first wife. Soraya knew he'd respect and care for her. *But it wasn't enough.*

She'd been an innocent ever to think devotion to her country or even her career was enough.

Why couldn't she have love too?

The dangerous thought eddied in her brain.

There were a multitude of reasons she couldn't have Zahir's love. She couldn't ask him to run away with her and betray the man he looked on as his father.

Yet she yearned for him with every cell in her body.

Was it too much to ask for a taste of that forbidden dream? For a morsel to comfort her in the long days ahead when she lived not for herself but for her country and the man who, however decent, could never be Zahir?

Soraya's breath escaped in a whoosh. She'd feared she shared her mother's weakness. But her mother had been in love with the idea of falling in love. Instinctively Soraya knew there'd be no other man after Zahir. He was the one. As for the future—that was immutable. She'd be faithful to the man she married.

But couldn't she allow herself a taste of love to sustain her through a future that loomed barren and bare? Just one night?

Zahir was unbuttoning his sleeves as he pushed open the door to his room. He needed a cold shower. Better yet, a couple of hours in the hotel's gym, then a cold shower. Though he knew it wouldn't help. His mind would be full of...

'Soraya!'

He slammed to a stop just inside the room.

Like an answer to forbidden cravings there she was, standing silhouetted by the glow of a bedside lamp. The soft light lingered lovingly on her ripe figure and his throat closed as all his blood drained south. Her hair was down in dark, rich waves that begged for his touch.

'What are you wearing?' His voice was a hoarse rasp.

She fiddled with the tie at her waist but said nothing. She didn't need to. It was obvious that beneath the embroidered silk wrap she was naked. No strap line marred its smooth texture and she'd done it up so firmly the fabric pulled tight across breasts and hips, cinching in at her waist.

His body raced into sexual overdrive, pulse humming, heat escalating, arousal burgeoning. His breath was choppy as he fought to drag in air.

'Soraya!' Somehow he was walking towards her, though he told himself to keep his distance.

Their gazes collided and he almost groaned at the familiar blast of connection between them.

Her nipples pebbled and his palms ached to reach out and cup the proud bounty of her breasts. Yet he managed to stop a pace away. Desire scorched him. More than desire; a yearning that was as much of the mind as the body. It engulfed him with a force that left him shaking.

'You shouldn't be in here.' It emerged as a plea.

'I couldn't stay away.' She swallowed convulsively and the pulse at the base of her neck raced out of control.

His blood beat just as fast. Just as haphazardly.

How many nights had he dreamed of her coming to him? How many mornings had he lashed himself with guilt over the imaginings he hadn't been able to conquer?

It was wrong. But he couldn't overcome it. He felt too much for her. He wanted her as he'd never wanted in his life. That alone told him how dangerous this was.

Soraya trembled as his gaze devoured her. A muscle worked in Zahir's jaw and she felt the tension come off him in great waves. His hands twitched and she wanted them on her. Surely his touch would relieve the ache deep inside?

'I want to make love with you, Zahir.' A weight lifted off her chest with the words and she dragged in her first free breath since she'd come to his room. 'Please.'

He stood stock-still. If she didn't know better, she'd swear he didn't even breathe.

Fear warred with hope. Grabbing the last of her courage she stepped forward, till the heat of his body encompassed her. Still he said nothing, didn't move a muscle. It was as if he'd locked down, rejecting her and what was between them.

Soraya refused to give in so easily. With a daring she didn't know she had, she reached out and grabbed his hand, placing it on her breast.

Instantly his fingers tightened, cupping her, and she swayed against him, captive to sweet, unfamiliar sensations. Fiery threads unravelled from her breast to her belly and lower, to the place where the ache was strongest and she felt hollow with need.

Gently he squeezed and she moaned as pleasure coursed through her. Much as she'd craved his touch, she just hadn't *known*...

She rose on tiptoe and pressed a kiss to his mouth. But at the last moment he moved and her lips landed on the sandpapery skin of his unshaved jaw.

An instant later his hands bit into her upper arms and he put her from him. Cruel fear invaded her bones as she looked into flinty eyes.

'Don't, Soraya.' His voice was harsh.

'Please, Zahir. I love you.' The words came out in a rush, but she couldn't regret them, even as she saw his head rear back in shock. She put her hands on his restraining arms and felt the muscles bunch and tighten. 'I thought—'

'You *didn't* think!' He almost spat the words as he let her go and strode away across the room. 'How could you even consider coming to my room like this?' He braced himself against the far wall, his head hanging down between wide shoulders that rose and fell with each huge breath.

Despair welled. He was rejecting her.

Soraya knew this was her only chance. She had to make him understand.

A moment later she stood beside him, her hands busy with the tie of her robe.

'What are you doing?' His voice was hoarse.

'Showing you I know exactly what I'm doing.' She paused

and hefted in a shuddery breath. 'It's true, Zahir. I love you.'
The whispered words sounded loud in the stillness. 'I didn't
want to. I didn't plan it. But I…' Welling emotion choked her.
'I can't pretend it hasn't happened. I can't face the future without knowing just once what it's like to be yours.'

Finally her clumsy fingers managed to unknot the belt. She
tore it open and shrugged the silk wrap off her shoulders. It slid
down sensitised flesh that tingled as if from a lover's caress.

She jutted her chin high; trying not to cower at the realisation she was naked before his gaze. She felt vulnerable and
weak, yet at the same time strangely buoyed, freed for now of
the oppressive weight of duty and fear of the future.

Zahir's eyes turned hot and hungry and flames licked her
deep inside.

'Please.' Her voice was thick. 'I'm only asking for tonight.
Just one night.'

He said nothing. Had she made a terrible mistake?

But Zahir's expression told her she hadn't been mistaken.
He did care, did want, just as she did.

She lifted one trembling hand and placed it on his chest.
Beneath her palm he felt strong and warm. His heart thudded
as quickly as hers. They both felt this yearning. She dragged
in a deep, relieved breath and with it Zahir's intoxicating scent.

'Don't!' In a blur of movement he grabbed her hand and
threw it off.

Shocked, Soraya stared up at a face of fury. The glitter in his
green eyes was lethal, the twist of his mouth scornful.

She backed away a pace.

He followed, his face a mask of contempt.

'Don't think you can come to my room like some…some
whore and tempt me into betraying Hussein.' His coruscat-
ing glare lashed her from top to toe and Soraya shrivelled as
if under a whip.

'I thought better of you, Soraya.'

Despite the roar of blood in her ears, she thought she heard
anguish in his voice. She must have imagined it.

'You go to your husband tomorrow and it won't be with my touch still warm on your body.' He looked away as if the sight of her sickened him. 'Get dressed and go to your room.' He was still speaking as he strode away and yanked the door open.

A moment later the door of the suite slammed behind him.

Blessed silence descended but in Soraya's head his words ran over and over.

A whore. He'd called her a whore!

With a muffled cry of pain Soraya lifted a shaky hand to her mouth, trying to keep back the bile that surged in her throat. Her legs gave way and she found herself huddled on the carpet.

Hours later Zahir stalked across the square towards their hotel. Even the Italians, who seemed to come alive in the evening, had vanished from the streets.

He was alone. Except he bore in his heart the image of Soraya, naked and impossibly tempting, offering herself to him as if he deserved such bounty.

Soraya, flinching under the despicable words he'd thrown at her in a last-ditch effort to shore up his rapidly failing control, when all he'd wanted was to gather her to him and learn the secrets of her beautiful body.

He felt sick with a pain no distance or mindless exercise could numb. How could he have treated her so? In his heart he'd recognised her desperation and need, for didn't he feel them too? To lash out at her had been more than cruel—it had been unforgivable.

Nevertheless, he'd apologise as soon as she woke in the morning. Before they boarded the plane for Bakhara and her bridegroom.

In the hotel doorway he faltered, his hand going out to steady himself as turbulent emotions threatened to unman him. Grief, loss, shame and unrepentant longing.

'*Signor?*' The concierge moved forward but Zahir waved him away and made for the lifts.

He'd walked the streets for hours and was no nearer finding peace.

It was past time he returned, even if guarding Soraya from harm on this last night seemed like a contradiction in terms. With her pleading eyes, sweetly feminine body and throaty voice telling him she loved him, she was the most dangerous being on the planet.

She made him believe what he felt was meant to be.

Instead his logical brain reminded himself that he'd eschewed love since he was nineteen, preferring to deal with lust. That she was promised to Hussein. That he owed Hussein everything and couldn't betray him.

His heart was heavy as he opened the door of the suite. The lights were on. Hadn't she gone to bed yet?

He'd assumed she'd be locked in her room. Adrenalin surged at the prospect of seeing her again.

For he wanted—more than wanted. He needed her with every breath of his being. How he'd cope after he delivered her to Hussein, he had no idea.

The door to his room was open, the lights on. Surely she wasn't…? No. It was empty. A shuddering breath escaped. Was it relief or regret that made his heart pump faster?

He turned back into the foyer, intending to turn off the lights in the rest of the suite, when he noticed Soraya's door wide-open.

Frowning, he paced closer. The overhead light blazed on an empty room. A familiar splash of champagne silk sprawled across the corner of the bed, trailing onto the floor. He picked it up, inhaling the scent of wildflowers. The fabric was cold to the touch.

The hair on Zahir's nape rose as he knocked on her bathroom door. When there was no response he jerked it open, only to find it empty.

Apprehension skittered down his spine as his senses went on alert. There was no sound in the suite as he strode from room to room, flinging open doors, hauling curtains back from the wall, even checking cupboards.

By the time he'd rung reception to discover Soraya had left no message, and double-checked every hiding place, he was in a cold sweat.

Returning to her bedroom, he rifled through her belongings: suitcase, clothes, purse and laptop. Even her passport and mobile phone were there.

Where was she?

Zahir scowled at the meagre collection of belongings, as if they could tell him what he needed to know.

Twenty minutes later the hotel had been searched from top to bottom, but there was no sign of Soraya.

Dread curled within him, sending tendrils of fear through his frozen limbs.

He'd done this! With his defensive temper and his unforgivable words. He'd never known such guilt, such fear, as sliced through him now, leaving him bereft and trembling.

Soraya was alone in an unfamiliar city at a time when honest people were off the streets. Only the foolhardy or dangerous prowled the city at this time.

Panic swamped him.

He strode to the window and stared at the empty square as if sheer desperation could conjure her. Somewhere out there, distressed and defenceless, was the woman he'd sworn to protect. The woman he cared for.

If anything happened to her…

Soraya put one foot in front of the other and plodded on. She was near the hotel but the fact she couldn't remember its exact location didn't bother her. She'd prefer never to return.

Yet the future had to be faced.

A hollow laugh escaped her. Weeks ago she'd thought life couldn't get worse than an arranged marriage. She'd fretted over it till she had felt sick with anxiety.

Now she knew what real despair was.

To marry one man while loving another.
To have the man she loved despise her for wanting him.

Pain lanced her and she stumbled, putting out her hand to lean against a stone wall. Even now she couldn't stop trembling.

She couldn't remember dressing or leaving the hotel. All she recalled were Zahir's words.

Had she been so wrong? Did he feel nothing for her?

She bent her head till the world stopped spinning. Maybe the grappa had muddled her senses.

She'd been watching water spurt from an old fountain when a motherly looking woman asked if she was all right. According to her, Soraya had been standing there for over an hour.

She'd led Soraya into a tiny courtyard filled with the scent of geraniums and the rumbling purr of a ginger cat. The woman had invited her to sit then pressed a glass of grappa into her unresisting hands. Then she'd taken the other seat and tilted a lamp towards her embroidery.

How long she'd sat there, Soraya didn't know. She'd lost track of time, soothed by the rhythm of the cat's breathing as it stretched across her lap and the chatter of a late-night radio talk show.

Finally she'd noticed the weariness on the other woman's face and, thanking her for her kindness, made her way onto the deserted street. Now she just had to find her way back. A shudder racked her at the idea of facing Zahir's piercing disapproval. But she had no choice.

After all, what more could he do? Her heart had already splintered into raw, jagged pieces.

From somewhere she dredged the strength to walk on. She'd covered just a metre when a figure came in view. A tall man with a purposeful stride.

Instantly she shrank back, her heart battering her ribs. In her dazed state he looked too much like...

'Soraya!'

He sprinted, his feet pounding the pavement, and before she

could gather her wits to retreat he was there, his hands on her shoulders, gripping her tight.

'Are you all right?' He didn't wait for her answer but ran his hands lightly across her shoulders, arms and face, as if needing to feel for himself that she was whole.

'Don't touch me!' She stumbled back a step till she collided with a wall but he followed, hemming her in.

'Tell me you're unhurt.' His voice was as raw as hers. In the dim light she almost didn't recognise him. He seemed to have aged a decade in one evening. 'Please, Soraya!' His fingers shook as he smoothed the hair back from her face. Something sharp twisted inside.

'I'm fine,' she said over a lump of congealing emotion. 'Don't worry; you don't have to soil your hands by touching me.' Though for one precious moment she let herself believe his concern was for her personally, not because he'd committed to bring her back in one piece.

'Soraya. Don't.'

Before her stunned gaze, Zahir dropped to his knees. He gripped her fingers in an unbreakable hold and pressed fervent kisses to the back of one hand then the other.

'Zahir?' Her befuddled brain couldn't grasp the change in him. To have him literally at her feet was unthinkable. His arrogant rejection was too fresh in her mind. Yet there he was, wretchedness written on his once-proud features.

He made her heart turn over despite her anger.

'I'm sorry.' He looked up, his gaze fiercely direct and a wave of emotion rocked her back on her heels. 'What I said to you.' He shook his head. 'It was unforgivable, as well as being untrue.'

His hands tightened and with a sense of wonder she read desperation in his grim visage.

'I lashed out because I felt myself crumbling.' He tore in a ragged breath that pumped his chest hard. 'Every word you spoke pulled me closer to deserting my principles, my duty, my loyalty. You *scared* me.'

He shook his head, though his eyes never wavered from hers. 'I wanted you so badly—*still* want you—it was torture having you offer yourself when I was so weak.'

'You want me?' Her heartbeat stalled.

'How could I not?' His voice was hoarse, his breath hot against her hands. 'I've desired you from the moment I saw you in that club. Every day and every night you fill my waking thoughts as well as my dreams. Soraya. Can you ever forgive me? To call you that...' His breath shuddered out in a rattling rasp. 'You were being honest, when I couldn't even face what I felt.'

He threaded his fingers through hers, turned her hands to plant heated kisses on her palms. Tremors of sensation shot up her arms, to her breasts and down to her womb. Her knees shook so hard she thought they'd give way.

'What do you feel, Zahir?' Soraya was light-headed, overloaded on emotion. She gripped his fingers hard, knowing it was only the current of energy flowing between them that gave her strength to stand.

'This.'

He was on his feet, looking down at her with an expression that melted her bones. His palms were strong and warm on her cheeks, his breath a ripple of heady pleasure as it caressed her lips.

Instinctively her lips parted as, with a groan, he lowered his mouth.

Their lips met and the world exploded. Caution vanished, incinerated by the fierce need devouring them.

Soraya sagged against Zahir, clinging to his broad shoulders as he took her mouth in a kiss that devastated and fulfilled. It pulsed with raw, unvarnished desire and sweetest longing. Soraya couldn't get enough.

His body pressed against hers from thigh to chest, imprinting her with his heat, his hunger. And she was just as eager. Just as unrestrained.

Their lips mashed as she kissed him with more fervour than

expertise. He gathered her close, his hands proprietorial as they stroked down her back till she arched high against him, eager for greater contact.

An instant later he stepped back, despite her moan of protest. Before she could complain, he hoisted her into his embrace and held her close to his pounding heart.

'Not here,' he growled in an unrecognisable voice that set off sparks of excitement deep in her belly.

He turned and strode towards the hotel, a man on a mission. 'We need privacy.'

CHAPTER TWELVE

Zahir's hold remained unbreakable as they entered the suite and the door crashed closed behind them.

Soraya carried jumbled impressions of the hotel foyer and the gawping receptionist's stunned expression, though Zahir hadn't slowed his purposeful stride long enough for her to feel anything but excitement at his possessive hold.

The mirrored lift to the penthouse suite reflected Zahir's granite-set visage, his jaw angled in a way that warned he'd brook no interference. No wonder the receptionist had stayed safely behind his desk.

Zahir's expression sent a wave of pleasure coursing through her. A purely feminine pleasure of anticipation.

His pace didn't falter as they crossed the suite's foyer. Lamp-light beckoned them into his room where light spilled across the sprawling bed.

Zahir slammed to a stop and in the quiet Soraya heard only their breathing, merging like a single heartbeat, fast and eager.

'Soraya.' It wasn't Zahir's voice; not the easy, calm voice she'd come to know. This sound was dredged from the depths of a tortured soul.

She shivered luxuriously as it wrapped around her, connecting to a deep, visceral part of her.

This was unknown territory yet the world had never felt so right as in his arms. Doubt and uncertainty fled before the force of them together: Zahir the epitome of conquering male, and she all melting, wanting female.

He lowered her to her feet, sliding centimetre by slow centimetre down his taut frame till she was strung so tight with need she could barely stand. She leaned in, latching needy fingers around his strong neck so she could feel his hot flesh.

That simple contact was almost unbearably wonderful.

'If you don't want this, say so,' he groaned, his lips a caress against her hair that set a whole new set of nerve endings into spasms of delight. 'Soraya!' His chest expanded mightily as he dragged in air. 'I can let you go but you have to tell me. Now!'

The way his big hands claimed her hips, pulling her up against him so she felt the rigid length of his erection, it seemed impossible he'd ever release her. Yet she knew his formidable will-power.

'No! Don't let me go.' Part demand, part plea, her words were harsh in the thundering silence.

Don't let me go, ever.

For ever. That was how long she wanted Zahir. She needed him in her life always.

She loved him with a raw, soul-deep passion that cut so deep she knew she'd carry it with her the rest of her life.

Soraya felt a great sigh of relief pass through him and recognised the unsteadiness in his touch—it was the same for her. Zahir needed her so vehemently, so completely he burned up with it. His flesh was hot beneath her fingers and tremors coursed his body.

A lifetime's reserve and caution disintegrated under the onslaught of feelings that welled free at last. Zahir's hot skin against her fingers was a benediction. She watched his brilliant eyes, heavy-lidded and mysterious as he drank in the sight of her.

The way he looked at her…

She slid her hands to his collar and with one quick tug wrenched it open.

His chest, contoured muscle and flesh dusted with dark

hair, beckoned. Her heart galloped as she spread her fingers wide, learning him.

My love.

She leaned in, breathing deep the intoxicating essence of him. Of the man she loved with all her being.

'Soraya.' She felt the breath rise in his chest as his voice trailed across her skin. Still their gazes locked.

The world stopped as they trembled on the brink.

Then, with magnificent disregard for her wardrobe, Zahir copied her action. Yet when he took her dress in his big hands and yanked, the silk ripped. It tore so far it was the work of a moment for him to slide it off her shoulders. The fabric slithered down her body in a furtive caress that made goose bumps prickle her flesh.

She hardly noticed, for the look in Zahir's eyes blotted all else from her mind.

Words poured from his lips, a whispered stream of praise and thanks as his gaze followed her dress down, then rose again to her now-rosy cheeks. That hoarse litany of heartfelt appreciation was enough to make any woman blush.

'No woman is perfect, Zahir.'

Why she demurred, she didn't know, except perhaps that he overwhelmed her. She wished she could be perfect—for him. The heated intensity of his stare, the guttural depth of emotion in his voice made her feel for a moment like the goddess he described.

How could any woman live up to that?

'Yet you are perfect, *habibti*.' He looked into her eyes and she felt that half-familiar shudder rip through her from the impact of an unseen force. 'To me you are.'

The glow in his eyes made her heart swell.

He said more but it was muffled against her throat as he kissed her. She tilted her head back in ecstasy and he lashed an arm around her waist to keep her from falling.

Yet she fell. Into a vortex of tumbling emotion and sensations.

It wasn't just the pleasure of his kiss. It was the way he made her feel: treasured, appreciated, loved.

This time when his hand cupped her breast it wasn't at her clumsy invitation. Zahir's was an expert's touch, moulding, caressing, teasing till wildfire roared through her to rush in a whirlpool of heat between her legs.

Her hands slid to the smooth flesh of his shoulders as he bowed her back, further and further, till she lay draped across his arm. His mouth closed over her breast through the filmy lace of her bra and she whimpered in delight, her fingers clutching at him frantically.

'Zahir.' Did that low, keening throb of sound come from her?

'You have no idea how much I want you.' His lips moved across her breast and throat as he spoke. 'I've tried to resist but I'm only human.'

'I don't want you to resist,' she gasped.

'Just as well.' He licked her nipple and her breath clogged in her throat. 'I couldn't stop now to save myself.'

She felt the mattress beneath her and when his arms came away from behind her they dragged her bra too. Dazed, she watched it arc over Zahir's shoulder as he stripped her panties and shoes away.

She should feel nervous as he ate her up with his eyes. Despite a lifetime's modesty, she couldn't. Not when the pride and pleasure in his expression made her feel like a queen.

He braced his arms wide and a shiver of delicious trepidation shot through her at the sensation of being surrounded by such a virile, dominant male. But, instead of lowering himself to her, he retreated down the bed.

Anticipation hummed through her, knowing that soon, when he'd stripped his trousers off, they'd...

'Zahir?'

'It's all right, little one.' His deep voice reassured but she couldn't relax, not when he settled himself deep between the V of her legs, splayed wide by his gently insistent hands.

'What are you...?' A hiss of indrawn breath clotted the

words in her throat. First his hand and then his mouth stroked her there, where need throbbed strongest.

Soraya's whole body jerked hard, as if from an electric shock. But this was pleasure, pure pleasure so intense it overwhelmed her senses.

One caress, another, and she almost lifted off the bed, held in place only by Zahir's solid weight as a shower of sparks ignited in her blood.

She needed to escape, keep some fragment of control, but delight as well as his imprisoning body kept her there, splayed and open before him.

Her eyelids drooped. Her mouth sagged as she gasped in another raw breath and suddenly, like a roiling tide that grew till it blotted out the world, ecstasy engulfed her. She shook and sobbed with the force of it, abandoned to a delight so intense she could never have imagined it.

A delight of Zahir's giving. Through the maelstrom her hand gripped his where it rested on her thigh. That was her lifeline, her connection to him.

Finally, as she lay spent and gasping, he slid from her grasp. She roused herself to protest, but the press of his mouth to the flesh above her hipbone stifled her words. Just the touch of his lips there evoked a pleasure she should be too spent to feel. His hands skimmed her lightly and she shifted under his touch, like a cat curving into a petting hand.

Except Zahir's hands moved with deliberate, erotic delicacy that soon had fire running in her veins again.

'Come to me?'

At her husky plea, his head lifted. Soraya's heart somersaulted as she saw how the skin dragged taut over those strong features. His eyes held a febrile glitter that spoke of fierce yearning.

'Not yet.'

'Why not?' She grasped his shoulders and tried to haul him close. It was like trying to loosen bedrock. 'Please.'

'I can't.' He shook his head. 'I have no control left. Once I...'

'Don't you understand?' Her voice shook. 'I don't care about subtleties or control. *I need you.* Just you.'

Soraya's heart gave a great leap as she read relief in his face and eagerness. She watched, mesmerized, as he reared up, dragging his clothes off.

She'd seen his body before at the pool, but now, in the golden glow of the lamp, he was hers. Her gaze lingered on the strong, lithe form of the man she loved. Even his scars, reminders of the dangerous life he'd led, seemed precious. Her pulse raced as she read the taut power in his heavy thighs, the wide span of his shoulders and the arrogant jut of his erection. As she stared he smoothed on protection.

She licked her lips, her mouth dry. But as he prowled up the bed, caging her with his body, Soraya felt no hesitancy, just gratitude and fizzing anticipation.

A mew of delight escaped her as he settled over her. To feel his chest against hers, the fuzz of his hair tickling her nipples, the smooth heat of his belly against hers—she hadn't known that alone would be bliss.

Hands tunnelling through his thick hair, she kissed him with all the love and wonder burgeoning within. His response was all she could have hoped for. Tender yet urgent, lavishly satisfying, even as her body stirred anew at the masculine weight pressed high between her legs.

'Soraya.' It was a groan of need as he centred himself above her.

'Yes.' She kissed him feverishly, holding him tight, almost afraid to believe this was real.

Then anticipation shattered, as with one surging movement he thrust sure and strong.

Her eyes sprang open. She was stunned by his overwhelming weight, the fullness that surely was impossible despite being so patently real. She was pinioned in a way that made something like panic rise and spread.

Her breath hitched and she forgot how to breathe as her body locked in shock.

She heard Zahir's heartbeat, loud as her own, fast as her own, and his laboured breathing, harsh in the stillness.

Dazed, Soraya groped for the pleasure that till a second ago had hummed in her needy body. She found only blankness.

'Breathe, *habibti*.' Zahir nuzzled the tender skin below her ear. 'Breathe for me.'

It wasn't his command that broke her stasis but the tiny shimmy of delight raying from the point where he kissed her.

He kissed her again, taking his time to lave her pulse-point and she dragged in a shuddering breath, her chest rising beneath his. Her skin tingled at the friction between their bodies and her next breath was deeper, filled with the male scent of him.

Zahir insinuated his hand between them to touch her breast, plucking delicately at her nipple, and a judder of heat rippled through her. Her frozen limbs eased a fraction and her stunned rigidity eased, replaced by a different, delicious tension.

Slowly, lavishly, Zahir seduced her mouth with his till the hint of panic eased.

'That's my girl. It's all right, see?' He moved, withdrawing from her little by little, till she missed the press of his body above hers and even the strange, too-full sensation of his possession.

Instinctively she slanted her pelvis and he responded with another thrust, this time claiming her body centimetre by slow centimetre. Now the sensations he wrought brought fire to her blood and a different sort of tension.

'Zahir!'

He lifted his head to see her face. To her shock he looked to be in pain, his features pinched. Yet his eyes blazed with a brilliance that stole her breath all over again.

Her hand lifted to his cheek. Tenderness filled her as she read what it cost him not to take as his body dictated, but to harness his impulses.

'Tell me what to do.' She felt so useless.

His lips quirked in a brief smile that looked more like a grimace. 'Lift your legs.' He nodded as she complied. 'Higher. Around my waist.'

Soraya tentatively followed his instructions as Zahir once more slid away, then back with an ease that evoked a stab of pleasure.

Her eyes widened. 'That feels...'

'It does, doesn't it?' His eyelids drooped till she saw only slits of dark green. One more easy thrust and this time she anticipated him, rocking up and back with Zahir, eliciting another sharp pulse of pleasure.

She tightened her hold, wanting to comfort him even as another rush of erotic sensation undermined thought.

They rocked together, finding a rhythm so excruciatingly slow it alternately stoked her arousal to fever pitch and satisfied it with a blinding flash of searing pleasure. The pleasure was the greater for seeing its reflection in Zahir's face.

Each dazzling, joyous pinnacle was shared so intimately it seemed they were one, their bodies moving in tandem, their minds linked as they shared something profound.

Finally, after what seemed a lifetime, pleasure crescendoed. Soraya's eyes fluttered shut and she clung to Zahir as, with a rush, their mutual climax splintered thought in a crash of crystal shards.

The sound of her name on Zahir's lips echoed through the velvet darkness that claimed her.

Zahir paced back from the bathroom into the darkened bedroom.

Was she asleep? He hoped so. He had to think, had to come to grips with what they'd done.

What *he'd* done.

Never, since the day Hussein had rescued him from his father, had Zahir acted on pure instinct without thought or plan.

Never had he acted solely on what he felt.

Until now.

Even at nineteen, when he'd fallen hard for the daughter of

the palace's head groom, he hadn't behaved rashly. He'd thought himself in the throes of love yet he'd never put a foot out of line, courting carefully, respectfully—till her father had put an end to his aspirations, rejecting him as too young, too lacking in prospects, the son of a dishonourable man.

Yet as Zahir neared the bed and saw Soraya, her hair a lush curtain that allowed glimpses of her silvered skin in the moonlight, he felt more than ever in his life.

He wanted her, craved her with all the longing in his battered heart. A heart she'd reawakened.

He wanted to drown out the world in the heady pleasure of her soft embrace.

He wanted that searing sense of rightness, of homecoming, of ecstasy as he became more than just the man he was, stronger for being part of Soraya.

Something tugged hard in his chest as he halted by the bed. He groped for control. Then her eyes opened, dark and fathomless as a desert sky. Her lips curved in a smile so tender it made his heart throb in a new, unfamiliar rhythm.

'Zahir.' The whisper of her sweet voice saying his name was devastating as an earthquake. He trembled at the impact. When she reached out to him that last, almost-sane part of his brain shut down.

He snatched her hand, cupping it so he could press urgent kisses to her palm. Her luxuriant ripple of pleasure was enough to dislodge any foggy shreds of sanity.

'Soraya.' His voice was raw with all he felt and could no longer deny.

Then he was with her, flesh to flesh, his rough body grazing her softness, his aching groin against her tender belly. He tried to hold back, to restrain himself, but she confounded him, her lips at his throat, stalling his breath in his lungs. Then her hand, small and smooth, curled around his erection and his heart stopped.

He surged against her palm, unable to prevent himself, rev-

elling in her gentle, clumsy hold that was more erotic than that
of the most practised seductress.

Zahir tugged her close, hands sliding on rippling tresses
and satiny skin.

Now she found her rhythm, encircling him in long strokes
that drew him tight and rigid as a bow.

It was ecstasy so potent it bordered on agony.

'You have to stop.' He reached for her hand. The rest of his
words dried as he held her, holding him. A great shudder passed
through him as he groped for something, anything, that would
stop him succumbing.

'You don't like it?' Doubt or excitement in her voice? He
couldn't tell over the drumming pulse in his ears.

She moved and the caress of her long hair over his shoulders
and down his heaving chest drove his desperation to new levels. Her skin, her voice, her hair, her touch; everything about
Soraya destroyed him. His limbs lost their strength, his resistance shattered, as she pressed her lips to his collarbone and
chest, her nipples grazing his belly in swaying strokes that
drove spikes of raw need through him, puncturing resistance
and good intentions.

His hands fisted in her hair, holding her tight as she slithered lower.

Her tongue flicked him gently, tasting him, and he bucked,
helpless beneath her. Only his grip on her scalp remained
strong.

Her lips opened and he was lost.

CHAPTER THIRTEEN

IT WAS late when Soraya woke. She knew without looking that Zahir had gone. She sensed it, just as she always knew when he was near.

Through the night and the early hours they'd lain in each other's arms, always touching. The sound of his breathing had lulled her to sleep after their tumultuous lovemaking.

Her skin glowed, her heart sang, her body throbbed with a pleasurable ache. Her limbs were heavy as if they'd never move again, yet at the same time light, as though she still floated on a plane where nothing existed save herself and the man she loved.

She opened her eyes and saw it was broad daylight. Her heart missed a beat.

She'd tasted bliss but now the real world intruded. She'd known for one short night what it was to be in the arms of the man she loved.

How could she give that up?

She had no choice. Nothing had changed. All the reasons they couldn't be together still held sway. Zahir knew it too. He'd already gone.

Desperate to see him, she flung off the sheet and rose. Her knees wobbled, weak after last night's loving.

A surge of heat tingled from her feet up to her face. Last night there'd been no embarrassment or thought of modesty, yet this morning, without Zahir's embrace, she found she could still blush.

Her clothes were tumbled on the floor. Instead of wearing them, she hurried to the wardrobe and grabbed the robe hanging there. She fumbled as she shrugged it on and cinched it tight. Her fingers as well as her legs shook.

She needed to see Zahir, to cling to the magic just a little longer, before she closed the door on love for ever.

Just one look, one touch.

He was in the living room, fully dressed as he stared at the busy square below. Disappointment stirred as she took in his wide shoulders in the dark jacket, his powerful legs hidden from view in tailored trousers.

He looked so…formal. After last night's potent virility, these clothes made him appear curiously stiff.

She was halfway across the room when he swung round, an espresso cup in his hand. Her pace slowed as he lifted the cup and took a long sip.

He looked different. It wasn't just the clothes. There was an aura around him that reminded her of the fiercely self-contained man he'd been in Paris.

She blinked as shyness assailed her. How could she be daunted by his business clothes? This was Zahir. The man she adored. The man who, she knew in her heart, loved her too. Given his strength of character nothing but that could have prompted him to spend the night loving her as if there was no tomorrow. The knowledge was poignant pleasure and pain intermingled.

'Good morning.' Her voice was husky. The last time she'd used it was when she'd cried out his name in the throes of passion.

'Good morning.' His black eyebrows were a horizontal smudge above severe features and he gave no answering smile. 'How are you feeling today? Are you all right?' His quick concern warmed her. Zahir had been a demanding lover, passionate, but incredibly tender.

'I feel fabulous.' She refused to think of how she'd feel when it was time to say goodbye.

Soraya's steps faltered and her heart lurched as her eyes locked with his. She found blankness there where before there'd been passion, love and even—she could have sworn—wonder. Ice water trickled down her spine.

'What's wrong?' He held himself so rigidly.

His mouth twisted in a brief, brutal smile that spoke of pain not pleasure. 'You can ask that?'

'Has something happened?' she whispered. 'Is there news from Bakhara?'

His fingers clenched so tight on the coffee cup she thought its handle would snap. 'No news from Bakhara.'

Soraya hefted in a sigh of relief, her hand pressed to her chest. For a moment, reading his serious face, she'd wondered if something had happened to her father.

'You look pale, Soraya. You must be worn-out. Why don't you go back to bed and rest?' He took a couple of paces towards her then pulled up short as if yanked back by an invisible rope. The sight of him stopping that telling distance away made every hair on her body rise. His gaze shifted towards the bedroom and colour streaked his sharp cheekbones. 'You must be sore. Last night I should have…'

'Zahir, I'm okay, *really*. I'm just…' What? Feeling needy? She knew their time was almost over and needed Zahir's embrace just one more time to give her strength to do what she must.

She moved towards him then slammed to a stop as he retreated.

It was just a half-step and he covered it quickly, pretending to cast about for somewhere to put his coffee cup, though there was a table right beside him. Yet she couldn't mistake his instinctive movement.

Her heart crashed against her ribs as disbelief swamped her. She grabbed for the back of the sofa to support herself.

'We need to talk,' he said before she could speak.

She nodded. She could barely believe this was the man she

knew. He was so ill at ease and distant. As if last night had never happened.

Or as if he regretted what they'd done.

A knife twisted in her vitals.

Had he been disgusted by her enthusiasm or her untutored clumsiness? She squashed the idea as absurd. Last night had been indescribable pleasure for both of them. The love between them had made each touch, each sigh, magic. It had been so much more than simple physical gratification.

Soraya flushed at the memories, but another look at Zahir's sombre face made the blood drain from her own.

She told herself he only did what he had to—created the distance that must forever more be between them.

Yet her poor heart yearned for one last touch, one embrace, one whispered word of reassurance. How weak she was.

'I'll make the necessary arrangements. You can leave it all to me.'

'Arrangements?' She tilted her head.

'For our wedding.' His gaze meshed with hers, but Soraya saw only flinty determination in eyes that looked curiously flat. 'In the circumstances it will be a small ceremony, and soon.'

'Wedding?' The word emerged as a breathless gasp. She couldn't be hearing this. Yet a flutter of excitement rippled through her, sabotaging her determination to be stoic as she faced the future.

'We're getting married.' She knew that determined look. He was a man set on a course of action and nothing would deter him. The flutter became a tidal wave of excitement.

'But we can't. There's no way...' She spread her arms, encompassing all the reasons they couldn't be together.

'After last night we must.' Strangely he didn't smile at the memory of what they'd shared. 'I've spent the morning working out a way we can be together.'

'It's impossible.'

'I'll make it possible.' A thrill ripped through her. Zahir would move heaven and earth to achieve what he wanted. Was it possible, after all, that there was a way for them to be together? She hardly dared believe it.

'I'll speak to your father as soon as possible and do my utmost to persuade him this will be in your best interests.' Zahir drew in a breath that made his whole chest rise, as if readying himself for some Herculean task.

Her dad. 'I'll talk to him.'

If there was explaining to be done, she'd do it. He'd be horribly disappointed, and worried—not to mention embarrassed that the royal engagement was off—but he loved her. Surely, eventually, she could make him understand, especially if Zahir had a plan that would lessen the fallout? After all, he understood love.

'No.' Zahir shook his head and straightened his shoulders to stand ramrod-straight. Soraya was reminded of a soldier on parade. 'It's my duty. I'll deal with it.'

It. He made news of their feelings sound like a crime. Soraya clasped clammy hands together as the nervous gyrations of her stomach grew worse.

She understood how dreadful this would be. The shock and dismay they'd cause with their relationship. The gossip. The scandal. But despite it all the promise of a future with Zahir at the end of the trauma made exultation bubble through her veins. For it seemed Zahir believed there really could be a future for them. Despite her best intentions excitement swelled.

No matter what sacrifice it took, she was ready. Nothing was more important than the love they felt.

Yet, she realised now, Zahir looked not like a uniformed officer so much as a man facing a firing squad.

'It's not about duty, Zahir. My father will understand better if I explain.' She wanted to take his hand but he'd shoved his fists deep in his trouser pockets.

What was wrong? If he'd found a way for them to be honest about their love…

His grim expression doused her excitement.

He did love her, didn't he?

The way he'd murmured endearments last night, the fact that he'd taken her to bed despite all she knew of his honour-bound code of conduct, had convinced her he shared the same deep emotion she did.

'Zahir?'

'Of course it's about duty.' Zahir's jaw clenched so hard his face looked painfully tight. A laugh jerked from his lips. The sound of it made the hairs on her nape prickle. 'I was going to say it's a matter of honour, but I have no claim to honour now. Not after last night.'

Raw pain stared out from his face as he turned to her and the bright, fierce joy she nursed close to her heart dimmed. Sensation plunged from her chest right down to her abdomen, like a lift plummeting to catastrophe.

'Of course you do.' She hauled in a difficult breath. 'Last night was about honesty and—'

'Don't!' The harsh syllable stopped her as she leaned forward. 'I dishonoured you last night. And I dishonoured Hussein.' Zahir tugged one hand free of his pocket and rubbed it round the back of his neck as if in pain. 'Not to mention your family and myself.'

Soraya's arm slumped to her side. She told herself it was natural he felt guilty. He wasn't the only one. Even now she felt torn.

'You didn't dishonour me. I chose—'

'Not dishonour you?' His bark of laughter was ugly. 'You were a virgin, Soraya. That privilege should have been your husband's.'

Frantically Soraya fought for calm, reminding herself he only spoke as many in Bakhara did.

'It wasn't a privilege, Zahir. It was a gift. *My* gift.'

He swung away as if he couldn't bear to look at her. 'Do you think I'd have taken you as I did if I'd known?'

Soraya froze. Her labouring lungs atrophied as his words sank in.

She opened her mouth and closed it, grasping for words.

Finally she dredged some from deep in her pain. 'You thought I'd already lost my virginity so it was safe to sleep with me?' A great tearing gasp ripped through her, widening with every second he remained silent. 'You're only offering marriage to make good the damage you've done my reputation?'

'No. Of course not.' Yet his face when he swung around wasn't that of a lover. It belonged to a stranger. A stranger who looked at her and felt only horror for the consequences of what they'd done.

He'd wanted her last night, but not enough to withstand the cold, clear light of a new day. There was no joy on his face at the idea of their future together.

No thought of *them*. Just of duty and dishonour.

Dishonour. The word tainted what they'd shared so gloriously.

What she'd thought they'd shared.

Soraya had shared everything. Herself, her hopes, fears and dreams. Her love.

And Zahir? He regretted last night with a fervour that couldn't be faked. Could it be that he'd shared no more than his virile body? She'd blurted her love for him but he hadn't, even in the most intimate of moments, reciprocated.

Finally she realised how significant that was.

She watched him turn to pace the room, his expression brooding. She had to know the truth. Yet still she hesitated, scared of what his answer might be.

'Zahir? Do you...*care* about me?'

His head jerked up. 'Care?' His brow pleated as if she spoke a foreign tongue. 'Of course I care. I want to *marry* you, Soraya. I want to look after you and protect you. Be assured, I will make it all right.'

All right. Hardly the words of a man in love. He made no mention of joy or anticipation.

Wave after wave of shock passed through Soraya. Her knees weakened and she plopped down onto a nearby chair. The leather was cold against her trembling palms.

Would she ever feel warm again?

That's what love gets you. Nothing but trouble!

Soraya shook her head, as if she could banish the voice of doubt in her head.

But she knew it for the truth. Soraya had always feared love with good reason. Wasn't that why an arranged marriage to the Emir had originally seemed such a safe, appealing option?

She looked up at the man with the closed face, pacing with such ferocious concentration. She couldn't focus on his words over the swelling roar of blood in her ears, but she could make out his tone: cool and clipped. No passion. No emotion. None of the love she'd been so sure he felt.

He was in damage-limitation mode. As if she was a diplomatic tangle to be sorted out. An indiscretion to be dealt with.

Her heart gave a single frantic thud that shook her to the core. To have him hold out hope to her of happiness and then dash it was the cruellest torture of all.

She'd do anything, go anywhere with him, if only he'd ask. *If only he loved her.* But she refused to be nothing more than a mistake to be rectified.

She'd thought his actions were proof of deeper feelings. Yet he'd never spoken the words. Never claimed to love her.

Marrying a man who felt compelled to 'do the right thing' by her could only lead to disaster. Zahir would end up resenting her and she—could she cope with loving him and knowing he didn't feel the same?

'Soraya?' She wasn't listening to him. Zahir jolted to a stop, his gaze straying over her: so sweet, so vulnerable in that oversized robe.

His woman.

Despite the untenable situation he'd put them in, he couldn't help but glory in the fact she was his. Incontrovertibly. Totally. His.

Wildfire shimmered in his blood as he remembered how they'd been together. He wanted to thrust the world aside and lose himself in her. But he had to be strong for both of them. He couldn't contemplate a future without her.

That meant dragging himself far enough away, mentally and physically, to be able to confront the implications of their passion. Touching her would addle his brain. It was imperative he think clearly. Besides, he had no right to touch her until he'd made this right for her.

He had to deal carefully with her family, the public and, above all, Hussein if Soraya was to be able to hold her head up in public.

His lungs squeezed tight as he thought of Hussein. Scalding guilt drenched him.

No matter what he felt for Soraya, nothing excused what he'd done. To Soraya. To his friend and mentor.

She might brush it off as 'honesty' but he knew it for selfish weakness. A strong man would have held back, waited till they got to Bakhara, then declared himself publicly.

What sort of man was he?

He'd prided himself on his loyalty, courage and honour. He was weak to the marrow, a hollow sham of the man he'd believed himself. His loyalty to Hussein, his honour, his intentions, had all disintegrated before Soraya.

Had he fooled himself when he'd pretended he wasn't his father's son? That he was stronger, better, honest? Surely his betrayal of Hussein was far worse than his father's disloyalty? *He was his father's son after all.*

The knowledge threatened everything he knew of himself, his life and aspirations. Yet he couldn't afford to dwell on that now. Not when Soraya needed him.

It hadn't been enough to dress, to avoid touching her, to force himself to focus on the ugly public repercussions. All his efforts to strengthen himself ready to face what must be faced crumbled before her potent presence. He wanted to shun the world and take her back to bed. But the world wouldn't go away.

'Soraya?'

Finally she looked up. Yet it was as if she didn't see him. Her gaze was unfocused, fixed on something far away.

She opened her mouth and spoke, but his brain refused to process what she said. He gazed blankly down at her, willing her to break the nightmare horror that suddenly engulfed him.

He crouched before her, hands planted on the leather sofa on either side of her, trapping her close.

'What did you say?' His voice was a hoarse crack of sound.

Her gaze shifted as if she couldn't bear to meet his eyes. His heart pounded. 'I said I won't marry you.'

Zahir stared, vaguely aware that he was still breathing despite the gaping hollow where his heart had been. How could that be?

'No!' Finally he found his voice. 'You must!' She was his. What they shared had transformed him. Made him realise there was more to life than honour, challenge and duty. What in his youth he'd imagined to be love was nothing compared with this all-consuming emotion.

'Must?' She arched a brow imperiously, like the princess Hussein wanted to make her. Her voice was cool, distancing him. 'You have no right to talk to me about *must*. You may be my bodyguard but you're not my keeper.'

Zahir reeled back on his heels, shock slamming into him. Fire exploded in his belly and crackled along his arteries at her attempt to fob him off.

Fury such as he'd never known blasted through him. She couldn't deny him!

'I'm a hell of a lot more than that.' Fear roughened his voice. He leaned in again, close enough to inhale her scent and feel the rapid flutter of her breath on his face. 'You smell of sex, Soraya. Did you know that? Of my skin on yours. My seed.'

Her eyes rounded, her reddened lips parting, and Zahir wanted more than anything to kiss her into capitulation. Seduce away the idea that they couldn't be together.

Instead he reached for the collar of her robe.

'Here.' He yanked it aside to reveal her collarbone. 'I've left my mark on you.'

He'd felt guilty when he'd realised his unshaven jaw had marked the delicate skin of her throat and breasts.

Now all he felt was primitive satisfaction. Despite his anger and shock, his erection surged against the confines of his clothes. He wanted her with every searing breath in his constricted lungs. Not just the sex. He wanted *her*: the woman who'd changed his life and taught him how to feel.

She shoved his shoulders so abruptly he almost lost his balance. As it was she had time to surge to her feet and stride away across the room before he scrambled to stand. He made to follow her and then stopped, reading the pain on her face. An ache filled his chest.

'So we had sex.' Her voice was bitter, unlike anything he'd ever heard from her lips. 'What do you want? Your name tattooed on my skin?'

He'd settle for her smile. Her heart beating next to his. The knowledge she'd be with him, always.

He shook his head. This wasn't Soraya. Not the loving, generous woman he knew. What had gone wrong? He'd worked so hard, spent hours working out how they could be together permanently, and she was throwing it all away.

'You said yourself last night wouldn't have happened if you'd known I was a virgin.' Contempt dripped from her words.

'No!' He paced closer. 'I said I wouldn't have taken you like that. So clumsily.' He waved a slashing hand at the thought of his uncontrolled possession. 'I should have been gentler.' He'd seen the shock of discomfort on her features, read it in every tensed centimetre of her body, and still he hadn't been able to pull away.

The closed expression on her face proclaimed she didn't believe him and he couldn't bear it. He strode across the room, reaching for her.

'No. Don't touch me.' She shrank back.

Instantly he stopped, his belly churning sickeningly.

'Soraya, please. I don't know what's wrong, but we need to talk. To sort this out.'

'Talking won't help.' Her long hair rippled around her shoulders and breasts, reminding him of the sensual delight they'd shared. 'There's nothing to sort out.'

'How can you say that?' Had the world flipped over on its axis? Everything was scrambled. Everything he felt, everything he thought she felt, turned on its head.

'Because there's no future for us, Zahir.'

For long seconds she gazed into his eyes and he read regret there. Regret and pain that tore him apart because he was helpless to stop it. Or did he imagine it? Now her expression was blank and austere.

'Of course there is. If you'll just listen. I've worked out a way—'

'There's no future because I'm going to marry the Emir as planned.'

Zahir swayed on his feet as his world imploded, collapsing around him.

'No! No, it's not possible.' He struggled to draw breath, to banish the wave of blackness that threatened to engulf him. 'You're not serious?'

But her face was set in determined lines. This was *real*. One of the things he loved about Soraya was her honesty. She meant it.

'You *can't* marry Hussein. Not now.' Not when they'd found each other.

'Why not?' Her chin tilted and her dark eyes, once soft as pansies, flashed fire. 'Because you plan to tell him I'm no virgin?'

Zahir shook his head.

'You said you loved me.' The words were torn from him. A desperate appeal in the face of pure torment.

She said nothing. His aching heart longed to hear the words again, to feel the balm of her love surrounding him once more.

Still she remained silent.

Had they been mere words? Lies?

She'd never lied before, screamed his battered soul.

'I'm going through with my betrothal,' she said at last.

He wanted to yank her into his arms and make love to her till she sobbed his name and clung to him, till she recanted and said she wanted him, not Hussein.

But the seed of knowledge he'd nurtured so long had finally burgeoned into full blossom. Once before he'd sought marriage and been rejected because he was the son of a miscreant, with no prospects. He'd vowed then to work harder, be stronger, more successful than any of his peers. To make a name for himself that would be respected.

He'd thought he'd succeeded. And it was true that his reputation, his talents, his position, had been won by sheer hard work and devotion to duty.

A duty he'd failed abysmally last night. Just as he'd failed the tests of loyalty and integrity.

Soraya had said she wanted to make the most of her last days of freedom. Now she'd tasted forbidden fruit. She'd sated her curiosity and her desire for him.

She'd made her choice. Zahir was good enough for a fling, a night's pleasure before a lifetime of fidelity.

But to marry the illegitimate son of a notorious traitor when she could have Bakhara's ruler? Why settle for less than the best?

Why settle for a man who'd proven himself without honour?

Zahir turned on his heel and strode from the room.

CHAPTER FOURTEEN

INSTEAD of escorting Soraya to the palace, Zahir found himself superfluous as her father, ecstatic at her return, met them at the airport and took her to their home.

A courteous man, he invited Zahir to accompany them for refreshment, but Zahir refused.

As for Soraya, she thanked him with formal courtesy. Raw pain skewered him as he watched her treat him like a stranger.

As if last night hadn't happened.

As if they meant nothing to each other.

But she wasn't an accomplished actress. Zahir didn't know whether to be buoyed or furious when he saw, for an instant, the betraying wobble of her lower lip. Her stiff, angular walk, unlike the gentle sway of her natural gait, told him she wasn't as indifferent as she pretended.

Then why…?

'Sir?'

Zahir turned, recognising one of the palace servants.

'Sir, the Emir asks that you attend the council chambers as soon as possible. The negotiations over disputed territories have commenced and you're needed.'

Zahir turned towards the main concourse. Through the glass doors he saw a royal limousine waiting. Yet he had to force himself not to follow Soraya and her father instead.

'Sir. It really is urgent.'

Zahir frowned. 'I'm sure the Emir is well able—'

'That's just it, sir. The Emir is away in his desert palace. He'd expected you earlier and in the meantime left the negotiations to his diplomatic staff.'

Zahir's frown became a scowl. Hussein was in the desert? Odd behaviour from a man expecting his bride-to-be. After a decade-long betrothal, surely he was eager now to claim the bride he'd ordered home?

'The Emir...' Zahir lowered his voice. 'He is well?'

His companion nodded. 'Yes, sir. So I understand. If you'll just come this way...'

It took two full days to turn the talks around into something productive, another day to develop an agreement for consideration by the various nations and a day to ensure the delegates were farewelled with formal courtesy.

Despite the heavy load placed on his shoulders, Zahir performed his official duties as if by rote. He was distracted. Tormented.

By Soraya, who'd said she loved him, only to reject him. Who'd turned from searing passion to icy detachment.

By the puzzle of Hussein's behaviour when he remained uncontactable during these vital discussions. It wasn't the action of the forthright, capable man he knew.

But, above all, by his own turbulent feelings.

Four days neck-deep in sensitive, world-changing negotiations and he'd felt none of his usual pleasure in a difficult job well done.

His priorities had changed.

Because he'd fallen for a woman who meant more to him than the life he'd carefully constructed. What did any of it matter when Soraya was denied him? Worse, when she herself denied what they'd shared?

Pride shredded, desperation welling, he could find no equanimity, could barely maintain a pretence of it.

Now, on the fourth night since his return, he finally had the luxury of solitude. Instinctively, he'd turned to the desert.

Behind him stretched the glittering city, lighting up the night. Before him, the moon-silvered open ground of the wilderness. He urged his horse forward, inhaling the evocative scent of wild herbs, dusty ground and the subtle indefinable scent of exotic spice borne from the east.

As they picked their way into the desert a perfume teased his senses, of some night-blooming flower, rare and fragile.

It reminded him of Soraya and her delicately perfumed skin, sweet as mountain blooms. Of her beauty and grace, how she made a simple smile a thing of rare joy. His heart crashed against his ribs at the thought of never seeing it again. Or seeing her smile at another man: Hussein.

Pain tore at him like great talons ripping his flesh.

It wasn't just her beauty or her smiles he wanted. It was her love. The way she made him feel. When she'd said she loved him, something inside had glowed incandescent: a hope, a dream he'd never known existed until Soraya.

She'd seduced him not with sex but with the wonder of herself. A woman like no other. Proud, determined, prickly, emotional, giving, warm-hearted, loyal. Loyal to the father she loved and the man to whom she'd promised herself.

But not to him.

Hadn't she felt the same joy at his love for her? Hadn't she—?

The horse whinnied and skittered to a halt as Zahir yanked on the reins.

She *must* know how he felt. It had been there in his every desperate caress, in every breath, each murmured endearment. His desire for marriage.

Yet, reeling back time to that night, the morning after, it struck him that he'd never said it aloud. Never declared his feelings.

He shook his head. Of course she knew he cared for her. Why else would he strategise so frantically to find a way they could wed?

But did she know he loved her?

He sat unmoving so long the stars wheeled in the darkness overhead and the moon inched towards the horizon. Finally his patient mount shifted and Zahir let him have his head, cantering down a slope into the network of valleys that marked the border of the great desert.

When finally they stopped, Zahir had reached a decision.

It was beyond him to believe he could win her for himself, though he couldn't completely stifle a sliver of outrageous hope. Yet he had to act. He had to declare what he felt so Soraya knew and Hussein too.

It wasn't in Zahir's nature to hide behind silence.

Suddenly Soraya's words about honour and honesty made sense. What he felt, however problematic, was honest and real.

He'd been honest with Hussein all his life. It was his honesty above all that had built his reputation as a man who could be trusted, especially in matters of state. He couldn't change now. He couldn't face his friend and benefactor hiding what he truly felt.

He couldn't let Soraya turn from him without knowing.

He couldn't live a lie. Not even if it meant banishment and loss of both the prestige he'd built and the dreams he'd held. Loving Hussein's wife doomed him to leaving all he'd once held close, even his best friend.

He would lose everything.

Yet hadn't he already lost the one thing that mattered?

He turned the stallion and headed back to the city, his heart lighter than it had been since Rome.

The royal audience-chamber was vast, richly ornamented and exquisitely decorated with murals and mosaics of semiprecious stones. Designed to reinforce the majesty of the nation's ruler, it could hold hundreds.

Zahir stopped on the threshold, surprised to find it virtually empty with only a few score in attendance.

There was Hussein, looking stately as ever and reassuringly fit, greeting guests. To one side was Soraya, gorgeous in amber silk with a gilt embroidered veil covering the back of her head. She was pale but composed.

His heart jerked with mingled delight and pain.

Would this be the last time he saw her?

After this he'd no doubt be escorted to the border and never allowed to enter the country again, much less approach the royal presence. The trembling in his belly spread to his limbs and for a moment he doubted he had the strength to go on.

Moving his gaze, he saw Soraya's father, hovering close to her. The rest of the guests he recognized: the country's most influential leaders, tribal elders and government ministers. Men he dealt with every day. Men he respected.

Men who'd shun him when this was over.

He watched Hussein, the benevolent, extraordinary man who was as precious to him as a father. Who trusted him implicitly. His stomach dived as he thought of the yawning rift he'd create between them and the hurt he'd cause.

Shifting his gaze back to Soraya, warmth stole through him. Not the heat of lust. This was stronger, fuller and more profound.

Taking a deep breath, he strode towards his fate.

Soraya held herself stiffly, beset by doubt.

She'd never been in the audience chamber and its brilliance daunted her, reinforcing the Emir's power and wealth. Reminding her she was to marry a stranger, as unfamiliar to her as the opulence that surrounded them.

When summoned to the palace this morning, she'd almost welcomed the invitation. For, despite what she'd told Zahir in her pride and hurt, she was less convinced than ever that she could marry the man who held centre stage in this auspicious gathering.

Yes, he was generous and decent, good-looking too, if you had a penchant for much, much older men.

But he wasn't Zahir.

It didn't matter that Zahir didn't love her. She'd given her heart to him and she knew that, like her father's, her love once given could not be rescinded.

She'd hoped for a chance to talk with the Emir in private. He had a right to know his bride loved another.

Instead she and her father had been ushered into a formal reception of VIPs so daunting she'd had difficulty doing more than respond to polite greetings. She very much feared the purpose of the gathering was to introduce her formally as a royal bride and announce a wedding date. Why else was she included amongst all these eminent people?

As soon as this was over she *had* to find a way to speak with the Emir privately. She owed him the truth, though she cringed, thinking of the consequences.

A stir in the crowd caught her attention. Heads turned towards the grand entrance. At the same time a frisson of awareness scudded down her spine, drawing her flesh taut and tingling, as if she'd been dipped in fizzing champagne.

Her breath caught. That sensation was unmistakeable.

It was Zahir. No one else made her feel that way.

Despair flowered deep inside as she realised there was no escape. She'd hoped to put off this first public meeting till she'd gathered her defences more strongly about her, ready to project an aura of disinterest.

Would she ever be able to pretend so well, when just the knowledge he was in the room made her knees weak?

Unable to resist, she turned and there he was, his long legs eating up the marble vastness as he strode towards the throne.

Her pulse rocketed as she took him in. Zahir as she'd never seen him. Zahir in a pure white robe that flowed from broad, straight shoulders, loose trousers tucked into traditional Bakhari horseman's boots. A belt secured a curved scabbard for the customary knife.

There was nothing ostentatious about him. His clothes were simple but of the finest materials. Yet no other man in the room matched him for sheer presence and masculine magnificence. Not even the Emir.

Zahir's face was drawn in harsh lines, as if he'd just come in from the blinding desert sun. Or as if he had momentous matters of state on his mind.

'Zahir! Welcome.' The Emir moved forward to greet him, arms outstretched for an embrace.

'My lord.' Zahir stopped several paces away, bowing deeply.

The Emir halted, his brow pleating as if Zahir's formality surprised him. 'It gladdens my heart to see you, Zahir. You are well?'

'I am, sire. And you are in good health?'

Soraya listened to the exchange of greetings with half an ear, all the while bracing herself for the moment Zahir looked past the Emir and noticed her. Would he come and greet her, or simply nod, as passing acquaintances might? She didn't know which would hurt more.

She must have missed part of their conversation. For suddenly the Emir was ushering him forward and Zahir was shaking his head.

'Before the business of the day begins, I have something I must tell you.' Zahir's eyes, like polished emeralds, flashed straight to her, piercing her where she stood. As ever, she felt the impact of his gaze from the roots of her hair to the tips of her feet in their embroidered silk slippers.

So he'd known she was there all along.

She shifted, a sense of terrible premonition welling.

'Of course.' The Emir gestured for him to continue. 'You are among friends. Let us hear what is on your mind.'

Zahir turned back to the Emir, his facial muscles so taut she wondered if he was in pain.

'It concerns the lady Soraya.'

Her heart skated to a halt then took up a quick, faltering rhythm. A murmur of interest resonated around the room but she barely registered it. Her whole being focused on Zahir.

What was he going to do—broadcast what he considered her shame to all and sundry? Accuse her of disloyalty? Unworthiness?

She found she'd clasped her hands together, fingers entwined and shaking. Her feet were rooted to the spot.

'Go on.'

'There is something you should know before you marry.' Zahir paused and you could have heard a pin drop in the massive room.

Soraya's father reached out and touched her arm but she couldn't tear her gaze from Zahir.

What was he doing? Why?

Her stasis shattered and she stumbled forward, her long dress sweeping around her unsteady legs.

The Emir half-turned to acknowledge her as she joined them. Yet Zahir didn't shift his gaze. He stared straight ahead at the man he'd called his best friend and mentor.

As if he blocked her out.

Panic swirled up from her stomach, prickling its way through her whole body. Or was it pain? The ache of waiting to be betrayed by the man who'd stolen her heart?

'I know you prize loyalty,' Zahir continued.

'I do.'

'Then you should know that I can no longer remain in Bakhara. Not once you marry this woman.' Zahir's voice was firm and strong, eliciting a ripple of gasps and whispers from the assembled group.

Heat roared through Soraya's cheeks then receded, leaving her cold and strangely empty. Then she felt the clasp of a sustaining hand on hers as her father moved to stand by her. That proof of his love almost shattered her, knowing how unbearably disappointed he would be at the news Zahir would break.

She opened her mouth but no sound emerged.

'Why is that, Zahir?' On her other side the Emir sounded unperturbed, as if he couldn't read the dark sizzle of emotion in Zahir's eyes or the thundering pulse at his temple.

'Because I love her.'

Silence descended, broken only by the rattle of Soraya's breath in her overburdened lungs. Surely she imagined the words? For Zahir to say them now, here, in front of the nation's elite... She tried to take it in but couldn't.

'I love her,' he said, louder this time, making himself heard over the immediate clamour of protest that rose around them. 'Therefore I can't be part of your court. I can't remain here, a loyal subject, when she—' he swallowed hard '—is your queen.'

Zahir's gaze flickered to her and she read haunting anguish in the depths of his eyes.

Her heart gave a great leap, battering up against her throat. She felt light-headed.

'You have never been precipitate before, Zahir.' The Emir spoke over the swelling roar behind them. 'I counsel you not to make rash statements now.

'Soraya?' At the Emir's questioning tone, she dragged her gaze to the weathered, stern face of the older man. 'What are your feelings for this man?'

He spoke with a gravity that confirmed all her fears for Zahir. Had he destroyed in one moment everything he'd worked for? She knew how much his position, his work—and above all this man's regard meant to him. Dismay gnawed.

She sensed the horror of the onlookers and knew he'd just willingly given up all he'd strived for. For *her*.

Yet she couldn't stop the elation singing in her bloodstream. Her lips curved in a smile she hadn't a hope of hiding.

'I love him.' She turned to Zahir. Pulling free of her father's hold, she stepped closer to the man who stood poised as if for battle, alone against the crowd. 'I love him with all my heart.'

She no longer heard the others. No longer noticed the older men. All she knew was the dawning light in Zahir's clear gaze. The pride and love that softened his severe features as his eyes devoured her. The sweet joy that filled her.

She could scarcely believe it. *He loved her.*

Not only that, he had declared it in defiance of protocol, of tradition, of everything that stood between them.

How long they remained there, gazes enmeshed, cocooned

from the uproar, Soraya didn't know. Finally the Emir's voice penetrated. He spoke in deep, carrying tones.

'My kinsman Zahir's announcement has rather pre-empted my own. I've brought you all here today as witnesses.'

Soraya spun around, alarm rising. He couldn't mean to continue with the wedding now? *Surely* he couldn't? She started forward in protest but a hand stopped her.

'Wait, Soraya.' It was Zahir's voice in her ear, quelling the worst of her panic. His fingers engulfed hers and she squeezed back. If they were to be parted now…

Her face flamed as she faced the crowd, read the strain on her father's features and the avid curiosity of so many strangers.

The Emir spoke again. 'I called you here because it's been my intention for some time to abdicate.'

Shocked silence greeted his words. Zahir's fingers spasmed on hers and she heard his swift intake of breath.

'That decision will affect others.' He turned and Soraya found herself meeting kindly hazel eyes. There was no trace of the anger she'd anticipated in his face.

'In the circumstances, it would be unreasonable of me to ask my betrothed to feel committed to me now I've taken a decision which will so substantially alter her future.'

He was letting her off the hook?

A buzz of questions and protests surfaced but Soraya couldn't take them in. All she could process was the solid warmth of Zahir beside her, his strength flowing into her from their linked hands and the knowledge she was free.

The Emir raised a hand as he turned back to the crowd and silence fell. 'I have of course thought carefully about a successor. A man of my own blood. A man who has proven himself capable and trustworthy in so many capacities. A man who just this week saved our peace negotiations when they were in danger of foundering.'

He turned and all eyes followed the direction of his gaze. 'I propose Zahir Adnan El Hashem as my most worthy successor.'

* * *

Soraya paced the antechamber, oblivious to its luxurious furnishings and breathtaking view over the city. What was happening? Her nerves crawled with impatience. She'd felt revolt in the air back there, fuelled by shock and Zahir's uncompromising stance over her.

Her father had ushered her here, away from curious eyes, while the future of the nation was decided. He'd been stunned by the scene in the audience chamber. But, once she'd confirmed she really was in love, he'd proved staunchly supportive, only leaving when she forced him to go and take his part in the deliberations.

The door to the antechamber opened and Soraya swung round, ready to throw herself into Zahir's arms. His eyes met hers, glittering with raw emotion, and her heart juddered in the aftershock of that connection.

He loved her...

But he wasn't alone. The Emir walked beside him.

Soraya clasped her hands together and forced herself to be still, dread rising as she saw Zahir's grim expression and the Emir's weary one.

'How could you do it?'

Soraya opened her mouth then realised the question came from Zahir's lips and that he was standing in front of the Emir, legs planted aggressively wide.

'It was necessary,' the older man said.

'Necessary!' Zahir's deep voice rose to a pitch she'd never heard before. He sounded on the verge of violence. 'You *used* her.'

'I regret that.' The Emir cast her a troubled look.

'Regret?' Zahir's hands fisted at his sides. 'You shackled a young, unsuspecting girl to you with no thought of what that might do to her? How *trapped* she might feel? How distressed?'

Soraya rushed forward and grabbed his arm. It trembled with repressed fury. His other hand covered hers possessively and she leaned into him, still dazed by the fact she could. He wanted her, loved her.

The tension in Zahir's strong frame shocked her. As if it would take just one careless word to unleash violence.

His anger on her behalf was like a comforting blanket, reminding her she wasn't alone any more.

'I'd lost my wife, the love of my life,' the older man said, his voice hollow. 'I think now you both have some idea how that felt.' Soraya felt a quiver of distress pass through Zahir. Or was it through her? The thought of losing him now she'd finally found him made her clutch tighter.

The Emir heaved a deep sigh. 'To rule, I had to be married.' His gaze shifted to Soraya. 'Or betrothed.'

He spread his hands wide. 'You remember how things were then, Zahir, how unready the nation was for another ruler. And there was no logical successor.' His lips quirked. 'Though one young man had caught my eye. I knew with experience one day he'd make a fine emir.'

'The illegitimate son of a brutal tyrant?' Zahir's words bit like bullets.

'The honourable, capable man I'm proud to call kin, however distant the connection.' The Emir paused. 'I've been weary a long time, Zahir. A ruler needs a helpmeet. I'm ready to retire to my country estate and study the stars, read my books and watch your children grow.'

Heat suffused Soraya's cheeks at his direct look. The idea of carrying Zahir's babies made a pulse beat deep in her womb.

'But Zahir isn't married. How could you know…?' Her voice trailed off in the face of the older man's smile.

'I knew Zahir would have no trouble finding a bride. It's time he was settled.'

But Zahir wasn't to be distracted. 'You brought Soraya into an untenable situation.'

The Emir nodded. 'I'd planned today to annul the betrothal on the grounds of my abdication. That would leave Soraya's reputation unblemished. I hadn't anticipated your announcement.'

'But it doesn't go anywhere near making up for the trauma she suffered.'

'Zahir!' She tugged at his arm. 'It's all right now, truly.'
And it was. Miraculously, it was. She'd have gone through far
more than anxiety over her royal betrothal if it meant having
the man she loved.

He turned and looked down at her. His breath on her face
was a soft caress. The look in his eyes sheer heaven.

'I owe you my deepest apologies, Soraya.' Dimly she was
aware of the Emir bowing, but she couldn't tear her gaze from
Zahir's. The way he looked at her was like dawn's fresh promise after an endless night. A moment later the door snicked shut
and they were alone. Finally.

'Is it true?'

Zahir lifted her hand and kissed it, turned it over and pressed
his lips to the centre of her palm. Lightning jagged through her
veins and lit up her senses. His eyes glinted with promise, like
cool oasis water in the desert.

'It's true, my love. I adore you. And I'll never let you go.'
His voice dropped to a gruff bass rumble that made her insides
melt. 'If you'll have me.'

'But in Rome…'

He pressed a finger to her lips.

'In Rome I was a fool. I was so caught up making plans and
anticipating problems I forgot the most important thing of all:
love.' He smiled and a sunburst exploded in her heart. 'I've
wanted you since the night I saw you in Paris.'

'But wanting isn't love.'

'And I've loved you almost as long. The more I learned about
you the less I could resist.' His finger on her mouth moved in
a slow, seductive stroke along her bottom lip that sent delight
shivering through her. 'The question is, do you want me?'

Stunned, her eyes widened. 'Of course I do. How can you
doubt it?'

'Because right now the royal council of elders is debating
whether I should become Emir of Bakhara. It's by no means
a done deal, and there'll be a lot of negotiating, but I need to
know what you think. You didn't want a royal life. You wanted

more than royal duty and who can blame you?' He paused and gathered her close so her heart beat against his, that single pulse all the stronger for being shared. 'I'll step away from it if that's what you want. I couldn't accept without your agreement.'

'Zahir!' She pulled away as far as his encircling arm allowed. 'You can't do that. You're made for the position.' She couldn't imagine anyone better suited. The knowledge filled her with pride. 'Unless you don't want it?'

Green eyes held hers, unblinking. 'I won't lie. The challenge of it is all I could ever want. Except for you.' His voice deepened and sent threads of gossamer silk trawling over her sensitive skin till she quivered. 'I'd rather have you, Soraya. That's my choice.'

Her heart swelled as she stopped his words with her lips. 'Then it's just as well you don't have to choose.' Something inside broke at the thought he'd give up all he'd worked for if it meant keeping her. She felt humbled. At the same time determination filled her. She'd be the best wife an emir could have. 'I'd rather be yours than anything else in the world, my darling.'

'You'll be mine? Even if it means being wife to the Emir?' His voice was raw with disbelief. His hands shook as he pulled her closer. 'You can pursue your engineering, whatever you want. It won't be all duty. I swear.'

She cupped his beautiful, questioning face in her hands, marvelling that he was hers. 'Well, there will be hardships, I know. Think of all the shopping I'll have to do to look the part if you're made Emir. The shoes, the clothes...' Her breath escaped in a gasp as his marauding hands investigated the sheer silk of her bodice. 'Zahir!'

'The attentions of your virile husband?'

'That will never be a hardship.' Soraya smiled with all the joy in her heart. She couldn't believe the world could hold such happiness.

'Just as well.' His head lowered, blotting out the elegant room, and the world faded away.

EPILOGUE

THE oasis encampment vibrated with the hoof beats of so many horses, all beautifully caparisoned, all bearing horsemen in traditional garb. Their white robes shimmered in the moonlight, their heirloom weapons glinting.

The women had just left in a fleet of luxury four-wheel drives back to the capital.

Soraya's breath caught at the spectacle of Bakhara's strongest and finest wheeling their horses out of the oasis.

The slightest of breezes feathered her dress and she shivered, not with cold, but with delight at the scene that wouldn't have looked out of place in some old romantic tale. An instant later warm hands clasped her arms, pulling her back against a strong, solid body.

A sigh of pleasure escaped her lips. It had been so long, a month in fact, since she'd felt Zahir so close.

Even through her silks and his fine cottons, his heat branded her. She snuggled back against him, revelling in the possessive tightening of his grip, the hitch in his breathing and his burgeoning hardness against her buttocks.

She shimmied back as delicious languor filled her.

'Minx,' Zahir growled as a salute of rifle shots thundered in the night sky. 'Wave for our audience, *habibti*.'

Soraya lifted her arm then moaned softly as he ground his pelvis hard against her. Rills of desire ran through her body, pooling deep inside.

The last of the riders disappeared over the ridge, leaving them sole occupants of the oasis.

'I thought today would never end.' Zahir's lips were hot on her neck. 'Why do Bakhari weddings take so long?'

She turned, wrapping her arms around his neck.

'Not any wedding. The Emir's.'

His hooded eyes glinted in the light of the nearby braziers. 'No regrets, my love?'

'None. Except…' She chewed her lip, feeling delight shimmer within as Zahir's hungry gaze honed in on her mouth. It was a wonder she didn't explode from the heat.

'What?' A frown pleated his brow.

'Except you're wasting valuable time talking.'

With a grin that stole her heart all over again, Zahir scooped her into his arms and strode into the richly decorated tent. Antique lamps spilled multicoloured light over thick, silk rugs, embroidered cushions and the widest bed Soraya had ever seen raised on a dais at the centre of the space.

Tenderly Zahir laid her on the satin cover, then propped himself beside her.

The lamplight cast his strong features in bronze, highlighting their severe strength and above all the shimmering emotion in his eyes.

Soraya's heart welled, reading the reflection there of all she felt.

'Your wish is my command, lady. But be warned.' He nuzzled the base of her neck as his fingers slid over the thin silk of her dress. Delicious tension bowed her taut body. 'I intend to tell you often how much I love you.'

It was a promise he kept through their lifetime together.

* * * * *

JOIN US ON SOCIAL MEDIA!

Stay up to date with our latest releases, author
news and gossip, special offers and discounts, and
all the behind-the-scenes action
from Mills & Boon...

 millsandboon

 millsandboonuk

 millsandboon

It might just be true love...

GET YOUR ROMANCE FIX!

MILLS & BOON
—— *blog* ——

Get the latest romance news, exclusive author interviews, story extracts and much more!